42

The Fiction Factory

JACK DANN

With Susan Casper, Gardner Dozois, Gregory Frost,
Jack C. Haldeman II, Barry N. Malzberg,
Michael Swanwick, Janeen Webb, and George Zebrowski

GOLDEN GRYPHON PRESS • 2005

LIBRARY OF CONGRESS CATALOGING–IN–PUBLICATION DATA
Dann, Jack.
    The fiction factory : stories / by Jack Dann ; with Susan Casper . . . [et al.].
        p.   cm.
    ISBN 1-930846-36-3 (hardcover : alk. paper)
    1. Science fiction, American.   I. Title.
PS3554.A574 F53 2005
813'.54—dc22   2005007098

First Edition.

Contents

In Memory of Jack C. Haldeman II
and George Alec Effinger

What's All This Fiction Factory Business . . . ?

Jack Dann

WHEN I FIRST READ MICHAEL SWANWICK'S WISE and wonderfully tongue-in-check story notes for this volume, it occurred to me that collaborations are like cigars . . . and solo stories and novels could be likened to cigarettes. In the compressed, hot, electric good old days of my youth, my salad days, the days when I was having one long helluva good time, living fast and hard, and making my bones as a writer, I smoked like a chimney.

I was as addicted to cigarettes as any junkie is addicted to smack.

I remember writing my first solo story in about four hours . . . and smoking an entire pack of Tarryton filter cigarettes in the process.

I coughed and wheezed my way through those early stories; but when everything was going well, when I wanted company and good spirits, I would have a decided urge for a good Churchill size cigar.

I haven't smoked for over twenty years (I stopped when I couldn't breathe without wheezing); and although I don't miss the cigarettes one whit, I still long for a cigar. I long to sit in my leather couch and stink up the room with the blue fumes of a sweet tasting Macanudo. I long to sit with old friends and talk the talk . . . which, I suppose, is what I'm doing right now.

My solo work—the stories and novels—are still, like the cigarettes of yore, an addiction. I still dance and fight and glide (but no longer cough) my way through to the end of each tale, trying to somehow recreate on the flat whiteness of the page those first-imagined, dreamlike images of beauty, fear, dread, bliss, and fascination. There is a great joy in the daily battle to create worlds and characters and sagas that (I hope) live in readers' minds, but the work always gets done in prisonlike isolation. Every day I drive to my studio near the sea and battle with the demons. Blinds closed, cup of tea on the laminated side table, laptop on my lap.

The solitary life of every writer.

I live in Australia, some nine thousand miles away from Binghamton and New York and Philadelphia where it all started, far away from those dear friends with whom I wrote most (but not all!) of the stories in this volume. Collaborating on stories are joyous occasions; and if collaborations are also addictive (like those blasted cigarettes!), it is the addiction of being with dear friends at the best party going anywhere.

Fine cigars . . .

Although I've learned a few things about the techniques of collaborating with other writers on stories and novels, the process is still mysterious and magical after all these years. For one thing, collaborating *feels* easy. You're sitting around with dear friends, workshopping, discussing plots and contracts and money, or just being raucous and silly at a party—drinking cheap wine (everything had to be cheap in "the good old days"), staying up late, imagining the lucent, expansive futures that lay ahead of us, and suddenly someone would make a quip or tell a story or say something that would blaze into an idea.

"Hey, what if . . ."

Discussion, extrapolation, more wine, jokes, excitement, and then someone (usually me) would sit down at the typewriter—yes, there *were* typewriters in the Pleistocene!—and start banging out what would still be just an idea for a story. In the story notes, you'll read much slander from Gardner Dozois and Michael Swanwick about how I would jump the gun and start writing and thus embarrass everybody *else* into collaborating on a story.

We'd usually discuss the story arc first, and I would just happen to sit down and start typing a few pages; and then, magically, other hands would weave their magic. I'd go home, which in those days was in upstate New York, and some weeks later, I'd get drafts back. Sometimes the drafts would be clean and complete; sometimes I'd be asked to write more connective material.

You see, I was able to pull that scam off for years—a few hours of concentrated pain doing the beginning of a first draft, and then, sorry, everyone, my work is done. Just cut me in for the money. And we were selling our collaborations to *Playboy* and . . . oops, I'm getting ahead of myself. I need my collaborators to rein me in!

Have I mentioned that every collaboration is different . . . ?

When I collaborate with Barry Malzberg, I usually come up with an idea, tell Barry, and then wait for what usually seems like five minutes to receive a completed first draft in the mail . . . or, nowadays, via e-mail. (Aside from being a wonderful writer, Barry is a *fast* writer, and a towering figure in the field, both literally and figuratively.) I would then spend two weeks reworking and adding connective tissue, editing.

When I've worked with Gardner, or Gardner and Michael, or Gardner and Susan, Gardner would do the final, conforming draft. When I've worked with Barry, Janeen Webb, Greg Frost, and Jack Haldeman, I would usually do the final draft; and when I was collaborating with George Zebrowski, sometimes he wrote the conforming draft; sometimes I wrote it. These things can be pretty fluid. If the collaboration is one where all the writers are combining their strengths, rather than their weaknesses, it *feels* easy no matter how hard the actual writing.

Whether you're doing the final copy, or working from the rough draft material your collaborators have so kindly provided, it's just a question of fixing this and noodling a little with that, editing out this bit, adding this bit in, even if you do end up writing some five thousand words of connecting material. And if you get to write the first draft, well, it's not really like writing your own solo stories because if you screw up, your collaborator—or collaborators; yes, some of these stories have three bylines!—will fix all your mistakes, misguided plotting, and infelicities of style. Or, better yet, your collaborators will plot the story. After all, you got it started, right?

When I'm doing my solo work, I sit and stare glumly and uncertainly into the monitor, piles of research books and notes scattered all around me, as I puzzle and push my way through the usual morning writer's block. Once through that, the words flow . . . until I reach the next plot twist. Slowly, slowly, I work through the creative blocks. But when I collaborate, my unconscious is fooled into thinking it has complete creative freedom. I don't worry about style and plot problems; I just rush ahead, the unconscious (what author Richard McKenna called "The Little Man") freed of obstacle and insecurity. And the words simply spill out . . .

My first two stories were collaborations (with George Zebrowski), and, for me, there is a direct linkage from talking shop, hanging out, and workshopping to collaborating on stories. Much of my early solo work was also, in a very real sense, collaborative, in that I usually had input from other writers.

I met George at the State University at Binghamton, SUNY as it was known, and he was kind enough to rent me crash space in his west side Binghamton apartment. In those days I was "crashing" in several apartments with a number of people, but *that's* a story for another day. George and I would sit opposite each other, typewriters back-to-back on George's old oak library table, and we would write. I can still hear the clatter of George's old Remington typewriter, can still see George glancing up and grinning at me, his face wide and handsome, high cheekbones, a curl of his silvery blond hair falling across his forehead, and that special intensity, as if right then, at that very second, we *were* going to write prose worthy of all the ages.

That was in 1968, and George was absolutely sure that he was going to be a full-time, successful writer. No, he was sure that he was *already* a writer, and his dark, high-ceilinged apartment was filled with books, books on philosophy, science, science-fiction, film, literary fiction, popular fiction, criticism, and history. George would walk around his little apartment, hands waving—a Mahler symphony playing in the background—as he expounded theories of writing and art; and, hell, to my mind this guy had figured *something* out, and I wanted to know all about it. So we talked endlessly, shared books and ideas . . . and stories. I had been trying to teach myself to write for years, had memorized and copied out into spiral notebooks favorite passages from some of my favorite authors: John Fowles, J. D. Salinger, J. G. Ballard, Vladimir Nabakov, Brian Aldiss, Jerzy Kosinski. George lent me Strunk and White's classic, *The Elements of Style.*

I memorized it. I was a sponge, and I was determined to become a real writer.

Well, George was a real writer. I sure as hell was going to be one, too; and I remember, I remember one summer's day when I ran madly through George's railroad apartment, shouting, "I wrote a real sentence, I wrote a real sentence," and although it embarrasses me to admit it today, especially now that Gardner refers to me as "the gray-haired eminence of Australia," I still remember that first real (and terrible) sentence: "A fused mass of beryllium fled from Deneb." A sentence I would surely cut now, but it takes some experience to know how and when to murder your darlings.

We sold that story to *Worlds of If,* and sumbitch, I was a writer!

It was only natural to continue sharing ideas . . . to sit down at the old clackers we called typewriters, and do more stories together. I remember when I had finally stopped crashing in other people's apartments and rented my own, I was writing fifteen hundred words a day of a novella called "Junction," a novella that I would later turn into a novel; and at the end of each day, I would traipse over to see George and his partner, author Pamela Sargent, who would read what I had written and workshop the text and brainstorm new ideas.

In those days, writing was part of everything I did; it was thought; it was breath; it was social; it was a waking dream that allowed me to live in simultaneous worlds and times; and it entwined with friendship and family . . . and I suppose, in many respects, that still holds true for me today. Even as I have a life apart from writing, I'm still that sponge. I'm still living in simultaneity, still that kid running through George's house screaming, "I wrote a sentence." After I finished my latest novel, *The Rebel: An Imagined Life of James Dean*, my wife Janeen asked me if I didn't think it was time to finally leave the 1960s and come back to the present.

And now I'm plotting out a new novel and once again living in simultaneity, half submerged in the lightning strobe world of dreams and story arcs.

It was in the early seventies that I met Gardner Dozois and Susan Casper. In those days, Gardner was a skinny, hippy-looking youth with shoulder-length blond hair. And Susan was a smart, beautiful, no-nonsense, dark-haired hippy chick. They rented an apartment on South Street in Philadelphia, and later on Quince Street. And during those halcyon years before some nine thousand miles and the exigencies of mature life and career conspired to separate us, I used to visit . . . often.

During those formative growing-up-as-a-writer years, Gardner was my story doctor. I can still remember taking a rough-cut copy of my novel *The Man Who Melted* with me on one of my many sojourns to Philadelphia; and I clearly remember staying long past the proverbial guests-become-like-fish-in-three-day's-time limit. In fact, I refused to leave until Gardner had workshopped the novel with me. (It's a good thing that Susan was a dear friend, for she never threw me out the window until the work was finished.)

I imposed upon them for shorter periods after Gardner became the editor of *Asimov's Magazine*. The dime finally dropped that maybe, just maybe, Gardner might have *other* people's work to edit.

I think of the seventies as the Guilford years.

Gardner brought me into the Guilford Writers Workshop, which used to meet in Jack C. Haldeman II's decaying four-story

Victorian mansion in the Guilford section of Baltimore; and I became a regular member of the group called the Guilford Gafia (nicknamed after "The Milford Mafia," which was what some people were calling Damon Knight's and Kate Wilhelm's now legendary Milford Writers Conferences). Our group comprised Jack and his brother Joe W. Haldeman, George Alec Effinger, Gardner, Ted White, Tom Monteleone, Robert Thurston, William Nabors, and myself.

Guilfords would last a weekend, a weekend of concentrated, exhausting work: staying up most of the night reading the stories to be workshopped the next day, then workshopping, reading, eating together, partying; we were creating our group mythology, creating fast friendships, as we honed our critical and writing skills. It was the Guilfords, and later the Philford Writers Workshops that paved the way for the frenetic, prolific, never-to-be-repeated Fiction Factory days of the eighties.

By the end of the seventies, the Guilfords had run their course. Jack Haldeman, known to his friends as Jay, got too busy, as, I suppose, we all did; we were swept up with the forward motion of our careers, yet, as I think about it, with all the excitement of trying to write novels and continuing to hone my skills, I was a bit at sixes-and-sevens about the direction my career should take. I wanted to write literate science fiction, but I was already starting to write stories on the edges of the genre and was beset with a vague uncertainty, which became a sort of ennui.

I was still making the pilgrimage to see Gardner and Susan . . . and through them I met Michael Swanwick. That would have been in the mid seventies, and I remember Gardner telling me that I've got to meet this guy Michael Swanwick, that even though he hadn't published anything yet, he always carried a notebook, and he *thought* like a writer; and I remember workshopping Michael's first story; and, yes, indeed, Gardner (as usual!) was right—this Michael Swanwick guy had the juice, the moxie, the chops. We would spend long sessions over those years—usually in Gardner and Susan's living room—discussing story ideas, working through the dark, symbolic stuff of the stories, and, probably working through the labyrinths of our unconscious. (For an example of the kind of thing I mean, take a look at our story "Ships," which is included in this collection, one of the strangest and most disturbing stories I've ever had a hand in writing. There, the mythic demons and ghouls of our unconscious selves are stomping and striding around, bigger than life.)

So now when I would come to Philadelphia, one of the first things we did was . . . call Michael; and we would hang out, talk and talk and talk, discuss stories, plots, the underlying architectures of stories and novels we were going to write. We revived the old Guilford and called it The Philford Writers Workshop. Although we only met twice, writers such as David Hartwell, Samuel R. Delany, John Ford, James Patrick Kelly, Timothy Sullivan, Tony Sarowitz, Gregory Frost, and Tom Purdom were in attendance. And it was but a natural segue to move from talking and workshopping to . . . collaborating.

From 1979 to 1985, I was collaborating intensively with Gardner, and with Gardner and Susan, and with Gardner and Michael; and, somehow, we became a miracle on wheels: we were selling everything we wrote, and selling to the slicks, to the most difficult magazines to sell to in their day: to *Playboy* and *Penthouse* and *Omni*. It seemed so easy to write those stories; and in the course of attending workshops, collaborating, and just hanging around Philadelphia for weekends of eating and drinking and having the best goddamn times I can remember, we secretly started calling ourselves "The Fiction Factory." In their notes before the stories, Gardner and Michael and Susan all tell the story of The Fiction Factory.

Later, after that six-year frenzy of collaborative production, I wrote a story with Greg Frost, another with Michael, and I continued to write stories with Barry Malzberg, stories such as "Blues and the Abstract Truth," "Life In the Air," and "Art Appreciation," but the wild and frantic fervor of collaboration had passed.

In 1994, I moved to Melbourne, Australia and married author and critic Janeen Webb. One of our collaborations is included in this collection.

Much of my work these days is out of genre, but in the odd times between writing this chapter or that, I find myself searching my files for story notes. There was this story idea Gardner and I had about an old man growing young. I remember writing a few pages. I remember we had notes.

Who knows . . . maybe another burst of collaboration?

And, hey, that may be just the story we need to write . . . a story about old guys getting younger, going back to their intense, prolific, joyful salad days.

After all, writers never get old.

They probably just start collaborating again.

The Fiction Factory

Introduction
Touring

Michael Swanwick

It was a clear, starry night and Jack Dann came breezing into town at the wheel of a limousine twenty feet long, with a big cigar stuck in one corner of his expansive grin . . . That's the way I remember it, anyhow. Maybe the details are a little off, but if so the blame lies not in me but in reality for failing to live up to those rare and wonderful times when Jack blew into Philadelphia and we all sat around in Gardner and Susan's tiny Quince Street apartment, laughing and talking big and kicking ideas around. Making literature.

There is no way to exaggerate what a glamorous guy Jack was when I first met him. No kidding, and not that he'd believe it, but I've seen drop-dead gorgeous women follow him down the street with their eyes. Gardner, on the other hand, was his bohemian opposite, a gargantuan figure with long blond hair, faded jeans, cowboy hat, and a black T-shirt reading PROPHET OF DOOM. They were each larger than life.

I, meanwhile, was a skinny young freak (hippiedom was gone by the time I came along) with raggedy clothes and hair down below my shoulders, still unpublished and desperate to connect with the live-wire core stuff of literature, that fiercely beating heart of language that makes prose. Now, keep in mind that Gardner and Jack didn't just write just any stories and novels but works that grappled with the key questions of existence, guilt, and identity. It didn't matter that Jack wasn't yet getting the big-buck contracts his fiction would later receive, or that Gardner was forever a breath away from penury. They were writing things that mattered, stories so intrinsic to their insights and experiences that nobody else could have written them.

Oh man, did I want to be like them!

Imagine how I felt, then, when Jack and Gardner informed me that we three were going to collaborate on "Touring" together. The two of them had plotted out a story that required a lot of specialized rock and roll lore and, by chance, I'd recently researched Janis Joplin for what was to be my first published story, "The Feast of Saint Janis." With the low cunning of working writers, they decided they could save themselves a mountain of work by dealing me in.

I was only too happy to oblige. I wrote down every word they told me and started in on the first draft. Which any writer will tell you is the hardest and least satisfying part of writing. It's where all the ugliest prose exists, the stuff that's got to be revised out of existence before the story is fit for human eyes. Later drafts are where all the fun and most of the art lies.

So Jack and Gardner got their money's worth out of the deal. But what was in it for me? The chance to learn from the best. Midway through the process, I made a major structural change—I forget now exactly what—and boasted to Jack that I'd done something surprising with the story. After a brief pause, Jack said, "I know what you did. But you're going to find that it doesn't work that way."

That's how sharp these guys were. Jack could see not only the way the story ought to go, but which false trails would present themselves to lead me astray. He was right, of course. I knew that instantly, just by his tone of voice. But I monkeyed around with the story for a week or so, doing it the wrong way just so I could see why it wouldn't work.

"Touring" was the beginning of my postgraduate education. And (this, too, is part of the working writer's education) I got paid for it, too.

Gardner Dozois

"It was a clear, starry night and Jack Dann came breezing into town at the wheel of a limousine twenty feet long, with a big cigar stuck in one corner of his expansive grin . . ." No, wait, that's Michael's *schtick.* Actually, I don't remember much about what kind of car Jack was driving, or (mercifully) about his cigars. I mostly remember him sleeping on our broken-down couch in our shabby, little Philadelphia apartment with the cats walking around on him, going next door to Just Ice Cream for ice-cream cones (when we got back, one of our cats would sit next to you and calmly lick one side of the ice-cream cone while you licked the other), drinking many bottles of cheap wine, and sitting around outside in the fenced-in square of broiling concrete we called a "backyard" when it got too hot to stay inside the apartment (which was most of the time, except for deep winter), plotting stories and throwing story ideas back and forth.

There was a definite social component to the collaborations. If Jack had stayed in Binghamton, instead of coming down to Philadelphia for visits that often stretched from days to weeks at a time, I doubt that any of them ever would have been written, even if we'd had e-mail and the internet back in those benighted long-ago days. It required all of us being in the same room, laughing, talking, throwing weird scraps of information or hooks or bizarre story-ideas that had just occurred to us (inspired by something that one of the *others* had just said) at each other to make the process work—what we used to call "bullshitting," in the old days. There, I've just given some hostile critic a stick to beat us with—and yet, we were looser and freer and more wildly creative in those bullshitting sessions than any of us have ever been before or since, and I do believe that, for better or worse, we wrote kinds of stories in those days that none of us alone would have ever have attempted to write, before or since. I believe that in most of them, we managed to combine our strengths rather than our weaknesses and write stories that none of us *could* have written by ourselves.

That was certainly true of "Touring," the first of the collaborations between the three of us. We'd been sitting around in my living room during one of these bullshit sessions, drinking and talking, discussing a story that Michael had just written about Janis Joplin, then moving on to talk about other dead rock legends, when Jack remarked that it would have been neat if Buddy Holly, Janis Joplin, and Elvis had ever gotten a chance to perform together, and the storyline for "Touring" blossomed in my head in an instant. A few minutes later, we were hammering out details of the plot, and figuring out (abortively, as it turned out; our initial scheme of assigning one writer to write about one rock star didn't work out, and we all ended writing about all of them at one point or another) who was going to write what. A day later, I was sitting on the white marble steps on an old brownstone building, writing furiously in longhand in a three-ring notebook while Jack and Michael and my wife Susan were playing pinball in the Fun Arcade next door, writing the scene where Buddy Holly goes to the laundromat—the first fiction writing of any sort that I'd done for several years.

That was another important part of the collaborative process—we were all at stages of our lives where we needed some kind of jolt or input psychologically, something we weren't getting in our individual lives. Michael to learn craft and gain confidence in his abilities, Jack to try new things and find new directions at a point in his career where he was drifting somewhat aimlessly, me (although it never occurred to me consciously that it would have this effect) to jump-start my creativity and shake me out of a creative dry spell that had lasted for several years. And although I've never been a high-volume prolific writer, before or after the collaborations, I've so far never entirely dried-up again creatively since either, always managing to eke out at least a slow trickle of work in spite of the press of other duties. So, if for nothing else, "Touring" was important to me for that—although I think that it is a good story, and a story that none of us would have been able to write or would ever have even *tried* to write on our own, my acid test for a good collaboration.

We sold it to *Penthouse*, a market none of us had ever thought of trying before and that we cracked our first time out of the box, and whose editor, Kathy Green, wisely talked us out of our plan to publish the story under the collaborative pseudonym of "Phil Ford," after the Philford Writers Workshop we'd run a few years before in Philadelphia. Everybody, including my agent, had assured us that no editor would buy a collaborative story with three individual bylines on it, but nobody ever gave us the slightest bit of trouble about that, so we put "Phil Ford" away in a box, and never opened it again.

Jack Dann

Ah, how we create our own mythologies. I was driving a powder blue Buick Le Sabre convertible, with miles of chrome and a big eight with overdrive—you could see the needle on the gas gauge tick down counterclockwise when you stepped hard on the accelerator. It wasn't a limo; it was just a big, beautiful American gas-guzzler the size of a limo; but then everything seemed larger, brighter, and more intense in those days. With the exception of the limo, Gardner's and Michael's memories of how we wrote the story jibe pretty much with my own; although I don't remember telling Michael he was taking a wrong turn. I *do* remember telling him how to rewrite a jam session scene, which he did; and then I realized (and had to tell him!) that he had done it absolutely right the first time. There was a lot of that in those days. And, yes, we did think we could each write *our* character—Michael: Janis, Gardner: Buddy, and I would write Elvis, as I was a big fan. I remember writing Elvis, but soon everyone was writing . . . everyone.

This story—one of those nifty ideas that one would *think* would be immediately grabbed up for television and a film—seemed to point right to the heart of American pop culture. It was story crafted out of the mythic stuff of sex, drugs, and rock 'n roll. It *seemed* to have the depths and layers, at least that's what I thought when we were in the throes of writing it. And reading it once again after all these years . . . it *still* feels right.

We passed the story back and forth after I (smelling profoundly of a guest who had transmogrified himself into a fish!) returned to my attic apartment in Binghamton, and then Gardner, I believe, sold it to the redoubtable Kathy Green at *Penthouse*. "Touring" had a pretty good run. It was reprinted in *The Year's Best Horror Stories*, *After Midnight*, *Ghosts*, and *Elvis Rising*.

But still no film! Wake up Hollywood!

Touring

Gardner Dozois, Jack Dann, and Michael Swanwick

THE FOUR-SEATER BEECHWOOD BONANZA DROPPED from a gray sky to the cheerless winter runways of Fargo Airport. Tires touched pavement, screeched, and the single-engine plane taxied to a halt. It was seven o'clock in the morning, February 3, 1959.

Buddy Holly duck-walked down the wing and hopped to the ground. It had been a long and grueling flight; his bones ached, his eyes were gritty behind the large, plastic-framed glasses, and he felt stale and curiously depressed. Overnight bag in one hand, laundry sack in the other, he stood beside Ritchie Valens for a moment, looking for their contact. White steam curled from their nostrils. Brown grass poked out of an old layer of snow beside the runway. Somewhere a dog barked, flat and far away.

Behind the hurricane fence edging the field, a stocky man waved both hands overhead. Valens nodded, and Holly hefted his bags. Behind them, J. P. Richardson grunted as he leaped down from the plane.

They walked toward the man across the tarmac, their feet crunching over patches of dirty ice.

"Jack Blemings," the man rasped as he came up to meet them. "I manage the dance hall and the hotel in Moorhead." Thin mustache, thin lips, cheeks going to jowl—Holly had met this man a thousand times before: the stogie in his mouth was inevitable; the sporty plaid hat nearly so. Blemings stuck out a hand, and Holly shuffled his bags awkwardly, trying to free his own hand. "Real pleased to meet you, Buddy," Blemings said. His hand was soggy and boneless. "Real pleased to meet a real artist."

He gestured them into a showroom-new '59 Cadillac. It dipped on its springs as Richardson gingerly collapsed into the backseat. Starting the engine, Blemings leaned over the seat for more introductions. Richardson was blowing his nose, but hastily transferred the silk handkerchief into his other hand so that they could shake. His delighted-to-meet-you expression lasted as long as the handshake, then the animation went out of him, and his face slumped back into lines of dull fatigue.

The Cadillac jerked into motion with an ostentatious squeal of rubber. Once across the Red River, which still ran steaming with gunmetal, predawn mist, they were out of North Dakota and into Moorhead, Minnesota. The streets of Moorhead were empty—not so much as a garbage truck out yet. "Sleepy little burg," Valens commented. No one responded. They pulled up to an undistinguished six-story brick hotel in the heart of town.

The hotel lobby was cavernous and gloomy, inhabited only by a few tired-looking, potted rubber plants. As they walked past a grouping of battered armchairs and sagging sofas toward the shadowy information desk in the back, dust puffed at their feet from the faded gray carpet. An unmoving ceiling fan cast thin-armed shadows across the room, and everything smelled of old cigar butts and dead flies and trapped sunshine.

The front desk was as deserted as the rest of the lobby. Blemings slammed the bell angrily until a balding, bored-looking man appeared from the back, moving as though he were swimming through syrup. As the desk clerk doled out room keys, still moving like a somnambulist, Blemings took the cigar out of his mouth and said, "I spoke with your road manager, must've been right after you guys left the Surf Ballroom. Needed his okay for two acts I'm adding to the show." He paused. "S'awright with you, hey?"

Holly shrugged. "It's your show," he said.

Holly unlaced one shoe, letting it drop heavily to the floor. His back ached, and the long, sleepless flight had made his suit rumpled and sour smelling. One last chore and he could sleep: he picked up the bedside telephone and dialed the hotel operator for an outside line so that he could call his wife, Maria, in New York and tell her that he had arrived safely.

The phone was dead; the switchboard must be closed down. He sighed and bent over to pick up his shoe again.

Eight or nine men were standing around the lobby when Holly stepped out of the elevator, husky fellows, southern boys by the look of them. Two were at the front desk, making demands of the clerk, who responded by spreading his arms wide and rolling his eyes upward.

Waiting his turn for service, Holly leaned back against the counter, glancing about. He froze in disbelief. Against all logic, all possibility, Elvis Presley himself was standing not six yards away on the gray carpet. For an instant Holly struggled with amazement. Then a second glance told him the truth.

Last year Elvis had been drafted into the army, depriving his fans of his presence and creating a ready market for those who could imitate him. A legion of Presley impersonators had crowded into the welcoming spotlights of stages across the country, trying vainly to fill the gap left by the King of Rock and Roll.

This man, though, he stood out. At first glance he was Elvis. An instant later you saw that he was twenty years too old and as much as forty pounds overweight. There were dissolute lines under his eyes and a weary, dissipated expression on his face. The rigors of being on the road had undone his ducktail so that his hair was an untidy mess, hanging down over his forehead and curling over his ears. He wore a sequined shirt, now wrinkled and sweaty, and a suede jacket.

Holly went over to introduce himself. "Hi," he said, "I guess you're playing tonight's show."

The man ignored his out-thrust hand. Dark, haunted eyes bored into Holly's. "I don't know what kind of game you're playing, son," he said. A soft Tennessee accent underlay his words. "But I'm packing a piece, and I know how to use it." His hand darted inside his jacket and emerged holding an ugly-looking .38.

Involuntarily Holly sucked in his breath. He slowly raised his hands shoulder-high and backed away. "Hey, it's okay," he said. "I was just trying to be friendly." The man's eyes followed his retreat suspiciously, and he didn't reholster the gun until Holly was back at the front desk.

The desk clerk was free now. Holly slid three bills across the counter, saying, "Change please." From the corner of his eye, he saw the imitation Elvis getting into the elevator, surrounded by his entourage. They were solicitous, almost subservient. One patted the man's back as he shakily recounted his close call. *Poor old man,*

Holly thought pityingly. The man was really cracking under the pressures of the road. He'd be lucky to last out the tour.

In the wooden booth across the lobby, Holly dumped his change on the ledge below the phone. He dialed the operator for long distance. The earpiece buzzed, made clicking noises. Then it filled with harsh, actinic static, and the clicking grew faster and louder. Holly jiggled the receiver, racked the phone angrily.

Another flood of musicians and crew coursed through the lobby. Stepping from the booth, ruefully glancing back at the phone, he collided with a small woman in a full-length mink. "Oof," she said, and then reached out and gave him a squeeze to show there were no hard feelings. A mobile, hoydenish face grinned up at him.

"Hey, sport," she said brightly. "I *love* that bow tie. And those glasses! — Jesus, you look just like Buddy Holly!"

"I know," he said wryly. But she was gone. He trudged back to the elevators. Then something caught his eye, and he swung about, openly staring. Was that a *man* she was talking to? My God, he had hair down to his shoulders!

Trying not to stare at this amazing apparition, he stepped into the elevator. Back in his room, he stopped only long enough to pick up his bag of laundry before heading out again. He was going to have to go outside the hotel to find a working phone anyway; he might as well fight down his weariness, hunt up a Laundromat, and get his laundry done.

The lobby was empty when he returned through it, and he couldn't even find the desk clerk to ask where the nearest Laundromat was. Muttering under his breath, Holly trudged out of the hotel.

Outside, the sun was shining brilliantly but without warmth from out of a hard, high blue sky. There was still no traffic, no one about on the street, and Holly walked along through an early-morning silence broken only by the squeaking of his sneakers, past closed-up shops and shuttered brownstone houses. He found a Laundromat after a few more blocks, and although it was open, there was no one in there either, not even the inevitable elderly Negro attendant. The rows of unused washing machines glinted dully in the dim light cast by a flyspecked bulb. Shrugging, he dumped his clothes into a machine. The change machine didn't work, of course, but you got used to dealing with things like that on the road, and he'd brought a handkerchief full of change with him. He got the machine going and then went out to look for a phone.

The streets were still empty, and after a few more blocks it began to get on his nerves. He'd been in hick towns before—had grown up in one—but this was the sleepiest, *deadest* damn town he'd ever seen. There was still no traffic, although there were plenty of cars parked by the curbs, and he hadn't seen another person since leaving the hotel. There weren't even any *pigeons*, for goodness sake!

There was a five-and-dime on the corner, its doors standing open. Holly poked his head inside. The lights were on, but there were no customers, no floorwalkers, no salesgirls behind the counters. True, small-town people weren't as suspicious as folk from the bigger cities—but still, this *was* a business, and it looked as if anyone could just walk in here and walk off with any of the unguarded merchandise. It was gloomy and close in the empty store, and the air was filled with dust. Holly backed out of the doorway, somehow not wanting to explore the depths of the store for the sales personnel who *must* be in there somewhere.

A slight wind had come up now, and it flicked grit against his face and blew bits of scrap paper down the empty street.

He found a phone on the next corner, hunted through his handkerchief for a dime while the wind snatched at the edges of the fabric. The phone buzzed and clicked at him again, and this time there was the faint, high wailing of wind in the wires, an eerie, desolate sound that always made him think of ghosts wandering alone through the darkness. The next phone he found was also dead, and the next.

Uneasily, he picked up his laundry and headed back to the hotel.

The desk clerk was spreading his hands wide in a gesture of helpless abnegation of responsibility when the fat southerner in the sequined shirt leaned forward, poked a hard finger into the clerk's chest, and said softly, "You know who I am, son?"

"Why, of course I do, Mr. Presley," the clerk said nervously. "Yessir, of course I do, sir."

"You say you know who I am, son," Elvis said in a cottony voice that slowly mounted in volume. "If you know who I am, then you *know* why I don't have to stay in a goddamned flophouse like this! Isn't that right? Would you give your mother a room like that? You know goddamned well you wouldn't. Just what are you people thinking of? I'm *Elvis Presley*, and you'd give me a room like that!"

Elvis was bellowing now, his face grown red and mottled, his features assuming that look of sulky, sneering meanness that had thrilled millions. His eyes were hard and bright as glass. As the frightened clerk shrank back, his hands held up now as much in terror as in supplication, Elvis suddenly began to change. He looked at the clerk sadly, as if pitying him, and said, "Son, do you know who I am?"

"Yessir," whispered the clerk.

"Then can't you see it?" asked Elvis.

"See what, sir?"

"That I'm *chosen!* Are you an atheist? Are you a goddamned atheist?" Elvis pounded on the desk and barked, "I'm the star, I've been given that, and you can't soil it, you atheist bastard! You *sonovabitch!*" Now that was the worst thing he could call anyone, and he never, almost never used it, for his mother, may she rest in peace, was holy. *She* had believed in him, had told him that the Lord had chosen *him*, that as long as he sang and believed, the Lord would take care of him. Like this? Is this the way He was going to take care of me?

"*I'm* the star, and I could *buy* this hotel out of my spare change! Buy it, you hear that?" And even as he spoke, the incongruity of the whole situation hit him, really hit him hard for the first time. It was as though his mind had suddenly cleared after a long, foggy daze, as if the scales had fallen from his eyes.

Elvis stopped shouting and stumbled back from the desk, frightened now, fears and suspicions flooding in on him like the sea. What was he doing *here?* Dammit, he was the King! He'd made his comeback, and he'd played to capacity crowds at the biggest concert halls in the country. And now he couldn't even remember how he'd gotten here—he'd been at Graceland, and then everything had gotten all foggy and confused, and the next thing he knew he was climbing out of the bus in front of this hotel with the roadies and the rest of the band. Even if he'd agreed to play this one-horse town, it would have to have been for charity. That's it; it had to be for charity. But then where were the reporters, the TV crews? His coming here would be the biggest damn thing that had ever happened in Moorhead, Minnesota. Why weren't there any screaming crowds being held back by police?

"What in hell's going on here?" Elvis shouted. He snatched out his revolver and gestured to his two bodyguards to close up on either side of him. His gaze darted wildly about the lobby as he tried to look into every corner at once. "Keep your eyes open! There's something funny—"

At that moment Jack Blemings stepped out of his office, shut the door smoothly behind him, and sauntered across the musty old carpet toward them. "Something wrong here, Mr. Presley?"

"Damn *right* there is," Elvis raged, taking a couple of steps toward Blemings and brandishing his gun. "You know how many *years* it's been since I played a tank town like this? I don't know what in hell the Colonel was thinking of to send me down here. I—"

Smiling blandly and ignoring the gun, Blemings reached out and touched Elvis on the chest.

Elvis shuddered and took a lurching step backward, his eyes glazing over. He shook his head, looked foggily around the lobby, glanced down at the gun in his hand as though noticing it for the first time, then holstered it absentmindedly. "Time's the show tonight?" he mumbled.

"About eight, Mr. Presley," Blemings answered, smiling. "You've got plenty of time to relax before then."

Elvis looked around the lobby again, running a hand through his greased-back hair. "Anything to do around here?" he asked, a hint of the old sneer returning.

"We got a real nice bar right over there the other side of the lobby," Blemings said.

"I don't drink," Elvis said sullenly.

"Well, then," Blemings added brightly, "we got some real nice pinball machines in that bar, too."

Shaking his head, Elvis turned and moved away across the lobby, taking his entourage with him.

Blemings went back to his office.

J. P. Richardson had unpacked the scotch and was going for ice when he saw the whore. There was no mistaking what she was. She was dressed in garish gypsy clothes with ungodly amounts of jewelry about her neck and wrists. Beneath a light blouse her breasts swayed freely—she wasn't even wearing a bra. Richardson didn't have to be told how she had earned the mink coat that was draped over one arm.

"Hey, little sister," Richardson said softly. He was still wearing the white suit that was his onstage trademark, his "Big Bopper" outfit. He looked good in it and knew it. "Are you available?"

"You talking to me, honey?" She spoke defiantly, almost jeeringly, but something in her stance, her bold stare, told him she was ready for almost anything. He discreetly slid a twenty from a jacket pocket, smiled, and nodded.

"I'd like to make an appointment," he said, slipping the folded bill into her hand. "That is, if you *are* available now."

She stared from him to the bill and back, a look of utter disbelief on her face. Then, suddenly, she grinned. "Why, 'course I'm available, sugar. What's your room number? Gimme ten minutes to stash my coat, and I'll be right there."

"It's room four-eleven." Richardson watched her flounce down the hall, and, despite some embarrassment, was pleased. There was a certain tawdry charm to her. Probably ruts like a mink, he told himself. He went back to his room to wait.

The woman went straight to the hotel bar, slapped the bill down, and shouted, "Hey, kids, pony up! The drinks are on Janis!"

There was a vague stirring, and three lackluster men eddied toward the bar.

Janis looked about, saw that the place was almost empty. A single drunk sat walleyed at a table, holding onto its edges with clenched hands to keep from falling over. To the rear, almost lost in gloom, a big stud was playing pinball. Two unfriendly types, who looked like bodyguards, stood nearby, protecting him from the empty tables. Otherwise—nothing. "Shoulda taken the fat dude up on his offer," she grumbled. "There's nothing happening *here*." Then, to the bartender, "Make mine a whiskey sour."

She took a gulp of her drink, feeling sorry for herself. The clatter of pinball bells ceased briefly as the stud lost his ball. He slammed the side of the machine viciously with one hand. She swiveled on her stool to look at him.

"Damn," she said to the bartender. "You know, from this angle that dude looks just like *Elvis*."

Buddy Holly finished adjusting his bow tie, reached for a comb, then stopped in mid-motion. He stared about the tiny dressing room, with its cracked mirror and bare light bulbs, and asked himself, *How did I get here?*

It was no idle, existential question. He really did not know. The last thing he remembered was entering his hotel room and collapsing on the bed. Then—here. There was nothing in between.

A rap at the door. Blemings stuck his head in, the stench of his cigar permeating the room. "Everything okay in here, Mr. Holly?"

"Well," Holly began. But he went no further. What could he say? "How long before I go on?"

"Plenty of time. You might want to catch the opener, though— good act. On in ten."

"Thanks."

Blemings left, not quite shutting the door behind him. Holly studied his face in the mirror. It looked haggard and unresponsive. He flashed a toothy smile but did not feel it. God, he was tired. Being on the road was going to kill him. There had to be a way off the treadmill.

The woman from the hotel leaned into his room. "Hey, Ace — you seen that Blemings motherfucker anywhere?"

Holly's jaw dropped. To hear that kind of language from a woman — from a *white* woman. "He just went by," he said weakly.

"Shit!" She was gone.

Her footsteps echoed in the hallway, were swallowed up by silence. And that was *wrong*. There should be the murmur and nervous bustle of acts preparing to go on, last-minute errands being run, equipment being tested. Holly peered into the corridor — empty.

To one side, the hall dead-ended into a metal door with a red EXIT sign overhead. Holly went the other way, toward the stage. Just as he reached the wings, the audience burst into prolonged, almost frenzied applause. The Elvis impersonator was striding onstage. It was a great crowd.

But the wings were empty. No stagehands or go-fers, no idlers, nobody preparing for the next set.

"Elvis" spread his legs wide and crouched low, his thick lips curling in a sensual sneer. He was wearing a gold lamé jumpsuit, white scarf about his neck. He moved his guitar loosely, adjusting the strap, then gave his band the downbeat.

Well it's one for the money
Two for the show
Three to get ready
Now go, cat, go!

And he was off and running into a brilliant rendition of "Blue Suede Shoes." Not an easy song to do, because the lyrics were laughable. It relied entirely on the music, and it took a real entertainer to make it work.

This guy had it all, though. The jumps, gyrations, and forward thrusts of the groin were stock stuff — but somehow he made them look right. He played the audience too, and his control was perfect. Holly could see shadowy shapes beyond the glare of the footlights, moving in a more than sexual frenzy, was astonished by their rapturous screams. All this in the first minutes of the set.

He's good, Holly marveled. Why was he wasting that kind of talent on a novelty act? There was a tug at his arm, and he shrugged it off.

The tug came again. "Hey, man," somebody said, and he turned to find himself again facing the woman. Their eyes met, and her expression changed oddly, becoming a mixture of bewilderment and outright fear. "Jesus God," she said in awe. "You are Buddy Holly!"

"You've already told me that," he said, irritated. He wanted to watch the man on stage—who *was* he, anyway?—not be distracted by this foul-mouthed and probably not very clean woman.

"No, I mean it—you're *really* Buddy Holly. And that dude on stage"—she pointed—"he's Elvis Presley."

"It's a good act," Holly admitted. "But it wouldn't fool my grandmother. That good ol' boy's forty if he's a day."

"Look," she said. "I'm Janis Joplin. I guess that don't mean nothing to you, but—hey, lemme show ya something." She tried to tug him away from the stage.

"I want to see the man's act," he said mildly.

"It won't take a minute, man. And it's important. I swear it. It's—you just gotta see it, is all."

There was no denying her. She led him away, down the corridor to the metal door with its red EXIT sign, and threw it open. "Look!"

He squinted into a dull, winter evening. Across a still, car-choked parking lot was a row of faded, brick buildings. A featureless, gray sky overhung all. "There used ta be a lot more out here," Janis babbled. "All the rest of the town. It all went away. Can you dig it, man? It just all—went away."

Holly shivered. This woman was crazy! "Look, Miss Joplin," he began. Then the buildings winked out of existence.

He blinked. The buildings had not faded away—they had simply ceased to be. As crisply and sharply as if somebody had flipped a switch. He opened his mouth, shut it again.

Janis was talking quietly, fervently. "I don't know what it is, man, but something *very weird* is going down here." Everything beyond the parking lot was a smooth, even gray. Janis started to speak again, stopped, moistened her lips. She looked suddenly hesitant and oddly embarrassed. "I mean, like, I don't know how to break this to ya, Buddy, but you're *dead*. You bought it in a plane crash way back in 'fifty-nine."

"This *is* 'fifty-nine," Holly said absently, looking out across the parking lot, still dazed, her words not really sinking in. As he watched, the cars snapped out of existence row by row, starting with the farthest row, working inward to the nearest. Only the asphalt lot itself remained, and a few bits of litter lying between the painted slots. Holly's groin tightened, and as fear broke through astonishment, he registered Janis's words and felt rage grow alongside fear.

"No, honey," Janis was saying, "I hate to tell ya, but this is 1970." She paused, looking uncertain. "Or maybe not. Ol' Elvis looks a deal older than I remember him being. We must be in the future or something, huh? Some kinda sci-fi trip like that, like on *Star Trek*? You think we—"

But Holly had swung around ferociously, cutting her off. "*Stop it!*" he said. "I don't know what's going on, what kind of trick you people are trying to play on me, or how you're doing all these things, but I'm not going to put up with any more of—"

Janis put her hand on Holly's shoulder; it felt hot and small and firm, like a child's hand. "Hey, listen," Janis said quietly, cutting him off. "I know this is hard for you to accept, and it is pretty heavy stuff . . . but, Buddy, you're *dead*. I mean, really, you are . . . It was about ten years ago, you were on tour, right? And your plane *crashed*, spread you *all* over some farmer's field. It was in all the goddamn papers, you and Ritchie Valens and . . ." She paused, startled, and then grinned. "And that fat dude at the hotel, that must've been the *Big Bopper*. Wow! Man, if I'd known *that* I might've taken him up on it. You were all on your way to some diddly-shit hicktown like . . ." She stopped, and when she started to speak again, she had gone pale ". . . like Moorhead, Minnesota. Oh, Christ, I think it was Moorhead. Oh, boy, is that spooky . . ."

Holly sighed. His anger had suddenly collapsed, leaving him feeling hollow and confused and tired. He blinked away a memory that wasn't a memory of torn-up, black ground and twisted shards of metal. "I don't *feel* dead," he said. His stomach hurt.

"You don't *look* dead, either," Janis reassured him. "But, honey, I mean, you really *were*."

They stood staring out across the now vacant parking lot, a cold, cinder-smelling wind tugging at their clothes and hair. At last, Janis said, her brassy voice gone curiously shy, "You got real famous, ya know, after . . . afterward. You even influenced, like, the *Beatles* . . . Shit, I forgot!—I guess you don't even know who they *are*, do you?" She paused uncomfortably, then said, "Anyway, honey, you got real famous."

"That's nice," Holly said dully.

The parking lot disappeared. Holly gasped and flinched back.

Everything was gone. Three concrete steps with an iron pipe railing led down from the door into a vast, unmoving nothingness.

"What a trip," Janis muttered. "What a trip . . ."

They stared at the oozing gray nothingness until it seemed to Holly that it was creeping closer, and then, shuddering, he slammed the door shut.

Holly found himself walking down the corridor, going no place in particular, his flesh still crawling. Janis tagged along after him, talking anxiously. "Ya know, I can't even really remember how I got to this burg. I was in L.A. the last I remember, but then everything gets all foggy. I thought it was the booze, but now I dunno."

"Maybe you're dead, too," Holly said almost absentmindedly.

Janis paled, but a strange kind of excitement shot through her face, under the fear, and she began to talk faster and faster. "Yeah, honey, maybe I am. I thought of that, too, man, once I saw you. Maybe whoever's behind all this are *magicians*, man, black magicians, and they conjured us all *up*." She laughed a slightly hysterical laugh. "And you wanna know another weird thing? I can't find any of my sidemen here or the roadies or *anybody*, ya know? Valens and the Bopper don't seem to be here either. All of 'em were at the hotel, but backstage here it's just you and me and Elvis and that motherfucker Blemings. It's like *they're* not really interested in the rest of them, right? They were just window dressing, man, but now they don't need 'em anymore, and so they sent them *back*. We're the headline acts, sweetie. Everybody else *they* vanished, just like they vanished the fucking parking lot, right? Right?"

"I don't know," Holly said. He needed time to think. Time alone.

"Or, hey—how about this? Maybe you're *not* dead. Maybe we got nabbed by flying saucers, and these aliens faked our deaths, right? Snatched you out of your plane, maybe. And they put us together here—wherever here is—not because they dig rock. Shit, they probably can't even *understand* it—but to study us and all that kinda shit. Or maybe it *is* 1959; maybe we got kidnapped by some time-traveler who's a big rock freak. Or maybe it's a million years in the future, and they've got us all *taped*, see? And they want to hear us; so they put on the tape, and we *think* we're here, only we're not. It's all a recording. Hey?"

"I don't *know*."

Blemings came walking down the corridor, cigar trailing a thin plume of smoke behind him. "Janis, honey! I've been beating the bushes for you, sweetie pie. You're on in two."

"Listen, motherfuck," Janis said angrily. "I want a few answers from you!" Blemings reached out and touched her hand. Her eyes went blank, and she meekly allowed him to lead her away.

"A real trouper, hey?" Blemings said cheerfully.

"Hey!" Holly said. But they were already gone.

Elvis laid down his guitar, whipped the scarf from his neck, and mopped his brow with it. He kissed the scarf and threw it into the crowd. The screams reached crescendo pitch as the little girls fought over its possession. With a jaunty wave of one hand, he walked offstage.

In the wings, he doubled over, breathing heavily. Sweat ran out of every pore in his body. He reached out a hand, and no one put a towel in it. He looked up angrily.

The wings were empty, save for a kid in big glasses. Elvis gestured weakly toward a nearby piece of terry cloth. "Towel," he gasped, and the kid fetched it.

Toweling off his face, Elvis threw back his head, began to catch his breath. He let the cloth slip to his shoulders and for the first time got a good look at the kid standing before him. "You're Buddy Holly," he said. He was proud of how calmly it came out.

"A lot of people have told me that today," Holly said.

The crowd roared, breaking off their conversation. They turned to look. Janis was dancing onstage from the opposite side. Shadowy musicians to the rear were laying down a hot, bluesy beat. She grabbed the microphone, laughed into it.

"Well! Ain't this a kick in the ass? Yeah. Real nice, real nice," There were anxious lines about her eyes, but most of the audience wouldn't be able to see that. "Ya know, I been thinking a lot about life lately. 'Deed I have. And I been thinkin' how it's like one a dem ole-time blues songs. Ya know? I mean, it *hurts* so bad, and it feels so *good!*" The crowd screamed approval. The band kept laying down the rhythm. "So I got a song here that kind of proves my point."

She swung an arm up and then down, giving the band the beat, and launched into "Heart and Soul."

"Well?" Elvis said. "Give me the message."

Holly was staring at the woman onstage. "I never heard anyone sing like that before," he murmured. Then, "I'm sorry—I don't know what you mean, Mr. Presley."

"Call me Elvis," he said automatically. He felt disappointed. There had been odd signs and omens, and now the spirits of departed rock stars were appearing before him—there really ought to be a message. But it was clear the kid was telling the truth; he looked scared and confused.

Elvis turned on a winning smile and impulsively plucked a ring from one of his fingers. It was a good ring; lots of diamonds and rubies. He thrust it into Holly's hands. "Here, take this. I don't want the goddamned thing anymore, anyway."

Holly squinted at the ring quizzically. "Well, put it on," Elvis snapped. When Holly had complied, he said, "Maybe you'd better tell me what you *do* know."

Holly told his story. "I understand now," Elvis said. "We're caught in a snare and delusion of Satan."

"You think so?" Holly looked doubtful.

"Squat down." Elvis hunkered down on the floor, and after an instant's hesitation, Holly followed suit. "I've got powers," Elvis explained. "The power to heal—stuff like that. Now me and my momma, we were always close. Real close. So she'll be able to help us, if we ask her."

"Your mother?"

"She's in Heaven," Elvis said matter-of-factly.

"Oh," Holly said weakly.

"Now join hands and concentrate real *hard*."

Holly felt embarrassed and uncomfortable. Since he was a good Baptist, which he certainly tried to be, the idea of a backstage seance seemed blasphemous. But Elvis, whether he was the real item or not, scared him. Elvis's eyes were screwed shut, and he was saying, "Momma. Can you hear me, Momma?" over and over in a fanatic drone.

The seance seemed to go on for hours, Holly suffering through it in mute misery, listening as well as he could to Janis, as she sung her way through number after amazing number. And finally she was taking her last bows, crowing "Thank you, thank you" at the crowd.

There was a cough at his shoulder and a familiar stench of tobacco. Holly looked up. "You're on," Blemings said. He touched Holly's shoulder.

Without transition, Holly found himself onstage. The audience was noisy and enthusiastic, a good bunch. A glance to the rear, and he saw that the backup musicians were not his regular sidemen. They stood in shadow, and he could not see their faces.

But the applause was long and loud, and it crept up under his skin and into his veins, and he knew he had to play *something*.

"Peggy Sue," he called to the musicians, hoping they knew the number. When he started playing his guitar, they were right with him. Tight. It was a helluva good backup band; their playing had bone and sinew to it. The audience was on its feet now, bouncing to the beat.

He gave them "Rave On," "Maybe Baby," "Words of Love," and "That'll be the Day," and the audience yelped and howled like wild beasts, but when he called out "Not Fade Away" to the musicians, the crowd quieted, and he felt a special, higher tension come into the hall. The band did a good, strong intro, and he began singing.

I wanna tell you how it's gonna be
You're gonna give your love to me

He had never felt the music take hold of him this immediately, this strongly, and he felt a surge of exhilaration that seemed to instantly communicate itself to the audience and be reflected back at him redoubled, bringing them all up to a deliriously high level of intensity. Never had he performed better. He glanced offstage, saw that Janis was swaying to the beat, slapping a hand against her thigh. Even Elvis was following the music, caught up in it, grinning broadly and clapping his ring-studded hands.

For love is love and not fade away.

Somewhere to the rear, one of the ghostly backup musicians was blowing blues harmonica, as good as any he'd ever heard.

There was a flash of scarlet, and Janis had run onstage. She grabbed a free mike, and joined him in the chorus. When they reached the second verse, they turned to face each other and began trading off lines. Janis sang:

My love's bigger than a Cadillac

and he responded. His voice was flat next to hers. He couldn't give the words the emotional twist she could, but their voices synched, they meshed, they worked together perfectly.

When the musical break came, somebody threw Janis a tambourine so she could stay onstage, and she nabbed it out of the air. Somebody else kicked a bottle of Southern Comfort across the stage, and she stopped it with her foot, lifted it, downed a big slug. Holly was leaping into the air, doing splits, using every trick of an old rocker's repertoire, and miraculously he felt he could keep on doing so forever, could stretch the break out to infinity if he tried.

Janis beckoned widely toward the wings. "Come on out," she cried into the microphone. "Come on."

To a rolling avalanche of applause, Elvis strode onstage. He grabbed a guitar and strapped it on, taking a stance beside Holly. "You don't mind?" he mumbled.

Holly grinned.

They went into the third verse in unison. Standing between the other two, Holly felt alive and holy and—better than either alive or holy—*right*. They were his brother and sister. They were in tune; he could not have sworn which body was his.

Well, love is love and not fade away

Elvis was wearing another scarf. He whipped it off, mopped his brow, and went to the footlights to dangle it into the crowd. Then he retreated as fast as if he'd been bitten by a snake.

Holly saw Elvis talking to Janis, frantically waving an arm at the crowd beyond the footlights. She ignored him, shrugging off his words. Holly squinted, could not make out a thing in the gloom.

Curious, he duck-walked to the edge of the stage, peered beyond.

Half the audience was gone. As he watched, the twenty people farthest from the stage snapped out of existence. Then another twenty. And another.

The crowd noise continued undiminished, the clapping and whooping and whistling, but the audience was *gone* now—except for Blemings, who sat alone in the exact center of the empty theater. He was smiling faintly at them, a smile that could have meant anything, and as Holly watched, he began softly, politely, to applaud.

Holly retreated backstage, pale, still playing automatically. Only Janis was singing now.

Not fade away

Holly glanced back at the musicians, saw first one, then another, cease to exist. Unreality was closing in on them. He stared into Elvis's face, and for an instant saw mirrored there the fear he felt.

Then Elvis threw back his head and laughed and was singing into his mike again. Holly gawked at him in disbelief.

But the *music* was right, and the *music* was good, and while all the rest—audience, applause, someplace to go when the show was over—was nice, it wasn't necessary. Holly glanced both ways and saw that he was not the only one to understand this. He rejoined the chorus.

Janis was squeezing the microphone tight, singing, when the last sideman blinked out. The only backup now came from Holly's guitar—Elvis had discarded his. She knew it was only a matter of minutes before the nothingness reached them, but it didn't really matter. *The music's all that matters*, she thought. *It's all that made any of it tolerable, anyway.* She sang.

Not fade away

Elvis snapped out. She and Holly kept on singing.

If anyone out there is listening, she thought. *If you can read my mind or some futuristic bullshit like that—I just want you to know that I'd do this again anytime. You want me, you got me.*

Holly disappeared. Janis realized that she had only seconds to go herself, and she put everything she had into the last repetition of the line. She wailed out her soul and a little bit more. *Let it echo after I'm gone*, she thought. *Let it hang on thin air.* And as the last fractional breath of music left her mouth, she felt something seize her, prepare to turn her off.

Not fade away

It had been a good session.

Introduction

The Gods of Mars

Michael Swanwick

It was a clear, starry night and Jack Dann came breezing into town at the wheel of a limousine twenty feet long, with a big cigar stuck in one corner of his expansive grin . . . And he and Gardner and I were sitting around, talking about Mars. Not many people remember what a crushing disillusionment the first Mars orbiter was. There had been fly-by photos of Mars, but they were sketchy and incomplete. The *Mariner* 9 probe sent back detailed photos of almost the entire planetary surface, and it was crystal-clear from them that the romantic old Red Planet of our dreams didn't exist. Mars lacked Lowell's canals or Bradbury's crystal towers or Brackett's decadent civilizations. It was, in short, lifeless. We're still in the process of getting over that one.

But here's the funny thing. As *Mariner* 9 approached camera range in late 1971, a planet-wide dust storm blew up, and—to the unspeakable frustration of the Mission Control guys—obscured the surface of our sister planet for weeks. "It's as if," one of us said, "the Martians had something to hide."

That was it. We all of us recognized a story idea when it was dumped in our laps, and we set to arguing it up and plotting it out. Picture us waving our hands in the air, interrupting each other, going back to make revisions, fleshing out characters, sketching out possibilities. Shot full of electricity and riding the lightning for all it was worth.

I did the first draft—the junior writer *always* does the first draft—Jack did the second, and Gardner did the final polish. That's the secret to a successful collaboration: Somebody has to be given final say, and the others have to trust him to do it right. It sounds easy, but many a collaboration has foundered on exactly that rock. We three always worked easily together, however. The chemistry was right.

"The Gods of Mars" was a finalist for the Nebula Award. It didn't win, of course—collaborations enter the list heavily handicapped—but the fact that it got onto the ballot at all suggests that we had hold of an idea that hit people where they lived.

Gardner Dozois

Another bullshitting/brainstorming session, another day of sitting around drinking in my "backyard" in the sweltering heat of Philadelphia in July. I was looking through my story-idea notebook, selecting one idea, and then throwing it out to Jack and Michael, like a keeper throwing fish to seals at the zoo. Most they let drop. A few we all tossed around, from one to the other, keeping them in the air for a while, before we ran out of steam and they bounced away. For some reason, the story-idea everybody caught fire about was one I'd had languishing in my notebook since the *Mariner* 9 mission in 1971: what if, under the screen of the planet-wide sandstorm that had frustratingly come up *just* before *Mariner* 9 got into camera range, Somebody had *changed* Mars, changed it before the probe could get a clear look at it, changed it from the Lowellian Mars we'd expected to see to the now-familiar Mars of the Mariner and Viking photos? And suppose, just before the first manned expedition gets there, Somebody changes it *back?*

I probably never would have attempted this story on my own, since it seemed to call for a hard-edged, *Analog*ish opening scene set in a realistically described NASA spacecraft in orbit around Mars, and that was way out of my area of expertise. So we tapped Michael, the only one of us with anything even resembling a scientific background, and whose father had actually worked in the space program, to handle that scene. Then Jack, who we regarded as our Phenomenology Expert, took over the story for a while. Then I did an extensive final draft, adding new scenes interstitially throughout, trying to deepen the characterization and add more psychological realism. The ending gave us fits, and we all took a crack at it, trying several different versions before we hammered out the version that you see here on the page. (Ironically, with the research I ended up doing for the final draft, including reading several books about NASA, I probably *could* have faked my way through the opening spacecraft scene . . . but I never would have done that research in the first place if the collaboration didn't call for it; the collaborations forced all of us to learn things we never would have bothered to learn, and stretch muscles we otherwise would never have used.)

During the writing of the story, I learned, to my amazement, that neither Jack nor Michael had ever read any of Edgar Rice Burroughs's Martian novels—so all the Barsoom nostalgia here was supplied by me.

We sold the story to Ellen Datlow at *Omni*, who talked us out of the title "Storm Warning," and made us do another minor tweaking of the text. It went on to *not* win the Nebula Award, although it came close enough (making the Final Ballot) to dismay several critics who were not at all fond of it.

Jack Dann

In *Being Gardner Dozois*, a fascinating, book-length interview conducted by Michael, Gardner said, "Neither Jack nor I would have written that story by ourselves, because . . . Well, I can't speak for Jack. Jack has showed himself in the past willing to tackle just about any project, no matter how daunting or formidable. So *he* might have bluffed his way through it."

Nah, I wouldn't have the temerity to try to write a hard science *Analog* story, which isn't what this story ended up being; but it needed the tropes of science, enough to convince the reader that this was . . . real stuff. I've taken on projects with enormous research—such as my historical novels, *The Memory Cathedral*, *The Silent*, and *The Rebel*—but I just don't have the right foundation to try to write hard science fiction. What I'm probably saying is I'm just too chickenshit to do so.

But Michael, ah, Michael *can* turn his hand to writing hard science, and he blocked out the opening, wrote about spanners and all the technical stuff, and then I ran with it for a while. I guess I was the phenomenology expert, whatever that means, but I'd been fascinated with Schrödinger's paradox and the Copenhagen Collapse and all that stuff since I wrote my early novel *Junction*.

However, as I think about it, Gardner and I—if pushed against the wall—could probably *approximate* the act of writing *Analog*ish science fiction. I remember writing the novel *High Steel* with Jay Haldeman, who kept pouring Drambuie into my glass as I worked on the novel at his house in Gainesville, Florida. He would write for a while, until he got blocked, and then I would take over. Although Jay was a scientist, who had worked on NASA's space station project, he suddenly started becoming the literary guy and writing all the literary stuff . . . and I found myself writing the hard science.

So, perhaps the prescription for writing hard science is ever-increasing amounts of Drambuie.

As I recall, we didn't have any at Gardner's.

But it was summer.

We were young and a hundred percent full of the hot, creative juices.

And *we* had Michael!

The Gods of Mars

Gardner Dozois, Jack Dann, and Michael Swanwick

THEY WERE OUTSIDE, UNLASHING THE MARS LANDER, when the storm blew up.

With Johnboy and Woody crowded against his shoulders, Thomas snipped the last lashing. In careful cadence, the others straightened, lifting the ends free of the lander. At Thomas's command, they let go. The metal lashing soared away, flashing in the harsh sunlight, twisting like a wounded snake, dwindling as it fell below and behind their orbit. The lander floated free, tied to the *Plowshare* by a single, slim umbilicus. Johnboy wrapped a spanner around a hex-bolt over the top strut of a landing leg and gave it a spin. Like a slow, graceful spider leg, it unfolded away from the lander's body. He slapped his spanner down on the next bolt and yanked. But he hadn't braced himself properly, and his feet went out from under him in a slow somersault. He spun away, laughing, to the end of his umbilicus. The spanner went skimming back toward the *Plowshare*, struck its metal skin, and sailed off into space.

"You meatballs!" Thomas shouted over the open intercom. The radio was sharp and peppery with sun static, but he could hear Woody and Johnboy laughing. "Cut it out! No skylarking! Let's get this done."

"Everything okay out there?" asked Commander Redenbaugh,

from inside the *Plowshare*. The commander's voice had a slight edge to it, and Thomas grimaced. The last time the three of them had gone out on EVA, practicing this very maneuver, Johnboy had started to horse around and had accidentally sent a dropped lug-nut smashing through the source-crystal housing, destroying the laser link to Earth. And hadn't the commander gotten on their asses about *that*; NASA had been really pissed, too—with the laser link gone, they would have to depend solely on the radio, which was vulnerable to static in an active sun year like this.

It was hard to blame the others too much for cutting up a little on EVA, after long, claustrophobic months of being jammed together in the *Plowshare*, but the responsibility for things going smoothly was his. Out here, *he* was supposed to be in command. That made him feel lonely and isolated, but after all, it was what he had sweated and strived for since the earliest days of flight training. The landing party was his command, his chance for glory, and he wasn't going to let anybody or anything ruin it.

"Everything's okay, Commander," Thomas said. "We've got the lander unshipped, and we're almost ready to go. I estimate about twenty minutes to separation." He spoke in the calm, matter-of-fact voice that tradition demanded, but inside he felt the excitement building again and hoped his pulse rate wasn't climbing too noticeably on the readouts. In only a few minutes, they were going to be making the first manned landing on Mars! Within the hour, he'd be down there, where he'd dreamed of being ever since he was a boy. On *Mars*.

And *he* would be in command. *How about that, Pop*, Thomas thought, with a flash of irony. *That good enough for you? Finally?*

Johnboy had pulled himself back to the *Plowshare*.

"Okay, then," Thomas said dryly. "If you're ready, let's get back to work. You and Woody get that junk out of the lander. I'll stay out here and mind the store."

"Yes, *sir*, sir," Johnboy said with amiable irony, and Thomas sighed. Johnboy was okay but a bit of a flake—you had to sit on him a little from time to time. Woody and Johnboy began pulling boxes out of the lander; it had been used as storage space for supplies they'd need on the return voyage, to save room in *Plowshare*. There were jokes cracked about how they ought to let some of the crates of flash-frozen glop that NASA straight-facedly called food escape into space, but at last, burdened with boxes, the two space-suited figures lumbered to the air lock and disappeared inside.

Thomas was alone, floating in space.

You really were alone out here, too, with nothing but the gaping immensity of the universe surrounding you on all sides. It was a little scary, but at the same time something to savor after long months of being packed into the *Plowshare* with three other men. There was precious little privacy aboard ship—out here, alone, there was nothing *but* privacy. Just you, the stars, the void . . . and, of course, Mars.

Thomas relaxed at the end of his tether, floating comfortably, and watched as Mars, immense and ruddy, turned below him like some huge, slow-spinning, rusty-red top. Mars! Lazily, he let his eyes trace the familiar landmarks. The ancient dead-river valley of Kasei Vallis, impact craters puckering its floor . . . the reddish brown and gray of haze and frost in Noctis Labyrinthus, the Labyrinth of Night . . . the immense scar of the Vallis Marineris, greatest of canyons, stretching two thirds of the way around the equator . . . the great volcanic constructs in Tharsis . . . and there, the Chryse Basin, where soon they would be walking.

Mars was as familiar to him as the streets of his hometown—*more* so, since his family had spent so much time moving from place to place when he was a kid. Mars had stayed a constant, though. Throughout his boyhood, he had been obsessed with space and with Mars in particular . . . as if he'd somehow always known that one day he'd be here, hanging disembodied like some ancient god over the slowly spinning red planet below. In high school he had done a paper on Martian plate tectonics. When he was only a gangly grade-school kid, ten or eleven, maybe, he had memorized every available map of Mars, learned every crater and valley and mountain range.

Drowsily, his thoughts drifted even further back, to that day in the attic of the old house in Wrightstown, near McGuire Air Force Base—the sound of jets taking off mingling with the lazy Saturday afternoon sounds of kids playing baseball and yelling, dogs barking, lawn mowers whirring, the rusty smell of pollen coming in the window on the mild, spring air—when he'd discovered an old, dog-eared copy of Edgar Rice Burroughs's *A Princess of Mars.*

He'd stayed up there for hours reading it, while the day passed unnoticed around him, until the light got so bad that he couldn't see the type anymore. And that night he'd surreptitiously read it in bed, under the covers with a pencil flashlight, until he'd finally fallen asleep, his dreams reeling with giant, four-armed green men, thoats, zitidars, long-sword-swinging heroes, and beautiful princesses . . . the Twin Cities of Helium . . . the dead sea bottoms lit by the opalescent light of the two hurtling moons . . . the nomad caverns of the Tharks, the barbaric riders draped with glittering jewels and rich riding silks. For an instant, staring down at Mars, he felt a childish disappointment that all of that really wasn't waiting down there for him after all, and then he smiled wryly at himself. Never doubt that those childhood dreams had power—after all, one way or another, they'd *gotten* him here, hadn't they?

Right at that moment the sandstorm began to blow up.

It blew up from the hardpan deserts and plains, and as Thomas watched in dismay, began to creep slowly across the planet like a tarp being pulled over a work site. Down there, winds moving at hundreds of kilometers per hour were racing across the Martian surface, filling the sky with churning, yellow-white clouds of sand. A curtain storm.

"You see that, Thomas?" the commander's voice asked in Thomas's ears.

"Yeah," Thomas said glumly. "I see it."

"Looks like a bad one."

Even as they watched, the storm slowly and relentlessly blotted out the entire visible surface of the planet. The lesser features went first, the scarps and rills and stone fields, then the greater ones. The polar caps went. Finally even the top of Olympus Mons—the tallest mountain in the solar system—disappeared.

"Well, that's it," the commander said sadly. "Socked in. No landing today."

"Son of a *bitch!*" Thomas exploded, feeling his stomach twist with disappointment and sudden rage. He'd been so *close.* . . .

"Watch your language, Thomas," the commander warned. "This is an open channel." Meaning that we mustn't shock the Vast Listening Audience Back Home. Oh, horrors, certainly *not.*

"If it'd just waited a couple more hours, we would have been able to get *down* there—"

"You ought to be glad it didn't," the commander said mildly. "Then you'd have been sitting on your hands down there with all that sand piling up around your ears. The wind can hit one hundred forty miles an hour during one of those storms. *I'd* hate to have to try to sit one out on the ground. Relax, Thomas. We've got plenty of time. As soon as the weather clears, you'll go down. It can't last forever."

Five weeks later, the storm finally died.

Those were hard weeks for Thomas, who was as full of useless

energy as a caged tiger. He had become overaware of his surroundings, of the pervasive, sour human smell, of the faintly metallic
taste of the air. It was like living in a jungle-gym factory, all twisting
pipes and narrow, cluttered passages, enclosed by metal walls that
were never out of sight. For the first time during the long months of
the mission, he began to feel seriously claustrophobic.

But the real enemy was time. Thomas was acutely aware that
the inexorable clock of celestial mechanics was ticking relentlessly
away . . . that soon the optimal launch window for the return journey to Earth would open and that they *must* shape for Earth then
or never get home at all. Whether the storm had lifted yet or not,
whether they had landed on Mars or not, whether Thomas had
finally gotten a chance to show off his own particular righteous stuff
or *not*, when the launch window opened, they had to go.

They had less than a week left in Mars orbit now, and still the
sandstorm raged.

The waiting got on everyone's nerves. Thomas found Johnboy's
manic energy particularly hard to take. Increasingly, he found himself snapping at Johnboy during meals and "happy hour," until
eventually the commander had to take him aside and tell him to
loosen up. Thomas muttered something apologetic, and the commander studied him shrewdly and said, "Plenty of time left, old
buddy. Don't worry. We'll get you down there yet!" The two men
found themselves grinning at each other. Commander Redenbaugh was a good officer, a quiet, pragmatic New Englander who
seemed to become ever more phlegmatic and unflappable as the
tension mounted and everyone else's nerves frayed. Johnboy habit-
ually called him Captain Ahab. The commander seemed rather to
enjoy the nickname, which was one of the few things that suggested that there might actually be a sense of humor lurking somewhere behind his deadpan facade.

The commander gave Thomas's arm an encouraging squeeze,
then launched himself toward the communications console.
Thomas watched him go, biting back a sudden bitter surge of
words that he knew he'd never say . . . not up here, anyway, where
the walls literally had ears. Ever since *Skylab*, astronauts had flown
with the tacit knowledge that everything they said in the ship was
being eavesdropped on and evaluated by NASA. Probably before
the day was out somebody back in Houston would be making a
black mark next to his name in a psychological-fitness dossier, just
because he'd let the waiting get on his nerves to the point where
the commander had had to speak to him about it. But damn it, it

was *easier* for the rest—they didn't have the responsibility of being NASA's token Nigger in the Sky, with all the white folks back home waiting and watching to see how you were going to fuck up. He'd felt like a third wheel on the way out here—Woody and the commander could easily fly the ship themselves and even take care of most of the routine schedule of experiments—but the landing party was supposed to be *his* command, his chance to finally do something other than be the obligatory black face in the NASA photos of Our Brave Astronauts. He remembered his demanding, domineering, hard-driving father saying to him, hundreds of times in his adolescent years, "It's a white man's world out there. If you're going to make it, you got to show that you're *better* than any of them. You got to force yourself down their throats, *make* them need you. You got to be twice as good as any of them. . . ." *Yeah, Pop,* Thomas thought, *you bet, Pop* . . . thinking, as he always did, of the one and only time he'd ever seen his father stinking, slobbering, falling-down drunk, the night the old man had been passed over for promotion to brigadier general for the third time, forcing him into mandatory retirement. *First they got to give you the chance, Pop,* he thought, remembering, again as he always did, a cartoon by Ron Cobb that he had seen when he was a kid and that had haunted him ever since: a cartoon showing black men in space suits on the moon—sweeping up around the Apollo 58 campsite.

"We're losing Houston again," Woody said. "I jes cain't keep the signal." He turned a dial, and the voice of Mission Control came into the cabin, chopped up and nearly obliterated by a hissing static that sounded like dozens of eggs frying in a huge iron skillet. ". . . read? . . . not read you . . . *Plowshare* . . . losing . . ." Sunspot activity had been unusually high for weeks, and just a few hours before, NASA had warned them about an enormous solar flare that was about to flood half the solar system with radio noise. Even as they listened, the voice was completely drowned out by static; the hissing noise kept getting louder and louder. "Weh-ayl," Woody said glumly, "that does it. That solar flare's screwing *every*thing up. If we still had the laser link"—here he flashed a sour look at John-boy, who had the grace to look embarrassed—"we'd be okay, I guess, but with*out* it . . . weh-ayl, shit, it could be days before reception clears up. *Weeks,* maybe."

Irritably, Woody flipped a switch, and the hissing static noise stopped. All four men were silent for a moment, feeling their suddenly increased isolation. For months, their only remaining contact with Earth had been a faint voice on the radio, and now, abruptly, even that link was severed. It made them feel lonelier than ever and somehow farther away from home.

Thomas turned away from the communications console and automatically glanced out the big observation window at Mars. It took him awhile to notice that there was something different about the view. Then he realized that the uniform, dirty yellow-white cloud cover was breaking up and becoming streaky, turning the planet into a giant, mottled Easter egg, allowing tantalizing glimpses of the surface. "Hey!" Thomas said, and at the same time Johnboy crowed, "Well, *well*, lookie there! Guess who's back, boys!"

They all crowded around the observation window, eagerly jostling one another.

As they watched, the storm died all at once, with the suddenness of a conjuring trick, and the surface was visible again. Johnboy let out an ear-splitting rebel yell. Everyone cheered. They were all laughing and joking and slapping one another's shoulders, and then, one by one, they fell silent.

Something was wrong. Thomas could feel the short hairs prickling erect along his back and arms, feel the muscles of his gut tightening. Something was *wrong*. What was it? What . . . ? He heard the commander gasp, and at the same time realization broke through into his conscious mind, and he felt the blood draining from his face.

Woody was the first to speak.

"But . . ." Woody said, in a puzzled, almost petulant voice, like a bewildered child. "But . . . *that's not Mars.*"

The air is thin on Mars. So thin it won't hold up dust in suspension unless the wind is traveling at enormous speeds. When the wind dies, the dust falls like pebbles, fast and all at once.

After five weeks of storm, the wind died. The dust fell.

Revealing entirely the wrong planet.

The surface was still predominantly a muddy reddish orange, but now there were large mottled patches of green and grayish ocher. The surface seemed softer now, smoother, with much less rugged relief. It took a moment to realize why: The craters—so very like those on the moon both in shape and distribution—were gone, and so were most of the mountains, the scarps and rills, the giant volcanic constructs. In their place were dozens of fine, perfectly straight blue lines. They were bordered by bands of green and extended across the entire planet in an elaborate crisscrossing pattern, from polar icecap to polar icecap.

"I cain't *find* anything," Woody was saying exasperatedly. "What *happened* to everything? I cain't even see Olympus Mons, for Christsake! The biggest fucking volcano in the solar system! Where is it? And what the fuck are those lines?"

Again Thomas felt an incredible burst of realization well up inside him. He gaped at the planet below, unable to speak, unable to answer, but Johnboy did it for him.

Johnboy had been leaning close to the window, his jaw slack with amazement, but now an odd, dreamy look was stealing over his face, and when he spoke, it was in a matter-of-fact, almost languid voice. "They're canals," he said.

"Canals, my ass!" the commander barked, losing control of his temper for the first time on the mission. "There aren't any canals on Mars! That idea went out with Schiaparelli and Lowell."

Johnboy shrugged. "Then what are *those?*" he asked mildly, jerking his thumb toward the planet, and Thomas felt a chill feather up along his spine.

A quick visual search turned up no recognizable surface features, none of the landmarks familiar to them all from the *Mariner* 9 and *Viking* orbiter photomaps—although Johnboy annoyed the commander by pointing out that the major named canals that Percival Lowell had described and mapped in the nineteenth century— Strymon, Charontis, Erebus, Circus, Dis—*were* there, just as Lowell had said that they were.

"It's *got* to be the sandstorm that did it," Thomas said, grasping desperately for some kind of rational explanation. "The wind moving the sand around from one place to another, maybe, covering up one set of surface features while at the same time exposing *another* set. . . ."

He faltered to a stop, seeing the holes in that argument even as Johnboy snorted and said, "Real good, sport, *real* good. But Olympus Mons just isn't *there*, a mountain three times higher than Mount Everest! Even if you could cover it up with sand, then what you'd have would be a fucking *sand dune* three times higher than Everest . . . but there don't seem to be any big mountains down there at all anymore."

"I know what happened," Woody said before Thomas could reply.

His voice sounded so strange that they all turned to look at him. He had been scanning the surface with the small optical telescope for the Mars-Sat experiments, but now he was leaning on the telescope mounting and staring at them instead. His eyes were feverish and unfocused and bright and seemed to have sunken into his head. He was trembling slightly, and his face had become waxen and pale.

He's scared, Thomas realized, *he's just plain scared right out of his skull. . . .*

"This has all happened before," Woody said hoarsely.

"What in the world are you talking about?" Thomas asked.

"Haven't you read your history?" Woody asked. He was a reticent man, slow voiced and deliberate, like most computer hackers, but now the words rushed from his mouth in a steadily accelerating stream, almost tumbling over one another in their anxiety to get out. His voice was higher than usual, and it held the ragged overtones of hysteria in it. "The *Mariner* 9 mission, the robot probe. Back in 1971. Remember? Jes as the probe reached Mars orbit, before it could start sending back any photos, a great big curtain storm came up, jes like this one. Great *big* bastard. Covered *everything*. Socked the whole planet in for weeks. No surface visibility at all. Had the scientists back home pulling their hair out. But when the storm finally did lift, and the photos did start coming in, everybody was jes flat-out *amazed*. None of the Lowellian features, no canals, *nothing*—jes craters and rills and volcanoes, all the stuff we expected to see *this* time around." He gave a shaky laugh.

"So everybody jes shrugged and said Lowell had been wrong—poor visibility, selector bias, he jes *thought* he'd seen canals. Connected up existing surface features with imaginary lines, maybe. He'd seen what he wanted to see." Woody paused, licking at his lips, and then began talking faster and shriller than ever. "But that wasn't *true*, was it? We *know* better, don't we, boys? We can see the proof right out that window! My crazy ol' uncle Barry, *he* had the right of it from the start, and everybody else was *wrong*. He tole me what happened, but I was jes too dumb to believe him! It was the *space* people, the UFO people! The Martians! *They* saw the probe coming, and they whomped that storm up, to keep us from seeing the surface, and then they changed everything. Under the cover of the sandstorm, they changed the whole damn planet to fool us, to keep us from finding out *they* were there! This *proves* it! They changed it *back!* They're out there right *now*, the flying saucer people! They're *out* there—"

"Bullshit!" the commander said. His voice was harsh and loud and cracked like a whip, but it was the unprecedented use of obscenity that startled them more than anything else. They turned to look at him, where he floated near the command console. Even Woody, who had just seemed on the verge of a breakdown, gasped and fell silent.

When he was sure he had everyone's attention, the commander smiled coldly and said, "While you were all going through your little psychodrama, I've been doing a little elementary checking. Here's the telemetry data, and you know what? *Every*thing shows up the same as it did before the sandstorm. Exactly . . . the . . . same. Deep radar, infrared, everything." He tapped the command console. "It's just the same as it ever was: no breathable air, low atmospheric pressure, subzero temperatures, nothing but sand and a bunch of goddamn rusty-red rocks. No vegetation, no surface water, *no canals.*" He switched the view from the ship's exterior cameras onto the cabin monitor, and there for everyone to see was the familiar Mars of the Mariner and Viking probes: rocky, rugged, cratered, lifeless. No green oases. No canals.

Everyone was silent, mesmerized by the two contradictory images.

"I don't know what's causing this strange visual hallucination we're all seeing," the commander said, gesturing at the window and speaking slowly and deliberately. "But I do know that it *is* a hallucination. It doesn't show up on the cameras, it doesn't show up in the telemetry. It's just not real."

They adjourned the argument to the bar. Doofus the Moose— an orange, inflatable toy out of Johnboy's personal kit—smiled benignly down on them as they sipped from bags of reconstituted citrus juice (NASA did not believe that they could be trusted with a ration of alcohol, and the hip flask Woody had smuggled aboard had been polished off long before) and went around and around the issue without reaching any kind of consensus. The "explanations" became more and more farfetched, until at last the commander uttered the classic phrase *mass hypnosis*, causing Johnboy to start whooping in derision.

There was a long, humming silence. Then Johnboy, his mood altering, said very quietly, "It doesn't matter anyway. We're never going to find out anything more about what's happening from up here." He looked soberly around at the others. "There's really only one decision we've got to make: Do we go on down, or not? Do we land?"

Even the commander was startled. "After all this—you still want to land?"

Johnboy shrugged. "Why not? It's what we came all the way out here for, isn't it?"

"It's too dangerous. We don't even know what's happening here."

"I thought it was only mass hypnosis," Johnboy said slyly.

"I think it is," the commander said stoutly, unperturbed by Johnboy's sarcasm. "But even if it is, we still don't know *why* we're having these hallucinations, do we? It could be a sign of organic deterioration or dysfunction of some sort, caused by who *knows* what. Maybe there's some kind of intense electromagnetic field out there that we haven't detected that's disrupting the electrical pathways of our nervous systems; maybe there's an unforeseen flaw in the recycling system that's causing some kind of toxic buildup that affects brain chemistry. . . . The point is, we're not *functioning* right; we're seeing things that aren't there!"

"None of that stuff matters," Johnboy said. He leaned forward, speaking now with great urgency and passion. No one had ever seen him so serious or so ferociously intent. "We have to land. Whatever the risk. It was hard enough funding *this* mission. If we fuck up out here, there may never be another one. NASA itself might not survive." He stared around at his crewmates. "How do *you* think it's going to look, Woody? We run into the greatest mystery the human race has ever encountered, and we immediately go scurrying home with our tails tucked between our legs without even investigating it? That sound good to you?"

Woody grunted and shook his head. "Sure doesn't, ol' buddy," he said. He glanced around the table and then coolly said, "Let's get on *down* there." Now that he was apparently no longer envisioning the imminent arrival of UFO-riding astronaut mutilators, Woody seemed determined to be as cool and unflappable and ultramacho as possible, as if to prove that he hadn't really been frightened after all.

There was another silence, and slowly Thomas became aware that everyone else was staring at him.

It all came down to him now. The deciding vote would be *his*. Thomas locked eyes with Johnboy, and Johnboy stared back at him with unwavering intensity. The question didn't even need to be voiced; it hung in the air between them and charged the lingering silence with tension. Thomas moved uneasily under the weight of all those watching eyes. How *did* he feel? He didn't really know—strange, that was about the closest he could come to it . . . hung up between fear and some other slowly stirring emotion he couldn't identify and didn't really want to think about. But there was one thing he suddenly was certain about: They weren't going to abandon *his* part of the mission, not after he'd come this far! Certainly he was never going to get another chance to get into the history books. Probably that was Johnboy's real motive, too, above and beyond the jazz about the survival of NASA. Johnboy was a cool enough head to realize that if they came home without landing, they'd be laughing-stocks, wimps instead of heroes, and somebody *else* on some future mission would get all the glory. Johnboy's ego was much too big to allow him to take a chance on *that*. And he was right! Thomas had even more reason to be afraid of being passed over, passed by: When you were black, opportunities like this certainly didn't knock more than once.

"We've still got almost three days until the launch window opens," Thomas said, speaking slowly and deliberately. "I think we should make maximum use of that time by going down there and finding out as much as we can." He raised his eyes and stared directly at the commander. "I say we *land*."

Commander Redenbaugh insisted on referring the issue to Houston for a final decision, but after several hours of trying, it became clear that he was not going to be able to get through to Earth. For once, the buck was refusing to be passed.

The commander sighed and ran his fingers wearily through his hair. He felt old and tired and ineffectual. He knew what Houston would probably have said, anyway. With the exception of the commander himself (who had been too well known *not* to be chosen), de facto policy for this mission had been to select unmarried men with no close personal or family ties back home. That alone spoke volumes. They were *supposed* to be taking risks out here. That was what they were here for. It was part of their job.

At dawn over Chryse, they went down.

As commander of the landing party, Thomas was first out of the lander. Awkward in his suit, he climbed backward out of the hatch and down the exterior ladder. He caught reeling flashes of the Martian sky and it was orange, as it should be. His first, instinctive reaction was relief, followed by an intense stab of perverse disappointment, which surprised him. As he hung from the ladder, one foot almost touching the ground, he paused to reel off the words that some PR man at NASA had composed for the occasion: "In the name of all humanity, we dedicate the planet of war to peace. May God grant us this." He put his foot down, then looked down from the ladder, twisting around to get a look at the spot he was standing on.

"Jesus *Christ*," he muttered reverently. Orange sky or not, there were *plants* of some kind growing here. He was standing almost knee-deep in them, a close-knit, springy mat of grayish-ocher vegetation. He knelt down and gingerly touched it.

"It looks like some kind of moss," he reported. "It's pliant and giving to the touch, springs slowly back up again. I can break it off in my hand."

The transmission from the *Plowshare* crackled and buzzed with static. "Thomas," said the commander's voice in his ear, "what are you *talking* about? Are you okay?"

Thomas straightened up and took his first long, slow look around. The ocher-colored moss stretched out to the orange horizon in all directions, covering both the flat plains immediately around them and a range of gently rolling hills in the middle distance to the north. Here and there the moss was punctuated by tight clusters of spiny, misshapen shrubs, usually brown or glossy black or muddy purple, and even occasionally by a lone tree. The trees were crimson, about ten feet high; the trunks glistened with the color of fresh, wet blood, and their flat, glassy leaves glittered like sheets of amethyst. Thomas dubbed them flametrees.

The lander was resting only several hundred yards away from a canal.

It was wide, the canal; and its still, perfectly clear waters reflected the sky as dark as wine, as red as blood. Small yellow flowers trailed delicate tentacles into the water from the edging walls, which were old and crumbling and carved with strange geometrical patterns of swirls and curlicues that might, just possibly, be runes.

It can't possibly be real, Thomas thought dazedly.

Johnboy and Woody were clambering down the ladder, clumsy and troll-like in their hulking suits, and Thomas moved over to make room for them.

"Mother dog!" Woody breathed, looking around him, the wonder clear in his voice. "This is really something, ain't it?" He laid a gloved hand on Thomas's shoulder. "*This* is what we saw from up there."

"But it's impossible," Thomas said.

Woody shrugged. "If it's a hallucination, then it's sure as hell a *beautiful one.*"

Johnboy had walked on ahead without a word, until he was several yards away from the ship; now he came to a stop and stood staring out across the moss-covered plain to the distant hills. "It's like being born again," he whispered.

The commander cut in again, his voice popping and crackling with static. "Report in! What's going *on* down there?"

Thomas shook his head. "Commander, I wish I knew."

He unlashed the exterior camera from the lander, set it up on its tripod, removed the lens cover. "Tell me what you see."

"I see sand, dust, rocks . . . what else do you *expect* me to see?"

"No canals?" Thomas asked softly. "No trees? No moss?"

"Christ, you're hallucinating again, aren't you?" the commander said. "This is what I was afraid of. All of you, listen to me! Listen good! There aren't any goddamn *canals* down there. Maybe there's water down a few dozen meters as permafrost. But the surface is as dry as the moon."

"But there's some sort of moss growing all over the place," Thomas said. "Kind of grayish-ocher color, about a foot and a half high. There's clumps of bushes. There's even *trees* of some kind. Can't you see any of that?"

"You're hallucinating," the commander said, "Believe me, the camera shows nothing but sand and rock down there. You're standing in a goddamn lunar desert and babbling to me about trees, for Christ's sake! That's enough for me. I want everybody back up here, right *now*. I shouldn't have let you talk me into this in the first place. We'll let Houston unravel all this. It's no longer our problem. Woody, come back here! Stick together, dammit!"

Johnboy was still standing where he had stopped, as if entranced, but Woody was wandering toward the canal, poking around, exploring.

"Listen up!" the commander said. "I want everybody back in the lander, right now. I'm going to get you out of there before somebody gets hurt. Everybody back *now*. That's an order! That's a direct order!"

Woody turned reluctantly and began bounding slowly toward the lander, pausing every few yards to look back over his shoulder at the canal.

Thomas sighed, not sure whether he was relieved to be getting out of here or heartbroken to be going so soon.

"Okay, Commander," Thomas said. "We read you. We're coming up. Right away." He took a few light, buoyant steps forward—fighting a tendency to bounce kangaroo-like off the ground—and tapped Johnboy gently on the arm. "Come on. We've got to go back up."

Johnboy turned slowly around. "Do we?" he said. "Do we *really?*"

"Orders," Thomas said uneasily, feeling something begin to stir and turn over ponderously in the deep backwaters of his own soul. "I don't want to go yet, either, but the commander's right. If we're hallucinating . . ."

"Don't give me that shit!" Johnboy said passionately. "Hallucinating, my ass! You touched the moss, didn't you? You *felt* it. This isn't a hallucination, or mass hypnosis, or any of that other crap. This is a *world*, a new world, and it's *ours!*"

"Johnboy, get in the lander right now!" the commander broke in. "That's an order!"

"Fuck you, Ahab!" Johnboy said. "And fuck your orders, too!"

Thomas was shocked—and at the same time felt a stab of glee at the insubordination, an emotion that surprised him and that he hurried uneasily to deny, saying, "You're out of line, Johnboy. I want you to listen to me, now—"

"No, you listen to *me*," Johnboy said fiercely. "Look around you! I know you've read Burroughs. You *know* where you are! A dead sea bottom, covered with ocher-colored moss. Rolling hills. A *canal*."

"Those are the very reasons why it can't be real," Thomas said uneasily.

"It's real if we *want* it to be real," Johnboy said. "It's here *because of* us. It's made *for* us. It's made *out* of us."

"Stop gabbing and get in the lander!" the commander shouted. "Move! Get your asses in gear!"

Woody had come up to join them. "Maybe we'd better—" he started to say, but Johnboy cut in with:

"Listen to me! I knew what was happening the moment I looked out and saw the Mars of Schiaparelli and Lowell, the *old* Mars. Woody, you said that Lowell saw what he wanted to see. That's *right*, but in a different way than you meant it. You know, other contemporary astronomers looked at Mars at the same time as Lowell, with the same kind of instruments, and saw no canals at all. You ever hear of consensual reality? Because Lowell wanted to see it, it existed for him! Just as it exists for us—because we want it to exist! We don't have to accept the gray reality of Ahab here and all the other gray, little men back at NASA. They *want* it to be rocks and dust and dead, drab desert; they *like* it that way—"

"For God's sake!" the commander said. "Somebody get that nut in the lander!"

"—but we don't like it! Deep down inside of us—Thomas, Woody—we don't *believe* in that Mars. We believe in this one—the

real one. That's why it's here for us! That's why it's the way it is—
it's made of our dreams. Who knows what's over those hills: bone-
white faerie cities? four-armed green men? beautiful princesses? the Twin Cities of Helium? There could be *anything* out
there!"

"Thomas!" the commander snapped. "Get Johnboy in the
lander *now*. Use force if necessary, but *get him in there*. Johnboy!
You're emotionally unstable. I want you to consider yourself under
house arrest!"

"I've been under house arrest all my life," Johnboy said. "Now
I'm *free*."

Moving deliberately, he reached up and unsnapped his helmet.

Thomas started forward with an inarticulate cry of horror, trying
to stop him, but it was too late. Johnboy had his helmet completely
off now and was shaking his head to free his shaggy, blond hair,
which rippled slightly in the breeze. He took a deep breath,
another, and then grinned at Thomas. "The air smells *great*," he
said. "And, my God, is it clean!"

"Johnboy?" Thomas said hesitantly. "Are you *okay?*"

"Christ!" the commander was muttering. "Christ! Oh my God!
Oh my sweet God!"

"I'm fine," Johnboy said. "In fact, I'm *terrific*." He smiled brilliantly at them, then sniffed at the inside of his helmet and made a
face. "Phew! Smells like an armpit in there!" He started to strip off
his suit.

"Thomas, Woody," the commander said leadenly. "Put Johnboy's body into the lander, and then get in there yourselves, fast,
before we lose somebody else."

"But . . ." Thomas said, "there's nothing wrong with Johnboy.
We're *talking to* him."

"God damn it, *look at your med readouts*."

Thomas glanced at the chinstrap readout board, which was reflected into a tiny square on the right side of his faceplate. There
was a tiny red light flashing on Johnboy's readout. "Christ!" Thomas
whispered.

"He's *dead*, Thomas, he's *dead*. I can see his body. He fell over
like he'd been pole-axed right after he opened his helmet and
hemorrhaged his lungs out into the sand. *Listen* to me! Johnboy's
dead—anything else is a hallucination!"

Johnboy grinned at them, kicking free of his suit. "I may be
dead, kids," he told them quizzically, "but let me tell *you*, dead
or not, I feel one-hundred-percent better now that I'm out of

that crummy suit, believe it. The air's a little bit cool, but it feels *wonderful*." He raised his arms and stretched lazily, like a cat.

"Johnboy—?" Woody said, tentatively.

"*Listen,*" the commander raged. "You're hallucinating! You're talking to yourselves! Get in the lander! That's an *order.*"

"Yes, *sir*, sir," Johnboy said mockingly, sketching a salute at the sky. "Are you actually going to *listen* to that asshole?" He stepped forward and took each of them by the arm and shook them angrily. "Do I *feel* dead to you, schmucks?"

Thomas *felt* the fingers close over his arm, and an odd, deep thrill shot through him—part incredulity, part supernatural dread, part a sudden, strange exhilaration. "I can *feel* him," Woody was saying wonderingly, patting Johnboy with his gloved hands. "He's solid. He's *there*. I'll be a son of a *bitch*—"

"Be one?" Johnboy said, grinning. "Ol' buddy, you already *are* one."

Woody laughed. "No hallucination's *that* corny," Woody said to Thomas. "He's real, all right."

"But the readout—" Thomas began.

"Obviously wrong. There's got to be some kind of mistake—" Woody started to unfasten his helmet.

"No!" the commander screamed, and at the same time Thomas darted forward shouting, "Woody! Stop!" and tried to grab him, but Woody twisted aside and bounded limberly away, out of reach.

Cautiously, Woody took his helmet off. He sniffed suspiciously, his lean, leathery face stiff with tension, then he relaxed, and then he began to smile. "Hooie," he said in awe.

"Get his helmet back on, quick!" the commander was shouting. But Woody's medical readout was already flashing orange, and even as the commander spoke, it turned red.

"Too late!" the commander moaned. "Oh God, too *late*. . . ."

Woody looked into his helmet at his own flashing readout. His face registered surprise for an instant, and then he began to laugh. "Weh-ayl," Woody drawled, "now that I'm officially a corpse, I guess I don't need *this* anymore." He threw his helmet aside; it bounced and rolled over the spongy moss. "Thomas," Woody said, "*you* do what you want, but I've been locked up in a smelly ol' tin can for months, and what *I'm* going to do is *wash my face* in some honest-to-God, unrecycled water!" He grinned at Thomas and began walking away toward the canal. "I might even take me a *swim*."

"Thomas . . ." the commander said brokenly. "Don't worry

about the bodies. Don't worry about *anything* else. Just get in the lander. As soon as you're inside I'm going to trigger the launch sequence."

Johnboy was staring at him quizzically, compassionately—waiting.

"Johnboy . . ." Thomas said. "Johnboy, how can I tell which is real?"

"You *choose* what's real," Johnboy said quietly. "We all do."

"*Listen to* me, Thomas," the commander pleaded; there was an edge of panic in his voice. "You're talking to yourself again. Whatever you think you're seeing, or hearing, or even *touching*, it just *isn't real*. There can be tactile hallucinations, too, you know. It's not *real*."

"Old Ahab up there has made his choice, too," Johnboy said. "For him, in his own conceptual universe, Woody and I *are* dead. And that's real, too—for *him*. But you don't have to choose that reality. You can choose *this* one."

"I don't know," Thomas mumbled, "I just don't *know*. . . ."

Woody hit the water in an explosion of foam. He swam a few strokes, whooping, then turned to float on his back. "C'mon in, you guys!" he shouted.

Johnboy smiled, then turned to bring his face close to Thomas's helmet, peering in through the faceplate. Johnboy was still wearing that strange, dreamy look, so unlike his usual animated expression, and his eyes were clear and compassionate and calm. "It calls for an act of faith, Thomas. Maybe that's how every world begins." He grinned at Thomas. "Meanwhile, I think I'm going to take a swim, too." He strolled off toward the canal, bouncing a little at each step.

Thomas stood unmoving, the two red lights flashing on his chinstrap readout.

"They're both going swimming now," Thomas said dully.

"Thomas! Can you hear me, Thomas?"

"I hear you," Thomas mumbled.

They were having *fun* in their new world—he could see that. The kind of fun that kids had . . . that every child took for granted. The joy of discovery, of everything being *new* . . . the joy that seemed to get lost in the gray shuffle to adulthood, given up bit by incremental bit. . . .

"You're just going to have to trust me, Thomas. *Trust me*. Take my word for it that I know what I'm talking about. You're going to have to take that on faith. Now *listen* to me: No matter what you think is going on down there, *don't take your helmet off*."

His father used to lecture him in that same tone of voice, demanding, domineering . . . and at the same time condescending. Scornful. Daddy knows best. Listen to me, boy, I *know* what I'm talking about! Do what I *tell* you to do!

"Do you hear me? Do *not* take your helmet off! Under any circumstances at all. That's an *order*."

Thomas nodded, before he could stop himself. Here he was, good boy little Tommy, standing on the fringes again, taking orders, doing what he was told. Getting passed over *again*. And for what?

Something flew by in the distance, headed toward the hills.

It looked to be about the size of a large bird, but like a dragonfly, it had six long, filmy gossamer wings, which it swirled around in a complexly interweaving pattern, as if it were rowing itself through the air.

"Get to the lander, Thomas, and close the hatch."

Never did have any fun. Have to be twice as good as *any* of them, have to bust your goddamn ass —

"That's a direct order, Thomas!"

You've got to make the bastards respect you, you've got to *earn* their respect. His father had said that a million times. And how little time it had taken him to waste away and die, once he'd stopped trying, once he realized that you can't earn what people aren't willing to sell.

A red and yellow lizard ran over his boot, as quick and silent as a tickle. It had six legs.

One by one, he began to unclog the latches of his helmet.

"No! Listen to me! If you take off your helmet, you'll *die*. Don't do it! For God's sake, don't do it!"

The last latch. It was sticky, but he tugged at it purposefully.

"You're killing yourself! Stop it! *Please. Stop! You goddamn stupid nigger! Stop —*"

Thomas smiled, oddly enough feeling closer to the commander in that moment than he ever had before. "Too late," he said cheerfully.

Thomas twisted his helmet a quarter turn and lifted it off his head.

When the third red light winked on, Commander Redenbaugh slumped against the board and started to cry. He wept openly and loudly, for they had been good men, and he had failed all of them, even Thomas, the best and steadiest of the lot. He hadn't been able to save a goddamned one of them!

At last he was able to pull himself together. He forced himself to look again at the monitor, which showed three space-suited bodies sprawled out lifelessly on the rusty-red sand.

He folded his hands, bent his head, and prayed for the souls of his dead companions. Then he switched the monitor off.

It was time to make plans. Since the *Plowshare* would be carrying a much lighter-than-anticipated return cargo, he had enough excess fuel to allow him to leave a bit early, if he wanted to, and he *did* want to. He began to punch figures into the computer, smiling bitterly at the irony. Yesterday he had been regretting that they had so little time left in Mars orbit. Now, suddenly, he was in a hurry to get home . . . but no matter how many corners he shaved, he'd still be several long, grueling months in transit—with quite probably a court-martial waiting for him when he got back.

For an instant, even the commander's spirit quailed at the thought of that dreadful return journey. But he soon got himself under control again. It would be a difficult and unpleasant trip, right enough, but a determined man could always manage to do what needed to be done.

Even if he had to do it alone.

When the *Plowshare*'s plasma drive was switched on, it created a daytime star in the Martian sky. It was like a shooting star in reverse, starting out at its brightest and dimming rapidly as it moved up and away.

Thomas saw it leave, He was leaning against his makeshift spear —flametree wood, with a fire-hardened tip—and watching Johnboy preparing to skin the dead hyena-leopard, when he chanced to glance up. "Look," he said.

Johnboy followed Thomas's eyes and saw it, too. He smiled sardonically and lifted the animal's limp paw, making it wave bye-bye. "So long, Ahab," Johnboy said. "Good luck." He went back to skinning the beast. The hyena-leopard—a little bit larger than a wildcat, six-legged, saber-tusked, its fur a muddy purple with rusty-orange spots—had attacked without warning and fought savagely; it had taken all three of them to kill it.

Woody looked up from where he was lashing a makeshift flame-tree-wood raft together with lengths of wiring from the lander. "I'm sure he'll make it okay," Woody said quietly.

Thomas sighed. "Yeah," he said, and then, more briskly, "Let me give you a hand with that raft. If we snap it up, we ought to be ready to leave by morning."

Last night, climbing the highest of the rolling hills to the north, they had seen the lights of a distant city, glinting silver and yellow and orange on the far horizon, gleaming far away across the black midnight expanse of the dead sea bottom like an ornate and intricate piece of jewelry set against ink-black velvet.

Thomas was still not sure if he hoped there would be aristocratic red men there, and giant four-armed green Tharks, and beautiful Martian princesses. . . .

Introduction

Art Appreciation

Barry Malzberg

"Art Appreciation," a product of too many afternoons in the 70s stalking museums and seeking a set of responses which I simply could not frame, was rejected here and there before it sold to *Omni* for an amazing (to me) $2,500.00, the highest price for a short story of my (at least partial) composition.

Jack Dann

In my autobiography for *Contemporary Authors*, I wrote:
   "I'm standing in Barry Malzberg's living room. The walls are covered with books. Two couches and a coffee table seem to fill up the room. Across the room and to my right are the glass doors of Barry's office.
   "It is 1975 and summer. Barry and George Zebrowski and I have just driven back from New Jersey, where we attended a dreadful party at Roger Elwood's home. Half of the people at the party were writers and half were members of his church. We rode up and back in Barry's Cadillac. The party was so uncomfortable that Barry and I kept sneaking out to the car to nip at a bottle of bourbon that he kept in the glove compartment for just such emergencies.
   "George, who is in another room talking to Joyce, Barry's wife, has been quite optimistic all day. He and Barry have been arguing

about the fate of science fiction, the growing book market, and hardcover vs. paperback books. George has been telling Barry that he, Barry, has hurt his career because of his approach to the field, because of his pessimism. Barry became angry and left the room, then returned, only to pace.

"Now he is standing beside me. He is well over six feet tall and is dressed in a white shirt with a tab collar, the kind worn during the sixties that pushed out the knot of the necktie. He is wearing a black tie and jacket; he has not fastened the little tabs under the tie. He seems to loom beside me, a great black bird.

" 'You think you're like George,' he whispers, as if George is in the room and might hear. 'You think that by being diligent and producing a body of good work it will somehow work out.' He pauses to fit a cigarette into a holder, and I wonder if the pause is for effect. 'You wait and see, you'll feel differently. There's too much darkness in you, you won't be able to delude yourself much longer. You'll see, you're like me. . . .'

"I nod and feel the man's power, his unique charisma. It's as if the darkness he spoke of, which he represents, has become suddenly palpable."

By 1985—by the time Barry and I wrote "Art Appreciation"— Barry neither smoked nor drank. But the "essence of Barry," that particular darkness that seems to shroud him, was and still is as strong and powerful as ever. However, his darkness, his poised bleakness, is really a distilled form of black humor—and, in fact, much of Barry's work is very funny. His fiction is a metaphor for his life, and it contains the joy, wisdom, and humor of the aphorism, "Don't worry, everything will get worse."

Barry and I have lived an entire lifetime through correspondence, first with what is now called "snail-mail," and then with e-mail. For some thirty years, we have carried on a continuing discussion about life, fiction, pain, joy, and the constructs by which we live. Millions of words. Words written every day. And, every once in a great while, we manage to get together and talk the talk. It's always pure joy . . . and it's always intense because intensity is one of Barry's defining characteristics.

Although most would not describe Barry as joyful, he is. It is a dark, ultraviolet joy, but it is joy nevertheless.

Barry's particular intensity—and humor—can be found in this story, which was passed back and forth in the mail. I think he took a particular joy with all the munching and masticating. The "glops" are all Barry's.

"Art Appreciation" was meant to be funny, but in such a nasty way that one might be forgiven for missing it.

With this story, as with many others (but not all), I believe I suggested the idea, Barry did a draft, and I did interstitial material and the final draft. It is my recollection that I sent the story to Ellen Datlow at *Omni* first.

Barry and I have just completed (via e-mail) another story. This one was passed back and forth—I wrote an opening, Barry wrote a section, I reworked and wrote another section, and Barry did the final, conforming draft.

So, you see, even old dogs can learn new collaborative tricks.

Art Appreciation

Barry N. Malzberg and Jack Dann

*G*LOP.

There went another gallery-goer, an overweight, middle-aged woman, camera slung over the right shoulder, blue sunglasses, a peaked cap, long purple fingernails. The kind of woman you'd fantasize being eaten by a painting, perhaps. The kind of woman—a tip of the hat to Mencken here—who made you want to burn every bed in the world. *Glop. Glug.* Into the Giaconda smile.

The Mona Lisa seemed to wink at Evans and Evans struggled against the impulse to wink back. That would have made him a collaborator. He was definitely not that. He viewed with alarm. Horror, in fact.

Glop. Tourists disappeared head first into the maw of La Giaconda. This woman was the fifth within the hour. How long had this been going on? he asked himself once again, as if repetition could bring enlightenment. Had it been going on since the very first? Since Leonardo had painted the sphinxlike wife of the merchant Pier Francesco del Giocondo? Could he have been her first victim? There was a certain metaphysical satisfaction in that thought. Indeed. Leonardo da Vinci unleashes the atom bomb of archetypes. Hateful man. But, alas, he could certainly paint.

All of this had its comic aspects, of course, and the indignity of exit was provocative, but you were really dealing with tragedy here. Evans had to keep that in mind. This was his Blue Period, as he had decided to call it only a little while ago when the tourists started to slide away. It was no improvement upon the Yellow Period, which seemed to have gone on for several decades up to this point, but it looked as if it was going to be instructive. Alone in the gallery now, bereaved, he supposed, Evans could feel waves of satisfaction coming from the famous painting, along with the hint of a belch. Well, what was he supposed to do? Arrest the painting? Turn in La Giaconda to the authorities? What did you do with something like this?

There was a whole clump of guards just outside the gallery, standing sullenly, pacing around; they represented, Evans supposed, a kind of authority. Should he go to them, point out that La Giaconda was gobbling tourists, waiting until only Evans and a straggler were there, then snatching the incautious traveler who came too close to the frame and inserting the surprised victim into a mouth grown not ambiguous but suddenly huge? The screams from the tourists, however brief, were intense enough to travel, but the guards had shown no reaction. The dangers posed by this kind of cannibalism seemed immense. Still, there seemed no proper way to deal with the situation. "Excuse me," he could say to one of the union guys carrying batons and small radios, "I don't mean to interrupt your conversation, but there's *some very strange stuff* going on here, I don't quite know how to tell you this, but—"

Well, but what? This wasn't the kind of thing you could tell a stranger. The terms were imponderable. The worst sign would be indications of interest and credulity. That would mean that he was being humored while reinforcements were called in. Drastic things would happen. Evans himself might stand accused of killing tourists, corpus delicti or not.

Still. "Still now," he said to the Mona Lisa, the painting on special international loan, placed high on the wall opposite, buttressed by heavy frame and protected by guys in the anteroom with batons and receivers, "I've got my eye on you, lady. You're not going to get away with this, lady. Evans is on the job and sees exactly what's going on here, which is why I'm keeping a safe distance. You're not getting away with anything in front of *me*," he pointed out quietly, meanwhile trying to maintain a reserved, a glacial calm. He knew he was safe if he stayed more than six feet away. "This is my Blue Period," Evans confided in a whisper. To a theoretical stranger he would appear perfectly insane, he knew, but there were no strangers in the gallery itself, just Evans and the painting. Oh, how they squealed and kicked in their dismay. It was a grim thing to see. "I didn't intend it to be this way," Evans went on, talking to the painting as if it were an actual, a reasonable woman rather than an assassin. "I had plans, you know, but the economy got tight and now I have to fill up the days any way I can. You're not going to get away with this though, lady. We're going to take measures."

In truth, Evans knew this was pure bluff. He had no plans whatsoever. Shortly, the absence of the eaten would be noted and bureaucracy in its fumbling way would try to deal with the situation, but there was no way that this could fall within its lexicon. Detectives might get to the Guggenheim, but how could they possibly implicate a painting, even one which was priceless? She wore an expression of utter innocence and had a terrific provenance. Her scheme was not only diabolic, it appeared foolproof. But, futile as it might be, Evans at least was on the case. "You're going to be stopped," he said harshly. "We're going to bring this to a conclusion." One of the guards outside moved to the doorway, put a hand on the sill, leaned, peered in, an uncomfortable moment of glances brushing. Evens shrugged, shook his head, then stood. There was no point in appearing crazy, although this museum like millennial New York itself was filled with mumblers. He would fit right in. Everything fit right in, one way or the other.

It was time to go out on Fifth Avenue and ponder his next moves, anyway. Couldn't stay hammered in with La Giaconda all day, not without attracting undue attention. There was more space out there, he would work something out. Trust not in Evans to abandon the situation, he thought hopefully. He would do something to avenge those innocent lives, protect others. Just as soon as he could figure out some means of approach.

The Yellow Period (he had not called it then, had merely thought of it as his life itself) had apparently ended; Evans was vaulted into a new and difficult circumstance. Once, not so long ago either, Evans thought he had the whole project worked out, a series of activities (lack of activity, perhaps), which was a process of real accommodation. You couldn't be a remittance man *all* your life, not if you wanted to lead an active, useful existence in millennial times. You had to get out there to the mainstream, compete in some way. Furthermore, he had always been interested in painting, not creation exactly but certainly art appreciation, had felt that someday he would really pursue it. Take in all the museums, the better galleries, follow the more important exhibitions; and then when his head was filled with all of the finest in art, he would register at the School for Visual Arts and try some work of his own.

Well, why not? Look at what had happened to Pollock, Kandinsky, Van Gogh, Roualt. Bums all of them, Picasso too and that mystic Chagall, foundered lives, preposterous choices which to everyone's surprise had worked out. Picasso had derived his first major success by painting whores from his favorite cathouse in the shape of squares. There were thirty-year-old punks around who had been striping up subway cars not so long ago, now picking up big money from the downtown crowd. Evans had at least as much to offer as they did; he knew he had the talent. It was just a matter of bringing it out.

So the renovated Guggenheim with its imported La Giaconda seemed a good place to start. There had been a lot of controversy, of course, about using the Guggenheim for the site of the Mona Lisa loan, a lot of critics had thought that it should go somewhere else, someplace larger, more important. If not the Metropolitan, then at least the Frick.

But the Guggenheim needed an attention-getter to bring its audience back and make a statement for the contributors. In their fervor to make this coup, the Guggenheim administrators broke, or perhaps bent, museum rules about acquiring and exhibiting only modern art. No small amount of emoluments, kickbacks, pleas, grief, sexual promises, and maneuvers even less desultory had been employed to lever La Giaconda from the Louvre for a six-month enlistment. It was worth it all for the prestige and publicity. La Giaconda was something of a cliché, a joke really, Evans had perceived from his assiduous researches, certainly not to be taken as seriously as might have been the case earlier. Priceless maybe, but a tourist phenomenon. So La Giaconda had ended up in the Guggenheim and so had Evans, starting his grand tour of what he liked to think of as his post-Yellow Period, but he hadn't counted on the Yellow turning Blue so rapidly; he hadn't counted on La Giaconda grabbing solitary tourists while guards complained to one another in the hallway when the gallery was momentarily empty, except for the keenly observant Evans. That had not been part of the plan.

It was a disconcerting business, that was for sure, and Evans was hardly positive that he was handling this properly. It probably was not a police matter, though. His instincts on that seemed reasonable. People had been put away permanently, he suspected, for far less than the kind of reportage he was resisting.

* * *

Out on Fifth Avenue, watching traffic, Evans considered his ever-narrowing options. Not much movement on a cloudy Tuesday morning, even the remittance men were sleeping in. He discussed metaphysics with a pretzel vendor, wrote two letters to an old girlfriend in his head, the first filled with euphemism, the second desperate and scatological. He looked at a woman walking her poodle, feeling a thin and desperate lust, and shook his head. Undone by his own mindless need.

"Good, isn't she?" the pretzel vendor said politely. "You see a lot on these streets, don't you?"

"More than I would ever know," Evans said hopelessly.

"Know what?" the vendor asked. "Know who? As long as you figure that they were just put there to torment us, you've got the right handle on the situation. It has nothing to do with getting and keeping."

"But what is getting and keeping?" Evans asked and then, before the conversation could get out of hand, backed away from the vendor. "We'll talk about it later," he said. "It doesn't matter." The vendor shrugged. I should just go home, Evans thought, go back to remittance man's heaven, go to my studio condominium in a reconverted downtown loft, get away from all this before I start to take it seriously. After all, none of this is my problem. If they want to come by and get taken away by a demented painting, that's their business. I'm not involved. I just happened to be on the premises. The only point is this: they aren't snatching *me*. As long as I'm not being picked up, what's the difference?

But the argument seemed halting and unconvincing. It seemed to evade the issues, whatever those issues might be. Another good-looking woman, earphones clamped, stray notes of baroque streaming from the earphones like pennants, jogged by, heedless of Evans's stare. He looked after her with confusion and a longing born of years of deprivation. She should snatch him up. She should do to him, Evans thought, what La Giaconda was doing with the tourists. Oh, how he yearned to run after her, find a cab maybe, catch up, plead his case. It wasn't as if he was disfigured, or an idiot. It wasn't as if he had nothing to say.

He had plenty to say! Look at what was going on in the gallery. That certainly would be a way to make contact. The jogger was wearing pink sweat-pants and a red T-shirt; it made him crazy watching her slowly diminish, like a favorable weather condition being undone by cosmic dust. The clownishness of his desire overwhelmed Evans then as it so often did, and he shook his head, tried to push all of it away, and walked back into the museum, showing his handstamp. I don't know why I'm going back, he thought, I don't know why I'm bothering with all this. I've seen all there is to see: five tourists gobbled, and every angle of La Giaconda. And two women, one in red and pink, the other *avec* chin, who wouldn't look at me twice if I were up there on the wall with Mona. Maybe that *was* the point. Maybe that was what he was driving toward. He thought of the School of Visual Arts, what art itself meant to him. If he could only get on that wall, become a simulacrum of himself.

Hell, if Leonardo da Vinci could do it why couldn't he? Wasn't La Giaconda supposed to be a portrait of the artist? Hadn't Evans heard a gallery guide putting forth that very possibility to a group of disbelieving tourists? Hadn't someone in fact used a computer to prove a point-by-point congruence by juxtaposing La Giaconda with Leonardo's red chalk self portrait? Take one part Leonardo's face and one part of La Giaconda and *presto!* you have the world's most enigmatic smile, the simulacrum to end all simulacra, eternal art. One need only follow the recipe.

Glop. It was all too abstract for him.

The gallery was still empty; the guards hanging around the hall nodded to him as he walked by. There in the corner, invisible from his first angle, was yet another pretty woman. Indeed, this was his morning for them. This woman looked somewhat like his jogger, all in red, though, a red dress, yearning waxen expression, a hand bag clutched against her small breasts. She was arched like a bow, staring at the Mona Lisa. Somehow she had gotten into this room, gotten into the Guggenheim, gotten through all of her life up to this point without Evans having ever seen her. Maybe she had come from the upper corridors, examining Segal sculptures. Of whatever provenance, she was extraordinary; in his sudden and tottering mood Evans felt he had never been so struck by anyone. Sensitivity came from her eyes, from the angle of her hand bag, from the intelligent, anguished tilt of her head as she searched the eyes of La Giaconda for meaning.

"Hey," he said quietly. "You shouldn't do that. I don't mean to intrude, I mean I'm not trying to come on like a masher or something, but you shouldn't lean into the painting like that, it's dangerous, you know what I mean? You're alone, something might happen—" He was babbling, that was all. In any event, she did not hear him. "Please," Evans said, "I'm just trying to be helpful, that painting is a masterpiece all right but it is very threatening—"

Who was threatening? Who was acting like an idiot now? He

stopped talking, sized up the situation with shrewd and caring eyes, then began to move slowly toward her, thoughts of rescue in mind.

This is ridiculous, Evans thought. I'm making a fool of myself. It was humiliating not even to be noticed. If he was going to lose control like this, then he should at least shed anonymity, make some kind of *impression*. Was this the real problem? He had never really been observed, never been the object of love and focus and interest, never had a sense of real connection. No wonder La Gioconda wouldn't eat him. He couldn't even establish a relationship at the point of consumption.

"Excuse me," he said very loudly to the woman in red. "You shouldn't do that, please."

Now it seemed that he had caught her attention. She had fine white lips, an openness of expression, an enormity of mood into which Evans felt he could suddenly plunge. He suddenly and truly loved her. As he stared at her in this moment of revelation, he had never been at such a distance in his life.

"Do what?" she asked. "What are you talking about?"

"The painting," he said hopelessly. "I want to tell you about the painting."

The woman put both hands on her pocketbook, backed a crucial step away from the Mona Lisa. Her cheekbones cast light, cast swift intelligence. Oh, he was definitely communicating, getting something through now. He had taken her a step away from the painting, and that was definitely progress.

"I don't understand," she said. "What do you mean?"

Her face showed interest, but it was that of the student, of the appreciator of art, of the listener to a recorded guided tour. The handbag could have been a device whispering words of information as she rubbed it subtly against her face, her ear. All portent, no possibility. Evans thought of calling for a guard, then put that thought away. It was hopeless. There was simply no way of dealing with the situation. I should have followed the jogger instead, he thought. I would have had fresh air, and she would not have been in danger.

"I don't know what I mean," Evans said abruptly. "I'm just trying to tell you about that painting. You shouldn't be near—"

"Do you *want* something? What do you want?" Displeasure streaked her beautiful features now; she seemed to be plunging toward a turmoil of accusation. Evans could pick up on those signs too. He had had plenty of experience at a difficult mid-Yellow point of life.

"Why don't you just go away," the woman said.

Well, there was nothing to say to that. Evans had nothing to say. If he went away, which was a reasonable possibility, he would confirm her impression; but then he would leave her exposed to the Mona Lisa smash and grab. Meanwhile, the guards were no factor unless she began to scream. She could start screaming very soon, though. Evans had the feeling that he was working within narrow perimeters here. Although he had the smallest possibility of achievement, he had to plunge on.

"You're very pretty," he said. "You're beautiful in fact. But you're too close to that painting. Move back another step."

"Are you a member of security?"

"Yes. If you will. If you want to call me that. I'm trying to keep you secure, can't you see?"

"You don't act like a security person," the woman said, not pleasantly. Disgust seemed to be seeping, along with confusion, into her sensitive features. "I don't think you're on staff at all."

"You don't understand," Evans said. "The painting is only on loan."

"What does that have to do with anything?"

"It's not permanently ours. It's a bait and switch game. It picks up and reassembles in France, maybe. The population problem—"

But now she had clearly reached an opinion as she backed slowly away from him. But at least she was moving away from the painting. Opening up space. That was the important thing. Evans followed her irresistibly. They moved in tandem toward the door. Now for the first time the guards seemed to take an interest; they peered in.

"One moment," Evans said. "*Uno momento*, I have to tell you something. I wanted to say how beautiful you are. You're a whole gallery in yourself."

The woman turned, as if ready to break into a full run. At least I've saved her, Evans thought. This is a dangerous situation, very perilous, hardly explicable, but at least I think I got her out of this.

"So listen to me," he said. "Before you go away, before you talk to the guard, before you complain, you've got to understand my angle here. It's not just because you're beautiful. It's because—"

Well, he had not put this the right way, obviously. She ran away, the red and brown handbag flapping like a decapitated bird. The guards were crooning to one another, then they seemed to make a collective decision: they advanced.

Evans reversed his course, backed, moved toward the painting.

There was simply nowhere else to go. "Hold it," a guard said, "just hold it right there, pal, we want to talk to you." Talk did not seem to be properly in his mind, however. The guard seemed enormous, a club extended like a baton from his right hand. He was conducting the others into a massed assault.

"Oh, *damn* it," Evans said hopelessly.

He scuttled toward the painting. On his right shoulder, then, he could feel a burning touch, a grasp of enormous assurance and power and then smoothly, inevitably, he felt himself moved upward. *Glug*, he thought. *Glop*. He was too high now to see the guards or to judge their reactions. He seemed quite out of control; and yet, at the center, was an awful certainty.

He felt the pressure and the wind as he was drawn.

You don't understand, he thought. "You don't understand," he wanted to say to the guards. He wanted to explain somehow, tell them about the fleeting, righteous woman, the vanished jogger, all of the vanished women of his Yellow and Blue periods; but the words would not come. "This is dangerous," he wanted to say. "This is a dangerous place. I just wanted to save her, can't you understand that?"

"It's not lust, it's humanity," he wanted to say.

Glop.

No, it seemed that they could not understand that. Evans was plunged into a clinging darkness, damp, damp, cold certainty pressing around him and then, shocking, he was falling. I wonder if there's anything down there, he thought. I always wanted to see Venice in its seasons, see the colors of the old Renaissance. Maybe that's waiting for me, maybe the others are waiting there, too, he thought. He thought many other things as well, but they do not fall into the scope of this present narrative. He is still thinking. He will be thinking for a long time.

Alas, those further thoughts are not to be recorded.

He is not on exhibition, not exactly.

Evans is on permanent loan.

Introduction

Golden Apples of the Sun

Michael Swanwick

It was a clear, starry night and Jack Dann came breezing into town at the wheel of a limousine twenty feet long, with a big cigar stuck in one corner of his expansive grin . . . And, as usual, Jack and Gardner and I were having five conversations at once. Jack was telling me about his experiences as a cable salesman and talking with Gardner about an anthology they were putting together. I was telling Jack about the time I almost drowned and what I saw as I was dying, and consulting with Gardner about a fantasy story I was having trouble with. And Gardner was talking to the room, passing along an interesting story that a new acquaintance named Tatiana had told us.

"Who's Tatiana?" Jack asked.

Gardner ignored him, of course. When you've got three Talkers going at once, you don't dare go back over the finer points of a story you're telling or the other two will run roughshod over you. He was expanding the tale now and elaborating it with an occasional "At least that's what Tatiana said."

"Who's Tatiana?" Jack repeated.

But Gardner was moving the narrative into virgin territory and all of his attention was on the creation of convincing detail. About the only relation this version had with the original at this point was the occasional validating mention of Tatiana as its unimpeachable source.

"Who's Tatiana?" Jack said, in a tone indicating he knew exactly how slim his chances of ever getting an answer to that particular question were.

"She's the Queen of the Fairies," Gardner wisecracked, playing on the name's similarity to Titania. Which didn't lessen Jack's confusion one bit.

So, taking pity on him, I threw in, "She's also Don Keller's wife."

"Jeeze," Jack said. "That's kind of a letdown. 'I used ta be da Queen a da Fairies an' now I'm selling computers in Poith Amboy.'"

And we were off.

"Golden Apples of the Sun" originally appeared in *Penthouse* in grotesquely shortened form. We'd written it out at ten thousand words, and the people there said they'd buy it if we cut it down to five thousand. Which Gardner and I, over a long and blood-soaked day, proceeded to do. But that's a gruesome tale and one that isn't fit for mixed company.

Gardner Dozois

Michael's account of the origin of this story is fundamentally accurate. Since Jack had actually worked as a door-to-door salesman (something we'd been talking about earlier in the afternoon, in fact, which probably went into the gestalt that inspired this story), and so had real-life experiences that he could draw upon, he seemed like the logical one to start the story, which we figured should begin with a sequence describing the hapless computer salesman trying fruitlessly to peddle his wares. Jack sat down at the typewriter with his usual energy, writing at a white-hot pace, and within a couple of hours had produced the first seven or eight pages, carrying the story through to the end of the initial door-to-door selling sequence, which appear here fundamentally unchanged, except for some interstitial fluffing-up, mostly scene-setting, that I added later. Then he went back to Binghamton, leaving us with a salesman stranded in Faërie with a grass tail and a two-foot-long nose, and also leaving us with no idea what to do with the rest of the story.

Michael and I worked out the rest of the plot, with a few embellishments from Jack, such as the hopping one-eyed creature, who'd already had a guest-shot in an earlier solo story of Jack's. Morrig the Fearsome was Michael's idea; having him talk like a '30s Labor Union Organizer was my idea. We went back and forth over the ending until we came up with something we were satisfied with. My major contribution to the story was to fluff up the texture, adding lots of mythological references and coming up with the pseudo-Spenserian dialect that the Faërie folk speak. I also tried to add a few evocative touches here and there, lyrical descriptions of the setting, since it seemed to me that Faërie ought to be a mysterious and beautiful place, a place of wonders, at the same time that it was the setting for an Unknown Worlds-type knockabout comedy. I also added some new scenes retroactively, like the scene where Barry runs into the Queen of the Fairies in a rundown roadside bar in South Jersey.

The story appeared, in a drastically cut version, in *Penthouse* under the terrible and misleading title (meant to be wink-wink salacious, perhaps?) "Virgin Territory." Later, the uncut version, under the title "Golden Apples of the Sun," was picked up by Art Saha for *The Year's Best Fantasy Stories: 11*. (The title contains an appalling pun, entirely of Michael's invention, which perhaps would be made clearer if we rendered the title, as we originally intended to, as "Golden APPLES of the Sun"—assuming that anyone, this far away from 1984, remembers what APPLES were. For what it's worth, written as it was at the very beginning of the Computer Age, or at least the Home Computer Age, this may be one of the first stories to toss Faërie, magic, and computers into the same aesthetic mix; it wouldn't be the last.

Jack Dann

I can't help it, but I've always thought of this as my cable TV story.

We were indeed talking about cable television because I was griping about having to be a cold call, commission only, cable television salesman.

I had sold a series of science fiction novels with a ten-page proposal; or rather I *thought* I had sold a series of science fiction novels. On the basis of that assumption, I bought a house (I had a new family), moved in, and as one does who has no actual money, I used my credit card to pay the bills. After all, an advance would be forthcoming real soon now.

Then I got *the* call: the proposal was knocked down in committee, sorry Jack, I was sure this was a done deal; and so one warm, summer night I was sitting on my porch, trying to figure out what the hell I was going to do, when a salesman came to my door trying to sell me cable TV, which I could now ill afford. We chatted. It turned out that he had always wanted to be a writer. I told him that if he could get me into the cable company, I would teach him how to write. And so I became a cable television salesman. (And he *tried* to become a writer.)

I had never sold anything in my life, and when I gingerly knocked on that first apartment house door, I was so nervous that I offered the homeowner a fifteen year free-trial of either *Showtime* or *HBO*. (It was supposed to be a fifteen-day free trial!)

The homeowner, of course, accepted immediately.

And suddenly, I was a salesman!

I don't remember the conversation about Don Keller's wife, but it *sounds* right. I do remember getting excited about the idea of a poor schlep of a salesman who is stuck selling computers in a bad neighborhood where everyone is a troll, witch, ogre, or some other form of foul, bad-smelling, nasty, ugly, dangerous, ill-mannered misfit—indeed, there were nights when I was pounding the pavements and having multiple doors slammed on my face that I felt like I was in my own tortured version of Faërie.

And so, yes, I sat down in front of the old Remington typewriter on the table in Gardner and Susan's living room and started typing in a white heat.

I was off and running.

I was going to get my own back at every sumbitch troll that had ever slammed a door on my pointy, inquisitive little face. Once again, I suppose, I embarrassed Gardner and Michael into another collaboration. I piled all those pages into a neat stack on the table beside the typewriter, and then, quietly, softly, with the stealth of a ballet dancer or a practiced international spy, I . . . left.

And magically, a check came in the mail.

Now I ask you, ain't being a writer grand? . . .

Golden Apples of the Sun

Gardner Dozois, Jack Dann, and Michael Swanwick

FEW OF THE FOLK IN FAËRIE WOULD HAVE ANYTHING to do with the computer salesman. He worked himself up and down one narrow, twisting street after another, until his feet throbbed and his arms ached from lugging the sample cases, and it seemed like days had passed rather than hours, and *still* he had not made a single sale. Barry Levingston considered himself a first-class salesman, one of the *best*, and he wasn't used to this kind of failure. It discouraged and frustrated him, and as the afternoon wore endlessly on—there was something funny about the way time passed here in Faërie; the hazy, bronze-colored Fairyland sun had hardly moved at all across the smoky, amber sky since he'd arrived, although it should certainly be evening by *now*—he could feel himself beginning to lose that easy confidence and unshakable self-esteem that are the successful salesman's most essential stock in trade. He tried to tell himself that it wasn't really *his* fault. He was working under severe restrictions, after all. The product was new and unfamiliar to this particular market, and he was going "cold sell." There had been no telephone solicitation programs to develop leads, no ad campaigns, not so much as a demographic study of the market potential. Still, his total lack of success was depressing.

The village that he'd been trudging through all day was built on and around three steep, hivelike hills, with one street rising from the roofs of the street below. The houses were piled chockablock atop each other, like clusters of grapes, making it almost impossible to even find—much less *get* to—many of the upper-story doorways. Sometimes the eaves grew out over the street, turning them into long, dark tunnels. And sometimes the streets ran up sloping house-sides and across rooftops, only to come to a sudden and frightening *stop* at a sheer drop of five or six stories, the street beginning again as abruptly on the far side of the gap. From the highest streets and stairs you could see a vista of the surrounding countryside: a hazy, golden-brown expanse of orchids and forests and fields, and, on the far horizon, blue with distance, the jagged, snow-capped peaks of a mighty mountain range—except that the mountains didn't always seem to be in the same *direction* from one moment to the next; sometimes they were to the west, then to the north, or east, or south; sometimes they seemed much closer or farther away; sometimes they weren't there at *all*.

Barry found all this unsettling. In fact, he found the whole *place* unsettling. Why go *on* with this, then? he asked himself. He certainly wasn't making any headway. Maybe it was because he overtowered most of the fairyfolk—maybe they were sensitive about being so *short*, and so tall people annoyed them. Maybe they just didn't like humans; humans *smelled* bad to them, or something. Whatever it was, he hadn't gotten more than three words of his spiel out of his mouth all day. Some of them had even slammed doors in his face—something he had almost forgotten could happen to a salesman.

Throw in the towel, then, he thought. But . . . no, he *couldn't* give up. Not yet. Barry sighed, and massaged his stomach, feeling the acid twinges in his gut that he knew presaged a savage attack of indigestion later on. This was virgin territory, a literally untouched route. Gold waiting to be mined. And the Fairy Queen had given this territory to *him* . . .

Doggedly, he plodded up to the next house, which looked something like a gigantic acorn, complete with a thatched cap and a crazily twisted chimney for the stem. He knocked on a round, wooden door.

A plump, freckled fairy woman answered. She was about the size of an earthly two-year-old, but a transparent gown seemingly woven of spidersilk made it plain that she was no child. She hovered a few inches above the doorsill on rapidly beating humming-bird wings.

"Aye?" she said sweetly, smiling at him, and Barry immediately felt his old confidence return. But he didn't permit himself to become excited. That was the quickest way to lose a sale.

"Hello," he said smoothly. "I'm from Newtech Computer Systems, and we've been authorized by Queen Titania, the Fairy Queen *herself*, to offer a *free* installation of our new home computer system—"

"That wot I not of," the fairy said.

"Don't you even know what a computer *is?*" Barry asked, dismayed, breaking off his spiel.

"Aye, I fear me, 'tis even so," she replied, frowning prettily. "In sooth, I know not. Belike you'll tell me of't, fair sir."

Barry began talking feverishly, meanwhile unsnapping his sample case and letting it fall open to display the computer within. "—balance your household accounts," he babbled. "Lets you organize your recipes, keep in touch with the stock market. You can generate full-color graphics, charts, graphs . . ."

The fairy frowned again, less sympathetically. She reached her hand toward the computer, but didn't quite touch it. "Has the smell of metal on't," she murmured. "Most chill and adamant." She shook her head. "Nay, sirrah, 'twill not serve. 'Tis a thing mechanical, a clockwork, meet for carillons and orreries. Those of us born within the Ring need not your engines philosophic, nor need we toil and swink as mortals do at such petty tasks an you have named. Then wherefore should I buy, who neither strive nor moil?"

"But you can play *games* on it!" Barry said desperately, knowing that he was losing her. "You can play Donkey Kong! You can play *PacMan! Everybody* likes to play PacMan—"

She smiled slowly at him sidelong. "I'd liefer more delightsome games," she said.

Before he could think of anything to say, a long, long, *long* green-gray arm came slithering out across the floor from the hidden interior of the house. The arm ended in a knobby hand equipped with six grotesquely long, tapering fingers, now spreading wide as the hand reached out toward the fairy . . .

Barry opened his mouth to shout a warning, but before he could, the long arm had wrapped bonelessly around her ankle, not once but *four* times around, and the hand with its scrabbling spider fingers had closed over her thigh. The arm yanked back, and she tumbled forward in the air, laughing. "Ah, loveling, can you not wait?" she said with mock severity. The arm tugged at her. She giggled, "Certes, me-seems you cannot!"

As the arm pulled her, still floating, back into the house, the fairy woman seized the door to slam it shut. Her face was flushed and preoccupied now, but she still found a moment to smile at Barry. "Farewell, sweet mortal!" she cried, and winked. "Next time, mayhap?"

The door shut. There was a muffled burst of giggling within. Then silence.

The salesman glumly shook his head. This was a goddamn tank town, was what it was, he thought. Here there were no knickknacks and bric-a-brac lining the windows, no cast-iron flamingoes and eave-climbing plaster kitty cats, no mailboxes with fake Olde English calligraphy on them—but in spite of that it was still a tank town. Just another goddamn middle-class neighborhood with money a little tight and the people running scared. Place like this, you couldn't even *give* the stuff away, much less make a sale. He stepped back out into the street. A fairy knight was coming down the road toward him, dressed in green jade armor cunningly shaped like leaves, and riding an enormous frog. Well, why not? Barry thought. He wasn't having a lot of luck door-to-door.

"Excuse me, sir!" Barry cried, stepping into the knight's way. "May I have a moment of your—"

The knight glared at him, and pulled back suddenly on his reins. The enormous frog reared up, and leaped straight into the air. Gigantic, leathery batlike wings spread, caught the thermals, carried mount and rider away.

Barry sighed and trudged doggedly up the cobblestone road toward the next house. No matter what happened, he wasn't going to quit until he'd finished the street. That was a compulsion of his . . . and the reason he was one of the top cold-sell agents in the company. He remembered a night when he'd spent five hours knocking on doors without a single sale, or even so much as a kind *word*, and then suddenly he'd sold $30,000 worth of merchandise in an hour . . . suddenly he'd been golden, and they couldn't say no to him. Maybe that would happen today, too. Maybe the next house would be the beginning of a run of good luck . . .

The next house was shaped like a gigantic ogre's face, its dark wood forming a yawning mouth and heavy-lidded eyes. The face was made up of a host of smaller faces, and each of *those* contained other, even smaller faces. He looked away dizzily, then resolutely climbed to a glowering, thick-nosed door and knocked right between the eyes—eyes that, he noted uneasily, seemed to be studying him with interest.

A fairy woman opened the door—below where he was standing. Belatedly, he realized that he had been knocking on a dormer; the top of the door was a foot below him.

This fairy woman had stubby, ugly wings. She was lumpy and gnarled, and her skin was the texture of old bark. Her hair stood straight out on end all around her head, in a puffy nimbus, like the Bride of Frankenstein. She stared imperiously up at him, somehow managing to seem to be staring *down* her nose at him at the same time. It was quite a nose, too. It was longer than his hand, and sharply pointed.

"A great ugly lump of a mortal, an I mistake not!" she snapped. Her eyes were flinty and hard. "What's toward?"

"I'm from Newtech Computer Systems," Barry said, biting back his resentment at her initial slur, "and I'm selling home computers, by special commission of the Queen—"

"Go to!" she snarled. "Seek you to cozen me? I wot *not* what abnormous beast that be, but I have no need of mortal kine, nor aught else from your loathly world! Get you gone!" She slammed the door under his feet. Which somehow was every bit as bad as slamming it in his face.

"Son of a *bitch!*" Barry raged, making an obscene gesture at the door, losing his temper at last. "You goddamn flying fat pig!"

He didn't realize that the fairy woman could hear him until a round, crystal window above his head flew open, and she poked her head out of it, nose first, buzzing like a jarful of hornets, "Wittold!" she shrieked. "Caitiff rogue!"

"Screw off, lady," Barry snarled. It had been a long, hard day, and he could feel the last shreds of self-control slipping away. "Get back in your goddamn hive, you goddamn pinocchio-nosed mosquito!"

The fairy woman spluttered incoherently with rage, then became dangerously silent. "So!" she said in cold passion. "*Noses*, is't? Would villify *my* nose, knave, whilst your *own* be uncommon squat and vile? A tweak or two will remedy *that*, I trow, and exchange the better for the worse!"

So saying, she came buzzing out of her house like an outraged wasp, streaking straight at the salesman.

Barry flinched back, but she seized hold of his nose with both hands and tweaked it savagely. Barry yelped in pain. She shrieked out a high-pitched syllable in some unknown language and began flying backward, her wings beating furiously, *tugging* at his nose.

He felt the pressure in his ears change with a sudden *pop*, and then, horrifyingly, he felt his face begin to *move* in a strangely fluid way, flowing like water, swelling out and out and *out* in front of him.

The fairy woman released his nose and darted away, cackling gleefully.

Dismayed, Barry clapped his hands to his face. He hadn't realized that these little buggers could *all* cast spells—he'd thought that kind of magic stuff was reserved for the Queen and her court. Like cavorting in hot tubs with naked starlets and handfuls of cocaine, out in Hollywood—a prerogative reserved only for the elite. But when his hands reached his nose, they almost couldn't close around it. It was too large. His nose was now nearly two feet long, as big around as a Polish sausage, and covered with bumpy warts.

He screamed in rage. "Goddammit, lady, come back here and *fix* this!"

The fairy woman was perching half-in and half-out of the round window, lazily swinging one leg. She smiled mockingly at him. "There!" she said, with malicious satisfaction. "Art *much* improved, methinks! Nay, thank me not!" And, laughing joyously, she tumbled back into the house and slammed the crystal window closed behind her.

"Lady!" Barry shouted. Scrambling down the heavy wooden lips, he pounded wildly on the door. "Hey, look, a joke's a joke, but I've got *work* to do! *Lady!* Look, lady, I'm *sorry*," he whined. "I'm sorry I swore at you, honest! Just come out here and *fix* this and I won't bother you anymore. Lady, *please!*" He heaved his shoulder experimentally against the door, but it was as solid as rock.

An eyelid-shaped shutter snapped open above him. He looked up eagerly, but it wasn't the lady; it was a fat fairy man with snail's horns growing out of his forehead. The horns were quivering with rage, and the fairy man's face was mottled red. "Pox take you, boy, and your cursed brabble!" the fairy man shouted. "When I am foredone with weariness, must I be roused from honest slumber by your hurble-burble?" Barry winced; evidentially he had struck the Faërie equivalent of a night-shift worker. The fairy man shook a fist at him. "Out upon you, miscreant! By the Oak of Mughna, I demand SILENCE!" The window snapped shut again.

Barry looked nervously up at the eyelid-window, but somehow he *had* to get the lady to come out and fix this goddamn *nose.* "Lady?" he whispered. "*Please*, lady?" No answer. This wasn't working at all. He'd have to change tactics, and take his chances, with

Snailface in the next apartment. "LADY!" he yelled. "OPEN UP! I'M GOING TO STAND HERE AND SHOUT AT THE TOP OF MY LUNGS UNTIL YOU COME OUT! YOU WANT THAT? DO YOU?"

The eyelid flew open. "This passes bearing!" Snailface raged. "Now Cernunnos shrivel me, an I chasten not this boisterous doltard!"

"Listen, mister, I'm *sorry*," Barry said uneasily, "I don't mean to wake you up, honest, but I've *got* to get that lady to come out, or my ass'll really be grass!"

"Your *Arse*, say you?" the snail-horned man snarled. "Marry, since you would have it so, why, by Lugh, I'll do it, straight!" He made a curious gesture, roared out a word that seemed to be all consonants, and then slammed the shutter closed.

Again, there was a *popping* noise in Barry's ears, and a change of pressure that he could feel throughout his sinuses. *Another* spell had been cast on him.

Sure enough, there was a strange, prickly sensation at the base of his spine. "Oh, no!" he whispered. He didn't really want to look —but at last he forced himself to. He groaned. He had sprouted a long, green tail. It looked and smelled suspiciously like grass.

"Ha! Ha!" Barry muttered savagely to himself. "Very funny! *Great* sense of humor these little winged people've got!"

In a sudden spasm of rage, he began to rip out handfuls of grass, trying to *tear* the loathsome thing from his body. The grass ripped out easily, and he felt no pain, but it grew back many times faster than he could tear it free—so that by the time he decided that he was getting nowhere, the tail trailed out six or seven feet behind him.

What was he going to do *now?*

He stared up at the glowering house for a long, silent moment, but he couldn't think of any plan of action that wouldn't just get him in *more* trouble with *someone.*

Gloomily, he gathered up his sample cases, and trudged off down the street, his nose banging into his upper lip at every step, his tail dragging forlornly behind him in the dust. Be damned if this wasn't even worse than cold-selling in *Newark.* He wouldn't have believed it. But *there* he had only been mugged and had his car's tires slashed. *Here* he had been hideously disfigured, maybe for life, and he wasn't even making any *sales.*

He came to an intricately carved stone fountain, and sat wearily down on its lip. Nixies and water nymphs laughed and cavorted within the leaping waters of the fountain, swimming just as easily up the spout as down. They cupped their pretty, little green breasts and called invitingly to him, and then mischievously spouted water at his tail when he didn't answer, but Barry was in no mood for them, and resolutely ignored their blandishments. After a while they went back to their games and left him alone.

Barry sighed, and tried to put his head in his hands, but his enormous new nose kept getting in the way. His stomach was churning. He reached into his pocket and worried out a metal-foil packet of antacid tablets. He tore the packet open, and then found—to his disgust—that he had to lift his sagging nose out of the way with one hand in order to reach his mouth. While he chewed on the chalky-tasting pills, he stared glumly at the twin leatherette bags that held his demonstrator models. He was beaten. Finished. Destroyed. *Ruined.* Down and out in Faërie, at the ulti-mate rock bottom of his career. What a bummer! What a *fiasco!*

And he had had such high hopes for this expedition, too. . . .

Barry never really understood why Titania, the Fairy Queen, spent so much of her time hanging out in a sleazy little roadside bar on the outskirts of a jerkwater South Jersey town—perhaps *that* was the kind of place that seemed exotic to *her.* Perhaps she liked the rotgut hootch, or the greasy hamburgers—just as likely to be "veni-son-burgers," really, depending on whether somebody's uncle or backwoods cousin had been out jacking deer with a flashlight and a 30.30 lately—or the footstomping honkey-tonk music on the jukebox. Perhaps she just had an odd sense of humor. Who knew? *Not* Barry.

Nor did Barry ever really understand what *he* was doing there—it wasn't really his sort of place, but he'd been on the road with a long way to go to the next town, and a sudden whim had made him stop in for a drink. *Nor* did he understand why, having stopped in in the first place, he had then gone *along* with the gag when the beat-up old barfly on his left had leaned over to him, breathing out poisonous fumes, and confided, "*I'm* really the Queen of the Fairies, you know." Ordinarily, he would have laughed, or ignored her, or said something like, "And *I'm* the Queen of the May, sleaze-ball." But he had done none of these things. Instead, he had nod-ded gravely and courteously, and asked her if he could have the honor of lighting the cigarette that was wobbling about in loopy circles in her shaking hand.

Why did he do this? Certainly it hadn't been from even the *remotest* desire to get into the Queen's grease-stained pants—in her earthly incarnation, the Queen was a grimy, gray-haired, broken-down rummy, with a horse's face, a dragon's breath, cloudy agate eyes, and a bright-red rumblossom nose. No, there had been no ulterior motives. But he had been in an odd mood, restless, bored, and stale. So he had played up to her, on a spur-of-the-moment whim, going along with the gag, buying her drinks and lighting cigarettes for her, and listening to her endless stream of half-coherent talk, all the while solemnly calling her "Your Majesty" and "Highness," getting a kind of role-playing let's pretend kick out of it that he hadn't known since he was a kid and he and his sister used to play "grown-up dress-up" with the trunk of castoff clothes in the attic.

So that when midnight came, and all the other patrons of the bar froze into freeze-frame rigidity, paralyzed in the middle of drinking or shouting or scratching or shoving, and Titania manifested herself in the radiant glory of her *true* form, nobody could have been more surprised than *Barry*.

"My God!" he'd cried. "You really *are*—"

"The Queen of the Fairies," Titania said smugly. "You bet your buns, sweetie. I *told* you so, didn't I?" She smiled radiantly, and then gave a ladylike hiccup. The Queen in her new form was so dazzlingly beautiful as to almost hurt the eye, but there was still a trace of rotgut whiskey on her breath. "And because *you've* been a most true and courteous knight to one from whom you thought to see no earthly gain, I'm going to grant you a *wish*. How about *that*, kiddo?" She beamed at him, then hiccuped again; whatever catabolic effect her transformation had had on her blood-alcohol level, she was obviously still slightly tipsy.

Barry was flabbergasted. "I can't believe it," he muttered. "I come into a bar, on *impulse*, just by *chance*, and the very first person I sit down next to turns out to be—"

Titania shrugged. "That's the way it goes, sweetheart. It's the Hidden Hand of Oberon, what you mortals call 'synchronicity.' Who knows what'll eventually come of this meeting—tragedy or comedy, events of little moment or of world-shaking weight and worth? Maybe even *Oberon* doesn't know, the silly old fart. Now, about that *wish*—"

Barry thought about it. What *did* he want? Well, he was a *salesman*, wasn't he? New worlds to conquer . . .

Even Titania had been startled. She looked at him in surprise and then said, "Honey, I've been dealing with mortals for a lot of years now, but nobody ever asked for *that* before. . . ."

* * *

Now he sat on cold stone in the heart of the Faërie town, and groaned, and cursed himself bitterly. If only he hadn't been so ambitious! If only he'd asked for something *safe*, like a swimming pool or a Ferrari . . .

Afterward, Barry was never sure how long he sat there on the lip of the fountain in a daze of despair—perhaps literally for weeks; it *felt* that long. Slowly, the smoky, bronze disk of the Fairyland sun sank beneath the horizon, and it became night, a warm and velvety night whose very darkness seemed somehow luminous. The nixies had long since departed, leaving him alone in the little square with the night and the splashing waters of the fountain. The strange stars of Faërie swam into the sky, witchfire crystals so thick against the velvet blackness of the night that they looked like phosphorescent plankton sparkling in some midnight tropic sea. Barry watched the night sky for a long time, but he could find none of the familiar constellations he knew, and he shivered to think how far away from home he must be. The stars *moved* much more rapidly here than they did in the sky of Earth, crawling perceptibly across the black bowl of the night even as you watched, swinging in stately procession across the sky, wheeling and reforming with a kind of solemn, awful grandeur, eddying and whirling, swirling into strange patterns and shapes and forms, spiral pinwheels of light. Pastel lanterns appeared among the houses on the hillsides as the night deepened, seeming to reflect the wheeling, blazing stars above.

At last, urged by some restless tropism, he got slowly to his feet, instinctively picked up his sample cases, and set off aimlessly through the mysterious night streets of the Faërie town. Where was he going? Who knew? Did it matter anymore? He kept walking. Once or twice he heard faint, far snatches of fairy music—wild, sad, yearning melodies that pierced him like a knife, leaving him shaken and melancholy and strangely elated all at once—and saw lines of pastel lights bobbing away down the hillsides, but he stayed away from those streets, and did his best not to listen; he had been warned about the bewitching nature of fairy music, and had no desire to spend the next hundred or so years dancing in helpless enchantment within a fairy ring. Away from the street and squares filled with dancing pastel lights and ghostly will-o'-the-'wisps— which he avoided—the town seemed dark and silent. Occasionally, winged shapes swooped and flittered overhead, silhouetted against the huge, mellow silver moon of Faërie, sometimes seeming to fly behind it for several wingbeats before flashing into sight again.

Once he met a fellow pedestrian, a monstrous one-legged creature with an underslung jaw full of snaggle teeth and one baleful eye in the middle of its forehead that blazed like a warning beacon, and stood unnoticed in the shadows, shivering, until the fearsome apparition had hopped by. Not paying any attention to where he was going, Barry wandered blindly downhill. He couldn't think at all—it was as if his brain had turned to ash. His feet stumbled over the cobblestones, and only by bone-deep instinct did he keep hold of the sample cases. The street ended in a long, curving set of wooden stairs. Mechanically, dazedly, he followed them down. At the bottom of the stairs, a narrow path led under the footing of one of the gossamer bridges that looped like slender, gray cobwebs between the fairy hills. It was cool and dark here, and almost peaceful . . .

"AAAARRRRGGHHHHH!"

Something *enormous* leaped out from the gloom, and enveloped him in a single, scaly green hand. The fingers were a good three feet long each, and their grip was as cold and hard as iron. The hand lifted him easily into the air, while he squirmed and kicked futilely.

Barry stared up into the creature's face. *"Yop!"* he said. A double row of yellowing fangs lined a frog-mouth large enough to swallow him up in one gulp. The blazing eyes bulged ferociously, and the nose was a flat smear. The head was topped off by a fringe of hair like red worms, and a curving pair of ram's horns.

"Pay *up* for the use a my bridge," the creature roared, "or by Oberon's dirty socks, I'll crunch you whole!"

It never ends, Barry thought. Aloud, he demanded in frustration. "What bridge?"

"A wise guy!" the monster sneered. *"That* bridge, whadda ya *think?"* He gestured upward scornfully. "The bridge *over* us, dummy! The Bridge a Morrig the Fearsome! *My* bridge. I got a royal commission says I gotta right ta collect toll from *every* creature that sets foot on it, and you better believe that means *you,* buddy. I got you dead to rights. So cough up!" He shook Barry until the salesman's teeth rattled. "Or *else!"*

"But I *haven't* set foot on it!" Barry wailed. "I just walked *under* it!"

"Oh," the monster said. He looked blank for a moment, scratching his knobby head with his free hand, and then his face sagged. "Oh," he said again, disappointedly. "Yeah. I guess you're right. Crap." Morrig the Fearsome sighed, a vast noisome displacement of air. Then he released the salesman. "Jeez, buddy, I'm sorry," Morrig said, crestfallen. "I shouldn't'a oughta have jerked ya around like that. I guess I got overanxious or sumpthin. Jeez, mac, you know how it is. Tryin' to make a buck. The old grind. It gets me down."

Morrig sat down, discouraged, and wrapped his immensely long and muscular arms around his knobby green knees. He brooded for a moment, then jerked his thumb up at the bridge. "That bridge's my only source a income, see?" He sighed gloomily. "When I come down from Utgard and set up this scam, I think I'm gonna get *rich*. Got the royal commission, all nice an' legal, everybody gotta *pay* me, right? Gonna clean *up*, right?" He shook his head glumly. "*Wrong*. I ain't making a lousy *dime*. All the locals got *wings*. Don't use the bridge at *all*." He spat noisily. "They're cheap little snots, these fairyfolk are."

"*Amen*, brother," Barry said, with feeling. "I know *just* what you mean."

"Hey!" Morrig said, brightening. "You care for a snort? I got a jug a hootch right here."

"Well, actually . . ." Barry said reluctantly. But the troll had already reached into the gloom with one long, triple-jointed arm, and pulled out a stone crock. He pried off the top and took a long swig. Several gallons of liquid gurgled down his throat. "Ahhhh!" He wiped his thin lips. "That hits the spot, all right." He thrust the crock into Barry's lap. "Have a belt."

When Barry hesitated, the troll rumbled, "Ah, go ahead, pal. Good for what ails ya. You got troubles too, ain'tcha, just like me —I can tell. It's the lot a the workin' man, brother. Drink up. Put hair on your *chest* even if you ain't got no dough in your *pocket*." While Barry drank, Morrig studied him cannily. "You're a mortal, ain'tcha, bud?"

Barry half-lowered the jug and nodded uneasily.

Morrig made an expansive gesture. "Don't worry, pal, I don't care, I figure all a us workin' folks gotta stick *together*, regardless a race or creed, or the bastards'll grind us *all* down. Right?" He leered, showing his huge, snaggly, yellowing fangs in what Barry assumed was supposed to be a reassuring grin. "But, say, buddy, if you're a mortal, how come you got a funny nose like that, and a tail?"

Voice shrill with outrage, Barry told his story, pausing only to hit the stone jug.

"Yeah, buddy," Morrig said sympathetically. "They really

worked you over, didn't they?" He sneered angrily. "Them bums! Just *like* them little snots to gang up on a guy who's just tryin' ta make an honest buck. Whadda *they* care about the problems a the workin' man? Buncha booshwa snobs! Screw 'em all!"

They passed the seemingly bottomless stone jug back and forth again. "Too bad *I* can't do none a that magic stuff," Morrig said sadly, "or I'd fix ya right up. What a shame." Wordlessly, they passed the jug again. Barry sighed. Morrig sighed too. They sat in gloomy silence for a couple of minutes, and then Morrig roused himself and said, "*What* kinda scam is it you're tryin' ta run? I ain't never heard a it before. Lemme see the merchandise."

"What's the point—?"

"C'mon," Morrig said impatiently. "I wantcha ta show me the goods. Maybe *I* can figure out a way ta move the stuff."

Listlessly, Barry snapped open a case. Morrig leaned forward to study the console with interest. "Kinda pretty," the troll said; he sniffed at it. "Don't smell too bad, either. Maybe make a nice planter, or sumpthin."

"*Planter?*" Barry cried; he could hear his voice cracking in outrage. "I'll have you know this is a piece of high technology! Precision machinery!"

Morrig shrugged. "Okay, bub, make it march."

"Ah," Barry said. "I need someplace to plug it in . . ."

Morrig picked up the plug and inserted it in his ear. The computer's CRT screen lit up. "Okay," Morrig said, "Gimme the pitch. What's it do?"

"Well," Barry said slowly, "let's suppose that you had a bond portfolio worth $2,147 invested at 8¾ percent compounded daily, over eighteen months, and you wanted to calculate—"

"Two thousand four hundred forty-three dollars and sixty-eight and seven-tenths cents," said the troll.

"Hah?"

"That's what it works out to, pal. Two hundred ninety-six dollars and change in compound interest."

With a sinking sensation, Barry punched through the figures and let the system work. Alphanumerics flickered on the CRT: $296.687.

"Can *everybody* in Faërie do that kind of mental calculation?" Barry asked.

"Yeah," the troll said. "But so what? No big deal. Who *cares* about crap like that anyway?" He stared incredulously at Barry. "Is that *all* that thing does?"

There was a heavy silence.

"Maybe you oughta reconsider that idea about the planters . . ." Morrig said.

Barry stood up again, a trifle unsteady from all the hootch he'd taken aboard. "Well, that's *really* it, then," he said. "I might just as well chuck my samples in the river—I'll never sell in *this* territory. Nobody needs my product."

Morrig shrugged. "What do *you* care how they use 'em? You oughta *sell* 'em first, and then let the *customers* find a use for 'em afterward. That's logic."

Fairy logic, perhaps, Barry thought. "But how can you *sell* something without first convincing the customer that it's useful?"

"Here." Morrig tossed off a final drink, gave a bone-rattling belch, and then lurched ponderously to his feet, scooping up both sample cases in one hand. "Lemme show you. Ya just gotta be *forceful.*"

The troll started off at a brisk pace, Barry practically having to run to keep up with his enormous strides. They climbed back up the curving, wooden steps, and then Morrig somehow retraced Barry's wandering route through the streets of Faërie town, leading them unerringly back to the home of the short-tempered, pinocchio-nosed fairy who had cast the first spell on Barry—the Hag of Blackwater, according to Morrig.

Morrig pounded thunderously on the Hag's door, making the whole house shake. The Hag snatched the door open angrily, snarling, "What's to—GACK!" as Morrig suddenly grabbed her up in one enormous hand, yanked her out of the house, and lifted her up to face level.

"Good evenin', maam," Morrig said pleasantly.

"A murrain on you, lummox!" she shrieked. "Curst vile rogue! Release me at once! At *once*, you foul scoundrel! I'll—BLURK" Her voice was cut off abruptly as Morrig tightened his grip, squeezing the breath out of her. Her face turned blood-red, and her eyes bulged from her head until Barry was afraid that she was going to pop like an overripe grape.

"Now, *now*, lady," Morrig said in a gently chiding tone. "Let's keep the party polite, okay? You know your magic's too weak to use on *me*. And you shouldn't'a' oughta use no hard language. We're just two workin' stiffs tryin' ta make a honest buck, see? You give us the bad mouth, and, say, it just might make me *sore*." Morrig began shaking her, up and down, back and forth, his fist moving with blinding speed, shaking her in his enormous hand as if she were a pair of dice he was about to shoot in a crap game. "AND YOU WOULDN'T WANT TA MAKE ME SORE, NOW, WOULD YOU, LADY?" Morrig bellowed. "WOULD YOU?"

The Hag was being shaken so hard that all you could see of her was a blur of motion, "Givors!" she said in a faint, little voice. "Givors, I pray you!"

Morrig stopped shaking her. She lay gasping and disheveled in his grasp, her eyes unfocused. "There!" Morrig said jovially, beaming down at her. "That's better, ain't it? Now I'm just gonna start all over again." He paused for a second, and then said brightly, "'Evenin', ma'am! I'm sellin' . . . uh . . ." He scratched his head, looking baffled, then brightened. ". . . compukers!" He held up a sample case to show her; she stared dazedly at it. "Now I could go on and on about how swell these compukers are, but I can see you're *already* anxious ta buy, so there ain't no need ta waste yer valuable time like that. Ain't that right?" When she didn't answer, he frowned and gave her a little shake. "Ain't that *right?*"

"A-aye," she gibbered. "Aye!"

Morrig set her down, keeping only a light grip on her shoulder, and Barry broke out the sales forms. While she was scribbling frantically in the indicated blanks, Morrig rumbled, "And, say, now that we're all gettin' along so good, how's about takin' your spell offa my friend's nose, just as a gesture a good will? You'll do that little thing for me, *won'tcha?*"

With ill grace, the Hag obliged. There was a *pop*, and Barry exulted as he felt his nose shrink down to its original size. *Part* of the way home, anyway! He collected the sales forms and returned the receipts. "You can let go of her now," he told Morrig.

Sullenly, the Hag stalked back into her house, slamming the door behind her. The door vanished, leaving only an expanse of blank wood. With a freight-train rumble, the whole house sank into the ground and disappeared from sight. Grass sprang up on the spot where the house had been, and started growing furiously.

Morrig chuckled. Before they could move on, another fairy woman darted out from an adjacent door. "What bought the Hag of Blackwater, so precious that straight she hastens to hide herself away with it from prying eyes?" the other fairy asked. "Must indeed be something wondrous rare, to make her cloister herself with such dispatch, like a mouse to its hole, and then pull the very hole in after her! Aye, she knew I'd be watching, I doubt not, the selfish old bitch! Ever has she been jealous of my Art. Fain am I to know what the Hag would keep from my sight. Let *me* see your wares."

It was *then* that Barry had his masterstroke. "I'm sorry," he said in his snidest voice, "but I'm afraid that I can't show it to *you*. We're selling these computers by *exclusive* license of the Queen, and of course we can't sell them to just *anyone*. I'm afraid that we certainly couldn't sell *you* one, so—"

"What!" the fairy spluttered. "No *one* is better connected at Court than I! You *must* let me buy! And you do *not*, the Queen's majesty shall hear of this!"

"Well," said Barry doubtfully, "I don't know. . . ."

Barry and Morrig made a great team. They were soon surrounded by a swarm of customers. The demand became so great that they had no trouble talking Snailface into taking his spell off Barry as part of the price of purchase. In fact, Snailface became so enthusiastic about computers, that he bought *six* of them. Morrig had been right. Who cared what they used them for, so long as they *bought* them? That was *their* problem, wasn't it?

In the end, they only quit because they had run out of sales forms.

Morrig had a new profession, and Barry returned to Earth a happy man.

Soon Barry had (with a little help from Morrig, who was still hard at work, back in Faërie) broken all previous company sales records, many times over. Barry had convinced the company that the flood tide of new orders was really coming from heretofore untouched backwoods regions of West Virginia, North Carolina, and Tennessee, and everyone agreed that it was simply *amazing* how many hillbillies out there in the Ozarks had suddenly decided that they wanted home-computer systems. Business was booming. So, when, months later, the company opened a new branch office with great pomp and ceremony, Barry was there, in a place of honor.

The sales staff stood respectfully watching as the company president himself sat down to try out one of the gleaming new terminals. The president had started the company out of his basement when home computers were new, and he was only a college dropout from Silicon Valley, and he was still proud of his programming skills.

But as the president punched figures into the keyboard, long, curling, purple moose antlers began to sprout from the top of his head.

The sales staff stood frozen in silent horror. Barry gasped; then, recovering swiftly, he reached over the president's shoulder to hit the cancel key. The purple moose horns disappeared.

The Old Man looked up, puzzled. "Is anything wrong?"

"Only a glitch, sir," Barry said smoothly. But his hand was trembling.

He was afraid that there were going to be more such glitches.

The way sales were booming—a *lot* more.

Evidently, the fairyfolk had finally figured out what computers were *really* for. And Barry suddenly seemed to hear, far back in his head, the silvery peals of malicious, elven laughter.

It was a *two*-way system, after all. . . .

Introduction

Niagara Falling

Janeen Webb

It was a hot summer's night. Jack and I were driving from New York to Toronto, and Jack thought a stopover at Niagara Falls would be a romantic setting for my birthday. It wasn't.

The hotel he'd booked was a disaster. We knew we were in trouble when porters dressed up as Teenage Mutant Ninja Turtles tried to hijack our luggage. A quick glance around the lobby revealed that the clientele was mostly under nine years old (though there were several tired parents skulking in the bar), and the only food was fast. We left.

Our second hotel was quieter, but unprepared for English-speaking guests. The reception staff spoke only Japanese, the signs were in Japanese, the lobby shops displayed their prices in yen. Japanese tourists were being herded about in groups that resembled weird multi-legged beasts mesmerized into following the raised, red umbrellas of their keepers. For Jack, who relishes negotiation as a contact sport, this was a serious challenge. The hondling began. Some considerable time later the concierge admitted defeat, and Jack and I took up residence in a lovely room with a view of the Falls. Things, we thought, were looking up. We were wrong.

We made the mistake of going out to dinner at the highly rec-ommended Award-winning "Italian" restaurant. The meal was seriously awful. We both got food poisoning, and spent a highly unromantic night taking turns in the bathroom. When we were well enough to travel, we left.

Some time later, Keith Ferrell suggested that it would be interesting to see what would happen if Jack and I tried writing a story together and offered to commission one for *Black Mist and Other Japanese Futures*. So we thought we'd extrapolate a Japanese Future from our own little holiday from hell.

After all we'd been through, we thought it would be easy. It wasn't. This was our first collaborative fiction, and it was almost our last. It's one thing to share a bathroom, but quite another to have one's partner messing with one's syntax. We found ourselves divided by a common language, the differences between Jack's American and my Australian stylistic sensibilities more difficult to reconcile than we'd imagined. But reconcile them we did, eventually.

In the end, "Niagara Falling" went on to win both the Aurealis and the Ditmar Awards for Best Short Story. So we must have done something right.

Jack Dann

Janeen's recounting is spot-on. Niagara Falls was just awful, egregious, unspeakably so. (But that won't stop me.)

Try as we might, we just could not get a decent meal. Only high-priced junk food (even if the offending vendor was trying to pass as a "restaurant"). We had a lovely suite, with lovely views, and as we looked down at the Falls and the gardens, we could see couples walking hand-in-hand through the lanes; they were all obviously newly married, ecstatically happy and in love. After strolling around the Falls and being duly impressed (and they *are* impressive!), we strolled on into town, which was a disaster. Downtown was nothing but fast food restaurants, tiny lanes filled with the concatenation of pinball parlors and cheap game rooms; so we escaped back to our hotel. But nothing really worked in the hotel. It *looked* like a hotel. It had a concierge, bellmen, a checkout desk, restaurants, but all these bits and pieces were simply for show. The concierge couldn't recommend a decent restaurant, the restaurant couldn't provide decent food, and the desk clerk seemed to be monolingual, and his language was Japanese.

So after the aforementioned food poisoning incident, we fled Niagara Falls and environs and left the region to newlyweds and giant Ninja Turtles. We were disappointed, ill, and angry; and although writers may often feel disenfranchised, we do have one neat little weapon: the pen. So pissed off as we were, we finished our working vacation in Canada and America and returned to Australia. We carried our grudge against the horror that was Niagara Falls . . . we carried it home like a suitcase we would open when we were properly rested.

The contents of that suitcase can be found in "Niagara Falling," our first fiction collaboration . . . but "Niagara Falling" wasn't our first collaboration.

We had written an article for *Omni Magazine* about Lawrence Hargrave, the Australian inventor of the box kite, and I remember sitting beside Janeen on our couch as I happily and obliviously recast and rewrote her text. Glancing sideways, I noticed that her beautiful, green eyes were squinting, squinting at *me*, squinting at what I was doing to her work. I looked again. Those eyes, those mirrors of the soul, were silently telling me that if I changed one more f-ing sentence, she would politely break my arms and legs, then snap my torso to make sure I would easily fit into the oven. (We didn't have a fireplace.)

I believe I ceased and desisted in time.

So I'm not going to blithely say that collaborating on "Niagara Falling" was easy as falling off a log, but I will say that it sure as hell was worthwhile. As Janeen recounted, we made certain interesting discoveries. Although we both speak English, we really speak—and write—two different languages. Australian English and American English have quite different takes on irony, humor, and even sentence structure. But I believe, as does Janeen, that we overcame those syntactical and ironical hurdles.

The heart of the "Niagara Falling" derives from an actual experience Janeen had when a wealthy sheik—seeing her in the elevator of the Bangkok Hilton—took a fancy to her. She had to flee her hotel to escape him. We extrapolated a North America ruled by Asian and Middle-eastern factions, and we derived some of the weird sex from a little book that we picked up in a Japanese gift shop in Melbourne. The book was a primer on nightlife and sexual mores in urban Japanese culture. My initial idea was to write something strange and exotic along the lines of Gene Wolfe's "Seven American Nights," and you can find some ironic and subtle—and some not-so-subtle—homages to Gene Wolfe, Ray Bradbury ("The Veldt"), and James Patrick Kelly ("Mr. Boy").

I will also cop to stealing some bits and pieces of technology from my novel *The Man Who Melted*; but the overarching story arc, and all the character interactions and details of scene and settings right from the middle through to the end of the story are all Janeen's.

And that weird sex scene . . .

Well, it surprised the hell right out of *me*.

Perhaps because I didn't write it!

Our editor's response to the story was "It is without doubt that most unusual of things, a science fiction story that works as real fiction, which is to say that you come perilously close to literature in this one, so BE CAREFUL!!!! You wouldn't want to spoil Jack's reputation."

"Niagara Falling" has been reprinted in *The Year's Best Australian Science Fiction and Fantasy, Wonder Years: the Ten Best Stories From a Decade Past,* and *The Best Australian Science Fiction Writing: A Fifty Year Collection.*

Niagara Falling

Janeen Webb and Jack Dann

THE WEDDING WAS THE BEST THAT MONEY COULD buy. A wooden platform was built right in the middle of Melbourne's Royal Botanical Gardens; it overlooked the swan lake that was surrounded by a blaze of yellow and orange and pink flowers specially lit for the evening party. Under a chandeliered tent, five hundred people dined at cozy tables aglitter with glassware and vintage bottles of Möet and danced to a full orchestra.

Helen Donoussa née Nisyros sat sweating in her gown at the head table beside her husband of exactly four hours and twenty-five minutes. It was unseasonably hot for April. "Kostas, you're not supposed to look bored, this is supposed to be the most exciting night of your life." Helen had a way of pulling away and looking down her nose when speaking, which had always mesmerized suitors, admirers, and acquaintances. Although, feature for feature, she was rather plain (except for her thick, golden blond hair), she looked regal; and everyone imagined her as being beautiful. Kostas, however, *was* beautiful: black, curly hair, square face, deep brown eyes, and a dimple in his right cheek, which made him look off-balance and vulnerable. He was twenty-five years old, had already tried seventeen cases before juries, and had won them all. But he didn't earn nearly as much money as Helen, who was a designer. She could turn an apartment into a virtual Georgian mansion.

"This is interminable," he said. "No one looks like themselves. Everyone's ugly. It's—"

"It's business," she said.

"I thought we were doing this for your family."

"Same thing," she said. "But it's really for you . . . for us." She extended her hand to an elderly man, one of her father's law partners, who had worked his way down the table, shaking hands and offering hearty congratulations. Kostas greeted Mr. Spiriounis, whose business he would eventually inherit, and then stood awkwardly before him while the old man chatted up the bride.

"You know, your father loves you very much," Mr. Spiriounis said.

"Why of course he does, Uncle Dimi," Helen said, gazing up at him, as if she was the one standing.

"No, no, no, I mean if he just loved you as fathers just love daughters, he would have given you a lovely wedding at Arbeena Court or Ballara or Ascot House, and everything would have been a virt: the flowers, the starry night. But this"—he motioned with his arms, gaining everyone's attention, and spoke loudly, playing to Helen's father—"this is *real*."

"Yes, Uncle Dimi, and it's hot, too," Helen said, as if she were complimenting her father for her discomfort.

"But this is wonderful. This is how it used to be, for everyone, not just for those who have achieved the success your father has." Uncle Dimi looked toward Helen's father, for whom he was talking loudly, but Mr. Nisyros was preoccupied with important Japanese clients who were bowing and presenting him with gifts. "Well, will you excuse me?"

Helen blew him a kiss and Kostas sat down as Uncle Dimi backtracked to glad-hand the clients still talking to Helen's father.

"Why is he always kissing your father's ass?" Kostas asked. "He's the principal partner."

"He thinks Daddy can help him stay in the firm, but he's already out."

"What do you mean, already out. There would need to be a vote by all the senior partners. I would have heard something."

"Daddy told me he's out, and when has he ever been wrong?" Helen asked.

"Maybe he should have taken *you* into the firm."

"He couldn't afford me, and now you're acting insecure and nasty. You don't have to stay. You could open up your own practice and make a fortune. Or you could ask me to dance."

Everyone stepped back to watch the bride and groom, who were not in the least self-conscious as they danced a perfect box step to a Strauss waltz. "You see, this is our perfect moment," Helen whispered into Kostas's ear. "You, my darling, are like a jet plane. When you stand still, you're awkward, but adorable. But when you're moving, you're like the music itself. You're beautiful. You're perfect."

Regaining his self-esteem, Kostas danced even better. He dipped her and twirled her and stood razor straight, cutting a fine figure.

"I wonder if Niagara Falls is a virt," Helen said.

"I'm sure the Falls are real."

Helen pulled back and looked at him contemptuously.

"What does it matter, anyway?"

"Professional curiosity."

"Well, we'll probably be the only professionals in Australia who've ever seen it," Kostas said. "Except for the guy who was bowing to your father and his family, friends, and associates."

Pleased, Helen giggled; and they left in the middle of the next dance, when everyone had crowded onto the floor. Daddy would be angry for a few minutes, and then he'd laugh that they'd "eloped."

By 3:00 AM Helen and Kostas were seated comfortably in Connoisseur Class on a 999 Quantas suborbital.

"I think we should put in an appearance at David's party," Helen said, as she gazed out the porthole window at the tarmac and the green runway lights. They were both seasoned travelers, resigned to spending as much time on runways as in the air.

"Well, it's too late now," Kostas said. The vibration of the engine was comforting and made him sleepy. He activated a privacy guard and the aisle and cruising automated stewards disappeared behind gray vibrating walls. "You didn't want to go, remember?"

"I was hungry."

Kostas didn't turn to look at her, but he could imagine her lips pursing into a pout. "Well, forget the party." He waited a beat and continued. "We did act like shits. The party was in our honor, after all."

"What you mean is that I'm a shit," Helen said.

"I didn't say that. I didn't want to go to a party either. I'll make up excuses when we get back."

"I'm sure the party is a bore and a half, and I'm tired, but we should put in an appearance," Helen said. "Come on, we'll virt in, apologize—you can make up one of your good excuses—and honor will be satisfied."

"We were specifically invited in person, remember?" Kostas said. "It's very bad form, especially for the guests of honor. I'll think of something when we get back."

"Well, *I'm* going to peep in," Helen said.

"You won't even get in."

Helen activated her privacy guard, walling herself away from Kostas. "*Oh, yes I will. . . .*"

Defeated, Kostas acquiesced; and Helen showed good form for their arrival. The guests at the party—if, indeed they would permit them to attend *en virt*—would see Kostas and Helen as Jan Van Eyck's "Giovanni Arnolfini and his Bride." Helen created their virtual images, her hands making tight motions on her lap, as if she were surreptitiously trying to conduct a symphony rather than manipulate data. She used an ancient geofiguration operating system, for she had trained with an old Mac designer, who died last year at 122, God rest his irritable soul.

Kostas lost his face to Van Eyck's financier Giovanni Arnolfini. His features became pale and sharp and thin, aristocratic, a spoiled little boy who had grown into selfish ennui. He wore an ermine cape and a large, velvet hat with a wide brim. But Helen retained her own features, now framed in a white lace shawl from which protruded two devil's horns of twisted blond hair. Her green dress, outlined with rabbit fur, cascaded to the floor in delightful folds.

"Come on, Kostas, stand up," Helen said, and she took his hand. "Stand up straight, there's enough room. There, that's close to the original painting. I just made us a bit better, that's all. What do you think?"

Kostas laughed. "You're beautiful, but are you sure you want to look pregnant?"

"I'm just being true to the painting. Let everyone think what they like." She giggled.

"You're not pregnant, are you?"

She shrugged. "Think whatever you like. Now what do you think of . . . you?"

"I can't see myself, but the frock feels nice and soft." Kostas said.

Kostas and Helen, like everyone else, wore self-cleaning virt body webs that were the texture of ancient nylon stockings.

"Well, you look very nice. Do you want a mirror?" She grinned at him, as she did when she was being provocative, when she was goading him.

"I'll trust you, but we don't have much room to move here."

"Stop being a baby," Helen said. "Once we're in, we'll sit," and she rang them into the party, leaving Kostas to make all the excuses while she waved hello to all their friends. They stood in a large living room that opened onto a pond and garden in the oriental style. Some of the guests were still dressed in the formal evening-ware that had changed so little since the nineteenth century; most of the others were naked.

"Why, you didn't have to be embarrassed," said David, the host of the party. "This party was for you. We could have made it virtual, if that would have been easier."

"When we get back, we'll have to have a party for all of you," Helen said. "Our way of doing penance."

"Well, we can do it right now," one of the other guests said, and in a trice the room dissolved, giving way after a few long moments to endless veldt at twilight. The sky was blood red, darkening into clotted purple only at the horizon. The guests reappeared as golden pelted lions and padded around the Van Eyckian Kostas and Helen, who both seemed to be sitting on a cloud floating but a foot above the veldt.

Helen squealed with surprise. The rank smell of wet animal fur was overpowering. "You planned this all along."

"Well, we *were* getting a tad bored just standing about," David confessed, "so Ellen started working up a story we could play." Host and guests could only be distinguished by their voices now.

"It was interesting to get on for a while *au fond*," another said. "Somehow, though, it feels . . . naughty."

"Well, we're not being naughty now," said another.

"Tell us about the story," Helen asked.

"First tell us if you're pregnant," said Ellen, who settled back on her haunches before the newlyweds. "Your virt's pregnant, anyway." Everyone laughed, and she continued, "And where are you going on honeymoon. It seems that none of those who love you know. Now isn't that just a little bit odd?"

"I'll tell you exactly what I told my husband," Helen said. "Think whatever you like."

"About which, your pregnancy or the honeymoon?"

Helen laughed. "Both." After a beat, she said, "Now let me

guess the game. It shouldn't be too difficult." Her friends circled them, and the scene took on a decidedly deadly cast. As it became darker, the other guests padded around Helen and Kostas in ever diminishing circles, feral eyes glowing.

Suddenly one of the guests leaped at Kostas, tearing at his legs, biting, ripping through to the virtual bone.

Kostas screamed in pain, and Helen said, "Okay, I'll give up . . . a little. I'm pregnant. Now, you see, you've spoiled it for Kostas. And I'll never really find out whether he's excited or upset."

"Well, tell her." The guests stopped pacing, all now watching Kostas, who was bleeding quite realistically, and was, indeed, in realistic pain.

"Oh, he won't reveal his true feelings in front of anyone," Helen said. "Not even me."

"You are pregnant?" Kostas said, angry and in pain.

"Would you like me to make the baby go away?" Helen asked. "Is that what you want?"

"No, of course not, but—"

"You see, I'm now married to this man, and I don't know him at all." With that, Helen transformed herself into an unpregnant bride. "And I'll tell you where we're going on our honeymoon. America!"

There was a gasp from the guests, and Helen disappeared, leaving her bleeding husband to the uncomprehending lions.

"Why did you lie about going to America?" Kostas asked Helen, who sat beside him sipping a champagne cocktail and reading *The Vision of God* by Nicholas of Cusa. As she was of a flamboyant nature, she read publicly, and the text, set in flames, hung in the air before her like the tablets of Moses. Nicholas was her saint, the saint of VR designers; he had dreamed of creating an image so potent as to be "omnivoyant"—all seeing. An icon of God.

Helen shrugged. "Give them something to talk about. And maybe I was angry at them for biting you. After all, you are the groom. And we'll practically be in America, so I didn't lie very much."

"Are you angry at me?" Kostas asked.

"Did you really think I might be pregnant?"

"For a second, maybe."

"You really didn't think I'd tell them before I told you," Helen said.

Kostas shrugged. "I asked you before, remember, and you wouldn't tell me. Who can know what you think."

That pleased her, and she smiled. "I worried that if I was pregnant . . . that you wouldn't be pleased."

"Of course I'd be pleased."

"Well, good. I assumed that you really truly loved me, so I took revenge on the party guests for you."

"What did you do?" Kostas asked.

"I drowned them. They stank from dampness anyway. That's what gave me the idea. They won't be able to turn off their game until they're all practically choking to death."

"Christ, they were giving us a wedding party."

"One that they'll never forget," Helen said.

"They'll hate us."

"They'll love us."

An hour later they landed at the Tad Wink International Airport, which was less than an hour from Niagara via the underground magnetic.

They were in the Confederacy of Canada.

And in love.

"Are you sure you want to go through with this?" Kostas asked, uneasy with the third world presence of human functionaries, each of whom was almost certainly carrying a cocktail of disgusting, transmittable diseases. He tried not to breathe too deeply.

"We've had all our shots," Helen said. "Stop obsessing about your health. Do you remember the survival rules? Never eat anything uncooked or anything that might have been left standing. Never eat fruit that you don't peel yourself. Never drink the water. But don't worry," she said unctuously. "This is supposed to be a bath house? I'm sure it's clean."

Irritated and humiliated, Kostas turned to the interpreter, who, though obviously a male, wore a black veil; he also wore traditional western clothes: suit, tie, and sneakers. The interpreter stammered a rehearsed apology: the lifts had failed. Again. As usual. They'd be working tomorrow. Maybe. But it wouldn't be so bad: only ten flights to climb. Helen just shrugged and watched a lime-green turtle struggle with her luggage. The glittering Regency foyer with its Corinthian doorways, black marble inseting, and domed alcoves was serviced by bears and seals and all manner of aquatic and terrestrial creatures. But for all the expensive touches, everything looked dusty and soiled. Even the light streaming in through the windows seemed gray.

"You see," Kostas said to Helen, "it's just as I thought. All the porters and clerks are virts."

Helen giggled. "No they're *not*. They're all wearing costumes. Can't you tell? It's just like America."

Kostas understood. She was right, damn her.

He watched the cartoonesque turtle pushing their suitcases on a trolley across the huge marbled lobby to the ornamented stairway. Something about the comfortable angle of the turtle's carapace betrayed the deformity beneath. A hunched back, maybe, or a twisted spine.

Yes, it was just as he had heard.

All the natives suffered some form of genetic damage.

And now that he knew what to look for, he could well imagine some subtle deformity covered by the translator's veil.

Their suite was shabby, the wallpaper aged a nondescript brown, the curtains faded, the obligatory Edo *ukiyo-e* prints of courtesans and erotica clung tiredly to the walls, a relief of form and figure fading one into the other. The traditional curtain-dais, latticed shutters, sliding doors, and screens seemed out of place in what would have passed for a cheap-jack motel room in any civilized country on the Pacific Rim. But these amenities were costing $12,000 a night, not including VAT tax.

Kostas checked the bathroom and was relieved to find that the plumbing worked after a fashion. Everything smelled of a recent application of disinfectant. But he was not pleased to see a hinged basket under the toilet paper dispenser and a metal sign screwed into the wall that read in Japanese, Arabic, and English: DISPOSE OF PAPER IN BASKET, NOT TOILET. He was, however, fascinated by the slightly out of focus moving figures and the ranked characters of the sexual services menu, printed on rather grubby paper that had slid into the porcelain bathtub. He hadn't had it in his hand a second when he heard Helen gasp and call his name.

He stepped back into the bedroom, where Helen stood staring at a wall of water. The Falls. The exhausted turtle had brought in all the luggage and depolarized the far wall to reveal the great horseshoe of foaming water that threatened to crash into their suite. Dismissed, the turtle was now bowing out of the room, and Kostas saw a clutch of real money in its bony hand. He remembered uncle Dimi slipping Helen a Japanese envelope at the wedding, and wondered if she had told the truth of their destination. He doubted it. The family was still traditional enough to disapprove of purchasing sexual games, no matter how fascinating and foreign, for its women. It wouldn't approve of his complicity, either.

"You called me in for *this?*" Kostas asked.

"Can't you hear it? Can't you feel it?"

The ancient waters roared their indifference, muted only by the heavy glass.

"Before the turtle turned off the wall, I just thought I was hearing the air-conditioning," Kostas said. "But I'm surprised that you're so taken with it all. Don't you think it's just a bit tacky?"

Helen pulled him toward a balcony. The doors sighed open, and the Falls sounded like constant thunder. "There. Can you feel it? Can you smell the ozone?"

"I smell *something,*" Kostas said.

Helen embraced him. "It's supposed to act like an aphrodisiac. That's why it's so popular."

"Do you believe that?" Kostas felt dizzy looking out at the Falls and down at the Japanese gardens below. From this vantage, everything below looked small and perfect and at rest . . . and about to be overwhelmed by the Falls.

"No, but this is all real. I can tell the difference."

"No you *can't,*" Kostas said.

"You're being very unromantic," Helen said. "This was a sacred place. You can still feel it."

"You're being very silly."

"And you're acting like a lawyer." Helen pulled away from him and went back inside.

Kostas followed. "I *am* a lawyer." The balcony shut out the noise behind them.

"I can see that. Here we are on our honeymoon and you're still clutching paperwork." She gestured at the sexual services menu that he was still holding.

"I found it in the bathroom, but I can't make out a damn thing . . . except for a few of the pictures, and they're fuzzy."

She took the menu.

"Could your Mac scan something that wrinkled?"

"No," she said, sitting down on the bed, her head propped on the large, hard pillows.

"There should be some clean copies in the desk," Kostas said.

"Uh, huh, I already looked. No computer, no postcards, not even a pencil. And no screen. Can't call out, can't see in."

"It's probably just a style thing. The stuff is there somewhere, just opaqued."

"Uh, huh," Helen said. "You could run downstairs and find out."

"I'm not—"

"Or you could just tick a box, any box, from each section. It's like those 'authentic' oriental restaurants . . . half a dozen basic items, with hundreds of minor variations. Look at the back page to see if there's a banquet." There wasn't. "So, here, let me surprise you."

Helen thumbed some of the items at random, and pink circles appeared around the Japanese ideographs. "There. This is supposed to be an adventure. Now . . . don't you feel adventurous?"

As if responding to Helen, the room replied, in English, "Please forgive the inexcusable lapse of hospitality, Mrs. Donoussa. Hotel Niagara is undergoing complete renovation. All hospitalities are being upgraded. It was most unfortunate that the hospitalities on this wing were down when you arrived. To make up for any inconvenience, we'll provide a special supper for you on the private roof garden and free run of all our bath and pink facilities. To answer your questions, you need not fill out any paperwork to use our facilities. Just tell us and all will be arranged. Postcards will soon be delivered and the room properly cleaned. If you need to make any calls, you need just ask."

"So where did *this* come from?" Kostas asked, waving the wrinkled services menu in the air.

"Our apologies, sir. The brochures for our pink salon do not usually find their way upstairs. But all your preferences have been noted."

"What is your pink salon?" Kostas asked.

"We're very proud of it, Mr. Donoussa. It is an exact reproduction of the famous *Futago no Kyabetsu*, which thrived in Osaka before the Millennium. But unlike the ancient Osaka club, we offer intercourse as well as massage and violence service. It's very authentic and down-market. We had a customer murdered just this week. That caused quite a sensation."

"How do we turn you off?" Helen asked.

"Would you prefer privacy?"

"Yes," Helen said. "Immediately, if you please."

The room was silent, but this place definitely did not feel private.

Helen's belle epoch high heels clacked against the marble floor of the lobby as she and Kostas left the hotel to have dinner in the fabled streets of Niagara Falls. Perhaps they would dine in the private roof garden tomorrow. Tonight they wanted privacy. They wanted to explore. In her crimson striped jacket and her gown that pushed her rouged bosom up and out like a pouter pigeon, Helen looked like a main character in a costume drama taking place in the mock period style of the hotel lobby. She was tall and confident and full of herself, in marked contrast to the groups of pin-neat Japanese businessmen hurrying through the lobby with their tour handlers like multi-legged beasts scurrying out of the way of predators. Kostas wore pegged trousers and an apricot yellow ascot ruffled in his shirt. It would be sticky out in the streets, so he dressed casually. But the thrill for Helen was to be seen, discussed, and complimented.

As she and Kostas reached the door, they had to step back, for a Muslim potentate entered with his entourage of bodyguards, servants, wild noisy children, and wives and concubines wearing silk headdresses and ornamented veils. The potentate was turbaned and dressed in white; he had a handsome, pockmarked face, shaven cheeks, and a black mustache and beard. He stopped when he saw Helen, as if he recognized her; and he nodded to her as she and Kostas stepped past.

"Do you know him?" Kostas asked.

"No, I never saw him before," Helen said. "Why do you ask?"

"Because he looked at you as if he recognized you."

Helen took his arm, obviously pleased, and they made their first foray out of the hotel. They walked down Bender Street to Falls Avenue, through the checkpoint guards and into the formal gardens of combed sand where pumice white rocks seemed to float like islands in a stationary gray sea, past the European gardens with turf walks bordered by strawberry beds, through copses of elm, chestnut, and fir that hid the sight but not the sound of the Falls. They walked beside the long wall that overlooked the crashing, steaming waterfall. Mist rose into the sky, creating soft clouds that turned to neon as the kliegs came on to illuminate the Falls. It became dark very quickly, and the damp, chilly air smelled of ozone and chestnuts and grilling soymeat. Vendors called out to Helen and Kostas as they passed. "American hot-dogs, California hamburgers, real-authentic." Children played tag and ate realauthentic soy and vermiform dogs and burgers. Lovers leaned against the stone wall and necked or made love in the open. Natural Canadians strolled past, many veiled or masked or costumed in cloaks or coats too warm for the cool evening. The Confederacy had declared this perimeter by the Falls public land, and the Japanese Trade Corporation had not been allowed to purchase it.

Around the horseshoe of the Falls, neon beckoned: geometrical lines and clouds of suffusing light rising into columns, cliffs, and spires. Along the narrow public streets money and organs were gambled for a burst of white ecstasy; telefac booths took junkies through their personal and prerecorded stations of the cross, while five and dime virts provided empty dinners for those who had never seen or smelled real meat and dreamland sex for those who could only imagine the pleasures to be had beyond the public perimeter.

But Kostas and Helen were anxious to see the *real* Niagara Falls. They could come down to the strip to slum later in the week. After all, there wouldn't be anything much here that they couldn't see for a dime in Sydney or Melbourne or Adelaide . . . except for the Falls. At the checkpoint beyond the Japanese gardens Kostas asked a guard dressed in an olive drab uniform where the best restaurants could be found. The guard pointed his Ouzi 5000 riot rifle at the ground and indicated that he did not speak English.

"Even if he did speak English, you can't ask someone like that to recommend a good restaurant," Helen said. "He'd just send you to the Japanese equivalent of a greasy spoon." Kostas didn't argue, although he'd always found the best food in foreign towns by asking the advice of policemen and outworkers. They walked hand in hand past the neat grounds of hotels and the much more grand corporate lodgings. But beyond the hotels were winding, narrow streets chockablock with blinking billboards, holos, videotects, and neon signs, an entire city turned into a twentieth century amusement park: Ferris wheels, parachute rides, the original steel-reinforced Cyclone roller coaster lifted right out of Coney Island, tunnels of love and death. And there were, of course, the dioramas that Niagara Falls was famous for: American city streets that were cracked and overgrown with the brown fronds of fleshweed were resurrected here in all their glory. There were the original Golden Gate Bridge (or rather one quarter of it; the rest had been moved to New Japan near Chile) and Lombard Street and an exact recreation of Washington Square Park and ancient Japanese red lamp districts such as 1950s Koganecho and Shiroganecho and Osaka's Tobita district, circa 1911. Beyond were the sandy beaches of 17th Century Watakano Island with its welcoming *funajoro* and *sentakunin*—ship whores and washer women. And on every street corner were holos blinking ketchup red and whispering in the three major languages: THE JAPANESE TRADE CORPORATION WELCOMES YOU. EVERYTHING YOU SEE IS REAL. THE NEW NIAGARA FALLS IS A VIRT FREE ZONE. ENJOY IT BUT BE CAREFUL! BE REMINDED: YOU HAVE SIGNED A DEATH WAIVER. WE HAVE

PROVIDED DANGEROUS SITUATIONS ESPECIALLY TO MAXIMIZE
YOUR ENJOYMENT. ALL CHILDREN UNDER SEVENTEEN MUST BE
BRANDED.

As danger simply was not on for the first night of their honeymoon, they decided to try a famous Philadelphia restaurant called
Locanda Veneta for a quiet supper and spend the rest of the night
inhaling ozone from the Falls and making love: Kostas, after all,
came from a traditional family. The ambiance of Locanda Veneta
was a kitchy interpretation of late twentieth century Italian (red
velvet chairs and red felt on the walls and well-lit but poorly exe-
cuted oil paintings). The lasagna della casa and the spinach and
ricotta cannelloni were execrable, as were the roasted quail and the
calf's liver with polenta. To add insult to injury, the food was
tremendously overpriced.

Helen credited the bill and Kostas suggested a safe cab to the
hotel and a judicious dose of mebeverine hydrochloride to elimi-
nate any possible irritable bowel syndrome that might have been
touched off by Locanda Veneta's poisonous cuisine. "Now I understand why they have danger signs at every corner," Kostas said,
once they were on the street.

Helen had decided they would walk. They had come here for
excitement. And anyway she had a special surprise waiting for
Kostas.

"What?"

"Don't worry. It's right at the hotel. We're going to take it easy
tonight." With that she grinned and stepped off into the crowds of
tourists and paid pickpockets, rapists, whores, and murderers.

Helen led Kostas across the hotel's lobby, past the banks of elevators, to Shinmachi Soaplands, the hotel's bath house. The
entrance—antique temple doors that reached almost to the ceiling—was behind a display of huge fans and screens, and a grand-
motherly old lady dressed in tenth century full court costume was
waiting for him. She shooed Helen away and said, "*Wasure nai,*"
which meant "Don't forget."

"What?" Kostas asked, pulling away from the grandmother, but
Helen simply blew him a kiss and left him there.

"I thought we were going to spend the night together," Kostas
shouted, immediately embarrassing himself, for everyone nearby
suddenly stopped talking.

Helen turned and said, "We will . . . now let the old lady do her
job." With that she disappeared behind a tour group of new arrivals
who had enough baggage to move house. And Kostas slipped

through the doorway to the pink salon with the old lady who introduced herself with a bow and a faint smile as Sei Shonagon, the boss and bitch of this court. Indeed, the spacious room resembled a royal court; no expense had been spared. Grandmother Bitch led him through indoor gardens under high, timbered roofs. They passed an old man playing a thirteen-pipe flute. Beside him was a naked woman playing a zither; she must have weighed at least three hundred pounds.

One by one Grandmother's nieces appeared with their enameled fans and hair ornaments and formal long-trained skirts. Kostas found himself smiling nervously as any bridegroom, as he was introduced to these shy women, several of whom looked prepubescent, all of whom had Canadian Confederacy Department of Agriculture and Health facial implants that glowed with a soft, green light: official proof that their blood was at this very minute clear of all communicable infections. Grandmother introduced each niece by her proper name, and Kostas would say, by rote, "*Taihen utsukushii desu*," or "*yubi na*," telling each woman, or girl —it was difficult to determine their ages—that she was very beautiful or very graceful. One of the nieces wore horn rimmed eyeglasses. Whether it was an affectation or a foil for some minor degenerescence, Kostas couldn't tell. He called her *riko na*, the last of the three compliments he could remember, and she beamed at him, for being called intelligent was the highest compliment one could receive in Japanese soiree society. Although unintentional, he had just made his selection. Grandmother's other nieces, looking properly crestfallen, excused themselves, and Grandmother recounted Pretty Girl's virtues and specialties. She was expert at pretend games such as pervert in the park and had invented and perfected *ososhiki supesharu*, which was now popular all over Japan: the funeral special. She could provide him with all the delicacies on the pink menu, from a simple bath to *ippo tsuko* (one-way street), *name-name pure* (lick-lick play), *paizure* (breast-urbation), or *sakasa tsubo hoshi* (upside-down pot service).

Grandmother bowed and excused herself.

Pretty Girl, although blushing, led Kostas through the gardens to a wonderfully hot and steamy bath, a huge improvement on the tepid water of his suite. Before she undressed him, he asked, "Why do you wear eyeglasses, Pretty Girl?" Kostas felt awkward, felt a need to communicate before being "served."

She kneeled before him, settling back comfortably on her haunches. She had very delicate features, except for her mouth, which was full. An application of lipstick would have made her look voluptuous, but she blurred her lip line with white face powder. Her hair was very long and lustrous; black, with brown highlights. "I'm blind, Mr. Donoussa."

"Kostas."

"Kostas." She said the word as if she were tasting it. "I like it very much."

"Do the glasses allow you to see?"

"No, they are for the comfort of others. They are like clothes to cover me. If you wish, you can see me without them?"

Kostas nodded, then realized she couldn't see him and said, "Yes." But he looked away when she took the glasses off and laid them carefully beside her. Her eye sockets were empty, brown hollows, dark gouges in her powered-white face.

"There are many who find my blindness attractive. If you find it repellent, I can put my glasses back on. Or perhaps you would rather one of my cousins instead?" She bowed her head.

"No, I wish to be with you," Kostas said, feeling an exotic rush of both attraction and repulsion as she undressed before him . . . as she bathed him and soaped him and efficiently fellated him. She was shy, yet able, and as he watched her serve him everything he had ordered on the menu, he dreamed of an eyeless, delicate Helen who would cater to his every wish. He dreamed of Helen as Pretty Girl performed *kuchu kimmu*, aerial service, which required that he only lie on his back while she climbed astride him. He dreamed of Helen as Pretty Girl led him back to the bath for a full body massage and pubic hair "brush wash" on a tatami mat. After a moment of ecstasy, his gaze drifted back to Pretty Girl's glasses, which rested neatly folded on the floor where she had left them.

Her lost, brown Bette Davis eyes gazed intently at him through tinted windows.

But Kostas was shocked out of his reverie by a glimpse of shiny black, nine-inch stiletto heels. Suddenly, his wrists were seized and handcuffed behind him, his ankles bound, and his knees pushed forward, so that Kostas found himself with his chest on the mat and his buttocks raised, pink and exposed. He glimpsed someone the size of a sumo wrestler moving gracefully toward the door. As he shouted for help, the diminutive Pretty Girl merely consulted the menu, then produced a gag, which she tied very carefully, so as not to bruise his gums. She brushed her hands across his face, as if seeing him with her caress.

There was nothing Kostas could do but resign himself to his fate.

After all, there's always *something* you don't like on the menu. And at least Pretty Girl was small.

He ground his teeth as she lashed his buttocks, carefully pressing down the ends of the whip so as not to leave welts on his soft, white skin. The whipping was mercifully short. When she teetered back into his line of vision to offer him his choice of authentic antique MADE IN TAIWAN battery operated dildoes for *anaru zeme* —anal attack, Kostas shook his head. He felt a cold blob of KY jelly followed by the tip of a boot heel as Pretty Girl gave him full measure, pumping, rotating her ankle, gradually working deeper inside him.

He was mortified to find his erection hardening as she increased the pressure. Then another woman wriggled onto the mat, sliding beneath his belly to take his penis in her mouth. Her technique was familiar, and Kostas's mortification turned to true humiliation as Helen sucked the juices from him in an explosive orgasm.

He stared at Pretty Girl's glasses, as if he could focus himself into one small object. He felt soiled, defiled. Sex was private. That's what they'd agreed. That was to be the only rule.

The image of Pretty Girl's brown eyes stared back at him.

And suddenly Kostas felt a shiver fan down his back.

Someone was watching them . . . and it wasn't Pretty Girl.

When Kostas woke up, he was alone in his suite. His head ached and there was a metallic taste in his mouth, as if he'd been drugged. He told the room to turn off the wall, and morning sunlight blazed through the window plate. Niagara Falls was a dull roar, a vibration that could be sensed rather than felt. From his bed he could only glimpse blue sky threaded with sheet white cirrus. He listened for bath noises; there were none.

"Where's my wife?"

"There was no message left for you, Mr. Donoussa," the room said.

"When did she leave?"

"She was previously in the room from 3:36 PM to 5:17 PM yesterday, Mr. Donoussa."

"Yes, go on."

"She has not returned, Mr. Donoussa."

Kostas was now sitting on the side of the bed, his hands shaking, his voice gravelly. Something had gone terribly wrong. He knew it. He could feel it. As he blinked, he imagined Pretty Girl's glasses staring at him. He tried to remember. He remembered calling to Helen, then . . . waking up here.

"When did *I* return?"
The room didn't answer.
"When did I return?"
Again, no answer.
The room was dead.

Kostas went down to the old Niagara Falls strip, which was already crowded with penny ante gamblers and the skinny junkies out for a small, cheap shot to their pleasure centers. The day-shift whores had been out since dawn, calling and revealing and heckling. Most were occidental and thick-featured, illegals from the US side and Canadians who couldn't qualify for the dole. One tried to hard-sell herself to a middle-aged, balding man who was with another woman and four children. The man ignored her, even as she danced in front of him; he put his arms around two of the children and looked straight ahead, as if the casinos, virt parlors, and pink palaces were gold-steepled cathedrals. Kostas noticed that the children were dressed in identical, garish-red outfits. They would certainly be easy to find. And just then Kostas felt suddenly homesick. He heard the internal thunder that always preceded tears and focused on the task at hand, as if he were in court.

He found a plastic booth near the toilets in the seediest looking casino on the strip. The sliding doors kept opening and closing until he hit the control panel hard with his fist, then the booth darkened. Activating his office's privacy code, he waited until sufficient phantom circuits were created and the image of his father-in-law resolved a few feet away from him. He wore a well-pressed suit and looked morning fresh, although he had probably already been in the office for fourteen hours. Mr. Nisyros was compulsive about shaving and washing, which he did every few hours.

"Christ, what kind of a hole are you calling from?" Mr. Nisyros asked. "I'm surprised the bugs managed to secure a line. Is everything all right?" He paused for a beat, then said, "I can see that it's not."

"Helen's missing."

"Then find her."

"I tried. I did everything—"

"You mean you reported it to the hotel and the corporation, don't you?"

"Yes," Kostas said. "What else would you have me do?"

"I would have had you call me and not alert the Yakuza mob."

"I most certainly did not—" Kostas controlled himself. "Do you have any suggestions?"

"Yes, go to the hotel and wait in your room."

"Don't you want to know the details of what happened?"

"Wait in your room, send for room service. Stay away from entertainments."

And Mr. Nisyros faded into the fetid, smeary darkness of the booth, leaving Kostas to wonder why he wouldn't talk on a secure line.

Kostas did as he was told. Actually, there was no choice, for if Helen's father was correct and the Yakuza mob was involved, he would be at risk. But if Angelos Maitland Nisyros told him to stay in his room, then there he would be safe.

But what about Helen?

If Kostas thought about her, if he imagined all the terrible possibilities, he would go mad. He paced the room—twenty-two steps from the door to the balcony, thirteen steps wide. Angelos had warned him to stay away from virts. No, he told himself, the old man told him to stay away from everything but food. At least the amenities were working. He ordered a BLT and hot sake. The plate was brought by one of the hotel officers, an occidental who wore a red, paisley tie and a blue uniform. The officer explained that the hotel provided authentic American-style bacon, then whispered out of the room as quickly and quietly as a robot . . . or a trained valet.

Kostas sat well away from the balcony, sipped the warm sake and watched the Falls. It was as if the air itself was vibrating; and as he gazed at the natural wonder, he felt himself falling as so many had done before him, sliding through the thundering storm of water and steam and foam, crashing onto the rocks below, to disappear. The day passed in increments of agony, for he could not escape memory and could not quiet his mind. He imagined all the possibilities, all the myriad deaths and tortures that Helen might be suffering right now as he drank and ate and remembered.

Yet she had manipulated him.

And he was helpless. He had tried to find her, and failed. Now her father was in control. As if in defiance, he opened the balcony doors and stepped out into the sunlight. He looked at the gardens below, perfectly laid out, as if he were an impotent god; and he felt a great surge of anger, of rage.

Helen was probably somewhere enjoying herself. And Kostas was being played the fool.

"Mr. Donoussa, would you kindly step back inside," the room said.

"Why?"

"It is the wish of your father-in-law, Mr. Donoussa."

Dawn.

Kostas sat in the back seat of an antique Rolls-Royce Silver Steamer and gazed out the bullet-proof window. The chauffeur wore a traditional *keffiyeh* head dress and *abayeh* and barely spoke, except when Kostas asked him a direct question. His cologne—oil of roses and sandalwood musk—permeated the cabin, overwhelming any lingering odors of strong tobacco, old leather, and sweat. There was no one else on the road. Empty tenements had given way to rocky scrub, and then the scrub and scrabble had disappeared; not even such hardy flora could grow in stone. Kostas was being driven across a stone desert. Gray escarpments rose in the distance, but the fused land was flat and pocked and utterly devoid of life. It was hard to believe that three hundred miles behind them was a living wall of water. And gardens of flowers and leaf wet to the touch.

But now he was in the *real* Canada, which wasn't very different from the arid lands of America.

Kostas thought he saw forest, but he had mistaken the grotesque stands of rock cones for trees. Yet this was still temperate climate; *something* should grow here. The pot-holed, broken roadway suddenly ended, but the driver only slowed down a little as the rubber-padded crawler tracks eased the Rolls over rocks and ridges. As rough as the ground was, there were only a few bone-shaking jolts. Although Kostas was worn out, he couldn't sleep; and the day seemed an eternity. Finally the noxious atmosphere deepened into sunset, which had become a crimson swirling of oil in a sea of turquoise. In the distance was a mirage of green, a forest of imported eucalyptus that could endure here better than the firs and deciduous oak and pine that had thriven for millennia.

And above the forest, on top of a smooth butte, was a fortress of polished, white marble burning in the last rays of the sun.

"Sheik Mohammed bin Dakhil-Allah el Faud awaits you in the gazebo," the chauffeur said as he hurried Kostas through formal avenues of green, where lush, scented foliage and splashing fountains bespoke a fortune vast enough to lavish water upon this parched earth. In the center of the gardens, the huge, stained-glass tent that roofed the gazebo glowed like a mosaic of jewels. Over the damp exhalations of plants and the evening smells of cooling stone came the rose perfumes of Arabia, and the unmistakable aroma of freshly ground coffee.

Once inside the gazebo, Kostas—nervous and exhausted—felt that he had somehow fallen into a kaleidoscope. Soft lighting revealed a floor strewn with gorgeous carpets: silk Herekes tossed over Bokharas and piled with plush, tasseled cushions. The finest weaving, achieved by master craftsmen calling patterns to swift-fingered children soon blinded by the task. Panels of gold filigree supported the netted glass and woven draperies on the walls, framing a profusion of shimmering reds, golds, and indigoes that shifted patterns and confused the eye.

The sheik waved the chauffeur away, then rose to meet Kostas.

"*Masalama*, Mr. Donoussa. My home is your home. The gazebo is at its best at moonrise, wouldn't you agree? A fitting welcome for an honored guest." Mohammed bin Dakhil-Allah el Faud looked to be in his mid-forties and moved with the assurance of one used to exercising the power conferred by wealth, and willing to be seduced by its luxuries. His immaculate white thobe revealed the rounded contours of a body overfond of the sweetmeats that glistened in their golden dishes at his feet. His heavy black mustache drooped over full lips, which parted in a smile of greeting to reveal teeth stained by a lifetime of betel and coffee. He extended pudgy, ringed fingers to Kostas, who was momentarily surprised by the strength he found there.

"Blessings upon you and your household, your excellency," Kostas said. He knew how to respond, as he had escorted many of his father-in-law's powerful Arab clients around Melbourne.

After an obligatory exchange of pleasantries, Kostas was invited to be seated on the carpets opposite his graceful host. The sheik poured coffee into tiny, exquisite cups.

Kostas sipped, and could not suppress a smile of pure delight. "This is wonderful, your excellency." He looked at the stained-glass tent above. "This . . . is truly magical."

"And it also has the virtue of being real, Mr. Donoussa. I leave virts to the infidel. In Islam, we do not reproduce images of the body, not even in art. And all my food, including the coffee, is hand-grown in safe soil. This is my personal blend. I have made it myself for you, to the traditional recipe: black as night, sweet as love, and hot as hell. It is a metaphor for your current situation, is it not?"

The coffee was like a jolt of amphetamine, clearing Kostas's head and sharpening his senses, which had been dulled by fatigue, grief, and frustration. He felt as if he were just coming out of a trance. . . .

The sheik continued to speak, his plump fingers now interlaced with the silken, black-tasseled cord of priceless, pure amber worry beads; their soft clicking punctuated his sentences.

"Your father-in-law has explained your situation to me, and here in my home you will be safe from the Yakuza." The sheik made a clucking noise of disapproval. "In Niagara, you would have disappeared just like your wife. As if you had never been."

"What do you know of my wife?" Kostas asked reflexively, realizing only after he spoke that he had broached courtesy, that the sheik would tell him in his own time.

Or perhaps would decide not to tell him anything.

"The Yakuza do not like bad publicity," the sheik continued, as if uninterrupted, "and news of an international abduction would be very bad for the tourist business. By now, the incident will not have happened. But they cannot come here. You are safe, *Inshallah*." The sheik nodded to Kostas, giving him permission to speak.

"I appreciate your concern, your excellency. Yet I must confess that I had expected to meet my father-in law here with you. I am a lawyer, and I wish only to negotiate the release of my wife."

"That would be unwise, my son. Your laws are of no consequence here. Your father-in-law, however, is a respected man of business. He has property rights to the abducted woman and can speak as an equal with Sheik Fauzin el Harith. The sheik is a reasonable man, a traditional man. Your wife will be safe under his protection."

Kostas remembered meeting the Muslim potentate and his retinue of slaves, wives, and concubines in the lobby of the hotel, remembered how he had looked at Helen . . . with recognition. Kostas felt soiled, for no doubt the man had watched everything, had watched Kostas and Helen making love in their room . . . had watched them later in the pink salon *à trois* with Pretty Girl. It was Fauzin el Harith's eyes that had been staring out at him from Pretty Girl's glasses. "Protection? He has kidnapped—"

"You are young, and emotional, as befits a bridegroom, but this is now a business matter for your elders. Sheik Fauzin el Harith has simply employed the means at his disposal to procure a woman who captured his fancy." Mohammed bin Dakhil-Allah el Faud shrugged, then continued. "He was of course not quite within the law, but he is a powerful man. And powerful men—such as your father-in-law and perhaps myself—are not within the law." He smiled, as if enjoying the idea. "It may be that the matter of your wife can be resolved with a negotiated ransom. Maybe yes, maybe no. Certainly Sheik Fauzin el Harith could be an important busi-

ness ally for your father-in-law. Pain is often the messenger of joy
. . . and wealth. But I will take care of you, as I promised your
father-in-law. I would do the same for my own sons. But it is better
that you should remain here where you are safe. It is important that
you are secure and available when the need arises. So you will be
my guest. I am honored to have Mr. Nisyros's adopted heir under
my protection. I have many children, praise be to Allah, and I will
introduce you to my family. But perhaps not just now. You will feel
much better after some rest."

The gentle tone admitted no argument.

Kostas realized that he was now, like Helen, a prisoner.

An honored prisoner in a cage of gold.

He could do nothing but wait.

The days passed like the long hours in the Rolls.

Servants attended Kostas at all times, and from them he learned
that it was an honor that Sheik Mohammed bin Dakhil-Allah el
Faud had received him privately and served him with his own
hands. It was an especial honor that he even allowed Kostas to
speak to his daughters, who were always dressed, or rather hidden,
in virgin-white gowns, headdresses, and veils. He thought it odd
that he had not met any of the sheik's sons, but would not broach
etiquette and ask.

Kostas waited for another audience with the sheik. When that
was not forthcoming, he became more insistent. The guards told
him that the sheik was busy.

The sheik was always busy.

Kostas kept to himself and waited for the all-important call from
his father-in-law or a summons from the sheik. Wrestling with the
dead weight of memory, he relived every moment of his last night
with Helen. Indeed, it was as if Helen were already dead and he
was in mourning. Then almost against his will, he began to come
back to life. He read in the sheik's library; rode the sheik's horses in
the scrub below the butte while a Sikorsky gunship helicopter flew
overhead; walked every inch of compound in the polite and distant
company of his guards; and found himself spending more and
more time with the sheik's eldest daughter Sagan. She was as tall
as Kostas, and was named after a man who had saved her father's
life. Although she, too, was always attended by servants and would
not remove her veil, she claimed to have visited the ruins of Man-
hattan and to have lived on her own in Toronto.

"Tell me about the man you are named after," Kostas asked as they sat in a long, lush garden. Beside them goldfish as large as trout swam back and forth along the edges of a brackish pond, as if waiting to be fed. Beyond—and white as Sagan's gown—were huge marble buildings built in the shape of tents: the soldiers' barracks. The architecture was as striking as the winged opera house in Sydney, Australia.

"I've already told you," Sagan said, her beautiful, dark eyes gazing out at him, as if from silken prisons.

"Was he an infidel?"

She laughed, and the guards standing a discrete distance away from them came to the alert, as if Kostas were about to do something untoward. "Do you think my father would name me after an infidel?"

Kostas shrugged.

"No, he is not an infidel. You won't find many infidels in Kentucky." She looked into the distance. "Have you been to America?"

"No."

She shook her head. "Better here."

"In the desert?"

"Better here."

"Didn't your father worry that you would be in the company of infidels when you lived in Toronto?" Kostas said.

"Why are you obsessed with infidels?" She smiled. "Are you asking if he would let me marry one?"

"Would he?"

"He allows you to keep me company."

Shocked, Kostas realized that he had been leading the conversation back to that, for if he lost Helen, he wanted Sagan. He wanted everything to end with physical intimacy, for then he could not be hurt. If language separated him from this veiled stranger, that would have been even better.

But what did he have with Helen? Emotional connection? Pain? Understanding? All of that, and he wallowed in the pain, yet he knew Helen little better than he knew this veiled princess, this outlander who was slumming with the infidel.

"I'm sorry, Kostas." That was the first time she had called him by his given name. "I was taking advantage of you, playing with you. You must be in great pain over your wife."

She watched him, waiting for him to speak; he had to say something. "I feel better when we're together."

"We can be together as much as you like."

Kostas nodded, thinking about Helen, wondering what she was

doing while he was having this conversation. He felt no anxiety now. He was empty, and content.

And as he sat there, holding Sagan's hand while the guards purposely looked the other way, he realized that he had been trapped once again. By Helen. By his father-in-law. By her father.

There was nothing to be done but relax and accept it.

An arrangement had been made.

In time, Sagan would remove her veil. . . .

Introduction

Ships

Michael Swanwich

It was a clear, starry night and Jack Dann came breezing into town at the wheel of a limousine twenty feet long, with a big cigar stuck in one corner of his expansive grin . . . Or, no, wait, we were talking online. This was back when dinosaurs roamed the Earth, before the days of the World Wide Web, when the Internet was text-based and bulletin boards charged stiff fees for the privilege of posting messages on them. One such BB (as they were then called, children) was GEnie, so named because it was owned and operated by General Electric. They'd had the clever idea of giving free access to science fiction writers, who would theoretically draw in star-struck paying members. In practice this meant that we hung around with each other, gossiping and joking and doing the BB no good whatsoever, but so what? It was fun.

So there was a batch of us exchanging witticisms and in response to some hit scored off him, Jack wrote: I died.

That would make a good opening for a story, I typed back. Off the top of my head, then, I wrote the next couple of lines.

So over the next hour or so, we bounced sentences and paragraphs off each other, like jazz musicians trading riffs, building a weird and wonderful fantasy world. I put the narrator in a coffin and Jack opened up his third eye. Jack sent the ships skimming over the sands and I put Aubrey Chang on one of them. Oh, baby. You can't imagine how good that felt.

The next day, I took everything we'd written, did a light, unifying rewrite to make it read smoothly, and sent it back to Jack, suggesting we work up the story for real. Jack, typically, was game, and we swapped the text back and forth by e-mail, neither of us knowing exactly where it was going to end up, but enjoying the hell out of the journey.

There was only one problem.

Jack was a newlywed at the time, deeply and madly in love with his wife Janeen, and his happiness tended to bleed into the story. I had created a genuinely sick relationship as its motive heart, and he kept trying to heal it. I'd hand off the text to him in a state of screaming negativity and he'd turn the protagonists into lovers, gentle co-conspirators against a cold universe. Then, when it came back to me I'd rip away the positive, redemptive elements and return the story to its original bracing nihilistic bleakness.

Weirdly enough, it was fun. Now that the story's done and brought safely to harbor, I can admit, too, that everything I like best about this story, every detail and turn of phrase I admire most, was written by Jack. Oh, man, those ships! Those grasshoppers! The guy's still got chops.

And I've still got things to learn from him.

Jack Dann

"Ships" started out as a game of writers' machismo. I remember Michael writing me a line and daring me to do one better. How could I resist? So I wrote something that was so over the top that it would silence even Michael.

Ha! Michael has a mind that is far too deviously brilliant and labyrinthine to be stopped so easily, and so, in typical Michael fashion, he did me one better, and—as they say—we were off and running.

But off and running where?

We kept trying to back each other into corners, and we ran full out on sheer ballsy cussedness and ego for as long as we could. But then there came the moment of truth, the moment that separates the men from the boys and the real writers from the wanabees: we had to actually figure out what the hell we were doing!

I have an e-mail from Michael dated April 26, 1994:

"Dear Jack:

"I really don't KNOW what's going on."

And neither did I, but we started brainstorming over e-mail, through the aether, and we wrote incomprehensible stuff that somehow pointed to the undercarriage of the story, or at least *we* thought so. Here is a smattering of those e-mails:

Jack:

"It is, perhaps a siege of Heaven with intent to kill God, but, perhaps not as you think. Perhaps we are looking, via the story, via Chang's viewpoint, at the 'many in the one.' Perhaps all these characters are manifestations of this god, who we will refer to as Chang, a god who is caught in a loop of death and resurrection, who, for reasons we need to work out, is so revolted with his 'be-ingness' that he is trying to revolt against himself . . . kill himself by creating one manifestation to kill the 'others.' "

Michael:

"I like what you've done and am already hard at work corrupting and diluting it. I've changed Julia's name to Anastasia (even cooler names welcomed). And I encourage you to write the Birth of Aphrodite scene . . .

"I'm convinced that the goal Chang thinks he has of killing God-and-the-Devil is delusory, that he is God and wants to kill himself. (Let's throw in lots of despairing angels in the assault on Heaven scene.) I like everybody being aspects of himself most especially since I've (that should be I'd) come to the conclusion that Starbuck was Chang's dark companion already.

"After Chang castrates Starbuck, amputates his arms and legs, cuts off his nose, gouges out his eyes (and casts them out a port-hole so that he'll see nothing but the vastness of space and stars and time for all eternity) and further mutilates him, let's put Starbuck in the darkest hold of the ship and keep him imprisoned there, miserable and wretched and prescient, a newly wise counsel for Our Hero to consult after his rash destruction of Sophonisba."

Jack:

"I thought the stuff you sent about disfiguring the figurehead was just brilliant. We can certainly use all the pieces (and we can throttle an angel). I'll take a shot at pulling some of this stuff together, but I'm not sure how you wish to integrate the material after Chang disfigures the figurehead. Do you want the scene where he finds Anastasia and Starbuck together in his cabin to replace the scene I had written, where Chang throws Starbuck's eyes into the void; or do you envision the scene you wrote to come after and simply raise the organ removal ante?"

Michael:

"Um . . . as a general rule, I'd like to keep you in the dark as to my fictive intentions since the stuff you've produced under exactly those conditions has been such a delight so far. But the gouging-out of eyes scene supersedes or is merged with or is used as a jumping-off point for your take on the mutilation scene. Feel free to muck about; I'd like to keep the reference to her 'sucking his soul out through his filthy little spigot' because that so well conveys his feelings toward Starbuck but even that's up for grabs."

Yes, it was all up for grabs, and in June I wrote Michael, "This is going to be a very strange story, even for the genre."

And it was.

Michael wrote the extraordinarily weird surrealistic bits, which I love. They shine through the story like arc lights through a window. My primary concern was the story arc, and we modeled the structure on Milton's "Paradise Lost."

What the hell; we figured we might as well go for broke.

Ships

Michael Swanwick and Jack Dann

I WAS DEAD. That before all: I was dead and buried. Time passed and I took no notice of it. My body rotted. The vermin of the Earth came and feasted upon my flesh.

It was then that my third eye opened up. An area in the center of my wallet-brown skull seemed to melt, and my questing vision stared upward, seeing through the coffin, through the soil, through the roots of the grass above, seeing as clearly as ever I had when I was alive.

I knew my mind's eye was blue, though I could not say how I knew. Perhaps it was some sort of sympathetic magic, for I was staring at a clear, blue sky that curved above me, flawless as the finest example of the ceramist's art. And though I well knew where I lay, I felt that I was at long last home.

I could remember my funeral, the incense, the last screams of . . . Anastasia? A woman, definitely. I could feel the wood and silk of the bier beneath me, mountains pressing upon me, even as the darkness swirled like wind, like smoke. I lay detached and emotionless, my thoughts slowly dissolving with death and my senses numbing into a synesthesia of color and sadness and memory and sound and

Then here. Blue eye. Open.

As the ships came toward me, skimming over sand, blowing slight tails in the dunes.

A kind of lightness seized me, lifting me up into the blue mirror of my eye. It was as if God had hooked a finger under my chin and held me dangling over the shimmering, the oceanic surface of my old life.

I waited.

The nearest of the ships, a three-decked frigate of a hundred guns, hove to, kicking up a light spray of the golden sand. I thought I felt a grain or two strike my face. The creatures aboard the ship — demons? angels? — crowded the rails and hung from the shrouds. A thin, almost skeletal figure stood on the raised quarterdeck, looking glass tucked under his arm.

With a pang of what emotion I now cannot say, I recognized him.

It was me. What I was seeing was either a doppelganger, a ghost . . . or else the real Auberon Chang.

For an instant, I felt a vertiginous turning, so that I became the other Auberon Chang, standing aboard the frigate, and I thought his thoughts, scanned the dunes with his baleful eyes, saw *me*. Our shared imagination quailed at the sight. He saw an open grave, violated brown bones, maggots caught as if in the webs of a hundred spiders. But the webbing was rotting musculature, and my skull was eyeless, for eyes were to the small workmen of the soil a delicacy beyond even flesh. Thoughts turned to darkness, emptiness, and when I awakened (as myself, as the captain of this impossible ship) I found myself on the forward deck, looking out into the starry darkness.

The sands were far behind us. Incredibly, we were sailing in the ebon blackness of space. The stars were so sharp and bright, so hot and cold in their redness and demon-fire blues that it hurt the eye to look into them. And below, far below, the Earth rotated like a blue dream, or a last thought.

"Sir! Permission to approach."

I turned, middle fingers linked behind my back, and nodded to the crewman waiting by the mainmast. He came to me, hauling by the scruff of its neck a wretched thing, pallid and afraid, but still undeniably human. *The cabin boy*, whispered a voice in my head.

"This'n here was caught stealing food, sir."

The cabin boy twisted his head around suddenly, snorted as if to clear his throat, and spat at me. It was a shocking gesture, wild and suicidal. Wiping my face in disgust, I could not but admire him for it.

"Take him aft," I said (and all the while thinking how pathetic a being this less-than-mannequin was, what a horrid existence he must lead, how deserving he was of compassion). "Have him hanged."

The hanging was held as a formal discipline, with a color guard and three drummers. The crew was assembled to watch as four demon sailors pulled the creature kicking and struggling into the air. They hauled on a rope that ran through a block-and-tackle hung from the fore yardarm and with each smooth motion the cabin boy was jerked another yard higher. His hands had been tied behind his back. His face darkened from red to blue, a knot of agony. It was a gruesome sight.

"Enjoying yourself, Captain?"

I turned into the grinning, many-toothed face of the first mate. *Starbuck*, my interior voice whispered, *a most dangerous subordinate.* "State your business, sir," I said coldly.

His smirk retreated from his face, but lingered beneath the skin, like a hyena waiting just beyond the lion's reach. "We've passed the beacon star, sir. It's time you opened our orders."

"I'll be the judge of that, Mr. Starbuck."

"Yes, sir."

"Have you so little to occupy your time, Mr. Starbuck, that you must involve yourself in second-guessing your superior? Do the men find your supervision wholly superfluous?"

An involuntary snarl distorted Starbuck's narrow face before he could hide it with a bow. Chastened, he made his respects and backed away.

The cabin boy's struggles were more desperate now. He had turned black, and blood poured from his nostrils—it made him seem a minor goblin. He could not die, of course—not here, not now—and so it was possible to extend his punishment as long as desired. Forever, if necessary.

"Cut him down," I said at last. "You know where to send him."

When I returned to my quarters, three bells later, the cabin boy was awaiting me. His eyes were red with hate, but he made no protest as I turned him around and pulled his ragged trousers from his smooth, young flanks. He allowed me to bend him over the cot submissively enough, and made only a single gurgling noise—a whimper, almost—when I entered him.

I took my pleasure of him.

When I had slaked my lust, I poured water in a basin and laved my privates. Then I adjusted my clothing. The cabin boy pulled up his rags and watched sullen and unblinking as I opened the ship's safe and removed the packet of instructions under which we sailed. It had been sealed in red wax with the Sigil of Baphomet. I tapped the parchment bundle thoughtfully against my lips.

"Brandy!" I snapped. "And then get out!"

Alone, I sprawled in the Captain's chair—mine was the only berth in the ship afforded this dignity—and drank deep from a cut-crystal tumbler. The liquor was as brown as amber and as delicious as old sins recalled in tranquillity.

I broke the seal.

The orders were brief and to the point. Nevertheless I studied them for a long time. Though I had long been expecting something of the sort, and had indeed argued for it in clandestine councils, still it was a shock to come upon the moment itself.

"Here it is, then," I murmured.

With sudden resolution I strode up on deck. "Starbuck!" I shouted. This was too great a moment for the master-of-arms, a sailing master, or indeed any officer of lesser rank than he. "Assemble the crew!"

He materialized at my elbow. "Twice in one watch? It's not good discipline, sir." Eyes glittering with an avaricious hunger for me to show weakness or indecision. But I had a trick up my sleeve worth two of his.

"Bugger discipline! Line 'em up and serve out three tots of rum-and-sulfur for every man-jack of them."

"Three!" Starbuck cried in involuntary amazement.

"Do it now, sir," I said quietly.

In minutes the crew was assembled in crude, undisciplined ranks before the mainmast. Their grog was served out, and this effectively divided their attention between curiosity and anxiety for the devilish liquor they knew better than to drink before my command to do so. At my direction, Midshipman Coffin stood by the mast. The cabin boy deposited a small chest at my feet.

"Mister Coffin!" I barked. "Strike the colors."

Demon mouths fell open in amazement, revealing arched rows of pointed teeth, fangs, tusks the hue of old ivory. Tattooed faces turned upward, aghast. A Babel of hoarse whispers arose from all sides. Out of the corner of my eye I saw Starbuck's hand surreptitiously close around the hidden dagger he thought I didn't know about. The silk flag of the Old Order floated gracefully down, as white and delicate as a hanky dropped from an old lady's hand.

From the chest I'd had removed from my cabin I drew forth new colors. Up they went.

The crew stared up at the banner under whose aegis we now sailed. It was as black and featureless as the black flag of anarchy. But the black of *our* flag held an infinitely more fearsome meaning.

A horror-struck silence descended upon the ship. Before it could break, I held out my hand. The cabin boy placed in it a leather cup identical to those the crew themselves held. I raised it in a formal toast.

"Blood and damnation! Fuck the grail."

I drained the thing in one gulp.

It took an effort to maintain my countenance, for the drink came from Hell's own cellars and was fit only for the degraded palates of such as sailed before the mast. But somehow I managed to keep a granite face. And the crew, nothing loath for a drink upon any occasion, knocked their own back.

While they were gasping and wheezing and laughing, I raised an eyebrow at Starbuck. He nodded to Coffin, who jumped atop the taffrail and whipped off his hat. "Hip-hip—" he cried.

"*Huzzah!*" the crew roared.

"Hip-hip—"

"*Huzzah!*"

"Hip-hip—"

"*Huzzah!*"

I allowed myself a tight, little smile of satisfaction. The moment when the men might have turned against me was past. They were mongrel curs to their very bones, with a cur's mentality: to attack upon show of weakness and to fawn and grovel before the hand that wielded the whip. I had acted with the high-handed assurance of a master of beasts. There would be no mutiny. My command was safe.

And we were rebels now.

Fuck the grail.

So began the great enterprise: With three cheers and a command to the steersman to abandon our prior course for a sharp veer into the starry wastes. Inevitably the first excitement of rebellion was swallowed up by the inescapable routines of duty, unchanged by our new status. Decks still needed swabbing, and sails trimming. Days, weeks, months, and years passed in the regular monotony of shipboard life, broken into dogwatches and the clocking tolling of bells and shrill of whistles. I grew to know and hate my officers and crew as intimately as they did me.

The strange transformation of the cabin boy escaped my attention for so immoderately long a time that when I at last had my revelation, it was already undeniable in its nature.

It happened at the end of the third watch. I had seized the cabin boy by the shoulders preparatory to entering him, and one hand slid forward and down to his chest, which I on occasion grasped and fondled during the act. Sliding under his loose tunic, it encountered what was unmistakably a woman's breast!

I drew back from him. He waited motionless, incurious.

"Strip," I commanded.

I watched avidly as he obeyed. In the gloom, he might have been mistaken for a slender woman. His hips had widened. He now had, as I have said, slight breasts. There had been a general shifting of fatty deposits. In other, less obvious ways he was no longer entirely male.

Wonderingly, I lit a lantern and scrutinized his body with care. There was an unforced femininity to his form and features. His neck was long and smooth. The gentle swell of his belly brought back ancient, longing memories. His penis, for which I had no use, had shriveled to the size of an infant's. He was all but hermaphroditic.

"How has this happened?" I demanded.

He shrugged. "It's what you wanted."

"Explain yourself!"

He gave me a look sharp as a fox's. "Yer the Captain and I'm just the cabin boy. You want something—what'm I sposed to do? Might not want to obey. Ain't got no choice."

I questioned him further, but he was a creature of little intellect. I was the captain and that meant I got my way. In his simple philosophy, that explained all. Still . . .

Was it possible? Had my desires—my *needs*—been slowly altering the creature in the course of the endless series of sodomies I visited on his body? It seemed inevitable. Those same lusts that overmastered me, it would appear, were capable of overwhelming their object as well.

I laid him down on the cot upon his back for the first time and studied his form with a cold and unsympathetic eye. Then I entered him from between his legs, as I would have a woman.

"Let's get to work," I growled. "You have a long way to go."

*   *   *

Within the year, the creature was no longer male. Its hair had, at my insistence, been left uncut and hung halfway down its back. Its breasts, pale as alabaster and pink-tinged at the tips, were full as ripe pears, the skin fine to the point of translucency. Its vagina was a detailed work of art, identical in every respect to that of one particular woman from my long ago and otherwise forgotten past.

On the day when it was at last clear that no trace of its penis, of its maleness, remained, I asked a question I had never directed at it before. "Do you have a name?"

It shook its head, not meeting my eyes. I took its chin between thumb and forefinger and lifted its gaze to meet mine. The coals of rebellion glowed therein, as hotly banked as ever. That I had very carefully left unchanged.

"I will call you Anastasia."

She flushed, but said nothing.

"The body's done," I told her then. "Let's start working on the face."

Already I could see the ghost of a different set of features lying just beneath the skin, like the face of a drowned woman glimpsed through murky water.

From that night on, Anastasia lived in my cabin; and like an artist who, knowing that a Madonna resides within the stone he's working, chips away blindly until he "finds" the form residing there, so did I mold her features, sometimes with fornications and sometimes with curses and beatings. I knew not what I wanted until the features manifested themselves in a series of tiny miracles of the flesh: Pale, blue eyes flecked with silver, hair as black as obsidian, a swarthy complexion. A narrow, aquiline nose and high cheekbones combined with a full mouth and a heart-shaped face to give her the appearance of a feral saint, the obscene sweetness of an angel blessed—or cursed—with free will.

She lay beside me when I slept, and upon awakening I would examine her to see what had changed, what had become defined, what had become more perfect, for her journey was to nothing less than perfection. Long before she was done, she was so beautiful that it hurt me to look upon her.

I talked with her for hours, teaching her to respond as Anastasia herself would. I gave her warmth and intelligence and a certain calculating curiosity. I gave her a smile so bewitching it made me want to wrap my hands lovingly about her throat and choke her senseless. I formed her mind as carefully as I did her body.

When she accompanied me topside, the crew would stare at her with the flat, cannibalistic gaze of a hungry rat considering its own children. She held herself stiffly then, chin high, trying in vain to hide her fear from me. She was never—never!—more deliciously desirable to me than she was then. Back in my cabin, I would take her while the terror still flowed from her body in great waves of pheromones.

I was living in a fool's paradise.

The watches passed, the men rotating like the dark hands of a clock that was the frigate itself, measuring out the futile parsecs of eternity. We sailed beyond the final dim stars of existence and into the void beyond. And there came at last a day when a thin line of light appeared in the distance, almost impossible to see, bisecting the universe.

The cliffs of Heaven.

The cliffs grew, incandescent white and brighter than any sun, for month upon month. By imperceptible degrees they towered so high over the ships that their tops could not be seen without looking up. Sunglasses were doled out to all the crew, and even so the cliffs could not be looked at directly for long without the eyes watering.

The mere sight of that ancient stronghold of the great Enemy sent the crew into frenzies of loathing. In their emotional state they committed even more atrocities than usual. Disciplines, floggings, torturings, became a daily entertainment. Yet, "We're detecting no more than one crime in ten," Starbuck reported.

"Then punish 'em ten times over for those you do."

Black specks against the more-than-Arctic dazzle, the gathering fleets were at first no more significant than a swarm of midges set upon attacking a continent.

But as more and more ships joined the gathering, by the dozens at first, and then the hundreds, congregating into the thousands and millions, the brightness diminished. We grew into the billions, and became a great cloud, a storm, and still we grew, into the trillions and beyond. Our numbers surpassed comprehension. The wave of hatred that preceded us was like a great fist smashing into Heaven's face. The cliffs cracked and shattered, crumbling, into the void even before we reached them.

By the time we passed the coastline our Armada seemed not just a threat but Fate itself.

*   *   *

Midshipman Coffin had good reason to believe that he would not prosper were Starbuck first-in-command. So it was he I chose to operate the capstan that lowered me in a rope-and-basket contraption alongside Sophonisba, the frigate's painted figurehead. She was an enormous carving, three times my own height, and I felt ridiculously diminished dangling before her, one hand clapped to my hat lest it blow away and the other clutching a little iron hatchet.

Imperiously, I rapped with the blunt end of the hatchet on the nearer of the figurehead's matronly breasts.

With a groan of pain her lips moved. "Why did you bring me to life?" she asked. "When will you let me die?" I swung slightly in the stellar breezes and quickly wrapped my hatchet-arm around one of the basket's guy wires. Her eyes remained dull and wooden.

"Prophesy for me."

"Death," she said. "Damnation. Eternity. Futility. All this you knew long ago and without my intervention. If you will not let me die, then at least let me sleep."

Outraged, I slammed her cheek. The hatchet bounced off, leaving behind a gash in the wood. "Awaken! The fleets are gathering. This is not the universe as it once was. Stretch your thoughts, look out across the plains of destiny. Give me tidings dire enough to glut my hunger for them. Tell me of horrors too fearsome to hear."

Now, as if a disguising mist had blown away from her, a knowing light kindled in Sophonisba's eyes and her wooden substance was transported briefly to flesh. Blood trickled down from the hatchet-scratch but she paid it no mind. A wondering expression came over her. Where her gaze went, mine could not follow.

"Speak!"

She said nothing at first, and then:

"I see angels dying. I see your ship destroyed and its crew as well. All that is good will be defiled; all that is evil will come to naught; I see destruction without purpose and desolation without end."

I could not help but gloat. This was better than I had dared hope for. "More!" I demanded. "Tell me more—and worse. Make me despair."

Sophonisba nodded, all-but-invisibly, and her lips moved.

"Why did you agree to this?" she said. It was Starbuck's voice, sullen and suspicious. "If Captain Chang were to discover us—and in his own berth!"

A trill of laughter such as could have come from but one throat. "What does it matter to you, little man? You'd spit in the captain's soup if you had the chance. Are you afraid to fuck his whore?" I screamed.

"You lie, you lie, you lie!" Sophonisba's face was lifeless again, and I was slamming it repeatedly with the hatchet. In my fury I smashed off her nose entirely and splintered both eyes blind, rendering her permanently useless to the ship. Then I was roaring to Coffin to crank up the basket, crank up the basket, the damnable basket, damn you sir, up!

Sophonisba did not lie.

Starbuck lay, hairy-bellied and naked, upon the formerly crisp linen of my own sheets while Anastasia crouched over him, sucking his soul out through the conduit of his filthy little spigot.

My thoughts were like rabbits fleeing from dogs, scattering across empty fields in futile quest of a safe cranny. A single lamp glowed, flickering with every movement of the ship, which was considerable, for our inverse tau was enormous now as we continually closed upon the limiting speed of light. Even as I stood, hatchet raised, before Starbuck and Anastasia, overwhelmed with blood lust and horribly, unspeakably, *enjoying* it, stars were being born before the bow and dying in our wake.

With a shriek Anastasia leaped from the bed, yanking the sheet after her. It hid one breast, one thigh, a parody of modesty. Leaving her lover uncovered and vulnerable to my eye. And helpless before my hatchet.

I chopped off his hands.

I hacked out his liver and his heart. I sliced through the tendons on the backs of his calves so that he must henceforward not walk as a man but crawl as does a serpent. His cock and balls I flung out the porthole into the great vacuum mouth of the universe.

Finally I gouged out both of Starbuck's eyes and cast them after his privates. Let him stare forever into infinitude and glory. Let him suffer.

Leaving his mewling remains behind, I seized Anastasia by the wrist. I could smell Starbuck's musky sweat all over her, like rot in salt-pork.

I hauled her, naked and squealing, to the forward hold. The only light came from a single green-glass bull's eye lantern. Demon sailors started to their feet at my entry, rolling down from hammocks, rising from dice games and rat-baitings. "You dog-fucking bastard!" Anastasia raged. "I'll make you crawl for this. Oh, sweet suffering, the things I'll make you do!"

I flung her down before the crew.

Some things are too vile to describe. I stood watching until there was not the least remnant of humanity left in the thing that had for a brief span been Anastasia.

Then I left.

Time passed. The watches accumulated like pearls deposited by divers.

One night I was wrenched awake from the cold dreamlessness of sleep by a great pain in my temples. I pressed my hands against them, as if the pressure could keep my head from bursting open. In the shaving mirror upon the wall I saw that my forehead was purple and bruised and my face swollen, as if from a hundred agonizing blows. I could hear my teeth cracking and feel my jaw begin to break as the side of my face tore open. Something inside my skull was struggling to get out, striving to be born.

In a frenzy, I threw open my medical kit and seized a vial of heroin. I cooked the solution and prepared a syringe with a long, curved needle designed for this express purpose. Then, peeling back an eyelid, I slid the needle between eye and socket and shot its load directly into my brain.

It took three slugs to lay the pain to rest.

I was sitting on my berth considering what to do next when the air was split by the shrilling and brazen clangor of every whistle and bell in the fleet being sounded at once. The thunder of cannons and demon drums swelled and merged into a roar the like of which had not been heard since that Word was spoken which began existence by shattering the primal monoblock. I leaped up, heart pounding, exultant.

The battle had at last begun.

We were in the vanguard of the fleet, right on the front line, but even so there was time to prepare. I had the ship's carpenter fasten an iron band about my forehead so that whatever lay within could not escape, and then turned my attention to the conversion of my ship. The internal bulkheads were taken down and the gunnery crew ran out the cannons. Weapons were served out to our marines and the fire-buckets filled with sand.

With a mighty creaking and groaning, the ship began to absorb the masts and extrude wings. Chitinous plates accreted over the hull and antennae sprouted above the mandibles at the prow. All around us ships were growing simple and compound eyes, proboscises, gaiters, stings and ovipositors, legs and tibia and spiracles, each according to its nature and genus. Steam issued from the cannon barrels and filthy holds still damp from piss and sweat. One by one the chittering voices of our unholy vessels rose up, merging into a single howl of despairing wrath.

My ship was the first to land on the icy desert plain.

Our multitudes rained down, frigates and cruisers and schooners and galleys and bomb vessels: ships of the line, swift chargers and cumbersome gunboats, all become locusts, hornets, wasps, mantises . . . Folding their wings and striding forward to ravage the fields of eternity. Marines crawled like ants down their ropes by the millions to defile the golden sands with shit and sacrilege. Briefly, we were unopposed.

Then the lookout screamed in rage and fear as a storm of angels kited up from the distant mountains. These were the lowliest of the Adversarial forces: its cherubim, those spirits so beautiful they were physically nauseating to look upon: gleaming towers of muscle and steel, wheels of whirling blades, hallowed and perfect; wings that billowed like sails, of such delicate construction that a soap bubble would be considered gross by comparison. Serene and pitiless eyes.

"Mister Coffin!" I cried. "Ready a salvo. On my word."

The closest of our enemies raised their lances. Needles of ruby light pierced carapace and armor plating. The boatswain's mate fell screaming to the deck, black bile gushing from his chest and back. Midshipman Coffin raised his hands to his mouth to form a megaphone. I glared them down. "Steady!" I barked. "Not yet."

The sacred *pneuma* rose up from our assailants in an invisible, lilac-scented cloud, driving the lesser demons mad and causing others to retch blood. "Not yet," I repeated. We could not fight them with bullets and shot, for we were *materia*, the real, the tangible, and that would be relinquishing one's essence, one's flesh and inner self to our opponents. But hermetic science (and swords and fists) would suffice to rid us of their oppression forever.

"Fire!"

The cannons blasted billows of black smoke into the attacking ranks. I had had them loaded with ancient injustices—the tears of the innocent, the screams of children, the prayers of the betrayed— and they wrought massive destruction upon the cherubim, who fell, broken, down the welling light to a land that blackened under them, each blasted angel staining and despoiling great swaths of the infinite plains.

So went the battle, bloody and disastrous for both sides. We were so perfectly matched that our struggle could only end in mutual and universal annihilation. But the advantage was ours, for it was the black flag of Annihilation under which we sailed, and the final end to suffering and punishment we sought. Our ships, driven by the strength of resentments older than the universe itself, cut through the Enemy in phalanxes, crushing with thoraxes wet with blood, spearing with claw and comb. An immense wasp exploded by our starboard bow and its crew were picked off before they hit the sands, eviscerated, mutilated, and eaten by the vengeful Defenders. A broadside caught an archangel square in the eye and he went down in explosions and gouts of blue flame.

I was the rattle and the saber. The fleets radiated out from my perfect fury like iron filings caught in a magnetic field. I was the very center, the focus, the eye of the hurricane. The children of wrath flocked to me like moths, and like moths they died in untellable numbers and unspeakable agony.

We fought for aeons.

Until finally, having exhausted all the ship's powder and its crew as well, Midshipman Coffin and I stood shoulder-to-shoulder on the blood-slick deck, faced with one final invading angel—a seraph. It was possible that he was the last of his kind.

The angel's strength was prodigious. With one blow of his fist he crushed Coffin and swept his body over the rail. With a second, he smashed my cutlass to flinders.

Dropping the hilt, I threw myself at the seraph; we locked arms about each other. My ribs splintered and cracked. Machine oil dribbled from his jaw and puffs of steam leaked from his joints. He forced that beautiful and pitiless face so close to mine I could see nothing else and murmured, "Look into my eyes."

Startled, I did. In all that inhuman visage of titanium and steel, only the eyes were organic. They were set into gimbals, held in place by pronged needles, and manipulated by gears and servomechanisms. Even so, I recognized them.

They were Starbuck's.

Those eldritch eyes blazed with amusement at my shocked recognition. Fleetingly I felt that what I fought was no more than an automaton, a marionette, the cat's-paw for forces beyond my comprehension. That all this, my glory and all-destroying triumph, were no more than a cruel and pointless shadow-play. Then I overbalanced and fell, pulling the seraph with me to the deck. For an instant my arm was free.

I seized the broken hilt of my cutlass and ran its twelve inches of jagged blade into the angel's abdomen. Hot ichor steamed over my clenched fist. For a long moment we lay thus, locked in homicidal embrace, and it was good, oh very good indeed, this moment was, far better than ever sex had been.

But even as I savored my victory, the Starbuck-eyed seraph rose up beneath me one last time. His blow was like lightning! I ducked its full force, but still his fist glancingly struck my forehead—and the iron band shattered!

Underneath me, laughing, the angel crumbled to nothing.

My pain was beyond expressing.

I rose to my knees, clutching my head in agony. I screamed as flesh extruded from flesh, essence from essence, physical being from the stuff of my own body. Weeping bloody tears, I could barely look at the separate thing that arose from me, even as it tore the umbilicus of flesh connecting us. Liquids gushed away, weakening me, strengthening *her*.

Anastasia.

She rose up before me, shaping herself even as I watched. Wet and slick as a newborn infant, but proud, fearless—a warrior queen. She was infinitely stronger than I; she had clarified. Her body, nude, was less flesh than light; radiance itself, a steady candle. I groped for a weapon, any weapon, even as the ship, creaking and groaning, shifted underfoot.

Anastasia kicked me in the side. Ribs splintered.

I screamed.

She seized me by the pigtail and hauled me, struggling, to my feet. "Where is my body?"

"I—"

She struck me in the face. Blood and spittle flew. "Don't talk—go!"

Half-blind with pain, I led Anastasia down into my dreadful vessel's hollow innards. The hold was lit only by the feeble phosphorescence of its dying flesh. In the trembling dark, a-reek with gore and maggots, I sought out the mutilated remains of what had once been Anastasia and before her the cabin boy.

It had been kept in an airless closet with a single bucket used to bring it slops and remove its leavings. When I unlocked the door, I was hit with the stench of gangrene. It had lost both legs and arms;

the stumps were tied up with leather thongs. Its dugs were empty sacks, its face a noseless horror black with necrosis. That blind and fish-mouthed face gaping up at me, idiotic in its misery, was all but unrecognizable.

Anastasia drew in her breath with a short, sharp hiss. But she only said, "Carry her."

I picked the body up and discovered that it was almost liquescent. It sloshed like an overripe pear. Anastasia walked us to the sailmaker's cupboard and from it took needles, canvas, and leather. Swiftly, she fashioned a kind of saddle for her onetime body and a harness for me.

"Strip," she commanded.

I obeyed.

Her body stirred slightly. A sort of coughing noise hacked and rattled in its chest and for a horrified instant I thought it was laughing at me. But then in a tiny, mewling voice, it said, "I want . . . I want . . ."

"Hush." Anastasia's voice and face were like stone. "I know what you want." She called upon her powers and was abruptly clothed again, in the good wool of my second-best dress uniform. She hung a gilt-framed mirror in the air and fluffed the jabot so that the lace stood up crisp and white. Her hair she briskly brushed and pulled back into a ponytail. She dashed on a touch of scent and made certain that the bow was perfectly straight.

Smiling her wrath, she turned upon me.

When at last she was done amusing herself, I was strapped and saddled like a mule. Her body was placed on my back.

Anastasia slapped me on the rump. "Move!"

We made our way up on deck. The corpses of my crew were strewn about. I looked upon them and felt nothing. Beyond, the immense insect-ships were breaking up and burning on the sands. Brown as lacquered wood, they kicked and struggled like dying cockroaches, their substance shifting in the golden light, disintegrating, degrading, rotting. The stench was terrible, the stink of elimination pits and extermination camps. So far as I could see, only we two had survived the holocaust.

We passed through the silent battlegrounds.

Gagged, harnessed, and bent over by the weight of Anastasia's mutilated body, I made my painful way across the sterile plains of Heaven.

How long did we travel? Hours? Days? Centuries? We did not sleep and there were no events to divide the eternal emptiness of the desert sands. I began the trek rabid with humiliation and inwardly raving for revenge. But the unvarying drudgery of passage leached away my passions a breath at a time, until all my past took on the unreality of a story told one time too many and I began to forget even my own name.

Finally, my senses numbed and emotions at zero, we came to a place where the unvarying sands stretched to infinity to all points of the compass. A place where all directions were one.

Anastasia's body was finally and undeniably dead. She unsaddled it and lowered it to the ground. Then she created a shovel and thrust it in my hands.

"Dig!" she commanded.

I delved the hole true and to the square: eight feet long, four feet wide, and six feet deep, with straight edges and crisp corners. Even Anastasia could find no fault with my work.

Her corpse lay alongside the grave. When I was done, she edged a foot underneath and unceremoniously rolled it in. It fell face upward.

Dead blue eyes stared up at me.

In that dizzying, vertiginous instant I remembered everything. All this had happened before, not once but innumerable times. Always to the same weary conclusion.

Exhausted and drained of emotion as I was, I would have made my peace with Anastasia if I could. But after all I had done to her, what overtures of mine would she accept? What words were sweet enough, groveling enough, *true* enough? None that human tongue had yet spoken.

Still—the alternative was unthinkable. I had to try.

But as I turned to speak, I saw Anastasia fade away, like smoke, like wind, like darkness.

And when I looked back, there were ships coming across the sands. I saw and, seeing, understood and, understanding, despaired.

The ships skimmed lightly over the golden sands, blowing slight tails in the dunes. A fresh and untouched flotilla, amnesiac, flagged by a schooner whose rails and shrouds were thronged with grotesques who were all aspects of a single woman. One among them, I knew, would love me despite herself—and pay dearly for doing so. The captain stood on the raised quarterdeck, looking glass tucked under her arm, harshly beautiful, eyes stern beyond all reason. It was Anastasia's turn again.

This time the ships were hers.

This time we would sail to Hell.

Introduction
High Steel

Jack Dann

This book is dedicated to the memory of Jack Haldeman II, who passed away in January 2002. I'd known Jay (as he was affectionately known to his friends) since the early seventies, since the old Guilford Writers' Workshops that were held in his old manse in Baltimore, Maryland.

Jay and I had collaborated on novels and a handful of stories. We were natural collaborators. I remember talking to him on the phone when we were writing the climax of the novel *High Steel*. Some weeks before, he had sent me a rough draft of the scene, which I smoothed out and did some of my usual interstitial tweaking. But Jay had forgotten that *he* had written the key scene, and he was all excited. He told me that I had done a terrific job, that the scene really moved, that he couldn't stop turning the pages; and I kept trying to interrupt him, saying, "Jay, *you* wrote that. Jay, shut up for a second and listen. *You* wrote that scene."

We worked so well together we forget where one left off and the other began.

Jay and I were writing *High Steel* in 1981, and we easily turned the first section into a story with the same title. We sent it to Ed Ferman, who published it as the cover story of the February 1982 issue of *The Magazine of Fantasy & Science Fiction*.

When I was doing research for my novel *Counting Coup*, I spent a year with a group of traditional Sioux people and became

friends with a young medicine man. I thought I would use some of
that material in a young adult science fiction novel about a boy
becoming a medicine man. I think I had something in mind like
Robert Heinlein's *Starman Jones* or *Have Space Suit Will Travel*.

I wrote the first chapter of the novel, but didn't take it any
farther than that; and then Jay and I were discussing projects, and I
asked him if he was interested in looking at the chapter. He was,
and we incorporated that material into the novel and the story
"High Steel."

I should mention that Jay grew up in Alaska with Eskimo people. While we were writing the novel, he moved to a reservation to
immerse himself in the culture. But we knew we were going to
catch some shit from reviewers because we were writing about
Native Americans without actually *being* Native Americans.

And we certainly did.

But we also received praise from critics such as John Clute,
who wrote, "Reading *High Steel* by Jack C. Haldeman II and Jack
Dann was like breathing pure oxygen . . . Various imagined
futures—from hard SF through Cyberpunk—intersect en passant
in narrative sequences of astonishing equipoise and thrust . . . Most
of the book is a predator, like a cat with blazing eyes, gorging on
the good meat of genre."

I probably needn't mention that writers tend to thrive on
reviews like that.

Alas, Jay can't be here to comment on our story; but I found an
interview that Jay and I did for *Omni* in 1993 where Jay pretty
much sums up the strange and wonderful joys of collaborating:

"At one point we were working in the same room on different
scenes and Jack was sobbing at his scene and I was laughing at
mine. We looked at each other, traded machines, and in less than
five minutes, I was crying and he was cackling like a maniac."

"High Steel" was a Nebula finalist for best short story in 1982.

❧

High Steel

Jack C. Haldeman II and Jack Dann

0000	STRANGER, JOHN
0001	T.A.S.E. RESERVATION
	D5-SOUTH DAKOTA-116
0002	SOC 187735-NN-000
0003	4 APR 2177—1:46 PM
0004	
0005	IMMEDIATE REPLY MANDATORY
	BY LAW
0006	REFER T.A.S.E. DIRECTIVE 2045 E
	SECTION
0007	
0008	GREETINGS JOHN STRANGER
0009	FROM THE TRANS-AMERICAN
	SPACE ENGINEERING CORP
0010	
0011	CONGRATULATIONS UPON BEING
	SELECTED BY T.A.S.E.
0012	FOR ORIENTATION AND TRAINING
	ON STATION CENTRAL
0013	
0014	YOU WILL REPORT TO YOUR
	TERMINAL INDUCTION BLGD

```
0015      ON 7 APR 2177—6:00 PM
0016
0017
0018      DO NOT BRING TOLIET
          ARTICLES OR A CHANGE OF
          CLOTHES
0019      ALL WILL BE PROVIDED
0020
0021      WELCOME ABOARD
0022      FROM YOUR T.A.S.E DRAFT
          COUNCIL
0023
0024      YOUR PRESENCE IS REQUIRED BY
          LAW
0025      REFER USCC DIRECTIVE 27AI
          INDIGENOUS PEOPLES
0026
0027      /*ROUTE PRINT REMOTE 2
0028      /*ROUTE PRINT LOCAL 7
0029      1234567890123456
0030/*
END       SOC 187735—FILE—NN—000
```

The old man walked beside John Stranger, staring down at the rocky trail. It was not a time to talk. His face was leather, as wrinkled as the earth. His lips were chapped and parched, as if they had never touched water. Years beyond counting had marked him, molded him. Now he was ageless, timeless.

The stark landscape stretched out below them: muddy columns carved by wind, deep ravines, vertical dikes, fluted ridges. It was desolate country. But it was their country. The way down would be difficult, but Broken-finger could climb almost as well as John. He often boasted that the Great Spirit would not make him weak and sick before taking him "south"—the direction of death. He had always been strong. He was an Indian, not a *wasicun*, not a white man. He would take his strength with him to the outerworld of the dead. That was his belief. That was his reality. It had always served him well.

Broken-finger was a medicine man. Since John Stranger was a child, the old man had taught him, trained him. That would all change.

They climbed down a sharp basalt cliff face, carefully searching out toeholds and handholds. Their progress was slow, the sun baked them unmercifully. But they were used to it; it was part of their lives. When they reached a rocky shelf about halfway down the cliff face, they paused to rest.

"Here," Broken-finger said, handing John a thermos of bitter water. "We can wait while you regain your strength."

John felt dizzy again. Had it really been four days since he had climbed alone into the vision pit? Time had blurred, scattered like sand before the wind.

"You had a good vision," Broken-finger said. It was not a question, but a statement. He knew. It required no answer.

John blinked, focused his eyes. The spirit-veils were fluttering before him, shaking up the yellow grass and rocks and hills below like rising heat. He could see his village in the distance, nestled between an expansive rise and the gently rounded hills beyond. It had been his home since birth. Seventeen years had passed. It seemed like more. At times, it seemed like less.

The village was comprised of fifty silvery hutches set in a great circle, in the Indian way. Broken-finger used to say that a square could not have much power. But a circle is a natural power; it is the design of the world and the universe. The square is the house and risor of the *wasicun*, the squared-off, divided-up, vertical white man.

"Everyone down there is waiting for you," Broken-finger said, as if reading John's thoughts. "A good sweat lodge has been prepared to sear your lungs and lighten your heart. Then there will be a celebration."

"Why a celebration?" John asked as he watched a spotted eagle soaring in circles against the sharp blue sky. It was brother to the eagle in his vision. Perhaps the spirit-man was watching.

"The village is making you a good-time because you must make a difficult decision. Pray your vision will help you."

"What has happened?" John stoppered the thermos, passed it back to the old man.

"We received news from the *wasicun* corporation yesterday." He paused, saddened, and stared straight ahead. "They claim their rights on you."

John Stranger felt a chill crawl down his back. He stood up and walked to the edge of the shelf; there he raised his hands and offered a prayer. He looked for the spotted eagle and, as if in a vision, imagined that it was flying away from him like an arrow through the clouds.

"We must go now," he said to Broken-finger, but he felt afraid and alone, as if he were back in the vision pit. He felt hollowed-out inside, as isolated as a city-dweller. They climbed down toward the village together; but John was alone, alone with the afterimages of his vision and the dark smoke of his thoughts and fears.

Below him, the village caught the sun and seemed to be bathed in spirit-light.

With an easy, fluid motion John unsnapped the end of his tether and moved to the next position on the huge beam. His feet automatically found the hold-tight indentations at the adjacent work station. For a brief moment his body hung free of any support. He was weightless and enjoyed the feeling of freedom. This was one of the few pleasures up here to his liking. The Earth hung above his head: a mottled globe, half darkness, half light. The cross-strut he needed floated slowly toward him. Anna was right behind it. Of all the damn luck: Anna. Anybody else. He shifted the joiner to his right hand and attached the proper nipple. There were twenty other floaters out on this shift; they could have sent someone else. The chatter on the intercom bothered him. So he tongued down the gain.

"Bellman to Catpaw Five." The direct communication cut through the static and low-tone babble. Mike Elliot was bellman; John was Catpaw Five. The bellman directed the placing of the beams, the floaters did the work.

"Five here," slurred John. Mike was a stickler for rules and regulations. From the deck he could afford to be. It was different outside.

"Strut alpha omega seven-one-four on its way."

"I have eyes," said John.

"Acknowledge transmission, Catpaw Five." Always by the book.

"Transmission acknowledged. Visual confirmation of alpha omega seven-one-four has been achieved. Satisfied?"

"This transmission is being monitored, Catpaw Five."

"They're all monitored, so what's the difference? Fire me."

"I wish I could."

"I wish you would." Damn uppity bellman. They were all the same. "And while you're at it, why did you send Grass-like-light? She has second shift today."

"She goes by Anna, floater, and I put her out because I wanted to."

"You put her out because she's a royal pain in my—"

"You're on report, John."

"Stuff it."

"Firing on five. Mark."

The seconds ticked down in his head. It was automatic—and he had already forgotten Mike. At the count of zero, three low-grade sparklers fired. Aluminum trioxide, mined on the moon. These one-time rockets were cheap and dirty, but all they needed. The boron filament beam, its apparent movement stopped, hovered a meter to his left. Sloppy.

"You missed," John said.

"You're still on report."

John shook his head, reached out with the grapple and pulled the rear end toward the join. Mike was always excited, always putting floaters on report. It didn't mean a thing. People were cheap, but the ability to walk high steel wasn't common. They could hire and fire ten bellmen before they would touch a floater. Anyone could work the calculations, but walking the steel was a rare talent. There was no way he could ignore Anna.

"Down," he said, activating the local channel.

Anna fixed a firing ring around the far end of the beam and slowly worked it into position. She drifted easily, lazily. The beam slid gracefully into plumb.

"That's got it," he said. "Thanks," he added as an afterthought.

"You're welcome," she said in a dry voice. Without another word, she hit her body thrusters and moved away from him to her next position.

John ignored the snub and went to work with the joiner. Five of the color-coded joints were within easy reach; he didn't even have to move from the hold-tights. Some ground-based jockey had probably figured it all out before the plans were shipped up and the beams forged in space. As usual, they had blown the obvious cross-joints. He had to unhook for those, swing his body around to the other side. What looked easy on paper was often a different matter in space. His helmet lamp created a glare in his eyes as it reflected off the beam. The blind side joins were the worst: no support. He clipped his joiner back on his belt and took a breather.

The tube that connected the globes of the barbell was taking shape. He'd been on the job for almost a month, from the very beginning. The tube looked like a skeleton now, but soon the outer skin would be worked into place and this job would be finished. After that, it was on to the next assignment. He could see several other floaters working on the tube: anonymous, white-suited figures in the distance.

"That's got it, shift one," came the bellman's voice over the intercom. "Come on in."

John waited for the transport, really nothing more than a raft drifting by. It had been an uneventful shift; Most of them were. They were ahead of schedule. That, too, was normal. Damn Anna, anyway. Damn Mike for slipping her on his shift. He knew how much that bothered him. John was used to his regular crew, knew their habits and eccentricities by heart. He didn't need other people. He didn't need Anna.

When the transport drifted by, he reached out and hooked himself on by the grapple. It was showy, but he didn't care. He looked to see if Anna noticed. She didn't seem to.

It didn't matter, he told himself.

"The skids are arriving right on schedule," Anna said, pointing at the nearest port. Outside, the small crafts blinked and glittered against the darkness. John Stranger didn't look; he made a point of not turning his head. It was loud in the wardroom, too many people packed into too small a place. After the riggers left, they would put up partitions, make it comfortable for the small number of people who would man the manufacturing station. Now they were packed in like fish in a tin. Riggers got little respect and fewer comforts. She leaned toward him across the small table, and it made him uncomfortable, although it didn't mean anything. Everyone leaned forward while resting in zero-g. It was reflex. A pencil floated past her face.

"So go have a good time," John said. The independent whores, male and female, always arrived just before the topping-off party. They were direct competition to the T.A.S.E.-supplied whores, who were more expensive but classier. It was almost time for the party. The job was almost finished. Soon the flag would be secured. Then would come the release, the time for the crew to become as blind and as drunk for as long as possible at the bosses' expense.

"What I do is my business," Anna said. "As it happens, I plan to have a good time. That is still permitted."

John twisted his foot compulsively into the hold-tight grid on the floor. "You've turned white enough. Go ahead and have a good time with the *wasicun*."

"I'm not white," she said defensively, pulling away from him. Only the hold-tights prevented her from floating to the ceiling. "You're a hypocrite," she said bitterly. "You're no more Indian than the rest of your friends." She waved her arm at the others in the room. "Some medicine man. Are *these* your people?"

John's face burned with anger and embarrassment. "Yes," he said. He was to have been a *wichasha wakan*, a holy man, a healer.

Clearly half the riggers—the floaters—were his own, his own blood. They were Indian, yet they weren't. They had turned away from their heritage, forgotten the way of the Sacred Pipe. They had jumped at the chance of reward, of a path out of the restrictive life of the ever-dwindling reservations. He could not understand, nor could he forgive. He had been taken away from his people, while most of them had left to become white men. A few, it was true, had been drafted. Anna was one.

She grinned at John, as if she could see right into him. "Spend the night with me," she said, baiting him. "Or aren't you man enough?"

"Our ways are not the same."

"Up here we are all the same," she said. "We are no longer in the woods, we are no longer dirtwalkers." She unlocked her cleats from the grid. Before pushing off she said, "John Stranger, I think you're impotent. I don't think you could even do it with *wasicun*."

John winced. Perhaps he had studied the ways of the People too long and didn't know enough about the world. But the People were the world!

The lights flashed twice, a signal. Fred Ransome, one of the bosses, walked through the wardroom shouting, "All right, riggers. Play time's over. Now move. Get yourselves back into the dark."

John rose, cleared his head. He was pulling a double shift, like most of the other floaters. He didn't mind the work, just the people he worked for. While he was working, he could forget—forget that he was outside the sacred circle, forget Anna's face and her words.

He would not take Anna, nor any of the whores. He was a *wichasha wakan*, a medicine man, even here. He was. He was. They could not take that away from him, no matter where they moved him, no matter what they made him do.

But in his heart, he was not so sure.

The shifts seemed to blur, one melting into another, as constant and predictable as the stars. Somehow immense loads of planking moved into place. Endless floating mountains of beams were connected into struts and decking. Slowly the skeleton grew, took shape. The two massive globes at opposing ends of the station were each large enough to house a fair-sized city. They dwarfed the tube that connected them, even though the tube itself was over fifty meters in diameter. Pipes, endless mazes of twisted wires, and interlocking tunnels ran through the length of the tube. Waldos walked down large tracks where the men would not be able to stand the gravity. In the middle of the connecting tube was a smaller globe, ringed with ports. It would hold the personnel manning the station.

Now the silvery covering was in place, and what had once looked as light as a delicate mobile seemed to gain in mass as strut after strut had been overlaid with the metallic skin.

Like predators circling a great whale, the tiny skids and larger T.A.S.E. ships floated, patient as the coming and going of the seasons. Even from where he stood at the aft end of the barbell, John could make out the details of the jury-rigged skids, odd pieces of junk bought or stolen, thrown together almost casually. The skids were dangerous, the reason for the high mortality rate of the freebooters. But they were free; free to die, work, or skiff off toward the asteroids, there to mine and get by until caught.

The freebooters were the people who had slipped through the otherwise smoothly running cogs of life in space. They belonged to no nation-state, no corporation, no colony. They came and went as they pleased, selling services and paying for what they needed, stealing if they could not pay. They were rarely bothered by the officials—in this area the T.A.S.E. Patrol—as long as they maintained a low profile. Over a hundred thousand people lived and worked in space, and the freebooters were an insignificant percentage. They moved easily, usually unseen, from the richest condo to the roughest manufacturing complex. If they made waves, they were dealt with, usually by dumping them out into space. Without a suit. If they showed some ability, they would be legally drafted by the corporation, as John had been. They were usually sent to the belt where they could cause no trouble.

The skids held pleasures of a coarse and vulgar nature. The T.A.S.E. corporation men on site made much use of them, the illegality of the situation adding greatly to the excitement. The freebooters were one of the darker sides of life in space.

But their lives were free.

The rest of the crew caught up with John. He clipped himself to Sam Woquini and they started to crab their way across the silvery skin of this dormant creature they had helped create. They worked as one, easily, as they had for the last year, without giving danger a thought, for their interdependence was mutual.

The Boss had ordered this final walk-through. As usual, he had wanted it done immediately. Everything had to be rushed. They had finished three weeks ahead of schedule and still the Boss hadn't let up. John tried not to let it bother him; it was just the city-dweller mentality, the *wasicun* way of life. They had yet to learn patience, to learn how to flow easily with the life-forces.

All across the station the floaters drifted, making their final visual check. It was largely unnecessary but protocol required it. They were dwarfed by the gargantuan structure they had given birth to, small specks against their grandiose creation.

John let his mind wander as he and Sam made their lazy way across the surface. He recognized the small signs of his own work as well as those of others. It was strangely comforting. There was pride involved here, satisfaction at a job well done. That was one of the few rewards of his situation. It could almost make up for the static he caught from the Bosses—T.A.S.E. brass—clowns, every one of them. It could never make up for the time they'd stolen from him, the years lost, away from the ways of his people. He felt the bitterness rise. He felt cheated.

The geodesic had docked and the party had been in full swing for over an hour. John had no intention of going. He sat with Sam on a large skid that had been used to haul material around during the construction of the station. Since the job was, for all practical purposes, finished, it had been moved well away from the station. A large collection of equipment hung in space around them, ready to be moved to the next job.

"Stranger and Woquini, get your respective butts over here. Time to make an appearance." Mike Elliot's voice came through scratchy and loud on the voicebox inside John's helmet. Elliot, the bellman, always seemed to be shouting. He knew the floaters kept their volume controls at the lowest setting.

"We're not going to make an appearance," said John. *Wasicun* always have to make noise, he thought. Only Sam knows how to be quiet.

"You're coming, and right now," shouted Elliot. "There's brass over here that wants to meet you. If you no-show, it's an automatic extension at my option. You know the rules. Right now I'm of a mind to tack a few years on. Might teach you a lesson."

That was always the kicker. They had draftees by the short hairs and could extend their tour for nearly any reason at all. When the corporations had worked out the conscription agreement with the government, they had held all the power, all the cards. Most of the land, too.

"I can make things hard for your friend." Elliot was getting frantic. His voice cracked. Must be getting a lot of pressure. John would have stalled on general principles, but there was Sam.

"Don't do it on my account," said his friend. "How hard can they make it for me? I've got a contract."

John knew about contracts; they were no better than the treaties of the past. They could be bent, broken, twisted in a thousand ways. He shook his head.

"We'd better go," he said. He looked at the Earth below him. The horizon seemed to be made of rainbows. It shifted as he watched. An erupting volcano traced a lazy finger of smoke. He'd been watching it for a month. A storm, one of the great ones, twisted and flickered in the ocean. All this beauty, and he had to go into a crowded geodesic and make small talk with the T.A.S.E. brass, fatcats who had never been alone a moment in their lives and were driven to turn Earth and space into frogskin dollars.

There was a small cycle tethered to a docking adapter on the skid. John moved toward it. "Give me a hand," he said to Sam, and they swung the cobbled-up cycle into position.

The cycle was the usual floater variety; simple, made out of parts lying around. It was just a collection of spare struts joined together and a tiny thruster that powered it with bursts of nitrogen. Several other cycles of similar design were scattered around the construction site. Floaters used them to get wherever they were going and left them there for the next person.

John gripped one of the struts and aimed the thruster. "Hop on," he said to Sam.

"No, thanks," he said. "I'm going the fun way."

Sam grabbed a whipper and swung it over his head, catching it on the edge of the skid with a perfect motion that was a combination of long practice and an innate skill that could never be taught. He let it pull his body up in an arc and let loose of the whipper at the precise moment that would allow his angular momentum to carry him to the geodesic docked at one of the swollen ends of the manufacturing station. His body spun end over end with a beautiful symmetrical motion. He let out a loud whoop that rattled John's voicebox even with the volume turned all the way down. John smiled at his friend, then laughed. Sometimes Sam did crazy things, just for the fun of it. On the reservation he would have become an upside-down man, a joker, the holy trickster. Up here he had respect: he was very large and good with his hands, sometimes with his fists. Sam's whoop rose and fell. It was full of joy, the joy of living.

"Clear all channels," shouted Elliot. "What is *that*? Who's in trouble? Stranger, is Woquini okay? It sounds like he's dying."

"He's not dying," said John. "He's living." He doubted Elliot would know the difference. He squeezed the thruster and headed for the geodesic.

The T.A.S.E. geodesic globe was actually a pleasure station brought in for the topping-off party. It was expensive, but the corporation could well afford it. There was enough gambling, sex, and cheap thrills available to satisfy all but the most jaded palates.

Sleds, hitters, skids, and cycles clustered all around the end of the barbell-shaped station and the docked geodesic. Parties like this brought the whores and hucksters out in force, along with the independents looking for work, hoping to sign on with someone. Independents were always looking for work, existence was precarious without corporate patronage. There were even private cabs—small energy-squandering vehicles—bearing the insignia of other corporations. They had come to check out the competition, look over the terrain, make connections, wheel and deal.

Off in the distance solar collectors hung in silent, glittering beauty for kilometers and kilometers. To John, they were a bead-game in space, mirrors for Earth. They held beauty, they held usefulness. They were in balance. The image of a bird in flight, somehow frozen, came to John. It was perfect; harmony and balance. How could such things be made by the *wasicun?* All this for the frogskin.

John and Sam arrived simultaneously at the entrance to the geodesic. Sam's trajectory, which would have given a computer a headache, was perfect. They had both known it would be. They unsuited and allowed themselves to be dragged into the party.

The topping-off party was a tradition that went back hundreds of years, its origin lost in legend and fable. At completion of work on a project—be it bridge, barn, or skyscraper—a flag, or sometimes a tree, was placed on the highest part of the structure. It was a christening of sorts and accompanied by a party, nearly always at the company's expense. If the owners declined to supply the whiskey for the party, the flag was replaced by a broom, expressing the workers' displeasure and embarrassing the company.

Like much of man's life on Earth, this tradition was carried into space. It was never planned, it just happened. It gave the men roots, a sense of place. For the same reason, the person who directed the placing of the beams was called a bellman, though bells hadn't been used as a signal in hundreds of years.

It was loud in the geodesic, much too loud for John. A mixture of floaters and corporation brass milled around, along with a scattering of other hangers-on, independents, whores. The corporation brass were easy to pick out by their obvious inability to handle zero-g. He picked out the floaters, equally obvious by their advanced stages of intoxication. They were a mixed ethnic bag: Scandinavians, Germans, Irish, Scots, Hispanics, the ever-present English. Most of them, however, were his own people, in blood if not in thought. As usual, they were making fools of themselves before the white man. He fought a rush of hatred, not only for the *wasicun*, but for his own people as well.

He was immediately ashamed, for in his heart he felt he was no different than the others. He found his oblivion in his work, his dreams, his love of the immensities of space. They found their oblivion in booze, women, and drugs. He was a freak, the outcast, not they.

The only other person he had met up here that came close to holding to the ways of the People was Sam. But Sam had chosen space, not been drafted. He seemed to have struck a balance between the old life and the new. In a way, John envied him.

He sometimes thought he saw some of the signs of the old life in Anna, though they were deeply buried. He got the feeling that she had turned her back on her past. John was a constant reminder of those times to her. Perhaps, he thought, that was why they never got along.

A young woman drifted over to John, offered him a nipple of scrag. He politely refused—it would be a double-bind if he was high and anything happened. Most of the floaters could handle it, but he knew he couldn't. He would be leaving the party as soon as possible.

A well-dressed man in his late sixties was holding court with a man about half his age. The younger man was a dirtwalker by all appearances. He stood perfectly still, as if one wrong move would send him floating away forever. His legs were tense, his feet jammed firmly in the hold-tights on the floor grid. His knees were locked. It would take a collision with a skimmer running full-bore to dislodge him. Uncomfortable as he looked, he was hanging on every word.

"Great return," said the older man. "Great return. You just can't beat space for high percentage income. Less hassles, too. No eco-freaks to muck around with. Hard to be accused of polluting space. Even harder to prove."

John shook his head, pushed away. He'd heard that conversation a thousand times, was sick to death of it. If they dragged him into their talk, he'd say something wrong and get into trouble for sure.

There was new gossip from the belt, chatter about business interests on the moon, but mostly talk centered around the station they'd just finished. Everyone seemed to think it was a marvelous feat of engineering. When set into rotation, the station would produce a graduated gravity source, with a maximum of fifty-g's at the rounded ends. It could never have been achieved on Earth. What would eventually be manufactured there was a mystery to John: more square cities for all he knew or cared. It was a job, plain and simple. He was pleased that the floaters' end had worked out well; beyond that he had very little interest.

Two of the T.A.S.E. brass separated from a crowd and kicked over toward him. There was no easy way to escape, so he braced himself.

"So you're John Stranger," said one of them. "I hear you're one of our best men up here."

"Do you know me?" he asked, making an attempt to be civil.

The man smiled and tapped his ear, indicating that he wore a computer plug. He turned to his companion.

"Mr. Stranger here is an American Indian, as many of our floaters are. They work well on the beams, seem to have no fear at all. We recruit and draft heavily from the tribes. They seem to have natural ability in their blood. Wouldn't you say that was true, Mr. Stranger?" He took a sniffer from his pocket, inhaled deeply. Some sort of drug, a stimulant, most likely.

John was insulted. People made the most sweeping generalizations. He swallowed his anger. It would serve no purpose to start trouble with the brass. He'd spend the rest of his life in servitude that way.

"Some say that," said John, instantly sorry he'd compromised himself. A cowardly action. "I'd better get back into the dark," he added, moving away. The man caught his arm.

"Can't leave now," he said. "This party's for you, for all of you. Can't thank you enough. You men and women are the real backbone of our operation."

The thought turned John's stomach. "I really have to be going," he said. If he didn't get out, he was going to do something foolish. He almost didn't care.

"We're having a spin party later in the living quarters on the station when they start the rotation. Just a few of us old boys and some selected friends. Ought to be pretty spectacular. If you're free, consider yourself invited."

"I'll keep it in mind," said John, swallowing his contempt, backing off. No way he'd show up at something like that.

Breaking away from the two men, he caught a glimpse of Anna across the room. She was talking with a young man, a pretty whore. She met his stare arrogantly, as if they were two opposing forces, two incompatible states of mind. She turned her attention back to the boy.

John was depressed. There were things about Anna that he felt drawn to, others that forced him away. It was a complex feeling. It was unsettling.

He had to get out of the geodesic, back into the dark, into space. He felt closed in, trapped. It was almost a claustrophobic feeling, a vague sense of uneasiness that brushed his heart, the pit of his stomach. He had never felt those things before, not even in the sweat lodge. All he knew was that he had to get out of there.

He found Sam and together they left the party, suited up. It wasn't until they left the geodesic that the pressure lifted from John. He shook his head. It had been all out of proportion to the situation.

He was still angry with himself because he hadn't stood up to the T.A.S.E. bureaucrat. The sense that he had betrayed something weighed heavily upon him, yet on another level he felt there had been no choice. It was a bitter feeling. He was no better than the others.

He was a hypocrite.

It was the first time John had been inside the computer bubble, the mobile command center for this operation. He wouldn't be there now if Sam hadn't talked him into it. Sam was a friend of Carl Hegyer, who was running the board. The bubble hung well away from the station; they had a panoramic view. Sam had thought John might like to watch the spin from there. He admitted it was better than being with the brass in the center of the station, or watching it with the drunker revelers in the geodesic.

Spin was imparted to the station by an extremely simple and cheap method. The surface of the station was covered with thousands of small, one-shot aluminum trioxide rockets. The crew called them sparklers. They were dirty, but that didn't matter in space. What mattered was that they were cheap, composed of elements easily mined at the lunar complexes.

Through the programmed computer, Carl Hegyer could select the number and order of rocket firings. They would fire only a few at first, to get the station moving. Slowly they would increase the rotation by firing more and more rockets until the desired rate of spin was achieved. The point they were aiming for was that which would produce a fifty-g force at the rounded ends of the station. That would still leave the majority of rockets in reserve. The immediate area had been cleared in preparation for the firing. The geodesic party, still in full swing, had been undocked from the station and moved a short distance away. Most of the brass and dirtwalkers were in the swollen living quarters in the middle of the station.

The digital mounted next to the CRT screen on Carl's console ticked down. A signal flare soared across the darkness like an orange comet. The two-minute warning.

Carl broke the silence in the bubble. "All this will probably seem pretty anticlimactic," he said. "I'm not much more than the guy that pushes the plunger. It starts slow. Not much to see at first."

He was right. When the digital ran down to zero, John had difficulty even seeing the rockets fire. Carl pointed to a few scattered dots on the station's image on the CRT screen. "Those are the rockets firing," he said. "We ought to be seeing something soon."

John looked out the large, curved port at the station. There were more rockets firing now, sending out white sparks like small magnesium flares. As he watched, one edge of the station occulted a star. It was moving. Still slow, but the movement was perceptible.

Although John had worked on several projects since his training, this was the first time he had seen his handiwork put into motion. It impressed him, moved him, touched something deep in his heart.

For this was *wasicun*, the work of the white man. Yet somehow, as the ponderous station gradually picked up speed with its trail of metallic sparks, it seemed more like the work of the People.

There was symmetry here, balance, purpose. There were circles, closed circles linked with the circular Earth. For a moment he forgot about the dirtwalkers on the station, the brawling party in the geodesic. Here was purpose, direction, in a fluid way. Relationships were being expressed that he could only guess at, not yet hold.

"It's beautiful," said Sam softly. "No one told me it would be beautiful."

John could only nod. He was afraid if he spoke, his voice would crack. Carl was busy at the console, fingers flying over the keyboard. Once in a while he would touch the CRT with a lightpen, triggering an individual rocket passed over.

It was going faster now, as fast as John had ever seen anything swing in space. He knew the station needed fifty-g's at the ends, zero-g at the center. It was necessary for the centrifugation and sedimentation of the material they were manufacturing. That seemed like a lot of g-forces, but the station was large, strong. It would handle it.

John saw it first, looking through the port. Carl saw it an instant later, through the computer. An unevenness, a ripple spread through the pattern of the rockets firing. Suddenly the board went wild, every tell-tale in the room went from green to red. Outside the port, the universe was lit with a blinding white flash.

"Jesus Christ," cried Carl, frozen. "No!" A whole bank of rockets along one arm had fired at once. Not one rocket, not ten; but hundreds of them.

The station swung in a ballet of death, caught in an ungainly pirouette by the uneven forces. The wrenching stresses pulled at the station in a way that could have never been anticipated. The metal twisted, buckled, finally reached the breaking point and sheared. Before their horrified eyes, the station broke apart, one end of the barbell ripping away. It headed inexorably for the geodesic, a precise arc of destruction. The rest of the station, out of control, cartwheeled wildly away.

Time froze. John was held by fear, the old fear taught to him by Leonard Broken-finger. It was the fear of one who can see with his heart, who can sense the spirits in the sweat lodge and in the vision pit. As bits of steel, aluminum, and boron silvered through space, catching the sun in their terrible dance, John became a *wichasha wakan*. He saw through the eyes of his people, was one with everything around him, was in the center of the circle.

Those aboard the geodesic must have tried to get out of the way. Yet it happened too fast, they had no chance. John's people were in there, his spirit reached for them.

The terrible fear, the crawling fear broke through his heart. "Oh Wakan Tanka, Great Mystery, all those people, don't let them die. . . ." John felt the wings of Wakinyan-tanka, the great thunderbird. They were made out of the essence of darkness; they were as cold as ice, yet they burned his skin.

The geodesic was struck dead center. It burst apart as broken metal and broken people were ripped and scattered in a thousand different directions, tossing and tumbling end over end.

He heard himself screaming; it was as if he were back in the vision pit, and he remembered: *Wakinyan-tanka eats his young, for they make him many; yet he is still one. He has a huge beak filled with jagged teeth, yet he has no head. He has wings, yet he has no shape.*

From somewhere distant, Sam yelled: "Do something, Carl, do something."

From somewhere else, came Carl's voice: "I can't."

And Sam: "Save the others."

Carl: "I can't stop it. Calculations are too complex. I can't."

John felt the cold breaking of death, the death of all, Indian and *wasicun* alike. He broke, and was made whole. He pulled Carl from the chair, sat down in front of the computer console. Sam yelled, Carl screamed. These were disruptive forces, he blocked them out, ran his fingers lightly over the keyboard.

He touched a button and a single rocket fired on the wildly careening remains of the station. He touched another button and a rocket fired someplace else on the skin of the station. There was a rhythm, a balance. Action and reaction, all parts of the whole.

Gently he felt his way into the heart of the computer. He did things, things happened. Forces were moved, stresses transposed from one place to another. It was all a matter of balance, of achieving a point of equilibrium. The computer was a prayer and he was in the pit again, close to the spirits that flicked in the dark and the thunder beings that carried the fear. His fingers danced over the keyboard. He felt, rather than saw, the forces he was manipulating. It was internal, not external: he was part and parcel of the things he did. He grabbed the lightpen and stroked the image of the runaway station on the screen. Under his fingers more rockets burst into life, counter-balancing the undesired motion. With the sureness of an ancient hand painting a Hopi jar, he sought out the proper forms, the patterns. The station slowed.

The fear, the ancient fear carried by prayer, was breaking him. It gave him the emptiness the *wasicun* built, transforming it into a wisdom. He frowned, added a few last strokes with the lightpen, tapped a few more buttons. The station stopped, motion arrested.

John slumped forward, drained of energy. He shook himself, looked around, half expecting to see the rolling desert, the towering mesas. Instead he saw Sam and Carl, though he didn't recognize them at first.

They stared at him with amazement, with fear, unable and

unwilling to move, to break the spell. They could not comprehend what they had just seen.

John looked at them and understood that, and more. Much more. He stood.

"We'd better go," he said. "Some of them may still be alive."

They followed him. They would have followed him anywhere.

It was cold on the mesa top; the sky was just beginning to lighten. Leonard Broken-finger crouched at the opening of the vision pit. He held a bag in one hand and rested himself against the wall with the other. The boy in the vision pit made stirring noises. His name was Jonas Goodbird and he was barely more than a child. It was age enough.

"You've been here four days," said Broken-finger. "Your vision quest is over. I hope Wakan-tanka has helped you."

"I'm still alive," said Jonas in a quavering, unbelieving voice.

"Of course you are; though by all appearances, not by much." He laughed, but his lips were tightly closed, so the laugh could play only in his throat and not in his mouth. For as long as anyone in the tribe could remember, the medicine man could not smile because his lips would break and bleed. Children made a game of trying to get old Broken-finger to laugh and break his lips. They had never succeeded.

The boy was getting ready to leave the vision pit. It would take a few minutes for him to gather his wits. Broken-finger left him to this and walked to the edge of the mesa. He faced east, standing rigid, standing tall.

The dry, cracked gullies stretched out below him, their colors muted in the morning mist. He felt old, but was not distressed. All his life he had been surrounded by the canyons, the towering rock formations. Time meant nothing to them. A man did what he could.

He thought of others he had walked down from the vision pit. There had been many. Some blurred into the distant past, some stood out. He thought of John Stranger, gone now three winters, taken by the *wasicun*. He had been special; it seemed the spirits lived through him.

A field mouse nudged his foot, a lizard scuttled across his leg: he stood that still. The sun broke the horizon. He felt the presence of John Stranger.

He raised his arms to the heavens, stood that way for endless moments staring at the rising sun. He felt the cold brush of wings.

Wakinyan-tanka eats his own young, for they make him many;

yet he is one. He has a huge beak filled with jagged teeth, yet he has no head. He has wings, yet has no shape.

He felt these things, and more. There were terrible things happening. There were beautiful things happening. It was a time of changes, a shifting of the order. The cold wings brought him thoughts of John Stranger.

Arms still high, tears ran down his cheeks. There was sadness. But sadness was not the whole; there were other things brought to him on the icy wings of Wakinyan-tanka. They stirred him deeply.

He smiled for the first time in fifty years. It was a gentle smile, it came from his heart. There were good things happening for the People, he could feel it. They would come at high cost, but they would come.

His lips cracked and blood ran down his chin, dropped to his chest. His arms did not waver.

They arrived at the ruined station before the summoned rescue vehicles. From the outside it looked to be the disaster it was. The end that had torn off left jagged remains; a twisted mass of beams, wires, and pipes. John led them to the living quarters in what had once been the middle of the station. It appeared intact but had been under considerable stress. What g-forces it had been subjected to could only be guessed at.

It was pitch-black inside. There was still air inside, stale, but breathable. John flipped back his visor and turned on his lantern. He could hear low moans. Moans meant life.

And what of life, of death? His people had died in the geodesic, he had been unable to help them. These that lived, these he saved, were of the *wasicun*. He had done what had to be done, led by the thunder spirits. There were reasons for everything.

His lamp stabbed through the blackness. Bodies floated in horrible, contorted shapes. Here and there an arm waved, a leg moved. Twisted wreckage was everywhere.

They worked together quietly, with purpose. They separated the living from the dead, did whatever they could for those who hung in between. Some they lost, some they saved. John drifted to the floor grid. It was twisted and buckled, people were trapped there. He worked at freeing them.

A soft voice called his name. A hand touched his shoulder. Anna. She lived.

"I thought you were dead," he said. "Dead with the others on the geodesic."

"I . . . I came here. It was . . ." Her voice trailed off.

Suddenly the chamber was filled with light as the rescue crew entered. They were efficient and noisy, barking orders everywhere. They took over. A part of John relaxed. In the bright light, Anna looked terrible. The side of her face was purple with a large bruise, her left arm hung at a funny angle. She was staring intently at him.

"You've changed," she said slowly, reaching out with her other hand to stroke the side of his face. There was awe in her voice, tinged with fear. She saw in his face things of the People. It was like looking into the past through the eyes of her mother's mother. There were things there that frightened her, things that made her proud.

"I am what I always have been," said John.

He saw many things, good and bad. The *wasicun* controlled his body, but not his spirit. There were things to be done and he had been called to do them. It would be a difficult time, but a good time for the People.

The cold wings of Wakinyan-tanka brushed his soul. The thunderbird would be with him always, as it was in the instant of death, the instant of salvation. He was part of the circle, perhaps in the center.

A long road lay ahead. He had but taken the first step.

```
5641        //STRANGER, JOHN
5642        (3014,5002,1,1,0),'COL-1, CAP#3',
            CLASS=Q
5643        //EXEC WATFIV
5644
5645        $JOB
5646        STRANGER, JOHN SOC
5647        TASE BILLET OZMA
5648
5649        ACCESS CLASSIFICATION LEVEL
            THREE CONFIDENTAL
5650        PASSWORD: REDMAN
5651
5652        STOCHASTIC ANALYSIS
            FOLLOWS
5653
5654        INTUITIVE RIGHT CHOICES IN
            DOUBLE BLIND SITUATIONS
5655        TRIALS = 100
5656        SUCCESS RATE = 100%
```

```
5657
5658        KINESTHESIC AWARDNESS
5659        TRIALS = 100
5660        SUCCESS RATE = 100%
5661
5662        PROBABILITY THIS DUE TO
            CHANCE APPROACHES ZERO
5663
5664        CONCLUSION:
5665        SUBJECT INTUITIVELY MAKES
            RIGHT DECISIONS IN
5666        APPARENTLY AMBIGUOUS
            SITUATIONS.
5667        SUBJECT HAS HIGH AWARDNESS
            OF SURROUNDINGS AND
5668        RELATIONSHIPS BETWEEN OB-
            JECTS IN HIS ENVIRONMENT.
5669
5670
5671        NOTE: SUBJECT UNCOOPERATIVE
5672
5673        WEAKNESS: TRIBAL LOYALTY
5674        CLOSE RELATIONS:
5675        LEONARD BROKEN-FINGER SOC
            15782-NN-863
5676        ANNA GRASS-LIKE-LIGHT SOC
            16364-NN-347
5677        SAM WOQUINI SOC 13837-NN-676
5678        EXPLOIT WITH EXTREME CARE
5679
5680        THIS SUBJECT IS POTENTIALLY
            DANGEROUS
5681        THIS SUBJECT IS POTENTIALLY
            USEFUL
5682
5683        RECOMMENDATION: OBSERVA-
            TION, MANIPULATION & CON-
            TROL
5684        /*ROUTE PRINT REMOTE 7
5685        STOP
5686        END
5687        2 NOV 2180 — 9:14 AM
0END        SOC 187735FILE-NN-000
```

Introduction

Down Among the Dead Men

Gardner Dozois

One of the engines that drove these collaborations was Jack's ability, once he got the bit between his teeth and his enthusiasm was fired up, to sit down at the typewriter for several hours at a stretch (so I guess that Jack's strong bladder is also partially responsible for the existence of the collaborations) and pour out copy at a white-hot pace, often producing ten or twelve pages at a time. Being fundamentally lazy, especially me, or at least lazier than *Jack*, many of these collaborations would have remained in the theoretical talking stage forever if it had been up to Michael or me, without us ever getting around to doing anything proactive about them, like sitting down and actually *writing* something. Once Jack had done one of his marathon writing sessions, though, and stood up from the typewriter bathed in a virtuous glow, leaving behind him a pile of ten or twelve pages of a story, shame drove us to actually *do* something with that pile, contributing our own sections and actually finishing the story. Once Jack was no longer physically present much, this element was removed, and the collaborations mainly dried up—another indication that if Jack hadn't been restless and bored enough in Binghamton to keep dropping down to Philadelphia for visits, or if he'd moved to Australia earlier than he did, these collaborations would never have happened at all; there was a narrow window of opportunity for them, all the factors happening to be right at the right time, and then that window closed.

The genesis of this story was a sentence in my story-idea notebook that I'd written down sometime in the early '70s: "Vampire in Nazi death camp in World War II." Jack was down for another of his visits, and had just written his brilliant story "Camps," which I'd just read in manuscript, and we'd been talking about the story and about the death camps in general that morning, so when we were sitting around that afternoon, trying to come up with a story we could work on together, it seemed only natural that I should pick out that particular story-idea and throw it out for Jack. He'd already done the necessary historical research for "Camps," after all! (Although, as turned out to be true with most of these collaborations, I ended up duplicating most of his research by the time we were through with the story anyway.)

Jack's recollection and mine differ here. His is that he was initially dismissive of the idea and reluctant to do anything with it, and that I had to talk him into working on it. *My* memory is that he took fire with the idea at once, as he usually did in these cases, and immediately rushed inside to the typewriter. Whichever is true, the fact is that he spent the rest of the afternoon and much of the evening sitting at the typewriter, pouring out copy at white-hot speed, and that by the time he got up, he'd roughed out the opening part of the story, the first nine or ten pages, up through the opening Passover scene (which, except for a few lines I added retroactively, is much the same as what's on the page here).

Then he left for Binghamton the next day, and I was left with the usual big pile of paper sitting reproachfully on the table next to the typewriter, shaming me into working on it, although the aesthetic tightrope we'd have to walk in finishing the story successfully was daunting enough that I might never have attempted it on my own. I took over the story after the Passover scene and continued it from there. Later we worked out some story problems in the manuscript and passed a couple of drafts back and forth, and then I did my usual unifying draft. I took special care in feathering over the join between Jack's opening scene and my later continuation of the story, and did a good enough job that nobody's ever been able to pinpoint exactly where he left off and I started, even Michael, who's as familiar as anybody on the planet with both of our writing styles. Jack and I later had a slight disagreement over the ending. I preferred the story to end with the line "His mouth filled with the strong, clean taste of copper," which is the way I've reprinted it in my own collections, while Jack preferred it to end with an additional paragraph he inserted after that line, which I assume is the way it's reproduced here.

For me, the story boils down to the question of identity, which is what interested me in it in the first place. Although he's a vampire, he's perceived by the Nazis as being a Jew, and so that's the way they treat him, no better or worse than they treat any of the other Jews. We are what other people think we are, to some extent, whether we want to be or not.

This story was way too risky for the timid genre magazine market of the '80s, so it first appeared in *Oui* magazine; sometime later, it was reprinted in *The Magazine of Fantasy & Science Fiction*, and later reprinted again in Ellen Datlow's vampire anthology, *Blood Is Not Enough*. It's been reprinted a number of times since. In some ways, this was one of the most successful of the collaborations, but it was also one of the most controversial, stirring very strong reactions. People seem to either love it or hate it, with very little middle ground.

Jack Dann

This story was indeed Gardner's idea, as was the title.

Ah, memory is a dangerous and perhaps self-serving beast because I remember staying over at Gardner and Susan's Quince Street apartment, sleeping on the couch with their cats padding over me, sniffing me out, curling up on top of my knees; I also remember sitting on that same couch and drinking wine, one of many invited guests—the susurration of conversation, friends waving their arms, gesticulating and greeting one another, ten conversations crossing over, hysterical laughter, the humidity rising, the room warming; and now, in memory, these are the smells and sounds of youth, that momentary heartbeat when everything was concentrated and important; sounds were more distinct, ideas more important, and emotions were so strong that their glandular after-trails are still felt.

I can still see Michael, relaxed and yet fully focused as he tempts me to enter one of the labyrinthine fairways of his story plots and brainstorm this or that idea, and Gardner holding court, exuding the charisma that he still does not believe he has; and Susan is right there in the center of it all, having as much fun as any guest; and I seem to remember writing the opening of "Down Among the Dead Men" at just such a party, but I'm sure Gardner's right . . . I'm sure we were alone, and that I'm conflating this story with another, which has probably been conflated with yet another.

But . . . but I *do* remember having a negative reaction to Gardner's suggestion that we write a story about a vampire in a concentration camp. I had written what I considered my definitive concentration camp story in 1979. "Camps" was my most successful piece of short fiction. Why, I remember thinking, would I want to revisit the camps again?

Surely just as I had that thought, I was also caught by the idea of collaborating once again with Gardner. I wouldn't have to do any research. I'd already done it. And I probably saw how the story could be written. Well, obviously the opening of the story flashed before me because I remember sitting down at Gardner's antique typewriter and typing with the wild and furious joy of an Athenian soldier engaging the Trojans in battle. I remember the physicality of bashing on those shiny black keys, the reassuring *thunk* when you knocked the heavy carriage back, the squeak when you threaded another piece of paper, and the quietly powerful joy of being in that same flat, bright place I used to experience when I was a long-distance runner and the endorphins would kick in.

Words mysteriously appeared on Gardner's ultra-white corasable bond typing paper.

This was like automatic writing.

Endorphin writing.

And hours later, when it was over, there was a pile of paper neatly piled beside the typewriter. And it still beats the hell out of me how those pages got there!

Gardner had touched something important—I would say even profound—with his idea of the vampire, for the horrific, impossible conundrum of the camps—their terrible reality—was that to survive you could not *help* but prey on others. You could not survive without being soiled, corrupted, and in some way co-opted. The system didn't permit it. You worked in the factory that was the concentration camp, and the camp produced corpses, the corpses of your friends, family, and neighbors. As one of my characters says in "Camps," "Like everyone else who survives, I count myself first, second, and third—then I try to do what I can for someone else."

And so it is with our vampire protagonist.

Our vampire is a metaphor for ourselves . . . yes, even for the most well meaning among us.

"Down Among the Dead Men" won the *Premios Gilgamés de Narrativa Fantastica Award* for Best Short Story published in Spanish in 1986.

Down Among the Dead Men

Gardner Dozois and Jack Dann

Bruckman FIRST DISCOVERED THAT WERNECKE WAS a vampire when they went to the quarry that morning.

He was bending down to pick up a large rock when he thought he heard something in the gully nearby. He looked around and saw Wernecke huddled over a *Musselmänn*, one of the walking dead, a new man who had not been able to wake up to the terrible reality of the camp.

"Do you need any help?" Bruckman asked Wernecke in a low voice.

Wernecke looked up, startled, and covered his mouth with his hand, as if he were signing to Bruckman to be quiet.

But Bruckman was certain that he had glimpsed blood smeared on Wernecke's mouth. "The Musselmänn, is he alive?" Wernecke had often risked his own life to save one or another of the men in his barracks. But to risk one's life for a Musselmänn? "What's wrong?"

"Get away."

All right, Bruckman thought. Best to leave him alone. He looked pale, perhaps it was typhus. The guards were working him hard enough, and Wernecke was older than the rest of the men in the work gang. Let him sit for a moment and rest. But what about that blood? . . .

"Hey, you, what are you doing?" one of the young SS guards shouted to Bruckman.

Bruckman picked up the rock and, as if he had not heard the guard, began to walk away from the gully, toward the rusty brown cart on the tracks that led back to the barbed-wire fence of the camp. He would try to draw the guard's attention away from Wernecke.

But the guard shouted at him to halt. "Were you taking a little rest, is that it?" he asked, and Bruckman tensed, ready for a beating. This guard was new, neatly and cleanly dressed—and an unknown quantity. He walked over to the gully and, seeing Wernecke and the Musselmänn, said, "Aha, so your friend is taking care of the sick." He motioned Bruckman to follow him into the gully.

Bruckman had done the unpardonable—he had brought it on Wernecke. He swore at himself. He had been in this camp long enough to know to keep his mouth shut.

The guard kicked Wernecke sharply in the ribs. "I want you to put the Musselmänn in the cart. Now!" He kicked Wernecke again, as if as an afterthought. Wernecke groaned, but got to his feet. "Help him put the Musselmänn in the cart," the guard said to Bruckman; then he smiled and drew a circle in the air—the sign of smoke, the smoke that rose from the tall, gray chimneys behind them. This Musselmänn would be in the oven within an hour, his ashes soon to be floating in the hot, stale air, as if they were the very particles of his soul.

Wernecke kicked the Musselmänn, and the guard chuckled, waved to another guard who had been watching, and stepped back a few feet. He stood with his hands on his hips. "Come on, dead man, get up or you're going to die in the oven," Wernecke whispered as he tried to pull the man to his feet. Bruckman supported the unsteady Musselmänn, who began to wail softly. Wernecke slapped him hard. "Do you want to live, Musselmänn? Do you want to see your family again, feel the touch of a woman, smell grass after it's been mowed? Then *move*." The Musselmänn shambled forward between Wernecke and Bruckman. "You're dead, aren't you Musselmänn," goaded Wernecke. "As dead as your father and mother, as dead as your sweet wife, if you ever had one, aren't you? Dead!"

The Musselmänn groaned, shook his head, and whispered, "Not dead, my wife . . ."

"Ah, it talks," Wernecke said, loud enough so the guard walking a step behind them could hear. "Do you have a name, corpse?"

"Josef, and I'm not a Musselmänn."

"The corpse says he's alive," Wernecke said, again loud enough for the SS guard to hear. Then in a whisper, he said, "Josef, if you're not a Musselmänn, then you must work now, do you understand?" Josef tripped, and Bruckman caught him. "Let him be," said Wernecke. "Let him walk to the cart himself."

"Not the cart," Josef mumbled. "Not to die, not—"

"Then get down and pick up stones, show the fart-eating guard you can work."

"Can't. I'm sick, I'm . . ."

"Musselmänn!"

Josef bent down, fell to his knees, but took hold of a stone and stood up.

"You see," Wernecke said to the guard, "it's not dead yet. It can still work."

"I told you to carry him to the cart, didn't I," the guard said petulantly.

"Show him you can work," Wernecke said to Josef, "or you'll surely be smoke."

And Josef stumbled away from Wernecke and Bruckman, leaning forward, as if following the rock he was carrying.

"Bring him *back!*" shouted the guard, but his attention was distracted from Josef by some other prisoners, who, sensing the trouble, began to mill about. One of the other guards began to shout and kick at the men on the periphery, and the new guard joined him. For the moment, he had forgotten about Josef.

"Let's get to work, lest they notice us again," Wernecke said.

"I'm sorry that I—"

Wernecke laughed and made a fluttering gesture with his hand—smoke rising. "It's all hazard, my friend. All luck." Again the laugh. "It was a venial sin," and his face seemed to darken. "Never do it again, though, lest I think of you as bad luck."

"Eduard, are you all right?" Bruckman asked. "I noticed some blood when—"

"Do the sores on your feet bleed in the morning?" Wernecke countered angrily. Bruckman nodded, feeling foolish and embarrassed. "And so it is with my gums. Now go away, unlucky one, and let me live."

At dusk, the guards broke the hypnosis of lifting and grunting and sweating and formed the prisoners into ranks. They marched back to the camp through the fields, beside the railroad tracks, the electrified wire, conical towers, and into the main gate of the camp.

Josef walked beside them, but he kept stumbling, as he was once again slipping back into death, becoming a Musselmänn. Wernecke helped him walk, pushed him along. "We should let this man become dead," Wernecke said to Bruckman.

Bruckman only nodded, but he felt a chill sweep over his sweating back. He was seeing Wernecke's face again as it was for that instant in the morning. Smeared with blood.

Yes, Bruckman thought, we should let the Musselmänn become dead.

We should all be dead. . . .

Wernecke served up the lukewarm water with bits of spoiled turnip floating on the top, what passed as soup for the prisoners. Everyone sat or kneeled on the rough-planked floor, as there were no chairs.

Bruckman ate his portion, counting the sips and bites, forcing himself to take his time. Later, he would take a very small bite of the bread he had in his pocket. He always saved a small morsel of food for later—in the endless world of the camp, he had learned to give himself things to look forward to. Better to dream of bread than to get lost in the present. That was the fate of the Musselmänner.

But he always dreamed of food. Hunger was with him every moment of the day and night. Those times when he actually ate were in a way the most difficult, for there was never enough to satisfy him. There was the taste of softness in his mouth, and then in an instant it was gone. The emptiness took the form of pain—it *hurt* to eat. For bread, he thought, he would have killed his father, or his wife. God forgive me, and he watched Wernecke— Wernecke, who had shared his bread with him, who had died a little so he could live. He's a better man than I, Bruckman thought.

It was dim inside the barracks. A bare light bulb hung from the ceiling and cast sharp shadows across the cavernous room. Two tiers of five-foot-deep shelves ran around the room on three sides, bare, wooden shelves where the men slept without blankets or mattresses. Set high in the northern wall was a slatted window, which let in the stark, white light of the kliegs. Outside, the lights turned the grounds into a deathly imitation of day; only inside the barracks was it night.

"Do you know what tonight is, my friends?" Wernecke asked.

He sat in the far corner of the room with Josef, who, hour by hour, was reverting back into a Musselmänn. Wernecke's face looked hollow and drawn in the light from the window and the light bulb; his eyes were deep-set and his face was long with deep creases running from his nose to the corners of his thin mouth. His hair was black, and even since Bruckman had known him, quite a bit of it had fallen out. He was a very tall man, almost six feet four, and that made him stand out in a crowd, which was dangerous in a death camp. But Wernecke had his own secret ways of blending with the crowd, of making himself invisible.

"No, tell us what tonight is," crazy old Bohme said. That men such as Bohme could survive was a miracle — or, as Bruckman thought — a testament to men such as Wernecke who somehow found the strength to help the others live.

"It's Passover," Wernecke said.

"How does he know that?" someone mumbled, but it didn't matter how Wernecke knew because he *knew* — even if it really wasn't Passover by the calendar. In this dimly lit barrack, it *was* Passover, the feast of freedom, the time of thanksgiving.

"But how can we have Passover without a *seder*?" asked Bohme. "We don't even have any *matzoh*," he whined.

"Nor do we have candles, or a silver cup for Elijah, or the shankbone, or *haroset* — nor would I make a *seder* over the *traif* the Nazis are so generous in giving us," replied Wernecke with a smile. "But we can pray, can't we? And when we all get out of here, when we're in our own homes in the coming year with God's help, then we'll have twice as much food — two *afikomens*, a bottle of wine for Elijah, and the *haggadahs* that our fathers and our fathers' fathers used."

It *was* Passover.

"Isadore, do you remember the four questions?" Wernecke asked Bruckman.

And Bruckman heard himself speaking. He was twelve years old again at the long table beside his father, who sat in the seat of honor. To sit next to him was itself an honor. "How does this night differ from all other nights? On all other nights we eat bread and *matzoh*; why on this night do we eat only *matzoh*?

"*M'a nisht' ana halylah hazeah. . . .*"

Sleep would not come to Bruckman that night, although he was so tired that he felt as if the marrow of his bones had been sucked away and replaced with lead.

He lay there in the semidarkness, feeling his muscles ache, feeling the acid biting of his hunger. Usually he was numb enough with exhaustion that he could empty his mind, close himself down, and fall rapidly into oblivion, but not tonight. Tonight he was noticing things again, his surroundings were getting through to him again, in a way that they had not since he had been new in camp. It was smotheringly hot, and the air was filled with the stinks of death and sweat and fever, of stale urine and drying blood. The sleepers thrashed and turned, as though they fought with sleep, and as they slept, many of them talked or muttered or screamed aloud; they lived other lives in their dreams, intensely compressed lives dreamed quickly, for soon it would be dawn, and once more they would be thrust into hell. Cramped in the midst of them, sleepers squeezed in all around him, it suddenly seemed to Bruckman that these pallid, white bodies were already dead, that he was sleeping in a graveyard. Suddenly it was the boxcar again. And his wife Miriam was dead again, dead and rotting unburied . . . .

Resolutely, Bruckman emptied his mind. He felt feverish and shaky, and wondered if the typhus was coming back, but he couldn't afford to worry about it. Those who couldn't sleep couldn't survive. Regulate your breathing, force your muscles to relax, don't think. Don't think.

For some reason, after he had managed to banish even the memory of his dead wife, he couldn't shake the image of the blood on Wernecke's mouth.

There were other images mixed in with it: Wernecke's uplifted arms and upturned face as he led them in prayer; the pale, strained face of the stumbling Musselmänn; Wernecke looking up, startled, as he crouched over Josef . . . but it was the blood to which Bruckman's feverish thoughts returned, and he pictured it again and again as he lay in the rustling, fart-smelling darkness, the watery sheen of blood over Wernecke's lips, the tarry trickle of blood in the corner of his mouth, like a tiny, scarlet worm. . . .

Just then a shadow crossed in front of the window, silhouetted blackly for an instant against the harsh, white glare, and Bruckman knew from the shadow's height and its curious forward stoop that it was Wernecke.

Where could he be going? Sometimes a prisoner would be unable to wait until morning, when the Germans would let them out to visit the slit-trench latrine again, and would slink shamefacedly into a far corner to piss against a wall, but surely Wernecke was too much of an old hand for that. . . . Most of the prisoners slept on the sleeping platforms, especially during the cold nights when they would huddle together for warmth, but sometimes during the hot weather, people would drift away and sleep on the floor instead; Bruckman had been thinking of doing that, as the jostling bodies of the sleepers around him helped to keep him from sleep. Perhaps Wernecke, who always had trouble fitting into the cramped sleeping niches, was merely looking for a place where he could lie down and stretch his legs . . .

Then Bruckman remembered that Josef had fallen asleep in the corner of the room where Wernecke had sat and prayed, and that they had left him there alone.

Without knowing why, Bruckman found himself on his feet. As silently as the ghost he sometimes felt he was becoming, he walked across the room in the direction Wernecke had gone, not understanding what he was doing or why he was doing it. The face of the Musselmänn, Josef, seemed to float behind his eyes. Bruckman's feet hurt, and he knew, without looking, that they were bleeding, leaving faint tracks behind him. It was dimmer here in the far corner, away from the window, but Bruckman knew that he must be near the wall by now, and he stopped to let his eyes readjust.

When his eyes had adapted to the dimmer light, he saw Josef sitting on the floor, propped up against the wall. Wernecke was hunched over the Musselmänn. Kissing him. One of Josef's hands was tangled in Wernecke's thinning hair.

Before Bruckman could react—such things had been known to happen once or twice before, although it shocked him deeply that *Wernecke* would be involved in such filth—Josef released his grip on Wernecke's hair. Josef's upraised arm fell limply to the side, his hand hitting the floor with a muffled but solid impact that should have been painful—but Josef made no sound.

Wernecke straightened up and turned around. Stronger light from the high window caught him as he straightened to his full height, momentarily illuminating his face.

Wernecke's mouth was smeared with blood.

"My God," Bruckman cried.

Startled, Wernecke flinched, then took two quick steps forward and seized Bruckman by the arm. "Quiet!" Wernecke hissed. His fingers were cold and hard.

At that moment, as though Wernecke's sudden movement were a cue, Josef began to slip down sideways along the wall. As Wernecke and Bruckman watched, both momentarily riveted by the sight, Josef toppled over to the floor, his head striking against the floorboards with a sound such as a dropped melon might make. He had made no attempt to break his fall or cushion his head, and lay now unmoving.

"My *God*," Bruckman said again.

"Quiet, I'll explain," Wernecke said, his lips still glazed with the Musselmänn blood. "Do you want to ruin us all? For the love of God, be *quiet*."

But Bruckman had shaken free of Wernecke's grip and crossed to kneel by Josef, leaning over him as Wernecke had done, placing a hand flat on Josef's chest for a moment, then touching the side of Josef's neck. Bruckman looked slowly up at Wernecke. "He's dead," Bruckman said, more quietly.

Wernecke squatted on the other side of Josef's body, and the rest of their conversation was carried out in whispers over Josef's chest, like friends conversing at the sickbed of another friend who has finally fallen into a fitful doze.

"Yes, he's dead," Wernecke said. "He was dead yesterday, wasn't he? Today he has just stopped walking." His eyes were hidden here, in the deeper shadow nearer to the floor, but there was still enough light for Bruckman to see that Wernecke had wiped his lips clean. Or licked them clean, Bruckman thought, and felt a spasm of nausea go through him.

"But *you*," Bruckman said, haltingly. "You were. . . ."

"Drinking his blood?" Wernecke said. "Yes, I was drinking his blood."

Bruckman's mind was numb. He couldn't deal with this, he couldn't understand it at all. "But *why*, Eduard? Why?"

"To live, of course. Why do any of us do anything here? If I am to live, I must have blood. Without it, I'd face a death even more certain than that doled out by the Nazis."

Bruckman opened and closed his mouth, but no sound came out, as if the words he wished to speak were too jagged to fit through his throat. At last he managed to croak, "A vampire? You're a vampire? Like in the old stories?"

Wernecke said calmly, "Men would call me that." He paused, then nodded. "Yes, that's what men would call me. . . . As though they can understand something simply by giving it a name."

"But Eduard," Bruckman said weakly, almost petulantly. "The Musselmänn . . ."

"Remember that he *was* a Musselmänn," Wernecke said, leaning forward and speaking more fiercely. "His strength was going, he was sinking. He would have been dead by morning anyway. I took from him something that he no longer needed, but that I needed in order to live. Does it matter? Starving men in lifeboats have eaten the bodies of their dead companions in order to live. Is what I've done any worse than that?"

"But he didn't just die. You *killed* him. . . ."

Wernecke was silent for a moment, and then said, quietly, "What better thing could I have done for him? I won't apologize for what I do, Isadore; I do what I have to do to live. Usually I take only a little blood from a number of men, just enough to survive. And that's fair, isn't it? Haven't I given food to others, to help them survive? To you, Isadore? Only very rarely do I take more than a minimum from any one man, although I'm weak and hungry all the time, believe me. And never have I drained the life from someone who wished to live. Instead I've helped them fight for survival in every way I can, you know that."

He reached out as though to touch Bruckman, then thought better of it and put his hand back on his own knee. He shook his head. "But these Musselmänner, the ones who have given up on life, the walking dead—it is a favor to them to take them, to give them the solace of death. Can you honestly say it is not, *here?* That it is better for them to walk around while they are dead, being beaten and abused by the Nazis until their bodies cannot go on, and then to be thrown into the ovens and burned like trash? Can you say that? Would *they* say that, if they knew what was going on? Or would they thank me?"

Wernecke suddenly stood up, and Bruckman stood up with him. As Wernecke's face came again into the stronger light, Bruckman could see that his eyes had filled with tears. "You have lived under the Nazis," Wernecke said. "Can you really call me a monster? Aren't I still a Jew, whatever else I might be? Aren't I *here*, in a death camp? Aren't I being persecuted, too, as much as any other? Aren't I in as much danger as anyone else? If I'm not a Jew, then tell the Nazis—they seem to think so." He paused for a moment, and then smiled wryly. "And forget your superstitious boogey tales. I'm no night spirit. If I could turn myself into a bat and fly away from here, I would have done it long before now, believe me."

Bruckman smiled reflectively, then grimaced. The two men avoided each other's eyes, Bruckman looking at the floor, and there was an uneasy silence, punctured only by the sighing and moaning of the sleepers on the other side of the cabin. Then, without looking up, in tacit surrender, Bruckman said, "What about *him*? The Nazis will find the body and cause trouble. . . ."

"Don't worry," Wernecke said. "There are no obvious marks. And nobody performs autopsies in a death camp. To the Nazis, he'll be just another Jew who had died of the heat, or from starvation or sickness, or from a broken heart."

Bruckman raised his head then and they stared eye to eye for a moment. Even knowing what he knew, Bruckman found it hard to see Wernecke as anything other than what he appeared to be: an aging, balding Jew, stooping and thin, with sad eyes and a tired, compassionate face.

"Well, then, Isadore," Wernecke said at last, matter-of-factly. "My life is in your hands. I will not be indelicate enough to remind you of how many times your life has been in mine."

Then he was gone, walking back toward the sleeping platforms, a shadow soon lost among other shadows.

Bruckman stood by himself in the gloom for a long time, and then followed him. It took all of his will not to look back over his shoulder at the corner where Josef lay, and even so Bruckman imagined that he could feel Josef's dead eyes watching him, watching reproachfully as he walked away abandoning Josef to the cold and isolated company of the dead.

Bruckman got no more sleep that night, and in the morning, when the Nazis shattered the gray, predawn stillness by bursting into the shack with shouts and shrill whistles and barking police dogs, he felt as if he were a thousand years old.

They were formed into two lines, shivering in the raw morning air, and marched off to the quarry. The clammy dawn mist had yet to burn off, and marching through it, through a white, shadowless void, with only the back of the man in front of him dimly visible, Bruckman felt more than ever like a ghost, suspended bodiless in some limbo between Heaven and Earth. Only the bite of pebbles and cinders into his raw, bleeding feet kept him anchored to the world, and he clung to the pain as a lifeline, fighting to shake off a feeling of numbness and unreality. However strange, however outré, the events of the previous night had *happened*. To doubt it, to wonder now if it had all been a feverish dream brought on by starvation and exhaustion, was to take the first step on the road to becoming a Musselmänn.

Wernecke is a vampire, he told himself. That was the harsh, unyielding reality that, like the reality of the camp itself, must be faced. Was it any more surreal, any more impossible than the nightmare around them? He must forget the tales that his grandmother had told him as a boy, "boogey tales" as Wernecke himself had called them, half-remembered tales that turned his knees to water whenever he thought of the blood smeared on Wernecke's mouth, whenever he thought of Wernecke's eyes watching him in the dark. . . .

"Wake up, Jew!" the guard alongside him snarled, whacking him lightly on the arm with his rifle butt. Bruckman stumbled, managed to stay upright and keep going. Yes, he thought, wake up. Wake up to the reality of this, just as you once had to wake up to the reality of the camp. It was just one more unpleasant fact he would have to adapt to, learn to deal with. . . .

Deal with how? he thought, and shivered.

By the time they reached the quarry, the mist had burned off, swirling past them in rags and tatters, and it was already beginning to get hot. There was Wernecke, his balding head gleaming dully in the harsh morning light. He didn't dissolve in the sunlight—there was one boogey tale disproved. . . .

They set to work, like golems, like ragtag, clockwork automatons.

Lack of sleep had drained what small reserves of strength Bruckman had, and the work was very hard for him that day. He had learned long ago all the tricks of timing and misdirection, the safe way to snatch short moments of rest, the ways to do a minimum of work with the maximum display of effort, the ways to keep the guards from noticing you, to fade into the faceless crowd of prisoners and not be singled out, but today his head was muzzy and slow, and none of the tricks seemed to work.

His body felt like a sheet of glass, fragile, ready to shatter into dust, and the painful, arthritic slowness of his movements got him first shouted at, and then knocked down. The guard kicked him twice for good measure before he could get up.

When Bruckman had climbed back to his feet again, he saw that Wernecke was watching him, face blank, eyes expressionless, a look that could have meant anything at all.

Bruckman felt the blood trickling from the corner of his mouth and thought, *the blood . . . he's watching the blood . . .* and once again he shivered.

Somehow, Bruckman forced himself to work faster, and although his muscles blazed with pain, he wasn't hit again, and the day passed.

When they formed up to go back to camp, Bruckman, almost unconsciously, made sure that he was in a different line than Wernecke.

That night in the cabin, Bruckman watched as Wernecke talked with the other men, here trying to help a new man named Melnick—no more than a boy—adjust to the dreadful reality of the camp, there exhorting someone who was slipping into despair to live and spite his tormentors, joking with old hands in the flat, black, bitter way that passed for humor among them, eliciting a wan smile or occasionally even a laugh from them, finally leading them all in prayer again, his strong, calm voice raised in the ancient words, giving meaning to those words again. . . .

He keeps us together, Bruckman thought, he keeps us going. Without him, we wouldn't last a week. Surely that's worth a little blood, a bit from each man, not even enough to hurt. . . . Surely they wouldn't even begrudge him it, if they knew and really understood. . . . No, he is a good man, better than the rest of us, in spite of his terrible affliction.

Bruckman had been avoiding Wernecke's eyes, hadn't spoken to him at all that day, and suddenly felt a wave of shame go through him at the thought of how shabbily he had been treating his friend. Yes, his friend, regardless, the man who had saved his life. . . . Deliberately, he caught Wernecke's eyes, and nodded, and then somewhat sheepishly, smiled. After a moment, Wernecke smiled back, and Bruckman felt a spreading warmth and relief uncoil his guts. Everything was going to be all right, as all right as it could be, here. . . .

Nevertheless, as soon as the inside lights clicked off that night, and Bruckman found himself lying alone in the darkness, his flesh began to crawl.

He had been unable to keep his eyes open a moment before, but now, in the sudden darkness, he found himself tensely and tickingly awake. Where was Wernecke? What was he doing, whom was he visiting tonight? Was he out there in the darkness even now, creeping closer, creeping nearer? . . . Stop it, Bruckman told himself uneasily, forget the boogey tales. This is your friend, a good man, not a monster. . . . But he couldn't control the fear that made the small hairs on his arms stand bristlingly erect, couldn't stop the grisly images from coming. . . .

Wernecke's eyes, gleaming in the darkness . . . was the blood already glistening on Wernecke's lips, as he drank? . . . The thought of the blood staining Wernecke's yellowing teeth made Bruckman cold and nauseous, but the image that he couldn't get out of his mind tonight was an image of Josef toppling over in that sinister, boneless way, striking his head against the floor. . . . Bruckman had seen people die in many more gruesome ways during his time at the camp, seen people shot, beaten to death, seen them die in convulsions from high fevers or cough their lungs up in bloody tatters from pneumonia, seen them hanging like charred-black scarecrows from the electrified fences, seen them torn apart by dogs . . . but somehow it was Josef's soft, passive, almost restful slumping into death that bothered him. That, and the obscene limpness of Josef's limbs as he sprawled there like a discarded rag doll, his pale and haggard face gleaming reproachfully in the dark. . . .

When Bruckman could stand it no longer, he got shakily to his feet and moved off through the shadows, once again not knowing where he was going or what he was going to do, but drawn forward by some obscure instinct he himself did not understand. This time he went cautiously, feeling his way and trying to be silent, expecting every second to see Wernecke's coal-black shadow rise up before him.

He paused, a faint noise scratching at his ears, then went on again, even more cautiously, crouching low, almost crawling across the grimy floor.

Whatever instinct had guided him—sounds heard and interpreted subliminally, perhaps?—it had timed his arrival well. Wernecke had someone down on the floor there, perhaps someone he seized and dragged away from the huddled mass of sleepers on one of the sleeping platforms, someone from the outer edge of bodies whose presence would not be missed, or perhaps someone who had gone to sleep on the floor, seeking solitude or greater comfort.

Whoever he was, he struggled in Wernecke's grip, but Wernecke handled him easily, almost negligently, in a manner that spoke of great physical power. Bruckman could hear the man trying to scream, but Wernecke had one hand on his throat, half-throttling him, and all that would come out was a sort of whistling gasp. The man thrashed in Wernecke's hands like a kite in a child's hands flapping in the wind, and, moving deliberately, Wernecke smoothed him out like a kite, pressing him slowly flat on the floor.

Then Wernecke bent over him, and lowered his mouth to his throat.

Bruckman watched in horror, knowing that he should shout, scream, try to rouse the other prisoners, but somehow unable to move, unable to make his mouth open, his lungs pump. He was paralyzed by fear, like a rabbit in the presence of a predator, a terror sharper and more intense than any he'd ever known.

The man's struggles were growing weaker, and Wernecke must have eased up some on the throttling pressure of his hand, because the man moaned "Don't . . . please don't . . ." in a weaker, slurred voice. The man had been drumming his fists against Wernecke's back and sides, but now the tempo of the drumming slowed, slowed, and then stopped, the man's arms falling laxly to the floor. "Don't . . ." the man whispered; he groaned and muttered incomprehensibly for a moment or two longer, then became silent. The silence stretched out for a minute, two, three, and Wernecke still crouched over his victim, who was now not moving at all. . . .

Wernecke stirred, a kind of shudder going through him, like a cat stretching. He stood up. His face became visible as he straightened up into the full light from the window, and there was blood on it, glistening black under the harsh glare of the kliegs. As Bruckman watched, Wernecke began to lick his lips clean, his tongue, also black in this light, sliding like some sort of sinuous, ebony snake around the rim of his mouth, darting and probing for the last lingering drops. . . .

How smug he looks, Bruckman thought, like a cat who has found the cream, and the anger that flashed through him at the thought enabled him to move and speak again. "Wernecke," he said harshly.

Wernecke glanced casually in his direction. "You again, Isadore?" Wernecke said. "Don't you ever sleep?" Wernecke spoke lazily, quizzically, without surprise, and Bruckman wondered if Wernecke had known all along that he was there. "Or do you just enjoy watching me?"

"Lies," Bruckman said. "You told me nothing but lies. Why did you bother?"

"You were excited," Wernecke said. "You had surprised me. It seemed best to tell you what you wanted to hear. If it satisfied you, then that was an easy solution to the problem."

"Never have I drained the life from someone who wanted to live," Bruckman said bitterly, mimicking Wernecke. "Only a little from each man! My God—and I believed you! I even felt sorry for you!"

Wernecke shrugged. "Most of it was true. Usually I only take a little from each man, softly and carefully, so that they never know, so that in the morning they are only a little weaker than they would have been anyway. . . ."

"Like Josef?" Bruckman said angrily. "Like the poor devil you killed tonight?"

Wernecke shrugged again. "I have been careless the last few nights, I admit. But I need to build up my strength again." His eyes gleamed in the darkness. "Events are coming to a head here. Can't you feel it, Isadore, can't you sense it? Soon the war will be over, everyone knows that. Before then, this camp will be shut down, and the Nazis will move us back into the interior—either that, or kill us. I have grown weak here, and I will soon need all my strength to survive, to take whatever opportunity presents itself to escape. I *must* be ready. And so I have let myself drink deeply again, drink my fill for the first time in months. . . ." Wernecke licked his lips again, perhaps unconsciously, then smiled bleakly at Bruckman. "You don't appreciate my restraint, Isadore. You don't understand how hard it has been for me to hold back, to take only a little each night. You don't understand how much that restraint has cost me. . . ."

"You are gracious," Bruckman sneered.

Wernecke laughed. "No, but I am a rational man; I pride myself on that. You other prisoners were my only source of food, and I have had to be very careful to make sure that you would last. I have no access to the Nazis, after all. I am trapped here, a prisoner just like you, whatever else you may believe—and I have not only had to find ways to survive here in the camp, I have had to procure my own food as well! No shepherd has ever watched over his flock more tenderly than I."

"Is that all we are to you—sheep? Animals to be slaughtered?"

Wernecke smiled. "Precisely."

When he could control his voice enough to speak, Bruckman said, "You're worse than the Nazis."

"I hardly think so," Wernecke said quietly, and for a moment he looked tired, as though something unimaginably old and unutterably weary had looked out through his eyes. "This camp was built by the Nazis—it wasn't my doing. The Nazis sent you here—not I. The Nazis have tried to kill you every day since, in one way or another—and I have tried to keep you alive, even at some risk to myself. No one has more of a vested interest in the survival of his livestock than the farmer, after all, even if he does occasionally slaughter an inferior animal. I have given you food—"

"Food you had no use for yourself! You sacrificed nothing!"

"That's true, of course. But *you* needed it, remember that. Whatever my motives, I have helped you to survive here—you and many others. By doing so I also acted in my own self-interest, of course, but can you have experienced this camp and still believe in things like altruism? What difference does it make what my reason for helping was—I still helped you, didn't I?"

"Sophistries!" Bruckman said. "Rationalizations! You twist words to justify yourself, but you can't disguise what you really are—a monster!"

Wernecke smiled gently, as though Bruckman's words amused him, and made as if to pass by, but Bruckman raised an arm to bar his way. They did not touch each other, but Wernecke stopped short, and a new quivering kind of tension sprung into existence in the air between them.

"I'll stop you," Bruckman said. "Somehow I'll stop you, I'll keep you from doing this terrible thing—"

"You'll do nothing," Wernecke said. His voice was hard and cold and flat, like a rock speaking. "What can you do? Tell the other prisoners? Who would believe you? They'd think you'd gone insane. Tell the *Nazis*, then?" Wernecke laughed harshly. "They'd think you'd gone crazy, too, and they'd take you to the hospital— and I don't have to tell you what your chances of getting out of there alive are, do I? No, you'll do *nothing*."

Wernecke took a step forward; his eyes were shiny and black and hard, like ice, like the pitiless eyes of a predatory bird, and Bruckman felt a sick rush of fear cut through his anger. Bruckman gave way, stepping backward involuntarily, and Wernecke pushed past him, seeming to brush him aside without touching him.

Once past, Wernecke turned to stare at Bruckman, and Bruckman had to summon up all the defiance that remained in him not to look uneasily away from Wernecke's agate-hard eyes. "You are the strongest and cleverest of all the other animals, Isadore," Wernecke said in a calm, conversational voice. "You have been useful to me. Every shepherd needs a good sheep dog. I still need you, to help me manage the others, and to help me keep them going long enough to serve my needs. This is the reason why I have taken so much time with you, instead of just killing you outright." He shrugged. "So let us both be rational about this—you leave me alone, Isadore, and I will leave you alone also. We will stay away from each other and look after our own affairs. Yes?"

"The others. . . ." Bruckman said weakly.

"They must look after themselves," Wernecke said. He smiled, a thin and almost invisible motion of his lips. "What did I teach you, Isadore? Here everyone must look after themselves. What difference does it make what happens to the others? In a few weeks almost all of them will be dead anyway."

"You *are* a monster," Bruckman said.

"I'm not much different from you, Isadore. The strong survive, whatever the cost."

"I am *nothing* like you," Bruckman said, with loathing.

"No?" Wernecke asked, ironically, and moved away; within a few paces he was hobbling and stooping, vanishing into the shadows, once more the harmless, old Jew.

Bruckman stood motionless for a moment, and then, moving slowly and reluctantly, he stepped across to where Wernecke's victim lay.

It was one of the new men Wernecke had been talking to earlier in the evening, and, of course, he was quite dead.

Shame and guilt took Bruckman then, emotions he thought he had forgotten—black and strong and bitter, they shook him by the throat the way Wernecke had shaken the new man.

Bruckman couldn't remember returning across the room to his sleeping platform, but suddenly he was there, lying on his back and staring into the stifling darkness, surrounded by the moaning, thrashing, stinking mass of sleepers. His hands were clasped protectively over his throat, although he couldn't remember putting them there, and he was shivering convulsively. How many mornings had he awoken with a dull ache in his neck, thinking it was no more than the habitual body aches and strained muscles they had all learned to take for granted? How many nights had Wernecke fed on *him?*

Every time Bruckman closed his eyes he would see Wernecke's face floating there in the luminous darkness behind his eyelids . . . Wernecke with his eyes half-closed, his face vulpine and cruel and satiated . . . Wernecke's face moving closer and closer to him, his eyes opening like black pits, his lips smiling back from his teeth . . . Wernecke's lips, sticky and red with blood . . . and then Bruckman would seem to feel the wet touch of Wernecke's lips on *his* throat, feel Wernecke's teeth biting into *his* flesh, and Bruckman's eyes would fly open again. Staring into the darkness. Nothing there. Nothing there *yet.* . . .

Dawn was a dirty gray imminence against the cabin window before Bruckman could force himself to lower his shielding arms from his throat, and once again he had not slept at all.

That day's work was a nightmare of pain and exhaustion for Bruckman, harder than anything he had known since his first few days at the camp. Somehow he forced himself to get up, somehow he stumbled outside and up the path to the quarry, seeming to float along high off the ground, his head a bloated balloon, his feet a thousand miles away at the end of boneless, beanstalk legs he could barely control at all. Twice he fell, and was kicked several times before he could drag himself back to his feet and lurch forward again. The sun was coming up in front of them, a hard, red disk in a sickly yellow sky, and to Bruckman it seemed to be a glazed and lidless eye staring dispassionately into the world to watch them flail and struggle and die, like the eye of a scientist peering into a laboratory maze.

He watched the disk of the sun as he stumbled toward it; it seemed to bob and shimmer with every painful step, expanding, swelling, and bloating until it swallowed the sky. . . .

Then he was picking up a rock, moaning with the effort, feeling the rough stone tear his hands. . . .

Reality began to slide away from Bruckman. There were long periods when the world was blank, and he would come slowly back to himself as if from a great distance, and hear his own voice speaking words that he could not understand, or keening mindlessly, or grunting in a hoarse, animalistic way, and he would find that his body was working mechanically, stooping and lifting and carrying, all without volition. . . .

A Musselmänn, Bruckman thought, I'm becoming a Musselmänn . . . and felt a chill of fear sweep through him. He fought to hold onto the world, afraid that the next time he slipped away from himself he would not come back, deliberately banging his hands into the rocks, cutting himself, clearing his head with pain.

The world steadied around him. A guard shouted a hoarse admonishment at him and slapped his rifle butt, and Bruckman forced himself to work faster, although he could not keep himself from weeping silently with the pain his movements cost him.

He discovered that Wernecke was watching him, and stared back defiantly, the bitter tears still runneling his dirty cheeks, thinking, I *won't become a Musselmänn for you, I won't make it easy for you, I won't provide another helpless victim for you.* . . . Wernecke met Bruckman's gaze for a moment, and then shrugged and turned away.

Bruckman bent for another stone, feeling the muscles in his back crack and the pain drive in like knives. What had Wernecke been thinking behind the blankness of his expressionless face? Had

Wernecke, sensing weakness, marked Bruckman for his next victim? Had Wernecke been disappointed or dismayed by the strength of Bruckman's will to survive? Would Wernecke now settle upon someone else?

The morning passed, and Bruckman grew feverish again. He could feel the fever in his face, making his eyes feel sandy and hot, pulling the skin taut over his cheekbones, and he wondered how long he could manage to stay on his feet. To falter, to grow weak and insensible, was certain death; if the Nazis didn't kill him, Wernecke would. . . . Wernecke was out of sight now, on the other side of the quarry, but it seemed to Bruckman that Wernecke's hard and flinty eyes were everywhere, floating in the air around him, looking out momentarily from the back of a Nazi soldier's head, watching him from the dulled iron side of a quarry cart, peering at him from a dozen different angles. He bent ponderously for another rock, and when he had pried it up from the earth he found Wernecke's eyes beneath it, staring unblinkingly up at him from the damp and pallid soil. . . .

That afternoon there were great flashes of light on the eastern horizon out across the endless, flat expanse of the steppe, flares in rapid sequence that lit up the sullen, gray sky, all without sound. The Nazi guards had gathered in a group, looking to the east and talking in subdued voices, ignoring the prisoners for the moment. For the first time Bruckman noticed how disheveled and unshaven the guards had become in the last few days, as though they had given up, as though they no longer cared. Their faces were strained and tight, and more than one of them seemed to be fascinated by the leaping fires on the distant edge of the world.

Melnick said that it was only a thunderstorm, but old Bohme said that it was an artillery battle being fought, and that that meant the Russians were coming, that soon they would all be liberated.

Bohme grew so excited at the thought that he began shouting, "The Russians! It's the Russians! The Russians are coming to free us!" Dichstein, another one of the new prisoners, and Melnick tried to hush him, but Bohme continued to caper and shout— doing a grotesque kind of jig while he yelled and flapped his arms—until he had attracted the attention of the guards. Infuriated, two of the guards fell upon Bohme and beat him severely, striking him with their rifle butts with more than usual force, knocking him to the ground, continuing to flail at him and kick him while he was down, Bohme writhing like an injured worm under their stamping boots. They probably would have beaten

Bohme to death on the spot, but Wernecke organized a distraction among some of the other prisoners, and when the guards moved away to deal with it, Wernecke helped Bohme to stand up and hobble away to the other side of the quarry, where the rest of the prisoners shielded him from sight with their bodies as best they could for the rest of the afternoon.

Something about the way Wernecke urged Bohme to his feet and helped him to limp and lurch away, something about the protective, possessive curve of Wernecke's arm around Bohme's shoulders, told Bruckman that Wernecke had selected his next victim.

That night Bruckman vomited up the meager and rancid meal that they were allowed, his stomach convulsing uncontrollably after the first few bites. Trembling with hunger and exhaustion and fever, he leaned against the wall and watched as Wernecke fussed over Bohme, nursing him as a man might nurse a sick child, talking gently to him, wiping away some of the blood that still oozed from the corner of Bohme's mouth, coaxing Bohme to drink a few sips of soup, finally arranging that Bohme should stretch out on the floor away from the sleeping platforms, where he would not be jostled by the others. . . .

As soon as the interior lights went out that night, Bruckman got up, crossed the floor quickly and unhesitantly, and lay down in the shadows near the spot where Bohme muttered and twitched and groaned.

Shivering, Bruckman lay in the darkness, the strong smell of the earth in his nostrils, waiting for Wernecke to come. . . .

In Bruckman's hand, held close to his chest, was a spoon that had been sharpened to a jagged needle point, a spoon he had stolen and begun to sharpen while he was still in a civilian prison in Cologne, so long ago that he almost couldn't remember, scraping it back and forth against the stone wall of his cell every night for hours, managing to keep it hidden on his person during the nightmarish ride in the sweltering boxcar, the first few terrible days at the camp, telling no one about it, not even Wernecke during the months when he'd thought of Wernecke as a kind of saint, keeping it hidden long after the possibility of escape had become too remote even to fantasize about, retaining it then more as a tangible link with the daydream country of his past than as a tool he ever actually hoped to employ, cherishing it almost as a holy relic, as a remnant of a vanished world that he otherwise might almost believe had never existed at all. . . .

And now that it was time to use it at last, he was almost reluctant to do so, to soil it with another man's blood. . . .

He fingered the spoon compulsively, turning it over and over; it was hard and smooth and cold, and he clenched it as tightly as he could, trying to ignore the fine tremoring of his hands.

He had to kill Wernecke. . . .

Nausea and an odd feeling of panic flashed through Bruckman at the thought, but there was no other choice, there was no other way. . . . He couldn't go on like this, his strength was failing; Wernecke was killing him, as surely as he had killed the others, just by keeping him from sleeping. . . . And as long as Wernecke lived, he would never be safe: always there would be the chance that Wernecke would come for him, that Wernecke would strike as soon as his guard was down. . . . Would Wernecke scruple for a second to kill him, after all, if he thought that he could do it safely? . . . No, of course not. . . . Given the chance, Wernecke would kill him without a moment's further thought. . . . No he must strike *first*. . . .

Bruckman licked his lips uneasily. Tonight. He had to kill Wernecke *tonight*. . . .

There was a stirring, a rustling: Someone was getting up, working his way free from the mass of sleepers on one of the platforms. A shadowy figure crossed the room toward Bruckman, and Bruckman tensed, reflexively running his thumb along the jagged end of the spoon, readying himself to rise, to strike—but at the last second, the figure veered aside and stumbled toward another corner. There was a sound like rain drumming on cloth; the man swayed there for a moment, mumbling, and then slowly returned to his pallet, dragging his feet, as if he had pissed his very life away against the wall. It was not Wernecke.

Bruckman eased himself back down to the floor, his heart seeming to shake his wasted body back and forth with the force of its beating. His hand was damp with sweat. He wiped it against his tattered pants, and then clutched the spoon again. . . .

Time seemed to stop. Bruckman waited, stretched out along the hard floorboards, the raw wood rasping his skin, dust clogging his mouth and nose, feeling as though he were already dead, a corpse laid out in the rough pine coffin, feeling eternity pile up on his chest like heavy clots of wet, black earth. . . . Outside the hut, the kliegs blazed, banishing night, abolishing it, but here inside the hut it was night, here night survived, perhaps the only pocket of night remaining on a klieg-lit planet, the shafts of light that came in through the slatted windows only serving to accentuate the surrounding darkness, to make it greater and more puissant by comparison. . . . Here in the darkness, nothing ever changed . . . there was only the smothering heat, and the weight of eternal darkness, and the changeless moments that could not pass because there was nothing to differentiate them one from the other. . . .

Many times as he waited Bruckman's eyes would grow heavy and slowly close, but each time his eyes would spring open again at once, and he would find himself staring into the shadows for Wernecke. Sleep would no longer have him, it was a kingdom closed to him now; it spat him out each time he tried to enter it, just as his stomach now spat out the food he placed in it. . . .

The thought of food brought Bruckman to a sharper awareness, and there in the darkness he huddled around his hunger, momentarily forgetting everything else. Never had he been so hungry. . . . He thought of the food he had wasted earlier in the evening, and only the last few shreds of his self-control kept him from moaning aloud.

Bohme did moan aloud then, as though unease were contagious. As Bruckman glanced at him, Bohme said, "Anya," in a clear, calm voice; he mumbled a little, and then, a bit more loudly, said, "Tseitel, have you set the table yet?" and Bruckman realized that Bohme was no longer in the camp, that Bohme was back in Dusseldorf in the tiny apartment with his fat wife and his four healthy children, and Bruckman felt a pang of envy go through him, for Bohme, who had escaped.

It was at that moment that Bruckman realized that Wernecke was standing there, just beyond Bohme.

There had been no movement that Bruckman had seen. Wernecke had seemed to slowly materialize from the darkness, atom by atom, bit by incremental bit, until at some point he had been solid enough for his presence to register on Bruckman's consciousness, so that what had been only a shadow a moment before was now unmistakably Wernecke as well, however much a shadow it remained.

Bruckman's mouth went dry with terror, and it almost seemed that he could hear the voice of his dead grandmother whispering in his ears. Boogey tales . . . Wernecke had said *I'm no night spirit.* Remember that he had said that. . . .

Wernecke was almost close enough to touch. He was staring down at Bohme; his face, lit by a dusty shaft of light from the window, was cold and remote, only the total lack of expression hinting at the passion that strained and quivered behind the mask. Slowly, lingeringly, Wernecke stooped over Bohme. "Anya," Bohme said again, caressingly, and then Wernecke's mouth was on his throat.

Let him feed, said a cold, remorseless voice in Bruckman's mind. It will be easier to take him when he's nearly sated, when he's fully preoccupied and growing lethargic and logy . . . growing *full*. . . .

Slowly, with infinite caution, Bruckman gathered himself to spring, watching in horror and fascination as Wernecke fed. He could hear Wernecke sucking the juice out of Bohme, as if there were not enough blood in the foolish old man to satiate him, as if there were not enough blood in the whole camp . . . or perhaps, the whole world. . . . And now Bohme was ceasing his feeble struggling, was becoming still. . . .

Bruckman flung himself upon Wernecke, stabbing him twice in the back before his weight bowled them both over. There was a moment of confusion as they rolled and struggled together, all without sound, and then Bruckman found himself sitting atop Wernecke, Wernecke's white face turned up to him. Bruckman drove his weapon into Wernecke again, the shock of the blow jarring Bruckman's arm to the shoulder. Wernecke made no outcry; his eyes were already glazing, but they looked at Bruckman with recognition, with cold anger, with bitter irony and, oddly, with what might have been resignation or relief, with what might almost have been pity. . . .

Bruckman stabbed again and again, driving the blows home with hysterical strength, panting, rocking atop his victim, feeling Wernecke's blood spatter against his face, wrapped in the heat and steam that rose from Wernecke's torn-open body like a smothering black cloud, coughing and choking on it for a moment, feeling the steam seep in through his pores and sink deep into the marrow of his bones, feeling the world seem to pulse and shimmer and change around him, as though he were suddenly seeing through new eyes, as though something had been born anew inside him, and then abruptly he was *smelling* Wernecke's blood, the hot, organic reek of it, leaning closer to drink in that sudden overpowering smell, better than the smell of freshly baked bread, better than anything he could remember, rich and heady and strong beyond imagining.

There was a moment of revulsion and horror, and he tried to wonder how long the ancient contamination had been passing from man to man to man, how far into the past the chain of lives stretched, how Wernecke himself had been trapped, and then his parched lips touched wetness, and he was drinking, drinking deeply and greedily, and his mouth was filled with the strong, clean taste of copper.

The following night, after Bruckman led the memorial prayers for Wernecke and Bohme, Melnick came to him. Melnick's eyes were bright with tears. "How can we go on without Eduard? He was everything to us. What will we do now? . . ."

"It will be all right, Moishe," Bruckman said. "I promise you, everything will be all right." He put his arm around Melnick for a moment to comfort him, and at the touch sensed the hot blood that pumped through the intricate network of the boy's veins, just under the skin, rich and warm and nourishing, waiting there inviolate for him to set it free.

Introduction
Life in the Air

Barry N. Malzberg

"Life in the Air," based upon a single line in Cynthia Ozick's famous "Levitation" ('all the Jews were in the air') floats above its basic, terrible point while pretending that it isn't about Jews. Don't believe a word of it.

Jack Dann

I don't remember whether Barry or I came up with the idea for this story, but the image of two people becoming weightless as their relationship and marriage is breaking down fascinated me. It's as if the sadness, separation, and dislocation of marital discord could confound gravity itself.

As our protagonist Stephen says, "It must be a metaphor."

The story was published in the April 1992 issue of the resurrected *Amazing Stories*.

Life in the Air

Barry N. Malzberg and Jack Dann

STEPHEN AND LAURA FOUND THEMSELVES SLOWLY
rising into the air, levitating though the oppressive spaces of
their rent-controlled apartment with the slow and terrible precision
of swimmers, as their marriage came apart over that long and difficult summer.

"It must be a metaphor," Stephen would say to his dark-haired,
twenty-eight-year-old wife, as he did slow turns and circles in the
air, as he placed palms against the ceiling, reversing himself and
kicking toward the bedroom. But Laura would confront him, con-
cealing her anger in condescension, and explain that this was life
itself, that there was nothing more, that there had never been
anything more, except perhaps dreams.

Life itself: Outside their apartment, Laura and Stephen felt themselves more rooted to the pavement than ever before. It was as if
gravity was the illness, and heavy and jointless they would plod
their way through the various events of their day. Laura was a
psychological social worker at the state office, and Stephen was a
veterinarian, which one might think would give him a few ideas
about how to deal with flight. He had tended all manner of birds,
from toucans and macaws to hawks and doves and Leadbeater
cockatoos, and had often given tetracycline to budgerigar lovebirds

burning with fever, for his specialty was winged things. But he had no prescription for his own marriage, which was as dry and dead as an abandoned nest. It was his fault. It was her fault. He couldn't guess how it had deteriorated. They were just being carried along; it was the natural course of things, he supposed. After sex had begun to dry up, they were left with the uncomfortable realization that what they had was small talk. Now neither had anything to say to the other about their jobs, their goals and frustrations and feelings. Just as they had become feather-light inside the confines of their apartment, so had everything of import become a burden. It had become impossible to talk of matters of gravity in their weightless world.

During that poisoned summer their focus seemed to narrow. The colors and spaces of the day were only something through which to move until they could get back to the apartment. There they would eat Stouffers frozen dinners that had floated steaming in the microwave oven, and then they would hurl insults at one another as they dove through archways and flew in circles over their antique sleigh bed. Laura would accuse him of being just like his faithless sister, who was now a military dependent in Thailand. His sister had told him at their last painful meeting, over their father's grave, that he would never amount to anything. "You're shallow and unfeeling," she had said. "You can't deal with people, so you deal with cats and birds." He had said very little to her in response, a family tradition. Most of what he had wanted to say to his parents and sister, he had said to Laura in the first six years of their marriage. She had become a receptacle for his poison.

In the seventh year they began to levitate.

Now they needed to sleep in loose ropes of sheets, or risk the stunning wedge of ceiling that would welcome them to light at six in the morning.

First it had been the ashtrays, then the toothbrushes and silverware and bric-a-brac such as the crystal paperweights and Lalique china pieces; even the graphics and watercolors had lifted away from the walls and hung suspended in the air. The rising of smaller objects was like a warning, for shortly thereafter Stephen slowly tore free of the limitations of gravity, Stephen before Laura, for he had always been the leader in the relationship; she had never had a chance to set the conditions. As they floated around the apartment, the inanimate objects, the utensils and ashtrays and paintings, settled back down, regained their proper weight, as if in compensation. It was

only the occasional spoon or steak or matchbook that would lift
into the air, as if they had a mind to break the unspoken rules.

The more difficult the marriage became, the more Stephen and
Laura floated free. Now they weren't even able to touch carpet or
linoleum for a few minutes to regain perspective and balance. They
were like two astronauts in housedress and pajamas. But their arguments had lately gone so far out of control that Stephen contem-
plated flinging himself over the windowsill. He dreamed that he
would float gracefully from the twelfth floor to the concrete of
Amsterdam Avenue, but he had never done this, not once. Some
elemental caution, some core of what he called sanity, but what
was probably only fear, had kept him locked inside the apartment.
During the short but inevitable times of lesser strain, they would
caution each other on making public their circumstance. They
could both agree on something: that their dark and difficult lives
had to be worked out within the reaches of the apartment or not be
worked out at all. There were no middle grounds here, no careful
compromises with flight, no way in which he and Laura could exist
in gravity outside and levitation within; there would have to be
some reckoning within and without, and yet, somehow, poised for
decision as he might have been, Stephen found himself existing in
two ways: floating within, graven and grounded without. A choice
would have to be made, but he was unable to make it. He could
only see himself in this simultaneity . . . this trap.

And the arguments continued, but they were all somehow the
same argument, yet the core of their hatred and frustrations was so
deeply buried that it could not be found. Instead, Stephen and
Laura argued about misplaced combs and brushes, errands forgotten, overcharged bank cards, the inequality of the relationship,
Stephen's predilection for waitresses and shopgirls, Laura's puritan
sexual attitudes and morbid fear and loathing of all household pets.
They both had a vague recognition that a hidden subtext weaved
their many arguments together, but neither one could disarm, lest
they be vulnerable to the other. All that was left was argument and
familiar ritual, which in its way was another correlative of Laura's
maxim that *this* was life itself.

But, oh, if his devoted old ladies, who lived for their cats and
ribboned dogs, if her dangerous youths and food-stamp Epicureans
had been able to glimpse them in that apartment that summer! he
thought. They were such figures of authority. Then why couldn't
they keep their feet on the floor? Why couldn't they walk from bed
to refrigerator or toilet without taking off like helium balloons on a

Fourth of July field day? Why couldn't they bump up against one another in the dark without that sudden and shocking speeding away? It was a rich and dangerous, a dark and provocative time, and yet Stephen knew that when he thought back on this summer, as he surely, surely would, he would remember only the fatigue and panic of finding himself tangling in the sheets at dawn, strangling in the sheets, bobbing against the ceiling.

Their sex was as furtive and bounded as their movement otherwise was free. They had had to work out an intricate arrangement of restraints in order to couple. But Stephen was not much interested in sex, anyway. He had rationalized that what he called "the rigmarole" had made him dysfunctional, and he gave it up with a sense of relief; for sex had always been an effort for him anyway, and he had been looking for an excuse to quit ever since she suggested and then demanded mutual satisfaction. He just didn't have the patience, and he felt like a sexual Sisyphus straining against a cold, unyielding rock during those infrequent times when he tried to bring her to orgasm.

"You never desired me," Laura would say to him. "You were only interested in waitresses and girls on the street. And that's all right because now I'm not interested any more. I don't want to make love with you. I don't even want to *live* with you any more. I'd be out of here in a second, except for the rents and the fact that I was here first."

That was true. Stephen had moved in with her, and then they had gotten married. But although Stephen could fly through their apartment like any canary or finch or conure or cockatoo or his beloved budgerigars, he couldn't stabilize himself long enough to pack up and move out. Nor did he have the heart to leave.

Around and around that apartment they flew during that tortured summer, swimmers in space, Icarus in the dust and steaming Amsterdam Avenue air. As their screaming confrontations grew ever longer, their proficiency in flight became complete, so that as they moved toward something climactic, Stephen realized that the emotional abyss and the Icarian idea were the same thing.

But he did not know if he had the strength to confront them.

Asleep, Stephen is wrenched against a wall while Laura hangs just below the ceiling. Each dreams the other, but they cannot connect, cannot touch. In his fever dream, Stephen speeds out the bedroom window into the acrid, polluted night air, but it is like perfume to him as at last he commits himself to freedom and dreams and the impossible. He arcs through the ebony bowl of sky and then suddenly plunges into a New York dawn grown enormous; he passes through its rainbow thermoclines and speeds toward the Seacaucus Flats, the imagined freedom of New Jersey. While Stephen flies, Laura groans in her sleep, for she dreams that Stephen has left her, that he has gone. But she dreams that in his flight is her fall, and in that knowledge she finds herself cresting to some enormous height and function of her own; she dreams that if she were to open her eyes and emerge from this gasping, asphyxiating sleep, she would find at last what she so desperately needed . . . but so emerging, so waking, finds herself locked to herself on the bed, limbs drawn in. The apartment is empty at last. In the darkness, only the numbers of the silent digital clock glow malignantly.

But with simultaneous dread and hope, she strains to hear, and she discerns the sound of Stephen screaming in the distance, screaming all the way to sudden declination. Screaming all the way to the dull boom of impact.

Slowly she expands with knowledge, even as she is rooted with grief. Fly no more?

Laura can hardly breathe.

And Stephen is not at all.

Introduction

Afternoon at Schrafft's

Michael Swanwick

It was a clear, starry night and Jack Dann came breezing into town at the wheel of a limousine twenty feet long, with a big cigar stuck in one corner of his expansive grin. . . This time, though, he actually—and you have no idea how rare an event this was—came to my house for dinner. Because Jack's a serious cook, Marianne invented a new dish in his honor, a boned and roasted chicken stuffed with eggplant, peppers, and onion, that's served up at the table whole and then sliced like a loaf of bread. Metaphysically Referential Chicken, she named it, but that's another story and if you get me started we'll be here all night.

After dinner, happily stuffed and slightly vinous, we gathered in the library to talk. The memory of how well "Touring" had worked out was fresh in my mind, so I suggested we collaborate on another story.

"We don't have an idea for another story," said spoilsport Dozois.

"My idea is that it should be very short," I said with drunken cunning, "because we've all had a lot to drink and we don't have long attention spans." Then I jokingly suggested that since Gardner and Jack had earlier in the day been discussing three theme anthologies—one on dinosaurs, another on wizards, and a third on cats—we should build something around all three elements so we could sell the reprint rights to each one.

This was good enough for Jack. He decided we had to set the story in Schrafft's (why? because he'd always wanted to set a story in Schrafft's) and plonked the wizard and his cat down at a table there. We began riffing dialogue back and forth.

Gardner tried to stay out of it. He disapproved of the entire enterprise . . . it was way too low-art for him. But he couldn't resist correcting us whenever we started going off in the wrong direction, and from there it was a very short fall in grace to being a full collaborator. Our voices rose in a spiral to the sky, throwing out ideas, talking over each other, hooting with laughter.

All this happened a quarter-century ago, in the long-lost Lyonesse of my youth. Now Jack's living in Australia, a major literary lion and the author of big, best-selling novels. I hear he has a ranch there. I hear he's happy, too. But, oh man, do I miss those long-ago evenings when we had the excess time to sit around a bottle of wine, flinging ideas in the air and batting them around.

Making stone soup.

Gardner Dozois

This may have been the most cynically conceived of all the collaborations, arising not out of anything that any of us had been thinking about writing anyway, but, as Michael relates, artificially induced as a result of Michael's Cunning Plan to get us to write a story about cats, wizards, and dinosaurs that could potentially be sold to all three of the reprint anthologies that Jack and I were putting together at the time. That the Cunning Plan actually worked is a testimony not only to Michael the Silver-Tongued Devil and his persistence and persuasiveness, but to the really mammoth amounts of wine we'd put away that evening.

Oddly, considering its utterly cynical and calculating origins, it somehow came out as a rather sweet story. Kids like it, although our attempt to sell it as a children's book failed dismally.

Michael took first draft here, then Jack took a pass at it, and then I did my usual unifying draft, adding detail and texture, like the contents of the wizard's purse, trying to punch up the humor, and adding some of the comic Yiddish shtick dialog (which everybody usually assumes that *Jack* puts in). All of the cabalistic lore was put in by Jack, and, since it's all gibberish to *me*, I have no idea if it's used correctly or not—that was his department, and we left him to it.

It's a pleasant read, with, of course, no great depth to it, although the relationship between the wizard and the cat is nicely handled, and more complicated in subtle ways than it looks on the surface. The story has a nice Bradburyesque quality to it, although it would be probably closer to the truth, as far as my sections are concerned, to say Thurberesque. Jack's sections have more of an Isaac Bashevis Singer quality to them. So, as I once said, it's as if Thurber and Isaac Bashevis Singer got *really* drunk one afternoon and decided to write a story—the result would be sort of like "Afternoon at Schrafft's." They probably wouldn't have put a dinosaur in it, though.

Jack Dann

Well, of *course* we put a dinosaur in the story. It had become rather a shtick with us: when in doubt, drop in a dinosaur. (See our story "A Change In the Weather.")

Gardner is absolutely right; this story was an exercise in crass, commercial, cynical opportunism fueled by the alcohol content of some very good California wine. Michael was the pulsing engine of opportunism on this story. We had spent a lovely evening at Michael and Marianne's home. The food was delightful, the wine smooth, the conversation champagne itself. In other words three members of The Fiction Factory were having one helova good time and getting considerably shit-faced into the bargain. Whether Michael had worked out his cynical idea hours—or days—earlier, or whether it was simply one of those wickedly glorious inspirations of the moment, Michael was determined to co-opt, corrupt, and degrade our sensitive literary aesthetics.

I was, of course, the first to fall from grace. Yes, it initially sounded like a stupid idea, and I didn't believe for one moment that we were going to make thousands and thousands of dollars on this story; but I just couldn't help myself: the image of a cat and a wizard sitting around in a Schrafft's restaurant in New York City suddenly blossomed in my mind. (I really don't know why I wanted to set a story in Schrafft's; I think my grandmother had talked about the restaurant when I was a child.) Anyway, one thing led to another, and, completely against my will and better judgment, I found myself describing how the first scene of the story should go; and from there, it didn't take long for Gardner to take a deep breath, shake his head, and say something to the effect, "No, that won't work, Jack, what you'd need to do is . . ."

And we were off and running once again.

I remember that we passed the story back and forth over the next few weeks, and that Gardner and Michael turned it into a technical tour de force. I worked up the first scene, wrote a few other scenes, and did the Jewish shtick and the magical incantations. I think I might have researched all the magic bits. Research has always been a bad habit of mine. After all, I'm one of the few people to actually possess a copy of *A True & Faithful RELATION OF What paffed for many Yeers Between Dr. JOHN DEE (A Mathematician of Great Fame in Q. Eliz. and King James their Reignes) and SOME SPIRITS: Tending (had it Succeeded) To a General Alteration of moft STATES and KINGDOMES in the World*.

I should also mention that we only reprinted "Afternoon At Schrafft's" in *one* of our anthologies (*Magicats*).

We *do* have standards!

Afternoon at Schrafft's

Gardner Dozois, Jack Dann, and
Michael Swanwick

T HE WIZARD SAT ALONE AT A TABLE IN SCHRAFFT'S, eating a tuna sandwich on rye. He finished off the last bite of his sandwich, sat back, and licked a spot of mayonnaise off his thumb. There was an ozone crackle in the air, and his familiar, a large brindle cat, materialized in the chair opposite him.

The cat coldly eyed the wizard's empty plate. "And where, may I ask, is my share?" he demanded.

The wizard coughed in embarrassment.

"You mean you didn't even leave me a crumb, is that it?"

The wizard shrugged and looked uncomfortable. "There's still a pickle left," he suggested.

The cat was not mollified.

"Or some chips. Have some potato chips."

"Feh," sneered the cat. "Potato chips I didn't want. What I *wanted* was a piece of your sandwich, Mister Inconsiderate."

"Listen, aggravation I don't need from you. Don't make such a big deal—it's only a *tuna fish sandwich*. So who cares!"

"So who *cares?*" the cat spat. "So *I* care, that's who. Listen, it's not just the sandwich. It's everything! It's your *attitude.*"

"Don't talk to *me* about *my* attitude—"

"Somebody should. You think you're *so* hot. Mister Big Deal!

The Big-Time Wizard!" The cat sneered at him. "Hah! You need me more than I need you, believe me, Mister Oh-I'm-So-Wonderful!"

"Don't make me laugh," the wizard said.

"You couldn't get along without me, and you know it!"

"I'm laughing," the wizard said. "It's such a funny joke you're making, look at me, I'm laughing. Hah. Hah. Hah."

The cat fluffed itself up, enraged. "Without me, you couldn't even get through the day. What an ingrate! You refuse to admit just how much you really need me. Why, without me, you couldn't even—" the cat paused, casting about for an example, and his gaze fell on the check "—without me, you couldn't even pay the *check*."

"Oh yeah?"

"Yeah. Even something as simple as *that*, you couldn't do it by yourself. You couldn't handle it."

"*Sure* I could. Don't get too big for your britches. Stuff like this I was handling before *you* were even weaned, bubbie, let *alone* housebroken. So don't puff yourself up."

The cat sneered at him again. "Okay, so go ahead! Show me! Do it!"

"Do what?" said the wizard after a pause, a trace of uneasiness coming into his voice.

"Pay the check. Take care of it yourself."

"All right," the wizard said. "All right, then, I will!"

"So go ahead, already. I'm watching. This ought to be good." The cat smiled nastily and faded away, slowly disappearing line by line—the Cheshire cat was one of his heroes, and this was a favorite trick, although for originality's sake he left his nose behind instead of his grin. The nose hung inscrutably in midair, like a small, black rubber UFO. Occasionally it would give a sardonic twitch.

The wizard sighed and sat staring morosely down at the check. Then, knowing in advance that it would be useless, he pulled out his battered, old change-purse and peered inside: nothing, except for some lint, the tiny, polished skull of a bat, and a ticket stub from the 1876 Centennial Exposition. The wizard never carried money —ordinarily, he'd have just told the cat to conjure up whatever funds were necessary, an exercise so simple and trivial that it was beneath his dignity as a Mage even to consider bothering with it himself. That was what familiars were *for*, to have tasks like that delegated to them. Now, though . . .

"Well?" the cat's voice drawled. "So, I'm waiting. . . ."

"All right, all right, big shot," the wizard said. "I can handle this, don't worry yourself."

"I'm not worried—I'm *waiting*."

"All right, already." Mumbling to himself, the wizard began to work out the elements of the spell. It was a very *small* magic, after all. Still . . . He hesitated, drumming his fingers on the table. . . . Still, he hadn't had to do anything like this for himself for years, and his memory wasn't what it used to be. . . . Better ease his hand in slowly, try a still smaller magic first. Practice. Let's see now . . . He muttered a few words in a hissing, sibilant tongue, sketched a close pattern in the air, and then rested his forefinger on the rim of his empty coffee cup. The cup filled with coffee, as though his finger was a spigot. He grunted in satisfaction, and then took a sip of his coffee. It was weak and yellow, and tasted faintly of turpentine. So far, so good, he thought. . . .

Across the table, the nose sniffed disdainfully.

The wizard ignored it. *Now* for the real thing. He loosened his tie and white, starched collar and drew the pentagram of harmony, the *Sephiroth*, using salt from the shaker, which was also the secret symbol for the fifth element of the pentagram, the *akasha*, or ether. He made do with a glass of water, catsup, mustard, and toothpicks to represent the four elements and the worlds of Emanation, Creation, Formation, and Action. He felt cheap and vulgar using such substitutes, but what else could he do?

Now . . . he thought, that *is* the pentagram of harmony . . . isn't it? For an instant he was uncertain. Well, it's close enough. . . .

He tugged back his cuffs, leaving his wrists free to make the proper passes over the pentagram. Now . . . what was the spell to make money? It was either the first or the second Enochian Key . . . *that* much he did remember. It must be the second Key, and that went . . . *"Piamoel od Vaoan!"* No, no, that wasn't it. Was it *"Giras ta nazodapesad Roray I?"* That *must* be it.

The wizard said the words and softly clapped his hands together . . . and nothing seemed to happen.

For an instant there was no noise, not even a breath. It was as if he were hovering, disembodied, between the worlds of emanation.

There was a slow shift in his equilibrium, like a wheel revolving ponderously in darkness.

But magic didn't just disappear, he told himself querulously—it had to go *somewhere*.

As if from the other side of the world, the wizard heard the soft voice of his familiar, so faint and far away that he could barely make it out. What was it saying?

"Putz," the cat whispered, "you used the Pentagram of Chaos, the *Qliphoth*."

And suddenly, as if he really had been turned upside down for a while, the wizard felt everything right itself. He was sitting at a table in Schrafft's, and there was the usual din of people talking and shouting and pushing and complaining.

But something was odd, something was wrong. Even as he watched, the table splintered and flew to flinders before him, and his chair creaked and groaned and swayed like a high-masted ship in a strong wind, and then broke, dumping him heavily to the floor. The room shook, and the floor cracked and starred beneath him.

What was wrong? What ethers and spheres had he roiled and foiled with his misspoken magicking? Why did he feel so *strange?* Then he saw himself in the gold-flecked smoked-glass mirrors that lined the room between rococo plaster pillars, and the reflection told him the terrible truth.

He had turned himself into some kind of giant lizard. A dinosaur. Actually, as dinosaurs go, he was rather small. He weighed about eight hundred pounds and was eleven feet long—a pachycephalosaurus, a horn-headed, pig-snouted herbivore that was in its prime in the Upper Cretaceous. But for Schrafft's, at lunchtime— big enough. He clicked his stubby tusks and tried to say "Gevalt!" as he shook his head ruefully. Before he could stop the motion, his head smashed into the wooden booth partition, causing it to shudder and crack.

Across from him, two eyes appeared, floating to either side of the hovering black nose. Slowly, solemnly, one eye winked. Then —slowly and very sinisterly—eyes and nose faded away and were gone.

That was a bad sign, the wizard thought. He huddled glumly against the wall. Maybe nobody would notice, he thought. His tail twitched nervously, splintering the booth behind him. The occupants of the booth leaped up, screaming, and fled the restaurant in terror. Out-of-towners, the wizard thought. Everyone else was eating and talking as usual, paying no attention, although the waiter *was* eyeing him somewhat sourly.

As he maneuvered clumsily away from the wall, pieces of wood crunching underfoot, the waiter came up to him and stood there making little *tsk*ing noises of disapproval. "Look, mister," the waiter said. "You're going to have to pay up and go. You're creating a disturbance. . . ." The wizard opened his mouth to utter a mild remonstrance, but what came out instead was a thunderous, roaring belch, grindingly deep and loud enough to rattle your bones; the sort of noise that might be produced by having someone stand on the bass keys of a giant Wurlitzer. Even the wizard could smell the fermenting rotting-egg, bubbling-prehistoric-swamp stink of sulfur that his belch had released, and he winced in embarrassment. "I'm sorry," the wizard said, enunciating with difficulty through the huge, sloppy mouth. "It's the tuna fish. I know I shouldn't eat it, it always gives me gas, but—" But the waiter no longer seemed to be listening—he had gone pale, and now he turned abruptly around without a word and walked away, ignoring as he passed the querulous demands for coffee refills from the people two tables away, marching in a straight line through the restaurant and right out into the street.

The wizard sighed, a gusty, twanging noise like a cello being squeezed flat in a winepress. Time—and *past* time—to work an obviation spell. So, then. Forgetting that he was a dinosaur, the wizard hurriedly tried to redraw the pentagram, but he couldn't pick up the salt, which was in a small pile around the broken glass shaker. And everything else he would need for the spell was buried under the debris of the table.

"Not doing so hot now, Mister Big Shot, are you?" a voice said, rather smugly.

"All right, all right, give me a minute, will you?" said the wizard, a difficult thing to say when your voice croaks like a gigantic frog's—it was hard to be a dinosaur and talk. But the wizard still had his pride. "You don't make soup in a second," he said. Then he began thinking feverishly. He didn't really *need* the elements and representations of the four worlds and the pentagram of cabalistic squares, not for an obviation spell, although, of course, things would be much more elegant *with* them. But. He *could* work the obviation spell by words alone—*if* he could remember the words. He needed something from the Eighteenth Path, that which connects *Binah* and *Geburah*, the House of Influence. Let's see, he thought. "*E pluribus unum.*" No, no. . . . Could it be "*Micaoli beranusaji UK?*" No, that was a pharmacological spell. . . . But, yes, of *course*, this was it, and he began to chant "*Tstske, tstskeleh, tchotchike, tchotchkeleh, trayf, Qu-a-a-on!*"

That should do it.

But nothing happened. Again! The wizard tried to frown, but hadn't the face for it. "Nothing happened," he complained.

The cat's head materialized in midair. "That's what *you* think. As a matter of fact, all the quiches at Maxim's just turned into frogs. Great big ones," he added maliciously. "Great big, green, *slimy* ones."

The wizard dipped his great head humbly. "All right," he grumbled. "Enough is enough, I give up. I admit defeat. I was wrong. From now on, I promise, I'll save you a bite of every sandwich I ever order."

The cat appeared fully for a moment, swishing its tail thoughtfully back and forth. "You do know, don't you, that I prefer the part in the middle, without the crust . . . ?"

"I'll never give you the crust, always from the middle—"

The waiter had come back into the restaurant, towing a policeman behind him, and was now pointing an indignant finger toward the wizard. The policeman began to slouch slowly toward them, looking bored and sullen and mean.

"I mean, it's not really the sandwich, you know," the cat said.

"I know, I know," the wizard mumbled.

"I get insecure too, like everyone else. I need to know that I'm wanted. It's the *thought* that counts, knowing that you're thinking about me, that you want me around—"

"All right, all right!" the wizard snapped irritably. Then he sighed again, and (with what would have been a gesture of final surrender if he'd had hands to spread) said, "So, okay, I want you around." He softened and said almost shyly, "I *do*, you know."

"I know," the cat said. They stared at each other with affection for a moment, and then the cat said, "For making money, it's the new moon blessing, *"Steyohn, v's-keyahlahnough—"*

"Money I don't need anymore," the wizard said grumpily. "Money it's gone beyond. Straighten out all of *this*—" gesturing with his piglike snout at his—feh!—scaly, green body.

"Not to worry. The *proper* obviation spell is that one you worked out during the Council of Trent, remember?"

The cat hissed out the words. Once again the wheel rotated slowly in darkness.

And then the wizard was sitting on the floor, in possession of his own spindly limbs again. Arthritically, he levered himself to his feet.

The cat watched him get up, saying smugly, "And as a bonus, I even put money in your purse, not bad, huh? I told—" And then the cat fell silent, staring off beyond the wizard's shoulder. The wizard looked around.

Everyone else in Schrafft's had turned into dinosaurs.

All around them were dinosaurs, dinosaurs in every possible variety, dinosaurs great and small, four-footed and two-footed, horned and scaled and armor-plated, striped and speckled and piebald, all busily eating lunch, hissing and grunting and belching and slurping, huge jaws chewing noisily, great fangs flashing and clashing, razor-sharp talons clicking on tile. The din was horrendous. The policeman had turned into some sort of giant spiky armadillo, and was contentedly munching up the baseboard. In one corner, two nattily pinstriped allosaurs were fighting over the check, tearing huge, bloody pieces out of each other. It was impossible to recognize the waiter.

The cat stared at the wizard.

The wizard stared at the cat.

The cat shrugged.

After a moment, the wizard shrugged too.

They both sighed.

"Lunch tomorrow?" the wizard asked, and the cat said, "Suits me."

Behind them, one of the triceratops finished off its second egg cream and made a rattling noise with the straw.

The wizard left the money for the check near the cash register, and added a substantial tip.

They went out of the restaurant together, out into the watery city sunshine, and strolled away down the busy street through the fine, mild air of spring.

Introduction

The Clowns

Susan Casper

Writing a story with Jack Dann and Gardner Dozois was, in some ways, both the hardest and easiest thing I'd ever done. The hardest because Jack was a good friend and Gardner my husband. Both were long time professionals, while I was a novice writer. I wanted my work to be good, to be worthy of the prose and ideas they would contribute. While this made it harder for me, it also in some ways made it easier, knowing that I wouldn't be allowed to get away with bad work and that any ideas and writing I contributed would be vetted by those two before it was ever seen by the public. They surprised me by accepting my ideas and my contributions, even when I found it necessary to overwrite what they had done, or make small changes in the plot as we had outlined it. I never felt uncomfortable in turning my work over to one of them when I found myself unable to continue, or in picking it up again when it was given back to me. It was a true learning experience and one a neophyte writer doesn't often get.

As a confidence builder it was a first-rate experience. It started with the telling of an experience that Gardner had. Jack liked the idea and ran with it, building a plot and somehow roping me into it. Since Gardner had planned on writing this story himself, he certainly wasn't going to let us get away with putting it together without him, and so it became a three-way collaboration, going back and forth between us until it was finished. Then Gardner gave the whole thing a smoothing draft, adding a patina of single-writer prose that unified it as a whole.

After some negotiation (the story was too long and had to be shortened) we sold the piece to *Playboy* magazine, which not only embarrassed my parents by forcing them to buy a copy of a "girlie magazine," but allowed me to truthfully tell my friends and co-workers that I had gotten my picture in *Playboy*. (I never mentioned that it was in the contributor section.)

Gardner Dozois

Susan's story-note pretty much tells the tale here. We were sitting around in our living room, just having come back from an expedition to the ice-cream parlor across the street, and Jack and Susan were talking about how *they* ought to collaborate on a story, as Jack and Michael and I were all doing at the time in various combinations. (In addition to the stories collected in this book, there were also stories written during this period of intense collaboration by me and Michael, me and Susan, me and Jack C. Haldeman . . . while Jack later went on to collaborate with Barry Malzberg, George Zebrowski, Jack Haldeman, Janeen Webb, Jeanne Van Buren, and Gregory Frost, and Michael collaborated with Wllliam Gibson, and later with Jack on his own. It was something in the air, I guess. Something that in some ways has *remained* in the air, or at least returned again, since I've recently finished stories started twenty years before, during the old Quince St. Apartrment collaborating days, with Michael Swanwick—"Ancestral Voices," "The City of God"—and with George R. R. Martin and Daniel Abraham—"Shadow Twin." There are only a few unfinished stories with Jack left from those days, and, if we live long enough, we may get around to finishing them too. Waste not, want not.)

With the idea that Jack and Susan should collaborate in the air, we then went on to have one of those conversations about Weird Stuff that friends occasionally have (the kind where someone eventually starts humming the *Twilight Zone* theme in the background), and during this conversation, I mentioned a conversation I'd had in the East Village in 1970 or early 1971, with this guy who'd told me—with total conviction and a weird traced calm, as though he'd accepted that he was doomed—that he was being followed around everywhere he went by sinisterly smiling clowns that no one else could see: about how he'd been alone in his apartment, and had gone into the bathroom, and found a clown in there, sitting on the toilet and silently grinning at him . . . how they followed him wherever he went, how he'd be riding on his motorcycle and feel cold arms close around his waist, and look behind him, and see a clown there, clutching him around the waist, grinning at him. . . .

Jack immediately took fire. "Wow! What a great idea for a story! Susan, that can be the story that you and I write together!" And before I knew what was happening, they were plotting out the story together, and then Jack was sitting down at the typewriter and writing it—they were writing *my* story, one I'd intended to write for more than a decade, on *my* typewriter with *my* paper, and they hadn't even asked me to work on it with them! I sulked about this for a day, and then declared myself in on the collaboration in self-defense; I was damned if I wasn't going to get *any* mileage out of this material I'd been carrying around in my head since the early '70s!

My memory is that Jack wrote a version of the opening swimming-pool scene, and that Susan then wrote much of the rest of the story, certainly all the scenes with David and his parents (whose dialog she seemed to have a better feel for than either of the rest of us), and then I went back and did a fairly heavy unifying rewrite, adding new scenes interstitially and working on the pacing of the existing scenes to increase the feeling of suspense I wanted them to have, then working intensively on the ending. As usual with my own stuff, although Susan was strongly in agreement with this, I wanted it to be ambiguous in the reader's mind at the end whether this was "really" happening, whether there "really were" sinister supernatural clowns following David around, or whether the whole thing is in his mind as he experiences a psychotic break/psychological meltdown. I tried to set it up so there's no way you can tell at the end which interpretation of the story is "correct," something I've enjoyed doing throughout my career—which is no doubt one reason why I bestride the Bestseller list like a colossus.

The story sold to *Playboy*, the first market we submitted it to.

Jack Dann

I suppose it wasn't really very nice of me to grab Gardner's idea. I can only attribute it to youthful greed and exuberance; but I can still clearly remember the shock and shudder I felt when Gardner told us about the guy who saw clowns. It was the image of a man sitting on the toilet and seeing a demented clown appear out of nowhere that did it for me. I couldn't help myself. I had to some-how get that image or something like it down on paper; and as Gardner and Susan related earlier, Susan caught fire with the idea, too, while, unseen by us (who were now completely preoccupied with plotting out our newly stolen story), Gardner was doing a slow burn.

Once Gardner dealt himself into the project, *his* project, I had completed my preliminary work; and, once again, it was time to sneak away back to Binghamton.

One of my contributions to this story was the setting, as I imme-diately saw it taking place in the small towns of Johnson City and Binghamton where I grew up. Most of the small town descriptions are real; I spent my youth swimming at the C. Fred Johnson Municipal Pool, which is featured in the story. "Clowns" was a very smooth collaboration, and Susan did indeed have exactly the right feel for the young protagonist and the dialogue. We discussed how ambiguous we wanted this story to be, and, as I remember, the consensus was to set it up so the clowns could be read as "real," or as psychological manifestations.

I saw the story as a psychological thriller, but whichever way you read it, the idea of demented, dangerous clowns—archetypical creatures from the Id—seems to be more than little disturbing.

That damned clown in the toilet certainly scared the hell out of *me*!

The Clowns

Gardner Dozois, Jack Dann, and Susan Casper

THE C. FRED JOHNSON MUNICIPAL POOL WAS PACKED with swimmers, more in spite of the blazing sun and wet, muggy heat than because of them.

It was the dead middle of August, stiflingly hot, and it would have made more sense to stay inside—or, at the very least, in the shade—than to splash around in the murky, tepid water. Nevertheless, the pool was crowded almost shoulder to shoulder, especially with kids—there were children everywhere, the younger ones splashing and shouting in the shallow end, the older kids and the teenagers jumping off the high dive or playing water polo in the deep end. Mothers sat in groups and chatted, their skins glistening with suntan oil and sweat. The temperature was well above 90, and the air seemed to shimmer with the heat, like automobile exhaust in a traffic jam.

David Shore twisted his wet bath towel and snapped it at his friend Sammy, hitting him on the sun-reddened backs of his thighs.

"Ow!" Sammy screamed. "You dork! Cut it out!" David grinned and snapped the towel at Sammy again, hitting only air this time but producing a satisfyingly loud *crack*. Sammy jumped back, shouting, "Cut it out! I'll tell! I'll *tell!* I mean it."

Sammy's voice was whining and petulant, and David felt a

spasm of annoyance. Sammy was his friend, and he didn't have so many friends that he wasn't grateful for that, but Sammy was *always* whining. What a baby! That's what he got for hanging out with little kids — Sammy was eight, two years younger than David — but since the trouble he'd had last fall, with his parents almost breaking up and he himself having to go for counseling, he'd been ostracized by many of the kids his own age. David's face darkened for a moment, but then he sighed and shook his head. Sammy was all right, really. A good kid. He really shouldn't tease him so much, play so many jokes on him. David smiled wryly. Maybe he did it just to hear him *whine* —

"Don't be such a baby," David said tiredly, wrapping the towel around his hand. "It's only a *towel*, dickface. It's not gonna kill you if—" Then David stopped abruptly, staring blankly off beyond Sammy, toward the bathhouse.

"It *hurt*," Sammy whined. "You're a real dork, you know that, Davie? How come you have to—" And then Sammy paused, too, aware that David wasn't paying any attention to him anymore. "Davie?" he said. "What's the matter?"

"Look at *that*," David said in an awed whisper.

Sammy turned around. After a moment, confused, he asked, "Look at what?"

"There!" David said, pointing toward a sun-bleached wooden rocking chair.

"*Oh*, no, you're not going to get *me* again with *that* old line," Sammy said disgustedly. His face twisted, and this time he looked as if he were really getting mad. "The wind's making that chair rock. It can rock for hours if the wind's right. You can't scare me that easy! I'm not a *baby*, you know!"

David was puzzled. Couldn't Sammy *see?* What was he— blind? It was as plain as anything. . . .

There was a clown sitting in the chair, sitting and rocking, watching the kids in the swimming pool.

The clown's face was caked with thick, white paint. He had a bulb nose that was painted blood red, the same color as his broad, painted-on smile. His eyes were like chips of blue ice. He sat very still, except for the slight movement of his legs needed to rock the beat-up, old chair, and his eyes never left the darting figures in the water.

David had seen clowns before, of course; he'd seen plenty of them at the Veterans' Arena in Binghamton when the Barnum & Bailey Circus came to town. Sammy's father was a barber and

always got good tickets to everything, and Sammy always took
David with him. But this clown was *different*, somehow. For one
thing, instead of performing, instead of dancing around or cake-
walking or somersaulting or squirting people with a Seltzer bottle,
this clown was just sitting quietly by the pool, as if it were the most
normal thing in the world for him to be there. And there was something else, too, he realized. *This* clown was all in black. Even his
big polka-dotted bow tie was black, shiny black dots against a
lighter gray-black. Only his gloves were white, and they were a
pure, eye-dazzling white. The contrast was startling.

"Sammy?" David said quietly. "Listen, this is important. You
really think that chair is empty?"

"Jeez, grow *up*, will ya?" Sammy snarled. "What a dork!" He
turned his back disgustedly on David and dived into the pool.

David stared thoughtfully at the clown. Was Sammy trying to
kid him? Turn the tables on him, get back at him for some of
his old jokes? But David was sure that Sammy wasn't smart enough
to pull it off. Sammy *always* gave himself away, usually by giggling.

Odd as it seemed, Sammy really *didn't* see the clown.

David looked around to see who else he could ask. Certainly
not Mr. Kreiger, who had a big potbelly and wore his round,
wire-rimmed glasses even in the water and who would stand for
hours in the shallow end of the pool and splash himself with one
arm, like an old bull elephant splashing water over itself with its
trunk. No. Who else? Bobby Little, Jimmy Seikes, and Andy Free-
man were taking turns diving and cannon-balling from the low
board, but David didn't want to ask *them* anything. That left only
Jas Ritter, the pool lifeguard, or the stuck-up Weaver sisters.

But David was beginning to realize that he didn't really *have* to
ask anybody. Freddy Schumaker and Jane Gelbert had just walked
right by the old rocking chair, without looking at the clown, without even glancing at him. Bill Dwyer was muscling himself over
the edge of the pool within inches of the clown's floppy, oblong
shoes, and he wasn't paying any attention to him, either. That just
wasn't possible. No matter how supercool they liked to pretend
they were, there was no *way* that kids were going to walk past a
clown without even *glancing* at him.

With a sudden thrill, David took the next logical step. Nobody
could see the clown except *him*. Maybe he was the only one in the
world who could see him!

It was an exhilarating thought. David stared at the clown in
awe. Nobody else could see him! Maybe he was a *ghost*, the ghost

of an old circus clown, doomed to roam the Earth forever, seeking out kids like the ones he'd performed for when he was alive, sitting in the sun and watching them play, thinking about the happy days when the circus had played this town.

That was a *wonderful* idea, a lush and romantic idea, and David shivered and hugged himself, feeling goose flesh sweep across his skin. He could see a *ghost!* It was wonderful! It was magic! Private, secret magic, his alone. It meant that he was *special.* It gave him a strange, secret kind of power. Maybe nobody else in the *universe* could see him—

It was at this point that Sammy slammed into him, laughing and shouting, "I'll learn *you*, sucker!" and knocked him into the pool.

By the time David broke the surface, sputtering and shaking water out of his eyes, the clown was gone and the old rocker was rocking by itself, in the wind and the thin, empty sunshine.

After leaving the pool, David and Sammy walked over the viaduct —there was no sign of any freight trains on the weed-overgrown tracks below—and took back-alley short cuts to Curtmeister's barbershop.

"Hang on a minute," Sammy said and ducked into the shop. Ordinarily, David would have followed, as Sammy's father kept gum and salt-water taffy in a basket on top of the magazine rack, but today he leaned back against the plate-glass window, thinking about the ghost he'd seen that morning, *his* ghost, watching as the red and blue stripes ran eternally up and around the barber pole. How fascinated he'd been by that pole a few years ago, and how simple it seemed to him now.

A clown turned the corner from Avenue B, jaywalking casually across Main Street.

David started and pushed himself upright. The ghost again! Or was it? Surely, *this* clown was shorter and squatter than the one he'd seen at the pool, though it was wearing the same kind of black costume, the same kind of white gloves. Could this be *another* ghost? Maybe there was a whole *circus*ful of clown ghosts wandering around the city.

"David!" a voice called, and he jumped. It was old Mrs. Zabriski, carrying two bulging, brown-paper grocery bags, working her way ponderously down the sidewalk toward him, puffing and wheezing, like some old, slow tugboat doggedly chugging toward its berth. "Want to earn a buck, David?" she called.

The clown had stopped right in the middle of Main Street, standing nonchalantly astride the double white divider line. David watched him in fascination.

"David?" Mrs. Zabriski said impatiently.

Reluctantly, David turned his attention back to Mrs. Zabriski. "Gosh, I'm sorry, Mrs. Z.," he said. A buck would be nice, but it was more important to keep an eye on the clown. "I—ah, I promised Sammy that I'd wait out here for him."

Mrs. Zabriski sighed. "Okay, David," she said. "Another time, then." She looked across the street to see what he was staring at, looked back puzzledly. "Are you all right, David?"

"Yeah. Honest, Mrs. Z.," he said, without looking around. "Really. I'm fine."

She sighed again with doughy fatalism. And then she started across the street, headed directly for the clown.

It was obvious to David that *she* didn't see him. He was standing right in front of her, grimacing and waving his arms and making faces at her, but she didn't even slow down—she would have walked right into him if he hadn't ducked out of the way at the last moment. After she passed, the clown minced along behind her for a few steps, doing a cruel but funny imitation of her ponderous, waddling walk, pretending to spank her on her big, fat rump.

David stifled a laugh. This was better than the circus! But now the clown seemed to have grown bored with mocking Mrs. Zabriski and began drifting slowly away toward the far side of Main Street.

David wanted to follow, but he suddenly realized, with a funny little chill, that he didn't want to do it alone. Even if it was the ghost of a clown, a funny and entertaining ghost, it was still a *ghost*, after all. Somehow, he'd have to get Sammy to come with him. But how could he explain to Sammy what they were doing? Not that it would matter if Sammy didn't come out of the shop soon—the clown was already a block away.

Anxiously, he peered in through the window until he managed to catch Sammy's attention, then waved to him urgently. Sammy held up his index finger and continued his conversation with his father. "Hurry up, dummy," David muttered under his breath. The clown was getting farther and farther away, almost out of sight now. Hurry up. David danced impatiently from one foot to the other. Hurry *up*.

But when Sammy finally came running out of the barbershop with the news that he'd talked his father into treating them both to a movie, the clown was gone.

*   *   *

By the time they got to the movie theater, David had pretty much gotten over the disappointment of losing the clown. At least it was a pretty good show—cartoons and a space-monster movie. There was a long line in front of the ticket window, a big crowd of kids—and even a few adults—waiting to get into the movie.

They were waiting in the tail of the line when the clown—or *a* clown—appeared again across the street.

"Hey, Davie!" Sammy said abruptly. "Do you see what *I* see?" And Sammy waved to the clown.

David was startled—and somewhat dismayed—by the strength of the surge of disappointment and jealousy that shot through him. If *Sammy* could see them, too, then David wasn't *special* anymore. The whole thing was ruined.

Then David realized that it wasn't the clown that Sammy was waving to.

He was waving to the old man who was waiting to cross the street, standing just in *front* of the clown. Old Mr. Thorne. He was at least a million years old, David knew. He'd played for the Boston Braves back before they'd even had *television*, for cripes' sake. But he loved children and treated them with uncondescend-ing courtesy and in turn was one of the few adults who were really respected by the kids. He was in charge of the yo-yo contests held in the park every summer, and he could make a yo-yo sleep or do around the world or over the falls or walking the dog better than anyone David had ever seen, including the guy who sold the golden yo-yos for the Duncan company.

Relieved, David joined Sammy in waving to his old friend, almost—but not quite—forgetting the clown for a moment. Mr. Thorne waved back but motioned for them to wait where they were. It was exciting to see the old man again. It would be worth missing the movie if Mr. Thorne was in the mood to buy them chocolate malteds and reminisce about the days when he'd hit a home run off the immortal Grover Cleveland Alexander.

Just as the traffic light turned yellow, an old flatbed truck with a dented fender came careening through the intersection.

David felt his heart lurch with sudden fear—But it was all right. Mr. Thorne saw the truck coming, he was still on the curb, he was safe. But then the clown stepped up close behind him. He grabbed Mr. Thorne by the shoulders. David could see Mr. Thorne jerk in surprise as he felt the white-gloved hands close over him. Mr. Thorne's mouth opened in surprise, his hands came fluttering weakly up, like startled birds. David could see the clown's painted face grinning over the top of Mr. Thorne's head. That wide, unchanging, painted-on smile.

Then the clown threw Mr. Thorne in front of the truck.

There was a sickening wet *thud,* a sound like that of a sledge-hammer hitting a side of beef. The shriek of brakes, the squeal of flaying tires. A brief, unnatural silence. Then a man said, "Jesus Christ!" in a soft, reverent whisper. A heartbeat later, a woman started to scream.

Then everyone was shouting, screaming, babbling in a dozen confused voices, running forward. The truck driver was climbing down from the cab, his face stricken; his mouth worked in a way that might have been funny in other circumstances, opening and closing, opening and closing—then he began to cry.

All you could see of Mr. Thorne was one arm sticking out from under the truck's rear wheels at an odd angle, like the arm of a broken doll.

A crowd was gathering now, and between loud exclamations of horror, everyone was already theorizing about what had happened: Maybe the old man had had a heart attack; maybe he'd just slipped and fallen; maybe he'd tripped over something. A man had thrown his arm around the shoulders of the bitterly sobbing truck driver; people were kneeling and peering gingerly under the truck; women were crying; little kids were shrieking and running frenziedly in all directions. Next to David, Sammy was crying and cursing at the same time, in a high and hysterical voice.

Only David was not moving.

He stood as if frozen in ice, staring at the clown.

All unnoticed, standing alone behind the ever-growing crowd, the clown was laughing.

Laughing silently, in unheard spasms that shook his shoulders and made his bulb nose jiggle. Laughing without sound, with his mouth wide-open, bending forward to slap his knees in glee, tears of pleasure running down his painted cheeks.

Laughing.

David felt his face flame. Contradictory emotions whipped through him: fear, dismay, rage, horror, disbelief, guilt. Guilt. . . .

The fucking clown was *laughing*—

All at once, David began to run, motionless one moment and running flat-out the next, as if suddenly propelled from a sling. He could taste the salty wetness of his own tears. He tried to fight his way through the thickening crowd, to get by them and *at* the clown. He kept bumping into people, spinning away, sobbing and cursing, then slamming into someone *else*. Someone cursed him. Someone else grabbed him and held him, making sympathetic, soothing noises—it was Mr. Gratini, the music teacher, thinking that David was trying to reach Mr. Thorne's body.

Meanwhile, the clown had stopped laughing. As if suddenly remembering another appointment, he turned brusquely and strode away.

"David, wait, there's nothing you can do. . . ." Mr. Gratini was saying, but David squirmed wildly, tore himself free, ran on.

By the time David had fought his way through the rest of the crowd, the clown was already a good distance down Willow Street, past the bakery and the engraving company with the silver sign in its second-story window.

The clown was walking faster now, was almost out of sight. Panting and sobbing, David ran after him.

He followed the clown through the alleys behind the shoe factories, over the hump of railroad tracks, under the arch of the cement viaduct that was covered with spray-painted graffiti. The viaduct was dark, its pavement strewn with candy wrappers and used condoms and cigarette butts. It was cool inside and smelled of dampness and cinders.

But on the other side of the viaduct, he realized that he'd lost the clown again. Perhaps he had crossed the field . . . though, surely, David would have seen him do that. He could be anywhere; this was an old section of town, and streets and avenues branched off in all directions.

David kept searching, but he was getting tired. He was breathing funny, sort of like having the hiccups. He felt sweaty and dirty and exhausted. He wanted to go home.

What would he have done if he'd *caught* the clown?

All at once, he felt cold.

There was nobody around, seemingly for miles—the streets were as deserted as those of a ghost town. Nobody around, no one to help him if he were attacked, no one to hear him if he cried for help.

The silence was thick and dusty and smothering. Scraps of paper blew by with the wind. The sun shimmered from the empty sidewalks.

David's mouth went dry. The hair rose bristlingly on his arms and legs.

The clown suddenly rounded the corner just ahead, coming swiftly toward him with a strange, duck-walking gait.

David screamed and took a quick step backward. He stumbled and lost his balance. For what seemed like an eternity, he teetered precariously, windmilling his arms. Then he crashed to the ground.

The fall hurt and knocked the breath out of him, but David almost didn't notice the pain. From the instant he'd hit the pavement, the one thought in his head had been, *Had he given himself away?* Did the clown now *realize* that David could *see* him?

Quickly, he sat up, clutching his hands around his knee and rocking back and forth as if absorbed in pain. He found that he had no difficulty making himself cry, and cry loudly, though he didn't feel the tears the way he had before. He carefully did not turn his head to look at the clown, though he did sneak a sidelong peek out of the corner of his eye.

The clown had stopped a few yards away and was watching him—standing motionlessly and *staring* at him, fixedly, unblinkingly, with total concentration, like some great, black, sullen bird of prey.

David hugged his skinned knee and made himself cry louder. There was a possibility that he hadn't given himself away—that the clown would think he'd yelled like that *because* he'd tripped and fallen down and not because he'd seen him come dancing around the corner. The two things had happened closely enough together that the clown *might* think that. Please, God, let him think that. Let him believe it.

The clown was still watching him.

Stiffly, David got up. Still not looking at the clown, he made himself lean over and brush off his pants. Although his mouth was still as dry as dust, he moistened his lips and forced himself to swear, swear out loud, blistering the air with every curse word he could think of, as though he were upset about the ragged hole torn in his new blue jeans and the blood on his knee.

He kept slapping at his pants a moment longer, still bent over, wondering if he should suddenly break and run now that he was on his feet again, make a flat-out dash for freedom. But the clowns were so *fast*. And even if he *did* escape, then they would *know* that he could see them.

Compressing his lips into a hard, thin line, David straightened up and began to walk directly toward the clown.

Closer and closer. He could sense the clown looming enormously in front of him, the cold, blue eyes still staring suspiciously at him. Don't look at the clown! Keep walking casually and *don't look at him*. David's spine was as stiff as if it were made of metal, and his head ached with the effort of not looking. He picked a spot on the sidewalk and stared at it, thrust his hands into his pockets with elaborate casualness and somehow forced his legs to keep walking. Closer. Now he was close enough to be grabbed, if the clown wanted to grab him. He was right next to him, barely an arm's length away. He could *smell* the clown now—a strong smell of greasepaint, underlaid with a strange, musty, earthen smell, like old, wet leaves, like damp, old wallpaper. He was suddenly *cold*, as cold as ice; it was all he could do to keep from shaking with the cold. Keep going. Take one more step. Then one more. . . .

As he passed the clown, he caught sight of an abrupt motion out of the corner of his eye. With all the will he could summon, he forced himself not to flinch or look back. He kept walking, feeling a cold spot in the middle of his back, *knowing* somehow that the clown was still staring at him, staring after him. *Don't* speed up. Just keep walking. Papers rustled in the gutter behind him. Was there a clown walking through them? Coming up behind him? About to *grab* him? He kept walking, all the while waiting for the clown to *get* him, for those strong, cold hands to close over his shoulders, the way they had closed over the shoulders of old Mr. Thorne.

He walked all the way home without once looking up or looking around him, and it wasn't until he had gotten inside, with the door locked firmly behind him, that he began to tremble.

David had gone upstairs without eating dinner. His father had started to yell about that—he was strict about meals—but his mother had intervened, taking his father aside to whisper something about "trauma" to him—both of them inadvertently shooting him that uneasy, walleyed look they sometimes gave him now, as if they weren't sure he mightn't suddenly start drooling and gibbering if they said the wrong thing to him, as if he had something they might catch—and his father had subsided, grumbling.

Upstairs, he sat quietly for a long time, thinking hard.

The clowns. Had they just come to town or had they always been there and he just hadn't been able to *see* them before? He remembered when Mikey had broken his collarbone two summers ago, and when Sarah's brother had been killed in the motorcycle accident, and when that railroad yardman had been hit by the freight train. Were the clowns responsible for those accidents, too?

He didn't know. There was one thing he *did* know, though:

Something had to be done about the clowns.

He was the only one who could see them.

Therefore, *he* had to do something about them.

He was the only one who could see them, the only one who could *warn* people. If he didn't do anything and the clowns hurt somebody else, then *he'd* be to blame. Somehow, he *had* to stop them.

How?

David sagged in his chair, overwhelmed by the immensity of the problem. *How?*

The doorbell rang.

David could hear an indistinct voice downstairs, mumbling something, and then hear his mother's voice, clearer, saying, "I don't know if Davie really feels very much like having company right now, Sammy."

Sammy—

David scooted halfway down the stairs and yelled, "Ma! No, Ma, it's okay! Send him up!" He went on down to the second-floor landing, saw Sammy's face peeking tentatively up the stairs and motioned for Sammy to follow him up to his room.

David's room was at the top of the tall, narrow old house, right next to the small room that his father sometimes used as an office. There were old magic posters on the walls—Thurston, Houdini, Blackstone: King of Magicians—a Duran Duran poster behind the bed and a skeleton mobile of a Tyrannosaurus hanging from the overhead lamp. He ushered Sammy in wordlessly, then flopped down on top of the *Star Wars* spread that he'd finally persuaded his mother to buy for him. Sammy pulled out the chair to David's desk and began to fiddle abstractedly with the pieces of David's half-assembled Bell X 15 model kit. There were new, dark hollows under Sammy's eyes and his face looked strained. Neither boy spoke.

"Mommy didn't want to let me out," Sammy said after a while, sweeping the model pieces aside with his hand. "I told her I'd feel better if I could come over and talk to you. It's really weird about Mr. Thorne, isn't it? I can't believe it, the way that truck *smushed* him, like a tube of tooth paste or something." Sammy grimaced and put his arms around his legs, clasping his hands together tightly, rocking back and forth nervously. "I just can't believe he's gone."

David felt the tears start and blinked them back. Crying wouldn't help. He looked speculatively at Sammy. He certainly couldn't tell his *parents* about the clowns. Since his "nervous collapse" last fall, they were already afraid that he was a nut.

"Sammy," he said. "I have to tell you something. Something important. But first you have to *promise* not to tell anybody. No matter what, no matter how crazy it sounds, you've got to promise!"

"Yeah?" Sammy said tentatively.

"No—first you've got to promise."

"Okay, I *promise*," Sammy said, a trace of anger creeping into his voice.

"Remember this afternoon at the swimming pool, when I pointed at that rocking chair, and you thought I was pulling a joke on you? Well, I *wasn't*. I did see somebody sitting there. I saw a clown."

Sammy looked disgusted. "I see a clown right now," he grated.

"Honest, Sammy, I *did* see a clown. A clown, all made up and in costume, just like at the circus. And it was a clown—the same one, I think—who pushed Mr. Thorne in front of that truck."

Sammy just looked down at his knees. His face reddened.

"I'm not lying about this, I swear. I'm telling the truth this time; honest, Sammy, I really am—"

Sammy made a strange noise, and David suddenly realized that he was *crying*.

David started to ask him what the matter was, but before he could speak, Sammy had rounded fiercely on him, blazing. "You're nuts! You *are* a loony, just like everybody says! No wonder nobody will play with you. Loony! Fucking *loony!*"

Sammy was screaming now, the muscles in his neck cording. David shrank away from him, his face going ashen.

They stared at each other. Sammy was panting like a dog, and tears were running down his cheeks.

"Everything's . . . some kind of . . . *joke* to you, isn't it?" Sammy panted. "Mr. Thorne was my *friend*. But you . . . you don't care about *anybody!*" He was screaming again on the last word. Then he whirled and ran out of the room.

David followed him, but, by the time he was halfway down the stairs, Sammy was already out the front door, slamming it shut behind him.

"What was *that* all about?" David's mother asked.

"Nothing," David said dully. He was staring through the screened-in door, watching Sammy run down the sidewalk. Should he chase him? But all at once it seemed as if he were too tired to move; he leaned listlessly against the doorjamb and watched Sammy disappear from sight. Sammy had left the gate of their white picket fence unlatched, and it swung back and forth in the wind, making a hollow, slamming sound.

How could he make anyone else believe him if he couldn't even convince *Sammy?* There was nobody left to tell.

David had a sudden, bitter vision of just how lonely the rest of the summer was going to be without even Sammy to play with. Just him, all by himself, all summer long.

Just him . . . and the clowns.

David heard his parents talking as he made his way down to breakfast the next morning and paused just outside the kitchen archway to listen.

"Was the strangest thing," his mother was saying.

"What was?" David's father grumbled. He was hunched over his morning coffee, glowering at it, as if daring it to cool off before he got around to drinking it. Mr. Shore was often grouchy in the morning, though things weren't as bad anymore as they'd been last fall, when his parents had often screamed obscenities at each other across the breakfast table—not as bad as that one terrible morning, the morning David didn't even want to think about, when his father had punched his mother in the face and knocked two of her teeth out, because the eggs were runny. David's mother kept telling him that his father was under a lot of "stress" because of his new job—he used to sell computers, but now he was a stockbroker trainee. "What was?" David's father repeated irritably, having gotten no reply.

"Oh, I don't know," David's mother said. "It's just that I was thinking about that poor old woman all night. I just can't get her out of my mind. You know, she kept swearing somebody pushed her."

"For Christ's sake!" David's father snapped. "Nobody *pushed* her. She's just getting senile. She had heavy bags to carry and all those stairs to climb, that's all." He broke off, having spotted David in the archway. "David, don't *skulk* like that. You know I hate a sneak. In or out!"

David came slowly forward. His mouth had gone dry again and he had to moisten his lips to be able to speak. "What—what were you talking about? Did something happen? Who got hurt?"

"Marty!" David's mother said sharply, glancing quickly and significantly at David, frowning, shaking her head.

"Damn it, Anna," David's father grumbled. "Do you really think that the kid's gonna curl up and die if he finds out that Mrs.

Zabriski fell down a flight of stairs? What the hell does he care?"

"*Marty!*"

"He doesn't even know her, except to say hello to, for Christ's sake! Accidents happen all the time; he might just as well get used to that—"

David was staring at them. His face had gone white. "Mrs. Zabriski?" he whispered. "Is—is she *dead?*"

His mother gave her husband a now-look-what-you've-done glare and moved quickly to put an arm around David's shoulder. "No, honey," she said soothingly, in that nervous, almost *too* sympathetic voice she used on him now whenever she thought he was under stress. "She's going to be okay. Just a broken leg and a few bruises. She fell down the stairs yesterday on her way back from the grocery store. Those stairs are awfully steep for a woman her age. She tripped, that's all."

David bit his lip. Somehow, he managed to blink back sudden, bitter tears. *His* fault! If he'd carried her bags for her, like she'd wanted him to, like she'd *asked* him to, then she'd have been all right; the clown wouldn't have gotten her.

For Mrs. Zabriski hadn't tripped. He knew that.

She'd been *pushed.*

By the time David got to Sammy's house, there was no one home. Too late! His father had reluctantly let David off the hook about eating breakfast—the very thought of eating made him ill—but had insisted in his I'm-going-to-brook-no-more-nonsense voice, the one he used just before he started hitting, that David wash the breakfast dishes, and that had slowed him up just enough. He'd hoped to catch Sammy before he left for the pool, try to talk to him again, try to get him to at least agree to keep quiet about the clowns.

He made one stop, in the Religious Book Store and Reading Room on Main Street, and bought something with some of the money from his allowance. Then, slowly and reluctantly, trying to ignore the fear that was building inside him, he walked to the swimming pool.

Sammy was already in the water when David arrived.

The pool was crowded, as usual. David waved halfheartedly to Jas, who was sitting in the high-legged lifeguard's chair. Jas waved back uninterestedly; he was surveying his domain through aluminum sunglasses, his nose smeared with zinc oxide to keep it from burning.

And—yes—the clown was there! Way in the back, near the refreshment stand. Lounging quietly against a wall and watching the people in the pool.

David felt his heart start hammering. Moving slowly and—he hoped—inconspicuously, he began to edge through the crowd toward Sammy. The clown was still looking the other way. If only—

But then Sammy saw David. "Well, well, *well*," Sammy yelled, "if it isn't David Shore!" His voice was harsh and ugly, his face flushed and twisted. David had never seen him so bitter and upset. "Seen any more *clowns* lately, Davie?" There was real hatred in his voice. "Seen any more killer, invisible clowns, Davie? You loony! You fucking *loony!*"

David flinched, then tried to shush him.

People were looking around, attracted by the shrillness of Sammy's voice.

The clown was looking, too. David saw him look at Sammy, who was still waving his arms and shouting, and then slowly raise his head, trying to spot who Sammy was yelling at.

David ducked aside into the crowd, half squatting down, dodging behind a couple of bigger kids. He could *feel* the clown's gaze pass overhead, like a scythe made of ice and darkness. Shut up, Sammy, he thought desperately. Shut up. He squirmed behind another group of kids, bumping into somebody, heard someone swear at him.

"Da—vie!" Sammy was shouting in bitter mockery. "Where are all the clowns, Davie? You seen any clowning around here *today*, Davie? Huh, Davie?"

The clown was walking toward Sammy now, still scanning the crowd, his gaze relentless and bright.

Slowly, David pushed his way through the crowd, moving away from Sammy. Bobby and Andy were standing in line at the other end of the pool, waiting to jump off the board. David stepped up behind Andy, pretending to be waiting in line, even though he hated diving. Should he leave the pool? Run? That would only make it easier for the clown to spot him. But if he left, maybe Sammy would shut *up*.

"You're crazy, David Shore!" Sammy was yelling. He seemed on the verge of tears—he had been very close to Mr. Thorne. "You know that? You're fucking *crazy. Bats in the belfry*, Davie—"

The clown was standing on the edge of the pool, right above Sammy, staring down at him thoughtfully.

Then Sammy spotted David. His face went blank, as though with amazement, and he pointed his finger at him. "David! *There's a clown behind you!*"

Instinctively, knowing that it was a mistake even as his muscles moved but unable to stop himself, David whipped his head around and looked behind him. Nothing was there.

When he turned back, the clown was staring at him.

Their eyes met, and David felt a chill go through him, as if he had been pierced with ice.

Sammy was breaking up, hugging himself in glee and laughing, shrill, cawing laughter with a trace of hysteria in it. "Jeez-*us*, Davie!" he yelled. "You're just not playing with a full deck, are you, Davie? You're—"

The clown knelt by the side of the pool. Moving with studied deliberation, never taking his eyes off David, the clown reached out, seized Sammy by the shoulders—Sammy jerked in surprise, his mouth opening wide—and slowly and relentlessly forced him under the water.

"Sammy!" David screamed.

The clown was leaning out over the pool, eyes still on David, one arm thrust almost shoulder-deep into the water, holding Sammy under. The water thrashed and boiled around the clown's outthrust arm, but *Sammy wasn't coming back up*—

"Jason!" David shrieked, waving his arms to attract the lifeguard's attention and then pointing toward the churning patch of water. "Ja-*son!* Help! Help! Somebody's *drowning!*" Jason looked in the direction David was pointing, sat up with a start, began to scramble to his feet—

David didn't wait to see any more. He hit the water in a clumsy dive, almost a belly whopper, and began thrashing across the pool toward Sammy, swimming as strongly as he could. Half blinded by spray and by the wet hair in his eyes, half dazed by the sudden shock of cold water on his sun-baked body, he almost rammed his head into the far side of the pool, banging it with a wildly flailing hand instead. He recoiled, gasping. The clown was right above him now, only a few feet away. The clown turned his head to look at him, still holding Sammy under, and once again David found himself shaking with that deathly arctic cold. He kicked at the side wall of the pool, thrusting himself backward. Then he took a deep breath and went under.

The water was murky, but he was close enough to see Sammy. The clown's white-gloved hand was planted firmly on top of

Sammy's head, holding him under. Sammy's eyes were open, strained wide, bulging almost out of his head. Dreadfully, they seemed to see David, recognize him, appeal mutely to him. Sammy's hands were pawing futilely at the clown's arm, more and more weakly, slowing, running down like an unwound clock. Even as David reached him, Sammy's mouth opened and there was a silvery explosion of bubbles.

David grabbed the clown's arm. A shock went through him at the contact, and his hands went cold, the bitter cold spreading rapidly up his arms, as if he were grasping something that avidly sucked the heat from anything that touched it. David yanked at the clown's arm with his numbing, clumsy hands, trying to break his grip, but it was like yanking on a steel girder.

A big, white shape barreled by him like a porpoise, knocking him aside. Jas.

David floundered, kicked, broke the surface of the water. He shot up into the air like a Polaris missile, fell back, took a great racking breath, another. Sunlight on water dazzled his eyes, and everything was noise and confusion in the open air, baffling after the muffled underwater silence. He kicked his feet weakly, just enough to keep him afloat, and looked around.

Jas was hauling Sammy out of the pool, Sammy's eyes were still open, but now they looked like glass, like the blank, staring eyes of a stuffed animal; a stream of dirty water ran out of his slack mouth, down over his chin. Jas laid Sammy out by the pool edge, bent hurriedly over him, began to blow into his mouth and press on his chest. A crowd was gathering, calling out questions and advice, making little wordless noises of dismay.

The clown had retreated from the edge of the pool. He was standing some yards away now, watching Jas labor over Sammy.

Slowly, he turned his head and looked at David.

Their eyes met again, once again with that shock of terrible cold, and this time the full emotional impact of what that look implied struck home as well.

The clowns *knew* that he could see them.

The clowns knew who he *was*.

The clowns would be after *him* now.

Slowly, the clown began to walk toward David, his icy-blue eyes fixed on him.

Terror squeezed David like a giant's fist. For a second, everything went dark. He couldn't remember swimming back across to the other side of the pool, but the next thing he knew, there he was, hauling himself up the ladder, panting and dripping. A couple of kids were looking at him funny; no doubt he'd shot across the pool like a torpedo.

The clown was coming around the far end of the pool, not running but walking fast, still staring at David.

There were still crowds of people on this side of the pool, too, some of them paying no attention to the grisly tableau on the far side, most of them pressed together near the pool's edge, standing on tiptoe and craning their necks to get a better look.

David pushed his way through the crowd, worming and dodging and shoving, and the clown followed him, moving faster now. The clown seemed to flow like smoke around people without touching them, never stumbling or bumping into anyone even in the most densely packed part of the crowd, and he was catching up. David kept looking back, and each time he did, the widely smiling painted face was closer behind him, momentarily bobbing up over the sunburned shoulders of the crowd, weaving in and out. Coming relentlessly on, pressing *closer*, all the while never taking his eyes off him.

The crowd was thinning out. He'd never make it back around the end of the pool before the clown caught up with him. Could he possibly outrun the clown in the open? Panting, he tried to work his hand into the pocket of his sopping-wet jeans as he stumbled along. The wet cloth resisted, resisted, and then his hand was inside the pocket, his fingers touching metal, closing over the thing he'd bought at the store on his way over.

Much too afraid to feel silly or self-conscious, he whirled around and held up the crucifix, extended it at arm's length toward the clown.

The clown stopped.

They stared at each other for a long, long moment, long enough for the muscles in David's arm to start to tremble.

Then, silently, mouth open, the clown started to laugh.

It wasn't going to work—

The clown sprang at David, spreading his arms wide as he came.

It was like a wave of fire-shot darkness hurtling toward him, getting bigger and bigger, blotting out the world—

David screamed and threw himself aside.

The clown's hand swiped at him, hooked fingers grazing his chest like stone talons, tearing free. For a moment, David was enveloped in arctic cold and that strong, musty smell of dead leaves, and then he was rolling free, scrambling to his feet, *running*—

He tripped across a bicycle lying on the grass, scooped it up and jumped aboard it all in one motion, began to pedal furiously. Those icy hands clutched at him again from just a step behind. He felt his shirt rip; the bicycle skidded and fishtailed in the dirt for a second; and then the wheels bit the ground and he was away and picking up speed.

When he dared to risk a look back, the clown was staring after him, a look thoughtful, slow and icily intent.

David left the bicycle in a doorway a block from home and ran the rest of the way, trying to look in all directions at once. He trudged wearily up the front steps of his house and let himself in.

His parents were in the front room. They had been quarreling but broke off as David came into the house and stared at him. David's mother rose rapidly to her feet, saying, "David! Where *were* you? We were so worried! Jason told us what happened at the pool."

David stared back at them. "Sammy?" he heard himself saying, knowing it was stupid to ask even as he spoke the words but unable to keep himself from feeling a faint stab of hope. "Is Sammy gonna be all right?"

His parents exchanged looks.

David's mother opened her mouth and closed it again, hesitantly, but his father waved a hand at her, sat up straighter in his chair and said flatly, "Sammy's dead, David. They think he had some sort of seizure and drowned before they could pull him out. I'm sorry. But that's the way it is."

"Marty!" David's mother protested.

"It's part of life, Anna," his father said. "He's got to learn to face it. You can't keep him wrapped up in cotton wool, for Christ's sake!"

"It's all right," David said quietly. "I knew he *had* to be. I just thought maybe . . . somehow. . . ."

There was a silence, and they looked at each other through it. "At any rate," his father finally said, "we're proud of you, David. The lifeguard told us you tried to save Sammy. You did the best you could, did it like a man, and you should be proud of that." His voice was heavy and solemn. "You're going to be upset for a while, sure—that's only normal—but someday that fact's going to make you feel a lot better about all this, believe me."

David could feel his lips trembling, but he was determined not to cry. Summoning all his will to keep his voice steady, he said, "Mom . . . Dad . . . if I . . . *told* you something—something that was really *weird*—would you believe me and not think I was going nuts again?"

His parents gave him that uneasy, walleyed look again. His mother wet her lips, hesitantly began to speak, but his father cut her off. "Tell your tall tales later," he said harshly. "It's time for supper."

David sagged back against the door panels. They *did* think he was going nuts again, had probably been afraid of that ever since they heard he had run wildly away from the pool after Sammy drowned. He could *smell* the fear on them, a sudden bitter burnt reek, like scorched onions. His mother was still staring at him uneasily, her face pale, but his father was grating, "Come on, now, wash up for supper. Make it snappy!" He wasn't going to *let* David be nuts, David realized; he was going to *force* everything to be "normal," by the sheer power of his anger.

"I'm not hungry," David said hollowly. "I'd rather just lie down." He walked quickly by his parents, hearing his father start to yell, hearing his mother intervene, hearing them start to quarrel again behind him. He didn't seem to care anymore. He kept going, pulling himself upstairs, leaning his weight on the wrought-iron banister. He was bone-tired and his head throbbed.

In his room, he listlessly peeled off his sweat-stiff clothes. His head was swimming with the need to sleep, but he paused before turning down the bedspread, grimaced and shot an uneasy glance at the window. Slowly, he crossed the room. Moving in jerks and starts, as though against his will, he lifted the edge of the curtain and looked out.

There was a clown in the street below, standing with that terrible, motionless patience in front of the house, staring up at David's window.

David was not even surprised. Of *course* the clowns would be there. They'd heard Sammy call his name. They'd found him. They knew where he lived now.

What was he going to *do?* He couldn't stay inside all summer. Sooner or later, his parents would *make* him go out.

And then the clowns would *get* him.

David woke up with a start, his heart thudding.

He pushed himself up on one elbow, blinking in the darkness, still foggy and confused with sleep. What had happened? What had wakened him?

He glanced at the fold-up travel clock that used to be his dad's; it sat on the desk, its numbers glowing. Almost midnight.

Had there been a noise? There *had* been a noise, hadn't there? He could almost remember it.

He sat alone in the darkened room, still only half-awake, listening to the silence.

Everything was silent. Unnaturally silent. He listened for familiar sounds: the air conditioner swooshing on, the hot-water tank rumbling, the refrigerator humming, the cuckoo clock chiming in the living room. Sometimes he could hear those sounds when he awakened in the middle of the night. But he couldn't hear them now. The crickets weren't even chirruping outside, nor was there any sound of passing traffic. There was only the sound of David's own breathing, harsh and loud in his ears, as though he were underwater and breathing through scuba gear. Without knowing why, he felt the hair begin to rise on the back of his neck.

The clowns were in the house.

That hit him suddenly, with a rush of adrenaline, waking him all the way up in an eyeblink.

He didn't know how he knew, but he *knew*. Somehow, he had thought that houses were *safe*, that the clowns could only be outside. But they were here. They were in the house. Perhaps they were here in the *room*, right now. Two of them, eight, a dozen. Forming a circle around the bed, staring at him in the darkness with their opaque and malevolent eyes.

He burst from the bed and ran for the light switch, careening blindly through blackness, waiting for clutching hands to grab him in the dark. His foot struck something—a toy, a shoe—and sent it clattering away, the noise making him gasp and flinch. A misty ghost shape seemed to move before him, making vague, windy gestures, more sensed than seen. He ducked away, dodging blindly. Then his hand was on the light switch.

The light came on like a bomb exploding, sudden and harsh and overwhelmingly bright. Black spots flashed before his eyes. As his vision readjusted, he jumped to see a face only inches from his own—stifling a scream when he realized that it was only his reflection in the dresser mirror. That had also been the moving, half-seen shape.

There was no one in the room.

Panting with fear, he slumped against the dresser. He'd instinctively thought that the light would help, but somehow it only made things worse. It picked out the eyes and the teeth of the demons in the magic posters on the walls, making them gleam sinisterly, and threw slowly moving monster shadows across the room from the dangling Tyrannosaurus mobile. The light was harsh and spiky, seeming to bounce and ricochet from every flat surface, hurting his eyes. The light wouldn't save him from the clowns, wouldn't keep them away, wouldn't banish them to unreality, like bad-dream bogeymen—it would only help them *find* him.

He was making a dry, little gasping noise, like a cornered animal. He found himself across the room, crouching with his back to the wall. Almost without thinking, he had snatched up the silver letter-opener knife, from his desk. Knife in hand, lips skinned back over his teeth in an animal snarl, he crouched against the wall and listened to the terrible silence that seemed to press in against his eardrums.

They were coming for him.

He imagined them moving with slow deliberation through the darkened living room downstairs, their eyes and their dead-white faces gleaming in the shadows, pausing at the foot of the stairs to look up toward his room and then, slowly, slowly—each movement as intense and stylized as the movements of a dance—beginning to climb . . . the stairs creaking under their weight . . . coming *closer. . . .*

David was crying now, almost without realizing that he was. His heart was thudding as if it would tear itself out of his chest, beating faster and faster as the pressure of fear built up inside him, shaking him, chuffing out, "*Run, run, run!* Don't let them trap you in here! *Run!*"

Before he had realized what he was doing, he had pulled open the door to his room and was in the long corridor outside.

Away from the patch of light from his doorway, the corridor was deadly black and seemed to stretch endlessly away into distance. Slowly, step by step, he forced himself into the darkness, one hand on the corridor wall, one hand clutching the silver knife. Although he was certain that every shadow that loomed up before him would turn out to be a silently waiting clown, he didn't even consider switching on the hallway light. Instinctively, he knew that the darkness would hide him. Make no noise, stay close to the wall. They might miss you in the dark. Knife in hand, he walked on down the hall, feeling his finger tips rasp along over wood and tile and wallpaper, his eyes strained wide. Into the darkness.

His body knew where he was going before he did. His parents' room. He wasn't sure if he wanted his parents to protect him or if he wanted to protect *them* from a menace they didn't even know existed and couldn't see, but through his haze of terror, all he could think of was getting to his parents' room. If he could beat the clowns to the second floor, hide in his parents' room, maybe they'd miss him; maybe they wouldn't look for him there. Maybe he'd be safe there . . . safe . . . the way he used to feel when a thunderstorm would wake him and he'd run sobbing down the hall in the darkness to his parents' room and his mother would take him in her arms.

The staircase, opening up in a well of space and darkness, was more felt than seen. Shoulder against the wall, he felt his way down the stairs, lowering one foot at a time, like a man backing down a ladder. The well of darkness rose up around him and slowly swallowed him. Between floors, away from the weak, pearly light let in by the upstairs-landing window, the darkness was deep and smothering, the air full of suspended dust and the musty smell of old carpeting. Every time the stairs creaked under his feet, he froze, heart thumping, certain that a clown was about to loom up out of the inky blackness, as pale and terrible as a shark rising up through black midnight water.

He imagined the clowns moving all around him in the darkness, swirling silently around him in some ghostly and enigmatic dance, unseen, their fingers not quite touching him as they brushed by like moth wings in the dark . . . the bushy fright wigs puffed out around their heads like sinister nimbi . . . the ghostly white faces, the dead-black costumes, the gleaming-white gloves reaching out through the darkness.

He forced himself to keep going, fumbling his way down one more step, then another. He was clutching the silver knife so hard that his hand hurt, holding it up high near his chest, ready to strike out with it.

The darkness seemed to open up before him. The second-floor landing. He felt his way out onto it, sliding his feet flat along the floor, like an ice skater. His parents' room was only a few steps away now. Was that a noise from the floor below, the faintest of sounds, as if someone or something was slowly climbing up the stairs?

His fingers touched wood. The door to his parents' room. Trying not to make even the slightest sound, he opened the door, eased inside, closed the door behind him and slowly threw the bolt.

He turned around. The room was dark, except for the hazy

moonlight coming in the window through the half-opened curtains; but after the deeper darkness of the hall outside, that was
light enough for him to be able to see. He could make out bulky
shapes under the night-gray sheets, and, as he watched, one of the
shapes moved slightly, changing positions.

They were there! He felt hope open hot and molten inside him,
and he choked back a sob. He would crawl into bed between them
as he had when he was a very little boy, awakened by nightmares
. . . he would nestle warmly between them . . . he would be *safe*.

"Mom?" he said softly. "Dad?" He crossed the room to stand
beside the bed. "Mom?" he whispered. Silence. He reached out
hesitantly, feeling a flicker of dread even as he moved, and slowly
pulled the sheet down on one side—

And there was the clown, staring up at him with those terrible,
opaque, expressionless blue eyes, smiling his unchanging painted
smile.

David plunged the knife down, feeling it bite into the spongy
resistance of muscle and flesh.

Introduction

Playing the Game

Gardner Dozois

This started out as a story by Jack called "The Alpha Tree," which was something about a boy who could see into alternate realities. Jack had written three or four pages of it and gotten stalled on it, so the next time he came to Philadelphia, he gave it to me to see what I could do with it. Where Jack would have ultimately taken it if he'd finished it as a solo story, I have no idea, but I skewed the whole thing somewhat, turning it into a vehicle to explore a concept that I'd thought about many times before: an intuition of how easy it would be to become lost among the billions of probability-worlds that exist all around us, once you'd cut free of our reality and began to travel among them. Quantum uncertainty would seem to indicate that you could never really be *certain* that you were really back where you started from, no matter how close a match it initially seemed. How could you ever know for sure that you were really home again?

Most of my effort went into "hiding things in plain sight," making seemingly innocuous statements that the reader would take on face value while reading the story—"only rarely did a new building appear in Old Town, or an old building vanish"—but that would have a very different and literal meaning when he went back and looked at them again after realizing what the story was about—a favorite technique of mine. Jack's original draft survives most nearly intact in the opening two pages, and in the description of Jimmy's journey to the grassy knoll in the cemetery.

The story sold to *The Twilight Zone Magazine,* and was reprinted in Donald A. Wollheim's *The 1983 Annual World's Best SF.*

Jack Dann

Once again, I used my hometown as a backdrop. After reading a story by the South American magical realist Jorge Luis Borges, I had the idea to write a story about a place—a point—from which one could peer into a multiplicity of parallel universes. In the heat of the moment, I wrote the beginning of "The Alpha Tree," got blocked, and set it aside. I took it with me on my next sojourn to Philadelphia, and Gardner, of course, immediately saw how my fragment could be turned into a workable story. Gardner *is* the quintessential story doctor!

He found exactly the right path for this story. After that, I believe we passed the story back and forth a couple of times. If I hadn't shown "The Alpha Tree" to Gardner, it would probably still be languishing in a file called "Story Ideas."

Checking my notes, I see that the story was also reprinted in *Great Stories From the Twilight Zone, 101 Science Fiction Stories,* and *The Giant Book of Science Fiction Stories.* "Playing the Game" was also published twice without our permission—once in the Polish magazine *Fantastyka* and again in an unauthorized collection of my stories published by the Tohoku University SF Society in Japan.

Go figure. . . .

Playing the Game

Gardner Dozois and Jack Dann

THE WOODS THAT EDGED THE NORTH SIDE OF MAN-
ningtown belonged to the cemetery, and if you looked west-
ward toward Endicott, you could see marble mausoleums and
expensive monuments atop the hills. The cemetery took up several
acres of carefully mown hillside and bordered Jefferson Avenue,
where well-kept woodframe houses faced the rococo painted head-
stones of the Italian section.

West of the cemetery there had once been a district of brownstone buildings and small shops, but for some time now there had
been a shopping mall there instead; east of the cemetery, the row of
dormer-windowed old mansions that Jimmy remembered had been
replaced by an ugly, brick school building and a fenced-in school-
yard where kids never played. The cemetery itself, though—that
never changed; it had always been there, exactly the same for as far
back as he could remember, and this made the cemetery a pleasant
place to Jimmy Daniels, a refuge, a welcome island of stability in a
rapidly changing world where change itself was often unpleasant
and sometimes menacing.

Jimmy Daniels lived in Old Town most of the time, just down
the hill from the cemetery, although sometimes they lived in Passdale or Southside or even Durham. Old Town was a quiet residen-

tial neighborhood of whitewashed, narrow-fronted houses and steep, cobbled streets that were lined with oak and maple trees. Things changed slowly there also, unlike the newer districts downtown, where it seemed that new parking garages or civic buildings popped out of the ground like mushrooms after a rain. Only rarely did a new building appear in Old Town, or an old building vanish. For this reason alone, Jimmy much preferred Old Town to Passdale or Southside, and was always relieved to be living there once again. True, he usually had no friends or school chums in the neighborhood, which consisted mostly of first- and second-generation Poles who worked for the Manningtown shoe factories, which had recently begun to fail. Sometimes, when they lived in Old Town, Jimmy got to play with a lame Italian boy who was almost as much of an outcast in the neighborhood as Jimmy was, but the Italian boy had been gone for the last few days, and Jimmy was left alone again. He didn't really mind being alone all that much—most of the time, anyway. He was a solitary boy by nature.

The whole Daniels family tended to be solitary, and usually had little to do with the close-knit, church-centered life of Old Town, although sometimes his mother belonged to the PTA or the Ladies' Auxiliary, and once Jimmy had been amazed to discover that his father had joined the Rotary Club. Jimmy's father usually worked for Weston Computers in Endicott, although Jimmy could remember times, unhappier times, when his father had worked as a CPA in Johnson City or even as a shoe salesman in Vestal. Jimmy's father had always been interested in history, that was another constant in Jimmy's life, and sometimes he did volunteer work for the Catholic Integration League. He never had much time to spend with Jimmy, wherever they lived, wherever he worked; that was another thing that didn't change. Jimmy's mother usually taught at the elementary school, although sometimes she worked as a typist at home, and other times—the bad times again—she stayed at home and took "medicine" and didn't work at all.

That morning when Jimmy woke up, the first thing he realized was that it was summer, a fact testified to by the brightness of the sunshine and the balminess of the air that came in through the open window, making up for his memory of yesterday, which had been gray and cold and dour. He rolled out of bed, surprised for a moment to find himself on the top tier of a bunk bed, and plumped down to the floor hard enough to make the soles of his feet tingle; at the last few places they had lived, he hadn't a bunk bed, and he wasn't used to waking up that high off the ground. Sometimes he had trouble finding his clothes in the morning, but this time it seemed that he had been conscientious enough to hang them all up the night before, and he came across a blue shirt with a zigzag, green stripe that he had not seen in a long time. That seemed like a good omen to him, and cheered him. He put on the blue shirt, then puzzled out the knots he could not remember leaving in his shoelaces. Still blinking sleep out of his eyes, he hunted futilely for his toothbrush; it always took a while for his mind to clear in the mornings, and he could be confused and disoriented until it did, but eventually memories began to seep back in, as they always did, and he sorted through them, trying to keep straight which house this was out of all the ones he had lived in, and where he kept things here.

Of course. But who would ever have thought that he'd keep it in an old coffee can under his desk!

Downstairs, his mother was making French toast, and he stopped in the archway to watch her as she cooked. She was a short, plump, dark-eyed, olive-complexioned woman who wore her oily, black hair pulled back in a tight bun. He watched her intently as she fussed over the hot griddle, noticing her quick, nervous motions, the irritable way she patted at loose strands of her hair. Her features were tightly drawn, her nose was long and straight and sharp, as though you could cut yourself on it, and she seemed all angles and edges today. Jimmy's father had been sitting sullenly over his third cup of coffee, but as Jimmy hesitated in the archway, he got to his feet and began to get ready for work. He was a thin man with a pale complexion and a shock of wiry, red hair, and Jimmy bit his lip in disappointment as he watched him, keeping well back and hoping not to be noticed. He could tell from the insignia on his father's briefcase that his father was working in Endicott today, and those times when his father's job was in Endicott were among the times when both of his parents would be at their most snappish in the morning.

He slipped silently into his chair at the table as his father stalked wordlessly from the room, and his mother served him his French toast, also wordlessly, except for a slight, sullen grunt of acknowledgment. This was going to be a bad day—not as bad as those times when his father worked in Manningtown and his mother took her "medicine," not as bad as some other times that he had no intention of thinking about at all, but unpleasant enough, right on the edge of acceptability. He shouldn't have given in to tiredness and come inside yesterday, he should have kept playing the Game . . . Fortunately, he had no intention of spending much time here today.

Jimmy got through his breakfast with little real difficulty, except that his mother started in on her routine about why didn't he call Tommy Melkonian, why didn't he go swimming or bike riding, he was daydreaming his summer away, it wasn't natural for him to be by himself all the time, he needed friends, it hurt her and made her feel guilty to see him moping around by himself all the time . . . and so on. He made the appropriate noises in response, but he had no intention of calling Tommy Melkonian today, or of letting her call for him. He had only played with Tommy once or twice before, the last time being when they lived over on Clinton Street (Tommy hadn't been around before that), but he didn't even *like* Tommy all that much, and he certainly wasn't going to waste the day on him. Sometimes Jimmy had given in to temptation and wasted whole days playing jacks or kick-the-can with other kids, or going swimming, or flipping baseball cards; sometimes he'd frittered away a week like that without once playing the Game. But in the end he always returned dutifully to playing the Game again, however tired of it all he sometimes became. And the Game had to be played alone.

Yes, he was definitely going to play the Game today; there was certainly no incentive to hang around here, and the Game seemed to be easier to play on fine, warm days anyway, for some reason.

So as soon as he could, Jimmy slipped away. For a moment he confused this place with the house they sometimes lived in on Ash Street, which was very similar in layout and where he had a different secret escape route to the outside, but at last he got his memories straightened out. He snuck into the cellar while his mother was busy elsewhere, and through the back cellar window, under which he had placed a chair so that he could reach the cement overhang and climb out onto the lawn. He cut across the neighbors' yards to Charles Street and then over to Floral Avenue, a steep, macadam dead-end road. Beyond was the start of the woods that belonged to the cemetery. Sometimes the mud hills below the woods would be guarded by a mangy, black and brown dog that would bark, snarl at him, and chase him. He walked faster, dreading the possibility.

But once in the woods, in the cool, brown and green shade of bole and leaf, he knew he was safe, safe from everything, and his pace slowed. The first tombstone appeared, half buried in mulch and stained with green moss, and he patted it fondly, as if it were a dog. He was in the cemetery now, where it had all begun so long ago. Where he had first played the Game.

Moving easily, he climbed up toward the crown of woods, a grassy knoll that poked up above the surrounding trees, the highest point in the cemetery. Even after all he had been through, this was still a magic place for him; never had he feared spooks or ghouls while he was here, even at night, although often as he walked along, as now, he would peer up at the gum-gray sky, through branches that interlocked like the fingers of witches, and pretend that monsters and secret agents and dinosaurs were moving through the woods around him, that the stunted azalea bushes concealed pirates or orcs . . . But these were only small games, mood-setting exercises to prepare him for the playing of the Game itself, and they fell away from him like a shed skin as he came out onto the grassy knoll and the landscape opened up below.

Jimmy stood entranced, feeling the warm hand of the sun on the back of his head, hardly breathing, listening to the chirruping of birds, the scratching of katydids, the long, sighing rush of wind through oak and evergreen. The sky was blue and high and cloudless, and the Susquehanna River gleamed below like a mirror snake, burning silver as it wound through the rolling, hilly country.

Slowly, he began to play the Game. How had it been, that first time that he had played it, inadvertently, not realizing what he was doing, not understanding that he was playing the Game or what Game he was playing until after he had already started playing? How had it been? Had everything looked like this? He decided that the sun had been lower in the sky that day, that the air had been hazier, that there had been a mass of clouds on the eastern horizon, and he flicked through mental pictures of the landscape as if he were riffling through a deck of cards with his thumb, until he found one that seemed to be right. Obediently, the sky grew darker, but the shape and texture of the clouds were not right, and he searched until he found a better match. It had been somewhat colder, and there had been a slight breeze . . .

So far it had been easy, but there were more subtle adjustments to be made. Had there been four smokestacks or five down in Southside? Four, he decided, and took one away. Had that radio tower been on the crest of that particular distant hill? Or on *that* one? Had the bridge over the Susquehanna been nearer or further away? Had that Exxon sign been there, at the corner of Cedar Road? Or had it been an Esso sign? His blue shirt had changed to a brown shirt by now, and he changed it further, to a red pinstriped shirt, trying to remember. Had that ice cream stand been there? He decided that it had not been. His skin was dark again now, although his hair was still too straight . . . Had the cemetery fence been a wrought iron fence or a hurricane fence? Had there been the sound of a factory whistle blowing? The smell of sulfur in the air? Or the smell of pine . . . ?

He worked at it until dusk; and then, drained, he came back down the hill again.

The shopping mall was still there, but the school and school-yard had vanished this time, to be replaced by the familiar row of stately, dormer-windowed old mansions. That usually meant that he was at least close. The house was on Schubert Street this evening, several blocks over from where it had been this morning, and it was a two-story, not a three-story house, closer to his memories of how things had been before he'd started playing the Game. The car outside the house was a '78 Volvo—not what he remembered, but closer than the '73 Buick from this morning. The windshield bore an Endicott parking sticker, and there was some Weston Computer literature tucked under the eyeshade, all of which meant that it was probably safe to go in; his father wouldn't be a murderous drunk this particular evening.

Inside the parlor, Jimmy's father looked up from his armchair, where he was reading Fuller's *Decisive Battles of the Western World*, and winked. "Hi, sport," he said, and Jimmy replied, "Hi, Dad." At least his father was a black man this time, as he should be, although he was much fatter than Jimmy ever remembered him being, and still had this morning's kinky red hair, instead of the kinky black hair he should have. Jimmy's mother came out of the kitchen, and she was thin enough now, but much too tall, with a tiny upturned nose, blue eyes instead of hazel, hair more blond than auburn . . .

"Wash up for dinner, Jimmy," his mother said, and Jimmy turned slowly for the stairs, feeling exhaustion wash through him like a bitter tide. She wasn't *really* his mother, they weren't *really* his parents. He had come a lot closer than this before, lots of other times . . . But always there was some small detail that was *wrong*, that proved that this particular probability-world out of the billions of probability-worlds was *not* the one he had started from, was not *home*.

Still, he had done much worse than this before, too. At least this wasn't a world where his father was dead, or an atomic war had happened, or his mother had cancer or was a drug addict, or his father was a brutal drunk, or a Nazi, or a child molester . . . This would do, for the night . . . He would settle for this, for tonight . . . He was so tired. . . .

In the morning, he would start searching again.

Someday, he would find them.

Introduction

A Change in the Weather

Gardner Dozois

Although I hesitate to give some critic this much ammunition to use against us, the fact is that this story came about because I wanted to test a new typewriter which had (a heretofore unheard-of expense) a new typewriter ribbon (remember those? Probably not—they are now mysterious artifacts from another cycle of existence. Remember *typewriters*, for that matter?). Jack and Michael were over, we were joking and talking and partying, and, every so often, somebody would wander over to the typewriter and peck out a couple of lines on it to test it out. A few minutes earlier, Jack had used it to produce the opening sentence of a story we wanted to write, which involved an old man sitting on a park bench despondently, with rain beating down on him and soaking the piles of garbage around him. While Jack and I were having some particularly pretentious and intellectually overblown conversation about the deep inner meaning of this story (which we never have actually written, to date), Michael drifted over to the typewriter and wrote an additional paragraph of parody of the opening sentences, where the old man was surrounded by pterodactyls which were picking through the trash. This was obviously a satirical comment on both Jack's opening lines and the solemn pretentiousness of our discussion. When he read what Michael had written, though, Jack got excited: "My God! He's writing our story for us! This is terrific!"

"No it's not," Michael said. "I'm making fun of you!" But Jack's enthusiasm could not be dampened.

Sitting at the typewriter myself later that night, looking at the lines that Jack and Michael had written, I became interested in working out a rationale for the incongruity of the image of the old man sitting there with the pterodactyls wandering around him, and he's totally ignoring them—obviously they're commonplace. What was going on? So we worked it out. (I myself take all blame for the appalling pun at the end.) By the time Michael came back the next day, we had finished the rest of the story. We offered to cut Michael in for a third of the profits on the strength of his one-paragraph contribution. Seething with artistic integrity, though, Michael stood on his ideals and refused to have his name associated with such a tawdry bit of naked commercial hackwork.

A few weeks later, we sold it first crack out of the box to *Playboy*, for more money than either of us had ever gotten for a short story in our entire careers.

There's a lesson here of some sort, I suppose, but it probably is not one that should be repeated in front of impressionable young writers.

Jack Dann

I wrote this story while I was asleep.

Well, Gardner wrote it while I was asleep. I remember being jolted awake some time during the small hours of the morning. Gardner tapped me on the shoulder.

"Yeah . . . ?" I asked, cotton-mouthed and muzzy-headed.

"Congratulations, Jack," Gardner said. "You just wrote a story."

Yeah, it was a party at Gardner and Susan's, and I remember pecking away at Gardner's old typewriter with its newly installed, very black ribbon. It could only be considered a red-letter day when Gardner put a new ribbon in his typewriter. In those early days, Gardner's stories had a truly distinctive appearance: The text on the page ran from one edge of the paper to the other (Gardner believed margins were wasted space) and the type was usually so faint that at first glance it would appear to be mere shadows, ghosts on the paper. So on this red-letter night, as Gardner related earlier, Michael and I periodically sat down in front of his typewriter and tested the brand new ribbon.

I started writing the still-not-completed Old Man Growing Younger story, and Michael then sat down and wrote a few lines or paragraphs about pterodactyls pecking away like pigeons around the old man. Perhaps it was the wine or simply fatigue after partying with pals through the night, but I *liked* Michael's idea, and just couldn't keep my hands off those clattering keys.

Gardner and I noodled with the story in the clear light of day; but, as far as *I'm* concerned, this was the story that got written while I was asleep.

A month or so later, when I was back in my fleabag apartment in Binghamton, I got a call from Gardner.

"Jack, you've just sold a story."

"Yeah . . . ?" I asked.

"To *Playboy.*"

I remember that I didn't say a word, not one word.

"Jack . . . ? Really, you just sold a story to *Playboy.*"

Disbelief. Dumbfoundment.

That was the first of several stories we'd sell to *Playboy.* Well, we *offered* to cut Michael in for his share. At least he can rest secure in the knowledge that he has retained his artistic integrity.

The two other hacks?

They just cashed the check and spent the money.

※❦※

A Change in the Weather

Jack Dann and Gardner Dozois

IT LOOKED LIKE RAIN AGAIN, BUT MICHAEL WENT FOR his walk anyway.

The park was shiny and empty, nothing more than a cement square defined by four metal benches. Piles of rain-soaked garbage were slowly dissolving into the cement.

Pterodactyls picked their way through the gutter, their legs lifting storklike as they daintily nipped at random pieces of refuse.

Muttering, the old man shooed a pterodactyl from his favorite bench, which was still damp from the afternoon rain, sat down, and tried to read his newspaper. But at once his bench was surrounded by the scavengers: they half flapped their metallic-looking wings, tilted the heads at the ends of their snakelike necks to look at him with oily, green eyes, uttered plaintive, begging little cries, and finally plucked at his clothes with their beaks, hoping to find crusts of bread or popcorn. At last, exasperated, he got suddenly to his feet—the pterodactyls skittering back away from him, croaking in alarm—and tried to scare them off by throwing his newspaper at them. They ate it, and looked to him hopefully for more. It began to rain, drizzling out of the gray sky.

Disgustedly, he made his way across the park, being jostled and almost knocked over by a hustling herd of small two-legged dromaeosaurs who were headed for the hot dog concession on Sixteenth Street. The rain was soaking in through his clothes now, and in spite of the warmth of the evening he was beginning to get chilly. He hoped the weather wasn't going to turn nippy; heating oil was getting really expensive, and his Social Security check was late again. An ankylosaur stopped in front of him, grunting and slurping as it chewed up old Coke bottles and beer cans from a cement trash barrel. He whacked it with his cane, impatiently, and it slowly moved out of his way, belching with a sound like a length of anchor chain being dropped through a hole.

There were brontosaurs lumbering along Broadway, as usual taking up the center of the street, with more agile herds of honking, duckbilled hadrosaurs dodging in and out of the lanes between them, and an occasional carnosaur stumping along by the curb, shaking its great head back and forth and hissing to itself in the back of its throat. It used to be a person could get a bus here, and without even needing a transfer get within a block of the house, but now, with all the competition for road space, they ran slowly if they ran at all—another good example of how the world was going to hell. He dodged between a brachiosaur and a slow-moving stegosaurus, crossed Broadway, and turned down toward Avenue A.

The triceratops were butting their heads together on Avenue A; they came together with a crash like locomotives colliding that boomed from the building fronts and rattled windows up and down the street. Nobody in the neighborhood would get much sleep tonight. Michael fought his way up the steps of his brownstone, crawling over the dimetrodons lounging on the stoop. Across the street, he could see the mailman trying to kick an iguanodon awake so that he could get past it into another brownstone's vestibule. No wonder his checks were late.

Upstairs, his wife put his plate in front of him without a word, and he stopped only to take off his wet jacket before sitting down to eat. Tuna casserole again, he noticed without enthusiasm. They ate in gloomy silence until the room was suddenly lit up by a sizzling bolt of lightning, followed by a terrific clap of thunder. As the echoes of the thunder died, they could hear a swelling cacophony of banging and thudding and shrieking and crashing, even over the sound of the now torrential rain.

"Goddamn," Michael's wife said, "it's doing it again!"

The old man got up and looked out the window, out over a panorama of weed-and-trash-choked tenement backyards. It was literally raining dinosaurs out there—as he watched they fell out of the sky by the thousands, twisting and scrambling in the air, bouncing from the pavement like hail, flopping and bellowing in the street.

"Well," the old man said glumly, pulling the curtains closed and turning back from the window, "at least it's stopped raining cats and dogs."

Introduction
Time Bride

Gardner Dozois

Yet another afternoon where Jack and I were sitting around trying to come up with a story-idea to work on, me leafing through my story-idea notebook and making suggestions, waiting for some idea to strike Jack the right way and fill him with enough enthusiasm to push him to the typewriter. The plot of this story was sketched out pretty completely in my story-idea notebook, where it had slumbered for years, pretty close to the way it actually came out, waiting only for someone to actually *write* it, to have plot notes translated into an actual *story*, on the page.

My memory of the process this time is that Jack had to go home after we had worked out the plot but before he had a chance to do his usual sitting-down-at-the-typewriter-with-smoke-pouring-out-of-his-ears session, and that he started working in Binghamton on what would later become the middle sections of the story, starting with Mr. Meisner's first conversation with Arnold and the dinner scene where they explain the deal to Marcy, while at the same time I was writing what would become the opening scene of the story, after grilling Susan about what it was like to be a little girl and stealing large chunks of her childhood, including the jump-rope chant. Later, I wrote the long bus ride/seduction scene, and then we pieced the manuscript together, working my scenes in around Jack's middle sequences, and then bouncing drafts of the closing scene, the coda, back and forth for a while. I did a final unifying and homogenizing draft, as usual, and then later, at the request of Shawna McCarthy, another rewrite, working mostly on the coda. The story finally sold to *Isaac Asimov's Science Fiction Magazine*, something that would have been unthinkable before Shawna took over there (the version here is somewhat different than the one that appeared in *Asimov's*, since there was a limit to how sexually explicit we could get in that market).

I think that the fact that there are two distinct authorial voices shows a little more clearly here than it does in some of these collaborations, perhaps because of the way we pieced it together. It's perhaps not the strongest of the collaborations, although I think that it's a respectable enough addition to the long-running canon of Time Viewer stories (which canon, and what twists I could work on it, was doubtless what I'd been thinking about when I jotted the initial notes down in my story-idea notebook in the first place), and I like to think that most readers at least felt that they'd gotten their money's worth in entertainment value when they read it in that particular issue of the magazine.

Jack Dann

Of all the stories from The Fiction Factory days, this one is surely the nastiest. I remember Gardner having pretty extensive notes. We brainstormed the story, and then I went back to Binghamton to think about it. I *think* I had envisioned the first portion that I wrote as being the opening, but Gardner saw a better way and wrote the beautiful, lyrical opening, which really sets up the reader. Once I wrote my initial sections, I sent them to Gardner, secure that he would integrate them into a real story. That was the kick for me: I could write flat-out, without worry, without censure from the Little Man that crawled around in my head, because whatever infelicities of prose I might have inflicted upon the page, whatever plot faults I might not have caught would be magically fixed by Gardner.

The magic of collaboration—it leaves you free to write, to blue-sky, to crane your neck and let the dream take you wherever the hell it wants to go.

We passed the story back and forth, each writing new interstitial scenes, keeping the story focused, and twisting it ever tighter.

And that last twist . . . well, it's pure Gardner.

Time Bride

Gardner Dozois and Jack Dann

T HE MAN-WHO-WASN'T-THERE FIRST SPOKE TO MARCY when she was eight years old.

She had gone out to play with her friends Shelley Mitnich and Michelle Liebman, a rare time out from under the eyes of her strict and over-protective parents, and in later years she would come to remember that long, late-summer afternoon as an idyll of freedom and happiness, in many ways the last real moments of her childhood.

The sky was high and blue and cloudless, the sun warm without being blisteringly hot, the breezes balmy, and as they played time seemed to stretch out, slow down, and then stop altogether, hanging suspended like honey melting on the tongue. They played Mother May I, halfball, Chinese jump rope, and giant steps. They played jacks—onesies, twosies, threesies, sweepsies, and squeezesies. They played hide-and-go-seek. They played Red Light Green Light, and Red Rover, and Teakettle Hot Teakettle Cold. They played double-dutch. They played Mimsy, chanting:

A mimsy, a *clapsie*
I whirl my hands to *bapsie*
my *right* hand
my *left* hand

high as the sky
low as the *sea*
touch my *knee*
touch my *heel*
touch my *toe*
and under we *go!*

while they went through a complicated routine of throwing a ball up and clapping before catching it, throwing a ball up and whirling their hands and touching their shoulders *(bapsie)* before catching it, and so forth, until at last they threw the ball under their legs on the final word, their faces as grimly intent and serious as the faces of druids performing holy mysteries at the summer solstice. And when Shelley got mad and went home because she got stuck on the Qs while playing A My Name Is Alice, and Marcy *hadn't*—coming right out with "Q my name is Queenie, my husband's name is Quintin, we come from Queensbury where we sell *quilts*," cool as could be, making it look infuriatingly easy— Michelle and Marcy kept right on playing, playing hop-scotch, playing dolls, playing Movie Star, in which Michelle pretended to be Nick Charles and Marcy got to be Nora and walk a pillow named Asta on a leash. And when Michelle had to go in because it was time for her dumb piano lesson, Marcy kept on playing by herself, not wanting the afternoon to end, reluctant to go back to the gloomy, old house where there was nothing to do but watch television or sit in her room and play pretend games, which weren't any fun because she felt *locked up* in that house.

Marcy ran through the scrub lots behind the houses, swishing through the waist-high tangles of grass and wild wheat and weeds, pretending to be a horse. Usually when she played horses it was with Michelle and yucky old Shelley—Marcy's name was *Lightning*, and she was a beautiful, black horse with a white mane and white tail, and Michelle was Star, and Shelley was Blaze—and she hadn't been sure that she would like playing horses all by herself, with nobody to run from forest fires with or chase rustlers with, but she found that she *did* like it. Running alone and free, the wind streaming her hair out behind her, the sky seeming to whirl dizzily around her as she ran, running so fast that she thought that she could run right off the edge of the world, so far and fast that no one could ever catch her again—yes, she liked it very much, perhaps more than she had ever liked anything up to that moment.

She ran through the scrub lots and the patches of trash woods— pines and aspens growing like weeds—and down through the sunlit meadow to the river.

There she paused to catch her breath, teetering dramatically on the riverbank with her arms stretched out to either side. This time of year, the river ran nearly dry—just the barest trickle of water, perhaps an inch deep, worming its way through a dry bed littered with thousands of rocks of all sizes and shapes, from tiny, rounded pebbles to boulders the size of automobiles—but Marcy pretended that she was about to fall in and maybe drown, so that Mommy would be sorry, or maybe she'd have to swim like *anything* to escape, or maybe a mermaid would save her and take her to a magic cave. . . . She whirled around and around on the riverbank, her arms still outstretched to either side. She was one of those classically beautiful children who look like Dresden china figurines, with wide, liquid eyes and pale, blemishless skin and finely chiseled features, an adult face done in miniature. She was wearing a new, blue dress trimmed with eyelet lace, and her hair shone like beaten gold as she spun in the sunlight.

She whirled until she was too dizzy to stand, and then she sat down with a plop in the mud of the riverbank, which was still soggy from the morning's rain. She was dismayed for a second, realizing what she'd done; then she smiled, and began to pat her hands in the mud with a kind of studied perversity.

"You shouldn't play in the mud," an adult voice said sternly.

She flinched and looked up—expecting to see one of the neighbors, or perhaps a workman from the new house they were putting up on the far side of the meadow.

No one was there.

"You're getting your dress all muddy that way," the voice complained, "and I can just imagine how much your mother must have had to pay for it, too. Have some consideration for others!"

Marcy stood up slowly, feeling gooseflesh prickle along her arms. Again, no one was there. Carefully, she looked all around her, but there was no place for anyone to hide—the grass was too short here, and the nearest clump of trees was a hundred yards away—so she didn't see how anyone could be playing a trick on her.

She stood there silently, frowning, trying to figure it out, still composed but beginning to be a little scared. The wind ruffled her hair and fluttered the lace on her muddy dress.

"You're the one," the voice said gloatingly. It seemed to emanate from the thin air right beside her, loud and unmistakable. "I knew it as soon as I saw you. Yes, you're the right one—you'll do very nicely indeed, I can tell. Boy, am I going to get my money's worth out of this. Every cent—it's worth it."

The voice sounded smug, pleased with itself, somewhat pompous. Like the voice of one of those sanctimonious and not terribly bright adults who would always insist on telling her stories with a moral or giving her Words To Live By, the kind of adults who would show slides of their vacation trip, or pinch her cheeks and tell her how big she was getting, like her Uncle Irving, who always stunk up the house with cigar smoke and whose droning-voiced company was more annoying than the nickel he invariably gave her was worth. A *schlimazel*, as her father would say, a *schlimazel's* voice, coming at her out of the empty August sky.

"Are you a ghost?" she asked politely, more intrigued than frightened now.

The voice chuckled. "No, I'm not a ghost."

"Are you invisible, then, like on TV?"

"Well . . ." the voice said, "I guess I'm not really *there* at all, the way you mean it, although I can see you and talk to you whenever I want, little Marcia."

Marcy shook her head. In spite of him saying that he wasn't a ghost, she pictured him as one, as a little-man-who-wasn't-there, like in the poem Mommy had read her, and for a long time that would be the way she would think of him. "How did you know my name?" she asked.

The man-who-wasn't-there chuckled smugly again. "I know lots of things, Marcia, and I can find out nearly anything I want to know. My name is Arnold Waxman, and someday I'm going to marry you."

"No you're *not*," she said, startled.

"Oh yes I am. I'm going to be your husband, little Marcia, you'll see. With my guidance you're going to grow up to be a perfect young lady, the perfect bride, and when the time is right, you'll marry me."

"Oh no I *won't*," she said, more vehemently, feeling tears start in her eyes. "I won't, I *won't*. You're a liar, a yucky old *liar*."

"Have some respect!" the man-who-wasn't-there said sharply. "Is this a way to talk to your future husband?"

But Marcy was already running, whizzing suddenly away like a stone shot out of a sling, up the slope, across the meadow, past the foundations for the new house. Not until she reached the first line of trees, the riverbank far behind her, did she whirl and yell back, "I'm not going to marry you, you dumb old ghost! I'm not!"

"Oh, I think you will," said a voice beside her, from the thin and empty summer air.

*   *   *

Barry Meisner, Marcy's father, was putting on his *tallis* and *t'fillen*, preparing to pray, when a voice spoke to him out of the ceiling: "Mr. Meisner? I have a proposition to make to you."

"What?" Mr. Meisner said, turning around, as if the voice might have emanated out of the red leather bar across the room. He cautiously walked over to the bar and looked behind it, but found nothing but his collection of vintage wines, a towel that had fallen to the floor, and a bottle cap that the maid had overlooked.

"So now you're hearing things," Mr. Meisner mumbled, scolding himself.

"Mr. Meisner," said the voice clearly, "please, just listen to me for a moment, and I'll explain everything."

"Oh, my God!" Mr. Meisner said, now looking straight up at the ceiling light which spotlit the bar and the ivory collection that filled the narrow, mirrored shelves on the wall behind it. Mr. Meisner, a successful businessman who attributed his success to a personal God who took a particular interest in *him*, Mr. Meisner suddenly began to shake. "Oh, my *God*. I always *knew* you were real. I'm your son, Barry," and he raised his arms before him and intoned the *Shema*: "Hear O Israel, the—"

"*Please*, Mr. Meisner," said the voice, "I am most certainly *not* God. Now if you'll just listen—"

Mr. Meisner lowered his arms reluctantly. "You're not God?"

"Absolutely not."

"Then who are you, *what* are you?" Mr. Meisner looked this way and that. "Come out! Show yourself!"

"I can't show myself, Mr. Meisner, because I'm from the future."

"The future!"

"That's right," said the voice, sounding somewhat smug.

Mr. Meisner squinted suspiciously up at the ceiling. "So, you're from the future, huh? You have a time machine, maybe, like in the movies? So, you want to talk to a person, why don't you step out and say hello, instead of doing tricks like a ventriloquist with the ceiling?"

"Mr. Meisner," the voice said, and you could almost hear the sigh behind the words, "there is no such thing as a time machine. Not the kind that you're talking about, anyway. It's quite impossible for anybody to *physically* travel through time. Or so the scientists tell me—I must admit that I don't really understand it myself. But the point is that I *can't* step out and shake hands with you, because

I'm not really *there*, not physically. You understand? Now what I *do* have is a device that lets me *see* through time, and enables me to speak to you, and hear what you have to say in return. And let me tell *you*, Mr. Meisner, it's expensive. The timescopes were developed only a little while ago (from my point of view, of course), and you wouldn't *believe* how much it's costing me to talk to you right now."

"Long distance calls are always expensive," Mr. Meisner said blandly; he had regained some of his composure, and he wasn't about to let a voice from the ceiling think that it could impress him by bragging about its money. He idly fingered the loose leather strap of the *t'fillen* while he looked thoughtfully upward. "So, then, Mr. Voice—" he said at last.

"Mr. Meisner, *please*. I'm not a voice, I'm a person just like you, and I have a name. My name is Arnold Waxman."

Mr. Meisner blinked. "So, then, Mr. . . . Waxman," he began again. "So you're up there in the future, and you're calling me, and it's costing you a million dollars a minute, or whatever they use for money in the future, and any time now the operator is going to break in and start yelling you should put another dime in the slot. . . ." He paused. "So what do you want? Why are you bothering *me?*"

"I'd like to speak to you about your daughter, Marcy."

"What about my daughter?" demanded Mr. Meisner, startled again.

"I would like your permission to marry her."

"Marry her? Are you a pervert, is that it?" Mr. Meisner began shaking with anger and fear. No one was going to marry his daughter. She wasn't even *bat mitzvahed* yet. Suddenly he stopped, and buried his face in his hands. "I *am* hearing things," Mr. Meisner said flatly, satisfied that he had finally had a breakdown. "*Now* let my wife deny that I've been working too hard."

A sigh filled the room. "Mr. Meisner, you're not crazy. You're living in the Twentieth Century, please try to act like a civilized man, not some superstitious aborigine."

"*You* should talk about civilized! My daughter is *eight years old*. Is this what they do in the future, marry eight-year-old girls?" A thought struck him and he began to panic. "Where is she? Oh my God, is she all right? What—"

"Calm yourself, Mr. Meisner," Arnold said. "Your daughter is fine; in fact, she's on her way home right now."

"She'd better be okay," Mr. Meisner said ominously.

"Please let me explain, Mr. Meisner. I don't want to marry Marcy *now*. I want to marry her in the future, ten years from now, when she's eighteen. That is, I believe, an acceptable age. And I am, as I believe I've already mentioned, a very rich man. A very respectable man. She could do far worse, believe me."

Mr. Meisner shook his head dubiously. "I should arrange a marriage like my Grandmother who lived in a *shtetl?*"

"I think you will find that the old ways contained much wisdom."

"Are you Jewish?" Mr. Meisner asked suspiciously.

"Of course I'm Jewish. Would I want to marry your daughter if I wasn't?"

"We're not Orthodox," said Mr. Meisner.

"Neither am I," Arnold said.

"No—come back in ten years when you're real and we can talk again. Until then, you're a figment of my imagination."

"You know perfectly well that I'm real, Mr. Meisner," Arnold said angrily, "and in ten years it will be too late for Marcy."

"What do you mean?"

"Mr. Meisner, do you have any idea what's going *on* up here in the future?"

Mr. Meisner shrugged. "I should know the future? I have enough trouble with the present."

"Well, let me tell *you*, you think it's bad down there *now*, you just wait until you see the future! It's a zoo. A jungle. The complete breakdown of all moral values. Kids running wild. Lewdness. Indecency. Do you want to live to see the day when your daughter is *schtupping* every boy she passes on the street?"

"Don't you dare talk like that about my daughter!"

"Mr. Meisner, without my guidance, *she'll marry a goy!*"

There was a heavy silence. "That's a lie," Mr. Meisner said at last, but he said it without much conviction. He paused again, then sighed. "So if I make an arrangement with you, how will that change what happens to my Marcy?"

"I'll look after her. I'll help her through the pitfalls of life. I'll make sure she grows up *right*."

"I can do that myself, thank you," said Mr. Meisner.

"Ah, but you can't watch over her *all* the time, can you?" Arnold said triumphantly. "In fact, just today I caught her rolling in the mud, deliberately getting her dress dirty, and I sent her straight home. Can *you* know what other trouble she'll get into when your back is turned? Can you guard her from every bad influence she'll run into outside the home, point out every mistake to her as she makes it, help her to resist every temptation she'll ever run into, anywhere? *I* can do all that."

"But . . ." said Mr. Meisner, rather dazedly, "why are you willing to wait ten years for my daughter?"

"So that I can make absolutely *sure* that she's the kind of woman I want to marry." Arnold sighed. "I've been disappointed twice before, Mr. Meisner, with fiancées who were girls from good families, supposedly well brought up . . . and yet, underneath it all, it turned out that they were really . . . sluts. They had been *spoiled,* in spite of their good backgrounds, in spite of all their parents could do. Somewhere along the line, Mr. Meisner, *somewhere,* at some time, the germ of corruption had worked its way in." He paused broodingly, and then, his voice quickening with enthusiasm, said, "But *this* way, using the timescope, I can actually help to mold Marcy into the type of girl she should be, I can personally supervise every detail. . . ."

The study door opened, and Marcy was standing there, looking flushed and rather flustered, her dress splattered with mud. "Daddy—" she began breathlessly.

"There! See!" Arnold said smugly. "*There* she is, and she's perfectly all right. And look, there's the mud, just like I told you. . . ."

Marcy gasped and flinched, and fell back a step, her eyes widening. Her face filled with fright, and, after a moment, with guilt.

Her father was staring at her oddly. "Go upstairs now, Marcy," he said at last. "We'll talk about what you did to your dress later on."

"But *Daddy* . . ."

"Go upstairs now," Mr. Meisner said curtly, "I'm very busy."

As the door was swinging shut, he turned his face back up to the ceiling and said, "Now, then, Mr. Waxman—"

Marcy stood outside the door of her father's study for a long time listening to the voices rising and falling within, and then, troubled, she went slowly upstairs to her room.

That night, as she was getting ready to turn out her light and go to sleep, the voice spoke to her again. She shrieked and jumped into bed and pulled the covers up over her head. She lay there quivering, somehow shocked that the voice could follow her even into her very own room. The voice droned on for what seemed like an eternity while she hugged the covers tighter and tried not to listen, telling her stupid stories about how wonderful their lives together would be, the wonderful things they would do, how they would live in a castle. . . .

Later, after her room had become quiet again, she cautiously poked one eye and her nose out from under the blanket, looked warily around, and then snaked her hand over to turn out the light, hoping that *he* wouldn't be able to find her in the dark.

They were lies, she told herself as she stared up at the shadowy ceiling of her room, all the things he'd said, all lies. None of that was going to happen. Marcy already had her life planned anyway: she was going to live in the Congo and be like Wonder Woman who never had to marry anybody, even though everybody was in love with her because she saved people's lives all the time and was beautiful.

There would be no room in such a plan for *Arnold*.

The next day, at dinner, Marcy's mother said, "But Marcy, this *is* for your own good." She and Mr. Meisner and Marcy were seated at the kitchen table. "Arnold sounds like a very nice man, and Mommie and Daddy and Arnold are going to make sure that you have a wonderful life and have everything you want."

"I don't want everything I want," Marcy whined. "Not if I have to listen to that dumb old Arnold all the time. I won't, I won't, I *won't*."

"Now that certainly isn't the way a young lady speaks to her parents." Arnold's voice seemed to be coming from the radar range under the Colonial-style kitchen cabinets. "Little Marcia, do you—"

"Don't call me 'Little Marcia.' My name is Marcy, and I'm not little."

"Very well," said Arnold. "Marcy, do you remember the Ten Commandments?"

Marcy looked down at her bowl of strawberry ice cream, and then carefully mashed the artificially colored mounds flat with the back of her teaspoon.

"Well, *do* you remember the Ten Commandments?" Mrs. Meisner asked. Mrs. Meisner had once been beautiful, but she had allowed herself to gain weight, which clouded the once-strong features of her face. But she still had beautiful, pale skin and eyes as pale blue as Marcy's. She wore her thick, dyed red hair shoulder-length, but it was sprayed so heavily that it shone as if it were shellacked. "Marcy, stop playing with your ice cream and answer Arnold. And be polite!"

"I know you're not supposed to steal or kill anybody or eat lobster," Marcy said sullenly.

"But you *are* supposed to respect your parents . . . and your elders." Now Arnold's stern voice seemed to be coming from somewhere above the table. " 'Honor thy father and mother,' " the voice intoned ominously.

"Not if they try to make me marry a stupid old voice!" Marcy said, and she ran out of the kitchen, through the red-carpeted hallway, and up the stairs to her bedroom.

"I think you owe your parents an apology," the voice said to Marcy, who was lying on her bed, her arms extended as if she were flying or perhaps floating.

Marcy stuck her tongue out at the ceiling, which was where she thought Arnold might be.

"I think a spanking would be in order unless you apologize to your parents this very moment," Arnold said.

"Who's going to spank me?" Marcy asked petulantly. "You?"

"I think your father is very capable of taking care of that."

"Well, he's *never* spanked me ever, so shut up and go away."

Five minutes later, Marcy received her first spanking from her father.

The first few weeks under the new regime weren't *too* bad, although Arnold was an awful pest, and nagged her a lot, particularly when her parents weren't around. By now, everybody was talking about the Voices from the future—more than thirty different cases had been reported from all over the globe, the contacts initiated for a bewildering variety of reasons, most of them amazingly frivolous—but Arnold at first was reasonably discreet about lecturing her in front of other people, and only Marcy's parents knew about him.

All that ended, along with the last shreds of her old life, one night, perhaps a month later, when Marcy was having dinner at Shelley Mitnich's house.

"Are you *sure* your parents won't mind if you eat this?" Mrs. Mitnich asked Marcy as she served a platter filled with lobster tails. She also placed a little bowl of melted butter between Marcy and Shelley.

"No, they don't mind," March said. "We can't eat it at home, but I'm allowed to have it in restaurants or at my friends', like here." Lobster was Marcy's favorite food.

Mr. Mitnich mumbled something Marcy couldn't hear, and Mrs. Mitnich gave him a nasty look.

"Well, I know your parents aren't Orthodox," Mrs. Mitnich said; but before Marcy could put a piece of the pink meat into her mouth, a voice said, "Put that fork down this very instant!"

"Shut up, Arnold!" Marcy shouted. Her face turned red, and she looked around the dining room, as if Arnold would suddenly appear in the flesh to mortify her.

"You know better than to eat *traif*," Arnold said.

With shocked expressions on their faces, Shelley and her parents looked around the room and then at Marcy.

"I can eat whatever I want," Marcy whined. "My parents let me eat whatever I want when I'm out . . . and it's none of your business, you goddamn *geek!*"

"Little girls with breeding do not use such language," Arnold said.

"Who the hell are you?" Mr. Mitnich asked as he stood up and waved his hands over the table where the voice seemed to be coming from, as if he could brush it away like a spiderweb. "I've heard all about weirdos like you." Then he leaned over toward Marcy and asked, "Honey, when did this weirdo from the future start bothering you?"

"I *beg* your pardon, sir," said the voice, which seemed to be coming from the far side of the room now.

"Shut up, you," Mr. Mitnich said to the wall, and then he turned toward Marcy again. "Do your parents know about this pervert?"

"They most certainly do, sir," Arnold said smugly. "I've arranged to marry Marcy when she's of age. I'm simply trying to save her from *your* daughter's fate. If that's being a pervert, then so be it."

"And just what *is* my daughter's fate?" Mr. Mitnich asked, looking at the wall.

"I'd rather not say."

Mr. Mitnich was livid. "Get out of here, you! Oh . . . and Marcy . . . I don't think you should be playing with Shelley anymore. Your parents should be ashamed of themselves. Bringing such filth into their own home . . . and ours."

"You just wait and see what happens to *your* daughter," Arnold said nastily. "Boy! You should only be so lucky to have someone like me to look after her!"

Mr. Mitnich threw his coffee cup at the ceiling.

Then Marcy was outside, trudging along toward her house as the bitter tears runneled her cheeks, and Arnold was telling her that she didn't need friends like that anyway, because after all, she had *him.*

* * *

After that, the word got out and Marcy became a minor celebrity for a while, even appearing on a television news program. This was small comfort to Marcy, though—Arnold became more and more strict as time went by, reprimanding her constantly in front of the other kids, snapping at children and adults who he thought were "bad influences," until eventually no one would play with her at all. She had lost all her friends, and even her teachers tended to leave her alone, tucking her away in back of the class where they could safely ignore her.

Arnold was with her nearly all the time now, and Marcy soon learned that it was nearly impossible to hide from him. When she hid under the azalea bush in the backyard and "touched herself," Arnold was suddenly there too, thundering wrath from out of the cloudy sky, loudly telling her parents about the disgusting thing their daughter had been doing, and Marcy had to promise never to do it again, and cried herself to sleep from the shame of it every night for a week. When Marcy stole a chocolate-covered cherry from her mother's candy box, Arnold was there. When Marcy wiped her nose on the sleeve of her new jacket, Arnold was there. When Marcy tried to hide her report card, Arnold was there. When Marcy let Diane Berkowitz talk her into trying a cigarette, Arnold was there.

He came to her every day and lectured her about morality and sin and perversion. He loved to talk about etiquette and deportment, and he made her read thick, musty books to "expand her horizons."

He told her in secret that her parents weren't very smart or, for that matter, very well educated.

He told her that he was her only friend.

He told her that she was very lucky to have him, for he was her salvation.

Soon after Marcy's fifteenth birthday, someone finally invented the timescope, belatedly justifying the prophecy of its existence. The inventor had been prompted by hints and "pointers" from the future, but with the exception of a few nit-picking scientists, no one seemed particularly disturbed by the hair-raising tangle of paradoxes this implied. Within a year, timescopes were for sale on the commercial market, although they were indeed very expensive to own and operate.

Soon after Marcy's sixteenth birthday, Shelley Mitnich got pregnant, and by a *shvartzer* yet: Arnold crowed about that for months, and his stock with Mr. Meisner became unassailably high.

Soon after Marcy's seventeenth birthday, she tried talking to her mother about Arnold. Marcy still didn't see any way out of marrying Arnold if her parents said that she had to—although if she'd been a few years older, or less dominated by her parents and Arnold, or if her counselor at school had been sympathetic enough to really open up to, or if she'd had any real friends with whom to talk things over, she might have seen several other options—and the prospect terrified her. Mrs. Meisner put down the *Soap Opera Digest* and listened patiently to her daughter, but her tired, fat face was unsympathetic. "You don't love him," Mrs. Meisner said. She made a rotating motion with her hand and said, "So? You can't learn to love a rich man just as easily as a poor one?"

Marcy's eighteenth birthday was approaching. She lay unsleeping in the close darkness of her room, night after night, listening to the buzzing and clicking of the street lamp outside her window, watching the glow of car headlights sweep across the ceiling in oscillating waves, like phosphorescent surf breaking on a black midnight beach.

In the mornings, the face that looked back at her from her mirror was haggard and pale. She began to grow gaunt, the flesh pulling back tightly over her cheekbones, her eyes becoming hollowed and darkly bruised. She had almost stopped eating. During the day she would pace constantly, like a caged animal, unable to stand still, awash with a sick, directionless energy that left her headachy and nauseous. At night she would lie rigid and unmoving in her bed, still as a statue, the blankets pulled up to her neck, taut with dread and anticipation of the voice that might speak to her from the darkness at any moment, without warning, the voice and the watching presence she could never escape. . . .

On the third such night, lying tensely in darkness and watching leaf shadows shake and reticulate across the walls, she made her decision.

Slowly, cautiously, she pushed the blankets aside and got out of bed. She groped across the room to the dresser, not daring to turn on the light, finding her things by touch. Since puberty, since her body hair had begun to grow and her breasts had started to bloom, she had kept her room totally dark at night, unable to bear the thought of *him* staring at her while she undressed; she had taken to dressing under the sheet in the morning, hurrying through baths

and showers as quickly as she could, certain that he was staring at
her nakedness whenever he got the chance, convinced that she
could feel his eyes crawling over her whenever she was obliged to
take off the swaddling, smothering, all-concealing clothes she had
come to prefer. Tucked away under the shapeless, tentlike dresses,
though, she still kept a pair of jeans and a dark blue cardigan
sweater, perhaps unconsciously saved for an emergency like this.
She fumbled her way into the clothes, hesitating after every movement, trying to inch her dresser drawer open soundlessly and freez-
ing for a long, terrified moment when it emitted a loud raucous
squeak, glancing compulsively upward at the milky ceiling (where
he lived, or so the child in the back of her mind still believed),
more than half-expecting to hear his voice any second, asking her
in that snide and chilly tone just *what* in the world she thought she
was *doing*. But by the time she had tied the last lace on her sneakers, crouching in the deep shadow of the chiffonier, she had begun
to feel a little more confident—she had been quiet and unrebel-
lious for a long time now, she hadn't tried to sneak out of her room
at night for *years*, and even *he* couldn't watch her *all* the time,
every moment. He had to sleep *sometime*, after all.

Maybe it was going to work.

No longer moving with quite the same exaggerated stealth,
Marcy slid her window open and climbed out onto the slanting second-story roof. Surely if *he* were watching, he would say something
now . . . but then she was outside, feeling the slippery tile under her
feet, seeing the fat, pale moon overhead through a scrim of silhouetted branches, and still the alarm hadn't come. She walked sure-
footedly along the roof to the big elm that grew at the corner of the
house, leaped across to it, and shimmied down it to the ground in a
shower of brittle leaves and displaced twigs, and only when she was
standing on the ground, her feet planted firmly in the damp grass,
only then did she sway and become dizzy. . . .

The bus into the center of town stopped right across from her
house, but she caught it a few blocks down, just to be safe. She
held her breath until the bus doors sighed shut behind her, and
then she slumped into a seat, and was taken by a fit of convulsive
shivering. She had to wrap her hands around the edge of the seat in
front of her and squeeze it until her knuckles whitened before the
shivering stopped, and when it had, and she was calmer, she was
content to just sit for a moment and watch the pastel lights of the
city ticking by outside the window. But she mustn't allow herself to
be lulled. She mustn't allow herself to think that she was safe, not

yet. She had worked it all out a dozen times. There was no sense in just running away—sooner or later, Arnold would find out where she had gone, track her down no matter where she went, and then her parents would just come and get her, or send the cops to pick her up. And the next time they'd watch her more closely, make it far more difficult for her to get away. No, it was now or never; she must use this opportunity *now*, while she had the chance, and there was only one thing she could think of to do with the stolen time that *might* be effective enough to break her free of Arnold.

She had become uneasy again, thinking about it. How much time *did* she have? Maybe a few hours . . . at the most. . . . Possibly as little as a half an hour, twenty minutes, maybe *less*. Sooner or later, the alarm would sound. . . . She felt the tension building up inside her again, like a hand rhythmically squeezing her guts, and she began to look anxiously around her at the people getting on and off the bus. She had not worked out the logistical details, the practical details, of her plan—she had vaguely imagined going to a bar, or a nightclub (but what if they wouldn't let her in?), or maybe to a bowling alley, or a restaurant, or . . . but she didn't have *time* for all that! Any minute now, the alarm was going to come, she *knew* it. She was running out of *time*. . . . And now the bus was emptying out, there were fewer and fewer people getting on. . . .

There was a man sitting a few seats away, reading a magazine. *You're it*, she thought. *You'll have to be it*. Gritting her teeth, she somehow forced herself to stand up, take a swaying step down the aisle toward him. He was probably a goy, but he was clean-looking anyway, his hair a bit longer than she liked it (and—ugh!—a mustache), dressed in slacks and a workshirt and an Eisenhower jacket, hushpuppies, plastic eyeglasses. . . . She took another step toward him, feeling her legs turning to rubber, her knees buckling, the fluttery panic coming up inside her.

At least he was *old*—he must be twenty-one, maybe even twenty-two. An older man, that should make it easier. . . .

The bus accelerated with a jolt, and Marcy took the next few steps in a stumbling half-run, almost falling, sprawling into the seat next to the man and then lurching against him as the bus took a sharp curve, knocking the magazine out of his hands. He stared at her, startled, and Marcy drew herself up and said "Hi!" brightly, showing all of her teeth to him in what was supposed to be a smile. He kept staring at her, blankly, and so she leaned in until their faces were nearly touching, and said "Hiiiii there," making her voice low and drawly, fanning her eyelashes, trying desperately to remember what the vamps on television did. He blinked, and then said "Uh . . . hi."

There was a long silence then, and they stared at each other through it while the bus bounced and swayed around them.

My God, my god, *say* something.

What?

"You know," she said, her voice harsh with tension, so that she had to swallow and start speaking again, "you know, you're a very good-looking man."

"I *am?*" he said, gaping at her.

"Yes, you're a very attractive guy." She looked up sidelong at him, up from under her eyelashes. "I mean—really you are. You know, *really.*" She batted her eyelashes at him again. "What's your name, anyway? Mine's Marcy."

"Uh . . . Alan," he said. He was beginning to smile in a sort of tentatively fatuous way, although he still looked puzzled. "My name's Alan."

She leaned in even closer, until she could feel his breath on her face. It smelled faintly of pepperoni, faintly of mouthwash. She fixed him with a long, smolderingly significant look, then said, "Hi, Alan," in a breathless whisper.

"Hi . . . um, Marcy . . ." he said. He still looked nervous, glancing around to see if anyone else was watching him. She took his arm, and he jumped a little. She could feel herself blushing, but she couldn't stop now. "I was sitting over there watching you," she said, "and I said to myself, you can't let a guy this gorgeous get away without even saying *hello* or something, you know? No matter *how* forward he thinks you are. . . . I mean, I'd like to get to know you better, Alan. Would you like to get to know *me* better, too? Would you?"

Alan licked nervously at his lips. "Why sure. We could go out. . . . We could, uhhh, go to the movies or something, I guess, or go get a Coke. . . ."

Too long! This was all taking too long!

She gritted her teeth, and put her hand in his lap.

He goggled at her, and through buzzing waves of embarrassment she was surprised to see that he was blushing too, blushing red, as a beet.

"Jesus Christ . . ." he whispered.

No turning back now. "I . . . I want to be alone with you," Marcy said, her voice wavering, forcing herself to keep her hand there. "Don't you have someplace we can go?"

"Yeah," he said in a strangled voice, "we can go to my place. . . ."

They got off a few stops later, and walked down half-lit streets to Alan's apartment. Marcy was hanging on to Alan's arm as though he might float up and away into the evening sky if she didn't guy him down, and he was walking so quickly that he was dragging her along, her feet almost not touching the sidewalk. He was chattering nervously, talking a mile a minute, but she hadn't heard a word he'd said. She could feel the tension building higher and tighter inside her, she could almost *smell* it, a scorched smell like insulation burning. She was almost out of time—she knew it, she *knew* it. Dammit, hurry *up*.

Alan's apartment was a fifth-floor walk-up in a battered old brownstone building that had seen better centuries, let alone better years. There was a shag couch, a bookcase made of boards and bricks, a coffee table, empty wine bottles with candles melted into them, a lamp with a red light bulb in it, rock posters on the walls. He took her coat and threw it over a chair, and then turned to her, rubbing his hands on his hips, looking uncertain again. "Ah, would you like a drink, or . . ."

"Don't talk." She slid into his arms. "I . . . I *need you*, Alan," she said huskily, remembering lines from a romance novel, too young to realize that he was young enough not to giggle. "Take me, take me *now!*"

Then—thank God! At last!—he was kissing her, while she tried not to fidget with impatience. After a moment's reluctance, she opened her lips and let him put his tongue in her mouth; she could feel it wandering clumsily around in there, bumping into her teeth, wagging back and forth like some kind of spongy, organic windshield wiper. His tongue felt huge and bloated in her mouth, and it made her feel a little ill, but he was making a sort of low moaning noise while he was kissing her, so apparently she was on the right track.

After a moment, he began fumbling with the buttons on her cardigan sweater, so clumsily that she had to help him, her own fingers shaking with nervousness. Then he was easing her blouse off. It felt odd to be standing in a strange room, in front of a stranger, in her brassiere, but she didn't have time to worry about it. It *couldn't* be much longer before they caught up with her. . . . Somehow he had figured out how to get the hooks undone. He tugged her brassiere off, and ran his hands over her breasts. She still felt nothing but anxiety, but the room was chilly, and if he took the hardening of her nipples as a sign of passion, well, all the better. . . .

He leaned down and put his mouth to her breast, his tongue encircling the nipple, and that *was* pleasurable in a low-key way, as if there were a mild electric current shooting through her, but she didn't have *time* for all these frills. "Hurry *up*," she snarled, tugging clumsily at his belt, breaking a fingernail, finally getting his pants open.

Alan would have been gratified to know that to her his penis looked enormous — a terrifying purplish spear of flesh, a foot long at least.

He threw her down on the couch, and they wrestled inconclusively together for a while — she staring up at the waterpocked ceiling with dread, and thinking hurry *up*, hurry *up*, hurry *up*, banging her chin on his shoulder for emphasis — but of course he was too nervous, and he went soft. He smiled weakly at her and said something apologetic, but she ignored all that and reached for him determinedly. His penis felt warm and dry and rubbery under her hands. She was blushing furiously now, blushing to her hair-roots, but she worked grimly away at him, telling herself that it was not that much different from milking a cow, something she'd done one summer at 4H Camp.

He rolled onto her again, hovered fumblingly above her, poised, and at that moment a loud, furious voice said "You *slut!!*"

Alan jerked and gasped, startled, and began to pull away, but Marcy growled "Oh, no, you don't!" — not yet! not after all that trouble! — and grabbed him back down. "Whore!" Arnold was screaming, "Filthy strumpet!" and Alan was saying "What?! What?!" in a kind of wild, dazed panic, but she kept rubbing herself up against him, hugging him with her arms and legs, saying "Don't worry about that! Don't pay any attention!" until at last he gave a convulsive shudder and lunged forward. She felt a sharp, tearing pain, and then he was gasping stertorously next to her ear as Arnold screamed and raved and gibbered incoherently from the ceiling. After a few moments Arnold's voice fell silent, and she smiled.

At last Alan moaned and collapsed crushingly on top of her. She lay unprotestingly under his weight, not even caring if she'd gotten pregnant.

Free of him at last, she thought.

Alan sat up, still bewildered.

"You can put your pants on now," she said dryly.

A few minutes later, her father began to pound at the door.

There was the expected scene. Screaming, slapping, crying, hysteria. "You're not my daughter—you're no daughter of mine." Slut. Whore. Et cetera. Marcy remained dry-eyed and unmoved through it all. Alan cowered in a corner, wrapped in a sheet, looking tousled and terrified, occasionally opening his mouth to speak, only to shut it again when one of Marcy's parents advanced shrieking upon him. Her parents swore that they would press charges against Alan —especially if (God forbid) she was pregnant—and hurled sulfurous threats involving jail and lawyers back at him as they left, but eventually they would give up on the idea of prosecution, fearing more scandal. Fortunately, Marcy was *not* pregnant. She said goodbye politely to Alan—he gaped at her, still looking bewildered, still wrapped in a sheet, and said nothing—and calmly followed her sputtering parents out of his apartment. She never saw him again. She packed a bag, took the money she had been saving, and moved out of her parents' house that very night. She never saw them again, either.

She stayed that night in a Holiday Inn, and spent the next few weeks in an inexpensive boardinghouse. She got a job at a five-and-dime, later worked as a counter-girl in a second-rate greasy spoon. After a couple of months, she landed a better job in the accounting department of a moderate-sized engineering firm, and was able to afford a small apartment of her own in a shabby-genteel neighborhood on the far side of town.

For the first few weeks she stayed in her apartment every night, scared and lonely, still more than half-expecting to hear Arnold's voice at any second. Then she went into what she herself would later refer to as her "slut phase," haunting bars and discos, dragging a different man home with her nearly every night. Some of these men were much more attractive and skillful than Alan, but she felt nothing with any of them, no pleasure, not even the mild tingle she had felt during the tussle in Alan's apartment. She tried getting drunk, and stoned, let lovers ply her with cocaine and buzzing electric novelties and mildly kinky sexual variations, but nothing worked. After a few months of this, she got tipsy after work and let one of the sales girls coax her into bed—but sex was just as unexciting with Sally as it had been with the faceless parade of male pickups. No matter how desperately she tried to be abandoned and wild, it seemed that she could not make herself stop *listening* for Arnold's disapproving voice, listening for it and dreading it with some deep and unreasoned part of her mind, and for her sex remained only a mildly unpleasant form of exercise, like being forced to do a hundred sit-ups or jumping jacks in a row.

She got another, and better, job, with a larger engineering firm, and stopped dating at all. She worked with impressive efficiency and a total concentration that brought her rapid promotions; after a while she was doing very well financially, and she moved into a much better apartment in a quiet residential high-rise whose other occupants were almost all over fifty years of age. She was generally popular with her co-workers, although she only occasionally joined them on Bowling Night or went with them on their expeditions to movies or restaurants or bars, and never showed the slightest hint of romantic interest in anyone, not even engaging in the harmless "social flirting" that went on almost constantly in the office. Those few who resented her reserve sometimes called her "Little Mary Sunshine" or "The Nun," but most of her colleagues appreciated her even-tempered disposition and her calm, unflappable efficiency, and the speculation that she "just didn't go out much" because she was still recovering from an unhappy love affair soon became an unquestioned part of office mythology—some people could even tell you all about the guy and why they'd broken up (in one version he'd turned out to be married; in another, he'd died slowly and dramatically of cancer).

A few of the more perceptive of her friends noticed that occasionally, right in the middle of things—while she was chatting over morning coffee, or discussing an audit with a section head, or telling the latest Polack joke in a bar during Happy Hour—Marcy would suddenly fall completely silent and freeze motionless for a heartbeat or two, as if she had abruptly and magically been turned to stone. None of them noticed, however, that at such times her eyes would invariably and almost imperceptibly flick upward, as if she had suddenly sensed someone looking over her shoulder.

Marcy only ever actually saw Arnold in the flesh once, and that was years after she had left home, at a party.

It was a reception given for the opening of the new wing of the museum, and Marcy was sipping pale sherry and talking to Joanne Korman when she heard an unmistakable voice, a voice that she hadn't actually *heard* since she was eighteen, although it had often whispered through her dreams at night. She turned around, and there was Arnold, eating cucumber sandwiches and blathering pompously about something or other to a museum staffer. Arnold turned out to be a short, potbellied man with a large nose and a receding chin, impeccably groomed—his hair was slick and shiny and combed into photographically exact furrows—and expensively, if somewhat conservatively, dressed. He held his cucumber sandwich as if he was a praying mantis, holding it up near his chin with both hands and turning it around and around and around before taking a small, surgical bite out of it. His eyes were small, humorless, and opaque, and he never seemed to blink. Marcy watched him in fascination. It was so strange to see Arnold's lips move and hear that familiar voice—sanctimonious, self-righteous, self-satisfied—issue from them instead of from the empty air. . . .

Arnold felt her watching him, and looked up. They stared at each other for a moment across the crowded room. There was no doubt that he recognized her. She saw his lips purse up tight, as if he had tasted something foul, and then he sneered at her, his face haughty and smugly contemptuous. Slowly, deliberately, disdainfully, he turned his back on her.

Marcy could never remember how she got back to her apartment that night.

She woke from abstraction, hours later, to find herself sitting at her kitchen counter, her mind full of circular, tail-swallowing thoughts about rope, and razor blades, and a long, slow fall into dark water.

With an immense effort of will, she wrenched her mind out of this downward spiral, and forced herself to think about Arnold for the first time in a very long time, really *think* about him, and the more she thought about him the more her hands began to shake, until the coffee cup she was clutching (the cup she couldn't remember filling) cracked and clattered and spilled.

He was so *smug*. That was what was not to be borne—after everything that he'd done to her, *he* still considered himself to be the injured party! He was so goddamned sleek and smug and self-satisfied, it made her feel dizzy with hate just to think of it. Undoubtedly he was smirking at himself in the mirror right now and telling himself how *right* he had been about her, how he had tried and *tried* to help her lead a decent life, but she just wouldn't *listen*, how she had proved herself unworthy of him. . . .

She couldn't stand to think of it.

He had won! In spite of everything, he had won. He had shamed and warped and twisted her, tormented her for a decade, ruined her childhood, blighted her life, and then he had simply turned and walked away, congratulating himself that all his worst expectations had come true.

And she had let him get *away* with it. That was the worst thing of all, the most unbearable part. She had let him get away scot-free. . . .

She spent the long, sleepless night pacing restlessly up and down the length of her apartment, seeming with every step she took to hear Arnold's gloating voice saying "every cent—it's worth it," repeating obsessively to the rhythmic clicking of her heels, "every cent—it's worth it, every cent—it's worth it, every cent—it's worth it," until long before dawn she had decided that somehow—*any-how*—she would have to make him *pay*, pay more than he had ever been willing to spend.

Early the next day, she went shopping.

Later that night, long after the technicians had left, she sat in her darkened living room before the newly installed console and ran her fingers caressingly over the switches and keyboards. She had been practicing for hours, and now she thought that she'd gotten the hang of it. She touched the keyboard, and the viewscreen lit up with a misty collage of moving images. She punched in the coordinates, and then used the fine-tuning to hunt around until she found a place where the young Arnold Waxman—pimply-faced and fat, just barely post-pubescent—was standing alone in his bathroom at night. His pants were down around his knees, and he had a *Playboy* gatefold in one hand. He had a stupid, preoccupied look on his face, and there was a strand of saliva glistening in the corner of his half-opened mouth.

Marcy leaned forward and touched the Transmit button. "Arnold!" she said sternly, watching him jump and gasp, "Arnold, you mustn't *do* that!"

Then, slowly, she smiled.

Introduction

The Incomplete Ripper

Gregory Frost

Look, Jack Dann is a silly person. I'm sorry, but there it is. His friends have tried for years to make out that he's this deeply serious, no-nonsense, dedicated writer, while the truth is, he's a crazy man who was too dangerous for North America and had to be shipped to a penal colony in Australia. The U.S. got the religious fundamentalists; Australia got all the criminals and Jack Dann. This was not a fair trade.

Some years ago a small writing workshop took place at the home of Gardner Dozois and Susan Casper, referred to as a "Philford"—that is, a Milford-format workshop held in Philadelphia.

Jack attended. I attended. Michael Swanwick, Tim Sullivan, James Patrick Kelly, and John M. Ford attended. And over a period of days we took turns carving up each other's stories (everyone had to bring one—you can't play unless you pay). We also ate and drank and in general misbehaved as is the custom. Neither Jack nor I brought this story nor anything like it to the workshop. But eventually we did start talking about Jack the Ripper, because Gardner and Susan were editing an anthology of stories about The Ripper (which ended up being called, surprisingly, *Ripper!* in the U.S. and *Jack the Ripper* in the UK. I always thought it should be called "Encomium for a Stuffed Rhinoceros," but nobody listens to me). Both Gardner and Susan are serious Ripper-ologists themselves.

Gardner put forth the notion—with which I agree—that if anyone ever were to open a file at Scotland Yard that revealed the true identity of Jack the Ripper, we would all respond with "Who the hell is that?" because it will turn out not to be one of the likely suspects; it will be someone you've never heard of. And somewhere during this discussion either Jack or I commented about what would happen if the Ripper was Woody Allen. What if he was this hapless nebbish with neither the strength to overpower nor the skill to execute his schemes. We kept throwing more ideas at it and pretty soon we were engaged in plotting out this story. By the end of the day, we had agreed to collaborate.

Could such a thing have happened if Jack Dann were not a goof? I put it to you that it could not.

Jack Dann

Yes, Greg and I got caught up in Susan and Gardner's Jack the Ripper frenzy . . . and you see the comedic result before you. Greg's account is accurate. We were hanging out, having a great time, and we started doing riffs on the subject of Jack the Ripper. It didn't take us long to go through a myriad of "what-ifs" before we struck the obvious, compelling scenario . . . or at least it was obvious and compelling to *us*!

What if Jack the Ripper was a complete incompetent? What if the women he tried to eviscerate and mutilate beat the shit out of him instead? What if Jack was a *putz*, a *patzer*, a *schmuck*, a *schleimel?*

Now *that* would make a story.

In the final analysis, I think Greg and I are a mite too silly to be true-blue, officially recognized, serious science fiction guys—and Gardner also falls into this elevated category. I remember several millennia ago when George R. R. Martin asked Gardner and me to do a story for his popular *Wildcard* series of anthologies. We could write whatever we wanted to, just as long as the protagonist had a super power. Well, Gardner and I put on our collaborative thinking caps and came up with the idea of a guy who had the unique super power of making women magically fall out of the ceiling. Of course, the fatal flaw of the aforementioned superpower was that all the falling women were over seventy. I think Gardner came up with the idea of women falling out of the ceiling; I think I came up with the idea that they would have to be blue-haired, kindly, kinky, little old ladies. I'm not sure. I do, however, remember going back to Binghamton and writing the first fifteen pages of the story in a few hours.

When we told George the subject and theme of what we were working on for him, he politely rejected it . . . sight-unseen.

And, as I recall, Greg and I wrote "The Incompleat Ripper" for Gardner and Susan's *Ripper!* anthology. It met a similar fate as the Women Falling Out Of the Ceiling story. We did, however, sell it on the second try.

This story was great fun to write. I remember finessing the Ripper's nineteenth century expletives into the text and being particularly proud of such phrases as "Who are you, slimy, cacky shitsmelling thing?" and "Play not with me, faggoty fartleberry. They be occupants, pinchpricks, putains . . . whores!"

After reading Patricia Cornwell's fascinating *Portrait of a Killer: Jack the Ripper Case Closed*, I'm *still* thinking about Jack the Ripper; and I've got an idea for a biographical novel about the artist Walter Sickert, who just might have been Jack the Ripper. I envision the novel as a sort of Portrait of the Artist as Mass Murderer.

It's an idea for a serious novel.

The problem is I can't quite get our original story version of Jack the Ripper out of my mind.

Wait, I've got an idea: How about a deluge of cute little old Jack the Ripper Sickerts falling out of the ceiling? . . .

The Incompleat Ripper

Jack Dann and Gregory Frost

ND SO IT WAS THAT THE ANGRY SPIRIT OF THE monster they called Jack the Ripper was reincarnated into the mind and body of Leon Michael Schwartz, who lived on the squalid north side of a city in New Jersey. Schwartz was virtually the path of least resistance. Hadn't he imagined himself to be Joan of Arc just last week when he tried to set himself on fire, only to be bathed clean by the efficient sprinkler system that Code Enforcement had compelled his landlord to install in Schwartz's rat-trap apartment? And last month, as the most perfect incarnation of Gandhi, hadn't he given up sex and hamburgers and tacos and frankfurters forever?

But Schwartz, who was overweight and pear-shaped with a weak chin and watery blue eyes, would not be driven out of himself by the likes of the Ripper, who had awakened within him like a hungry bear from a hundred-year hibernation. No, Schwartz had become used to the psychic squatters that had come to inhabit him periodically over the years; he had learned to accept them, just as his mother had learned to accept her husband's constant flatulence.

"You'll never be anyone," his mother used to say; that was her all-purpose threat. Would that she were still alive to see that he was well on his way to being *every*one.

"Where am I?" demanded the Ripper. "On Cherry Street," Schwartz replied, as he tried to continue reading an article in *Midnight Capers* about a woman in Kansas who had given birth to a unicorn. "You're in my apartment, right over 'Barbara's Beauty Parlor and Boutique.' Can't you hear the dryers going? They're on all the time. Drives me crazy. I thought when she installed all those tanning machines that maybe she'd turn the dryers off. No such luck."

"I don't hear anything," the Ripper said.

"You got to know what to listen for. Then the noise drives you up a wall."

"Who *are* you, slimy, cacky, shitsmelling thing?" the Ripper demanded.

"Your roommate," Schwartz said. "And I'm clean enough."

But the Ripper could not be quieted. He ranted madly in what seemed to be mostly gibberish about doxies and dead pickers, harpies and hay-bags, and the great pestilence of whores. Schwartz half-listened; he was used to his 'roommates' being a bit discon-certed early on, but he began to view this new tenant with some apprehension. The previous personalities at least had the decency to leave other people alone while they wreaked havoc on his, Schwartz's, life. But the Ripper seemed monomanically hell-bent on harlots of every persuasion.

Images of torn viscera and clotting blood flashed through the fiend's mind and made Schwartz queasy.

"Stop it, you're making me sick."

"Blood!" cried the Ripper. "Jehovah wants purification, and I am his servant. I carve the canvasback snatchpeddling whores into holy offerings. Remove the impure parts, He tells me, and I, his servant, must obey."

Schwartz grimaced. "Is that from *Macbeth?*" He thought his new invader might be one of the Booth family.

"Yahweh wants a tool for his work. Where is the Blade of Wrath?"

"The *what?*" Schwartz asked. But even as he asked, Jack had him up on his feet and into the kitchen. This visitor was stronger than any of the others. Seeking the correct tool for the job, he opened the silverware drawer. Schwartz fought every time Jack reached for a cleaver or a boning or serrated edged knife and, in fact, managed to turn the groping fingers astray. Jack was infuriated, and he wrestled Schwartz around the kitchen in an awkward dance without music, right hand slapping left, and vice versa, as they smashed into walls, knocked over chairs and shelves of bric-a-brac in their battle for control.

Finally, weary of further conflict—and worried about further damage to the apartment that *would* have to be paid for—Schwartz let Jack have a corkscrew.

"All right, then, I'll unplug the harlots!" Jack proclaimed, although some of the wind had definitely been taken out of his sails. Surely, the Lord was testing him by imprisoning him within this pacific creature. It was, he thought, God's will that he convert the slothful, such as Schwartz, and bring them to a level of sublime understanding. But first, the true nature and corruption of whores must be revealed. That would be Schwartz's first revelation, thought the Ripper. "Where are they?" he demanded to know.

"Who?"

"Play not with me, faggoty fartleberry," said Jack. "*They* be occupants, pinchpricks, putains . . . whores! Have you not heard of them?"

"They 'be' cross town," Schwartz said. "They're certainly not *here.*"

"We must go out, then," and Schwartz found himself lurching across the room. The Ripper seemed to be gaining strength; if this kept up he would overpower Schwartz completely. No mean feat, for Schwartz considered himself a psychic acrobat of sorts. "We must seek them," said the Ripper.

"Look," Schwartz said, "this isn't working out at all. Go 'seek' your whores in someone else's body," and Schwartz pinched his eyes closed and tried to imagine someone else inside him. Maybe some great personage who was transcendentally kind and good.

Maybe someone like Walt Disney.

He certainly would never consider unplugging whores.

But that, alas, seemed a wish which would never come to fruition, for the Ripper was in command now, and at large; it was time, finally, to descend, reborn, upon the painted women of accommodating morals that walked the sin-sodden streets of the city.

Jack the Ripper stood outside the Vine Street underpass, a narrow, graffiti-covered walkway a few blocks from his—Schwartz's—apartment. Occasionally, a freight train would thunder across the tracks overhead, shaking earth and cement. Jack had revealed himself to his host, and that pestiferous presence, sufficiently awed at being in such overwhelming proximity to God's Tool, had finally retreated and let him, Jack, carry on in peace.

The alley lay in deep shadow; it was a beautiful, sunny, spring day, and here was a perfect place to hunt: he had but to drag the demimondaine of his choice into the foul-smelling underpass and disembowel her in a craftsmanlike manner. Dozens of people passed by every minute, but none of the women looked right. Jack would know when the right one came along. A few passers-by glanced over uneasily at the solitary, lumpish figure standing and leering and fondling the corkscrew in his hand. Schwartz, who was worried they were going to be picked up by a cop, was not yet quite so overwhelmed by the Ripper that he couldn't exert a force of his own. However, Schwartz was aware that he couldn't push his luck too far; that could be suicide. The Ripper wasn't used to being thwarted.

And once again they fought, dancing about the street like a hopped-up Fred Astaire. Nevertheless, Schwartz managed to maneuver him into the underpass, where no one would notice them.

"It's too dangerous right out in the open," Schwartz said, panting. "You can't just attack people in broad daylight. Anyway, the underpass is as good as the street; people come through here as a short-cut."

"Are you an expert on this, too?" the Ripper asked coldly.

"Just trust me," Schwartz said, and he could feel the burning, focused power and barely controlled anger of the Ripper. They were dark, malignant forces working inside him . . . against him. Schwartz shivered as a cold, wet blade of fear worked up him spine.

But except for a few children and old couples, no one walked through the underpass. It was after five; the offices had emptied out.

The street was empty.

The rush was over.

And the Ripper had missed his window of opportunity. It was entirely Schwartz's fault. "So you are an expert, hey," the Ripper said, as he went completely insane, turning into the monster that killed, maimed, tamped, pummeled, dissevered, whittled, slished, hackled, sliced, and diced, and used filthy language. He waved his arms, shouted, and wheezed, and called Schwartz a jank and a jerker and a shit-fire bunghole, peppering every sentence with more expletives than Schwartz could understand.

When Schwartz had had enough, when he opened up his mouth to bellow some reasonable, contemporary curses, the Ripper said, "Hush!"

Footsteps approached.

Schwartz fell silent. He peeked around the edge of the alley. A single woman was walking along toward the underpass. She was tiny, and skinny. She wore pre-washed jeans, a sweatshirt, and jogging shoes. The Ripper groaned and grumbled; this was not the sort of woman he had hoped for. Where was the thick make-up, where the low-cut dress? he wanted to know. And to add insult to injury, this chick-a-biddy was an ectomorph. No meat, just bones. He'd need a saw to send her to Hell.

"Well, I'm terribly sorry she won't do," Schwartz said, relieved.

"Oh, she'll do," the Ripper said as the woman walked into the underpass. "What kind of nodcock would I be to argue with providence?"

And with that Schwartz jumped out with a corkscrew and pinned the woman against the wall. He was aghast at what he was doing, but it was the Ripper who was in control now. He leaned right up against her, the corkscrew pointed above her navel, ready to puncture and rend. Schwartz found himself grinning in feral fashion, and growling deep down in his throat, as if his hay fever was acting up again, producing too much phlegm.

The woman blinked at him as if she couldn't believe this was happening to her. But she made no attempt to scream. Perhaps she was too frightened, although she didn't look particularly frightened. She looked more like an architect studying a building.

"Scourge of Flesh," Jack said as he reached for her jeans.

She, in turn, expertly slammed her knee into his crotch.

Schwartz choked and doubled over.

The woman clasped her fingers together and hammered both hands down on his back.

Schwartz dropped to the ground.

With the starry heavens reeling and sparkling around him, he felt her grab him by the hair and raise his face off the cool, moldy-smelling concrete. "If I ever catch you here again, buster, I'm going to break your arms and your legs and put your dick in a jar. Is that clear?"

Schwartz didn't know if he nodded or not, but she finally walked away. He was very glad that no one came along after that, for it took him an eternity to learn how to stand up again . . . and another to learn how to walk.

✵   ✵   ✵

The red light district. It was nicknamed "Haymarket Avenue," and was a seedy confusion of rum-dum bars that were so small that twenty people would have trouble squeezing into any one of them. Rum-bags stumbled down the street, their noses red as Santa's, even in the warm, balmy night air. Past the bars lined chockablock on both sides of a great stone viaduct that rose over factories and warehouses and slums, past the stumblers and runaways and vent people and kids looking for dope, past the throwback hippy vendors selling glow-in-the-dark necklaces and "real" Gucci wristwatches to the Yuppies slumming on a Friday night, a huge Victorian building came into full view. The Ripper gasped with astonishment and joy. Schwartz sighed, feeling his own presence becoming weaker while the Ripper grew more potent, and let the Ripper have his legs to rush there that much quicker.

The building was the old railroad station that was no longer in use, a rundown Victorian Gothic structure, copper-green and replete with smoked glass windows, corbeled turrets, and cinquefoil arches. "This is one-in-a-way!" cried the Ripper. "I can feel the machinations of the devil here. I can smell peccancy and depravement in the very air."

"It's called pollution," Schwartz said.

"Exactly," the Ripper said. "This is perfect!"

"This is death," Schwartz grumbled. Untold stabbings and muggings and rapes and perhaps even murders had occurred around here. It was a center for whores and pimps and dopers. But all the murder and rape and whatnot had all been hushed-up by the city council because it would tarnish the city's image, and the city needed to attract industry. Schwartz had heard all about that from someone who knew someone in city government, and just now he fervently believed it all.

"And which of these facilities might house the fuckery?" the Ripper asked, staring intently at the station as if he already knew the answer.

"The what?" asked Schwartz.

"The whores, you jolterhead."

"How would I know? If I've ever been here it was as somebody else."

The Ripper became skeptical of his host's sanity. "Then we will linger beside the station."

"But it's empty. There's no one around here at all. It'll be worse than the underpass."

"We shall *wait*. God shall provide."

"If God were involved here, we'd both be salt by now," Schwartz said, frustrated. He tried another tack. "Look, let's just give it up for a while. Nice people don't kill and cut up and mangle women. It's just not done a lot around here. I'll tell you what, since this place is deserted, I'll take you to a great place I know and show you how to play video games. That might take your edge off."

The Ripper ignored Schwartz's suggestions and strode over deserted, broken tracks, around to the rear of the station, and up onto the rickety, rotted platform. Wooden ties were stacked neatly in pyramids, and he wove in and out of them, bursting with the sweet promise of finding a choice victim. And Schwartz could overhear his thoughts. This station reminded the Ripper of his home in England. Sighing, Jack dwelled on sweet memories of carnage and death and his collection of fine clocks. Schwartz's sneakers made hardly a sound as this modern Ripper, dressed in Rugby shirt, torn jeans, and aviator jacket, prowled the city. He fingered the sharp tip of the corkscrew.

Reaching the edge of the building, peering around the corner, he espied a large, gray station wagon below. It was not five feet away. Its lights were off, and moonlit clouds passed across its windshield. The Ripper did not feel entirely comfortable around cars yet, but he stood motionless.

Waiting . . .

Suddenly a cigarette glowed in the front seat. A moment later, a high-pitched laugh could be heard. Then the door opened, and Jack saw the woman below in fine, artificially lit detail. Shiny, blond hair piled up on her head, a bosom as big as a dashboard, encased like a trophy in a frilly blouse . . . and make-up, she wore make-up on her face. *This* was what he had anticipated, what he had expected.

"She looks like Kim Novak," Schwartz said.

"And who might that be?"

"And old actress."

"An actress?" he said disgustedly, as if acting was as odious as whoring.

Then the car started up. It backed out and drove away. The woman paid no attention, but looked at the neon face of her gaudy, turquoise inlaid wristwatch. Then she began a circuit of the cinder-covered yard.

Jack kept back, near the building's wall, out of sight. The moment was quickly approaching. She would pass below him in a few seconds. But he was a good seven feet above her.

"You're *not* going to jump," Schwartz said, but there was a whine in that thought. Better a whine than two broken legs and various contusions and abrasions.

Once again the Ripper ignored Schwartz. He looked about the platform. A few feet away were several pylons and an ancient, frayed rope that at one time must have been used for loading.

"No," Schwartz said, "you're not going to—"

Like an overweight Tarzan, Schwartz found himself leaping for the rope, and then climbing down, hand over hand, or trying to. The Ripper had forgotten that this body contained more mass, was in fact a good hundred pounds heavier than the Ripper, who, in fact, had been rather a frail, delicate specimen. When he was corporeal, in his own body, he prided himself on his neurasthenic appearance—that of noble blood. But blood, fat, and spirit were all slipping, falling, thudding against the woman, who broke Schwartz's fall. Miraculously, no bones snapped, although it knocked the wind out of him.

They landed on the rough cinders. The woman made a grunting noise as she fell, but Jack, every thought focused on the task at hand, was even then trying to stab her with his corkscrew. The woman scrambled out of his grasp. She was a big one and seemed to be merely winded and surprised. But the Ripper was her equal. He jumped up to confront her.

And discovered that she had been wearing a wig, for it had fallen away. Her real hair, which was dyed the color of henna, was slicked back, but in its present dishevelment stood up in greasy cowlicks. "What the hell is this shit?" she shouted, her large hands balled into fists. "What are you, some kind of weird, flying pervert?" Her voice dropped an octave below her initial exclamation.

"Just what we need," Schwartz mumbled. "A transvestite." Jack was paralyzed with disbelief. A good time for Schwartz to run, but the Ripper was too powerful, and he, Schwartz, was rooted to the spot.

The transvestite looked at her torn stockings, her bleeding knee. "Look at me," she whined in an affected voice. "You lousy pervert, look what you did."

"I'm really sorry," Schwartz said. "Really, it was an accident."

Enraged, Jack shouted, "Sorry! We're not sorry. You must die, you cock-queen!" And he jumped at her.

"Eat it, you prick," she answered and punched him in the jaw. Once again Schwartz glimpsed explosions of stars in the heavens as he crashed back down onto the cinders, his jacket tearing. But the transvestite was not finished. She began kicking him, and then beating him with what could only be a bludgeon disguised as a purse.

Later, through what felt like a cauliflower ear, he heard a car drive away. He assumed it must be the transvestite leaving. Did he still have all his teeth? he wondered. Had he broken any bones? This was by far the worst of the personalities thus far, and he vowed that there would be no more. He was going to board up his mind, close off every crack where they might get in.

"Do you mind if we go home now?" Schwartz thought, addressing the Ripper.

"Home? How can you entertain such thoughts when demons and perverts torment you like this. This is not the time to go home."

Schwartz sat up groaning. "Yes, it is. Why don't you go live in somebody else? Make it easy on both of us. You know, somebody you can relate to. You should be able to find a murderer or—"

"It is my *will* that we try again."

"Look, I'm tired of all this. I think my nose is inside out, and—"

"Up, pustulant golem!"

And Schwartz felt an implacable force pulling him to his feet. It was as if he was a marionette—he could do nothing but resign himself to the circumstances.

Soon it would be dawn. Perhaps then Jack would fade away like a vampire in the first rays of sunlight.

The Ripper insisted that they take a breath of air in the park, and so Schwartz had to walk five miles cross-town to Recreation Park, another hotbed of rape, drugs, and street-gang goings-on. While Schwartz was concerned with the constant, thudding pain of his bruises, the Ripper began to manifest a new, albeit restrained, *joie de vivre*. He was invigorated by every bum and street person they passed. Here was the land of promise, hecaters of perversion to be burned and scourged. It was up to God to restock this place with innocents once Jack had completed his work.

And, indeed, the Ripper did give a little thought to the possibility of moving out of this wretched Schwartz and into a strong, vibrant host.

After an hour of walking through the moonlit park, which was all silver highlight and velvet shadow, they heard a noise. It was more a mewling than a cry—muffled. Then, as they stopped and strained to hear, they discerned a woman's harsh whisper. "Please," she implored.

Jack scurried down a cobbled path past two graffiti-covered benches. The corkscrew was like a knife-handle in his grip. He crouched, listening, and was rewarded with the sound of rustling fabric.

Jack stalked toward his prey, only momentarily losing the spoor. Then he saw movement ahead, near a large, black-shadowed plane tree. He edged closer.

A woman lay on the ground, leaning up on her elbows. Her blouse was torn and her breathing was loud and ragged from fright. She was wearing a tight-fitting, leather mini-skirt. The man standing over her had his pants down around his ankles. Schwartz could see that the man was tall and stocky and wore his hair in a Balboa: a bleached plume on the top, the sides long and greased-backed into a duck's-ass. He had a knife in his hand, a large, mother-of-pearl handled switchblade. Just now, Schwartz wished that he had let the Ripper have one of the large kitchen knives instead of the corkscrew.

This woman is perfect, the Ripper thought. He had no patience to wait for this overgrown child of the gutters to be done with her.

And with a leap, he sprang into view.

The rapist panicked and lunged for Jack, but his feet became caught in his undone trousers and he toppled with his first step. His knife went wide as he grabbed for air.

The Ripper had only to hold the corkscrew steady.

The rapist impaled himself, driving it into his own throat unassisted.

After a moment, the woman watched Jack suspiciously; for it wasn't immediately obvious what the Ripper's intentions were.

But Jack's only concern was a weapon with which to slice and dice.

"Ask her what's her sign," Schwartz suggested, trying to divert the Ripper.

"His knife!" Jack said, ignoring the pestiferous Schwartz and regarded the dying, burbling rapist. He bent to retrieve the knife.

This was the golden moment.

But then a loud voice shouted, "Hold it right there, buddy," and at the same instant a bright beam of light caught him like a deer in the road. "Don't even try to scratch your ass, mister," called another unfriendly voice.

Two policemen walked toward him cautiously, pistols drawn. One of them eyed him curiously, almost blinding Schwartz with his flashlight. Schwartz did what he was told. He was trembling with fright. It looked like he was a murderer and who knows what else.

How could he explain that the Ripper did it?

"You try to kiss a bus or something, scumbag?" one of the policemen asked sarcastically, as he gazed at Schwartz's multiple contusions and abrasions and the robin's egg swelling under his eye.

Schwartz was too terrified to speak. He had bought the farm. He was going to be electrocuted or, maybe with luck and a skillful court-appointed attorney, he might get life and a day. Either way it was death. Maybe he could go back to being Gandhi. He stifled that thought.

But the story came out, finally, from the woman, whom both officers knew as a local hooker. She worked without a pimp, which was even more dangerous than having one. This particular "john" had seemed safe enough at first (he carried a photograph of his mother in his wallet), but had turned into a maniac once they reached the park. The "tore-up wino," as she referred to Jack, had saved her life. Schwartz wanted to explain that he wasn't a wino, but the Ripper was gnashing his teeth. He was mortified that they could construe that he had *saved* this harlot.

The policeman nearest the body called his partner over and shined his flashlight on the dead rapist's throat. "Check this out," he said, indicating the crosspiece of the corkscrew, which shone in all its stainless steel radiance. "Looks like we've got a *high-rent* wino here."

While the police were talking, the hooker sidled up to Schwartz and said, "Anytime, like, you want a freebie or something, you come see me, okay? I owe you. And here," she said, handing him a twenty dollar bill. "You go buy yourself a bottle of good whitewash, it's on me." Before Schwartz could refuse or think of anything proper to say, she walked back over to the policemen.

Jack was seething with humiliation and frustration. He had been brought back from the grave to do God's work . . . and he had failed abysmally. "I must escape from this cow-sham's coffin, this prison of flocculence and humiliation!" the Ripper screamed, cursing his fate, but Schwartz managed to keep his jaw firmly locked. The words escaped as a muffled yowling. One of the policemen turned toward Schwartz, who, thinking quickly, said, "I sometimes get these spasms of the larynx, and people think I'm trying to say something." The policeman nodded, believing him, and turned his attention back to the hooker.

Schwartz stumbled to a nearby bench. He felt weak and woozy.

He didn't even notice when the first of several television news teams arrived with cameras and lights. Great changes were going on inside him. His mind and body were being shocked and pummeled by the Ripper's soul, which, in desperation, began to flay about like a sharp-taloned bird of prey caught in a snare. As if that weren't enough, Leon felt that another presence had entered him. Although his eyes were rolled up in his head, and he shook as if suffering terrible spasms, Schwartz felt removed from it all; he looked inside himself as if he were a doctor giving an examination with an opthalmoscope.

But he could find no Ripper.

Jack had fled, disappeared, had finally returned to his eternal reward; and a *woman* had taken his place. Schwartz could feel her strength and femininity pulsing through him, drawing him in, shriveling him like fat on a fire until all that seemed to be left of Schwartz were a few coruscating thoughts and short-term memories. Then the tremors subsided, replaced by an oceanic calm. The beautiful, fulfilling, beatific presence that surrounded him was Sister Aimee Semple McPherson, the founder of the International Church of the Foursquare Gospel, who had ended her life with an overdose of sleeping powders.

Schwartz had finally seen the light.

He was utterly, unselfishly, undeniably in love.

He was but a prayer in her cathedral.

"And what might all this be?" Sister Aimee asked, as a camera crew moved in with all their lights and equipment. Car doors slammed, people chattered—the park had been turned into chaos.

"*Action News*," Schwartz said, despairing more for her than himself. "This is the end. Tomorrow morning a million or so people are going to see us on the morning news, and we'll be known as the 'high rent wino' who hangs around in the parks at night."

"A *million* people will see . . . *us?*" Sister Aimee intoned, awed and overwhelmed by the thought. "A million people . . ." She searched Schwartz's mind for more information on television. "I thought I was the cat's meow when I started my own gospel radio station in Los Angeles, but a million people . . . And they can see us, as if we were right there in their living rooms leading them back to God. Why it's a new chance, a new beginning. The Foursquare Gospel *shall* be raised up again.

"We must meet our public," she proclaimed to Schwartz—her love and her host—as she lifted up his arms to the reporters.

And the cameras, flashing halos, swung toward them.

Here, tonight, in this park, their new ministry would begin.

Introduction
Yellowhead

George Zebrowski

Subways were a big thing in my boyhood and teen years. They got you anywhere you wanted to go in New York City, the center of the world. Big also, in my imagination, was the great monorail sequence that opens Arthur C. Clarke's novel, *Earthlight*.

As I pressed through my college years, my periodic returns to the City showed me more of its underside, through the graffiti explosions of the 1970s and the gaudily dressed teenage gang lovers displaying themselves during the roaring rides through the endless darkness of the subway tunnels.

"Look there," I said to Jack Dann as we rode one of the painted trains. "There's a pair of characters." We later named them Yellowhead and his love Yoy, when the story grew in our heads.

An observation, from Jack or myself, sometimes from Pamela Sargent, would set off a story idea. Jack or I might suddenly type an opening paragraph, sometimes a mere sentence, and abandon the story to the alien ways of the other. If the story ran to its end, one of us would revise the draft. If Jack or I didn't like it, one of us would try again. This could and did go on for years, and I think only one full story was ever abandoned. We don't count fragments. Sometimes a nip or a tuck years later would get a full story right enough to be accepted by an editor.

"Yellowhead" is, we both believe with fingers crossed behind our backs, the best of some dozen published stories that we did together. But it had a few more interesting bumps along the way to publication than the others. On paper it earned more than any of the others, but we collected much less, when my then agent, the esteemed Virginia Kidd, placed the story with a now long-dead slick magazine, which delayed a considerable payment long enough for the magazine to go out of business.

Unstoppable as we were in those days, Jack and I did some more polishing, critical as we were of our work, then had it retyped by a young woman who might have passed for Yoy, if she had dressed for the part. Unpaid, meanwhile, Jack and I wrote the "bad debt" off on our taxes, and looked around for a likely place to send the story next. Thomas M. Disch and Charles Naylor were editing a new anthology about "tomorrow's mythologies" for Harper & Row, *New Constellations*, and paying much less than the now dead slick magazine; but Tom spoke an interest, so we sent him the story. His interest more than made up for any possible financial reward by the regard in which his high standards were held. And it would be a hardcover book!

We did not expect that he would accept the story. The teeth of self-doubt bite deep with beginning writers. But he accepted it— with praise. And sent us a check, which we divided in two and topped off our bank accounts.

So you see, Yoy typed the story on an old IBM electric with oversized type. The story retold the Orpheus myth in a subway setting. It all made perfect sense.

Jack Dann

In the early seventies, when I was crashing in George's apartment in Binghamton, New York; when we kept two antique, black typewriters ready to go on George's oak library table; when the simple physical joy of banging away at those typewriter keys with flexed and calloused index fingers prompted us to write many of our stories in first person, present tense because that seemed to help the words flow faster; in those fast, frantic, compacted, concentrated, never-to-be-repeated days of writing and workshopping and living in a communal intellectual environment that was of its time and place, we used to periodically visit the Bronx.

George's blond and beautiful mother had an apartment in a five-story walk-up, and I have such fond memories of sinking into the upholstered couch in her living room and eating exquisitely prepared Polish food in her formal dining room. Although I was in my early twenties, I always felt safe and secure there. George's mother treated George and me as if we were brothers—which in the profound sense we were, and are—and that apartment was like our safe house, the quiet place from which we would venture out to explore the exciting, shifting, deliciously dangerous, cacophonous labyrinths of New York City.

In those days graffiti was being elevated into an art form, and the cars of the subway trains looked like painted dragons flickering past us, as they silently careened into mythic, tunneled darkness. We became train-spotters, aficionados of subway art, of the scrolls and shadowed coded letters, of the brightly colored images; and, of course, we were looking through the gauze of right-now reality into the possibilities of art and myth and story.

We took it all back to Binghamton and started writing.

Collaborating with George was so seamless that it is almost impossible for me to tell what lines and sections George wrote, and what I wrote. We never followed any one formula. As George indicated earlier, sometimes we would write the story together, one looking over the shoulder of the other; sometimes one of us would work in seclusion on a section, which we would leave for the other to find. Some stories took days, others took weeks and months, and, yes, some took years. Very large and vociferous egos melted away. All that was important was to capture the shared vision.

I think we did that with "Yellowhead."

And if I remember correctly, my old girlfriend Marcia—a dancer—became the template for Yoy . . . wild, willowy, exuberant Yoy.

✦✦✦

Yellowhead

Jack Dann and George Zebrowski

THE SUBWAY TRAIN WAS A FLASH OF SALAD COLORS
as Retro Five, recently acquired by The Henchmen's Sixth
Division, pulled into the Bedford Park Station. That was where
they let Yellowhead off for the last time, only twenty-three years
after the trains had been painted and taken over by the Pain 5
People, who run them to this day better than the uptop jobbers.
Black Satin and Stitch Tonto hijacked the first train one long-ago
summer, moved their Pilots into the last car, called it Smoke Three
and ran it up and down the line. Soon no one cared.

Yellowhead started with Retro Five, then left for Jerome Avenue
to run his own operation. All the best painters followed him. No
one saw him upside after he shaved his head and painted it yellow.
He had a red, freckled face, a long, overly thin nose, thick sensuous
lips, and a weak chin that showed a slight cleft. He was more than
six feet tall and lanky, always bending over, slouching as if he
needed to bend toward the security of a floor.

With his painted head and tinted body, he was an awesome
sight to the busy people—the fingermen and serfage workers and
layers and prompters and factory-sitters. Although their jobs were
high and low, they all dressed the same: white-roughed faces, eyes
lined, noses shadowed, hair bristled and bronzed—lacking all

natural color—starched white shirts and snake black ties, tricolor jackets and pantaloons.

But Yellowhead couldn't stand the sameness of ties and jobs, sametalk and samesex, so he smoked some of Mama's Pain 5 and cut his neatly cropped hair. To substitute for his lack of color, he dipped into a paint store and covered himself with yellow. He almost died that first time, for he didn't realize that the body, like the lungs, had to breathe. He was barked and beaten twice that day, and gang-raped once, before he fled to the subways—his secret dream, that "slum hole for degenerates and filth," as Mama used to say.

Yellowhead had a darling, but he didn't know it until too late. Her name was Yoy Cross and she was as fair as a white line.

Yoy Cross, straight as they came and full of clichés, was a seamworker in North Brunswick Section Factory on 53rd Street. She had glint-gilded hair, trussed and tied as was the summer fashion, a fair face like Yellowhead's, but with thin lips and dimple creases. She was short and slight, small-boned and delicate. She had been trained to drive country trucks and largecars, but she had fallen from grace by refusing to manage company affairs and had left in virgin haste. Her Borndaddy and sister had thrown her out of the house as an example to the neighbors. She would have the stigma of a "Cherry" even after she had been bobbed by as many men and loving women as she could hold. She was a tragic throwback.

Six days a week she rode the Retro Five and watched the painters working their designs and graffiti onto the metal walls—inside and outside. That was her break in the day's monotony, her flash of danger. The dark tunnels promised to swallow her, promised juicy, delicious night-terrors. And the bare, bright ceiling bulbs provided security.

"Okay, okay, okay, okay," shouted a twelve-year-old dressed in khakis and dirty shirt. He brandished a crowbar, but not menacingly. He was polite and pushed his way through the crowd until he could get near enough to a handhold. He hooked his crowbar onto the handhold and swung back and forth with one arm, kicking an uptown woman in the shoulder. She only sighed and moved away. It was the weekend; everyone wanted to get home and rest—the insecurity of the subway could be least tolerated on Saturday. Even Yoy looked down at the painted floor and wished for home and toilet.

"Okay, okay, okay," shouted another boy, older than the other, but dressed the same. He passed Yoy, purposely stepping on her foot and smiling and waving his crowbar. "Excuse me, pardon me, sorry, sorry . . ."

Yoy looked around for a Pilot but couldn't find one. This car was dislocated; there was not even a painter to add contrast and safety, just upsiders like herself, and no one to protect them from themselves.

The train pushed through the tunnels, curving, climbing, turning, then screeched—metal against metal—and slowed down before a red light. It bolted, ran for a few seconds, and jerked to another stop. Through the smeared windows Yoy could see the roundtop intersection: bare bulbs shining wanly in a garage pit, cement struts crisscrossed with metal tiebars, other tunnels—illusions of immensity, leaders of track and another waiting train pulled up. It was close enough to touch, a metal dragon of green and yellow and red, a sandblast paint job, car after car painted and pruned to look like a Wu-dragon, a metal centipede. That had been painted before Yellowhead had left Retro Five—a good time when the best painters could still be boasted by Stitch Tonto.

Yoy hoped this wouldn't be a long stop. The air would become thick and some old man would start coughing and wheezing and start everyone else crying and sneezing and screaming. Someone died in her car at least once every week. She thought perhaps she was a jinx, a laylow, but then so was everyone else.

"Hey, Cherry, Cherry," screamed a high-pitched male voice. Yoy turned around, saw it was an old neighbor's son. He was still fat and pimply, and his face was dirty except for paint spots and drool lines. She tried to ignore him. He had joined a gang of boys with crowbars, but he was young and green so was only permitted to carry a broken umbrella stick. She was sure that would make him mean.

"Hey, lolly, lolly, Yoy," sang another boy. They all pushed toward her, bars in hand, hair plastered back unstylishly, mouths puckered in polite smiles.

The youngest boy tried his luck on a young girl—slashed her face with an umbrella end, rubbed her belly and humped her. The crowd looked through the windows, grumbled and kept at small-talk. After all, the boys were still being polite.

Next an old man. His wife was too stiff to scream. Dress the same, rape the same—that was the time-honored jingo.

An older boy—sword scar across his face down to his neck, blue eyes that twinkled, greased hair in ringlets and unpainted mouth with no teeth—pushed into Yoy, ripped the front of her dress open and watched to see if the boy beside her intended to help her. He looked away, and the older boy ground glass knuckles into Yoy's face. With fairly good style, he bloodied both her breasts and then proceeded to rape her slowly.

Yoy screamed, pretended she wasn't there, stared out the window as the dragon train pulled away silently, its cars jerking under its painted carapace.

But it was too soon for Yoy to black out. Virginity can be taken only once, and she, through her tears and screams, was enjoying her betrothal to society. Offspring from such a union would be considered holy, but she knew she wouldn't tell her family. Let them cross and snuffle in their rotten rooms.

With a jerk, the train started moving. She could feel him shaking like a weak child and was amused that such a fragile husk was forcing itself into her.

More screams—her own.

And unknown to her, a few boys, painted and plumed, jumped across from the rear car to the tunnel catwalk, heading for the club cave near the old pipe junction.

He got off her as the train started to roar into the tunnel. The car was empty, and she could tell that he was disappointed. His audience had fled into the forward parts of the train.

That was when Yellowhead came into the car, walking forward on his rounds, checking the car links and open-close door whooshers. She saw him come up behind the thief and bring his fist down on his head, crumpling him with one blow.

She opened her eyes and tried to sit up. She tried to grab Yellowhead's hand, but he only smiled.

"You'll be happy without him," he said to her.

And she felt that he wanted her. He had fought for her, however slightly. He continued into the next car as she fixed herself up. She watched him go, but she knew that when next they met, it would be different. He was being kind now, leaving her to her rites, content to wait for when they would meet on more individual terms.

But he never spoke to her again.

She rode his train week after week, hoping to catch a glimpse of him. She listened to conversations about him on the other lines. And she followed him when rumor told her that he was riding elsewhere in the city with friends in their living cars at the ends of their trains. Once through a car window she saw him change his clothes. For a moment she caught a glimpse of his tattooed body topped by his yellow skull. He was thin and wiry and could not see her in the dark tunnel where she stood. She had come up to the window too late for him to see her.

As time went on her love became more anxious. He did not notice her even when she smiled at him. She became desperate when he disappeared for a whole month during the short war with the out-city trains. He came back with a bandage over his right eye and his arm in a sling, and she cried for his pain.

Now his indifference was slowly turning into betrayal in her mind. The saddest songs come from this part of her life. The train howls in the tunnel and the wheels whine more sweetly than an electric violin. The air in the tunnels vibrates with the tears of heroes.

And a train comes rolling forward toward the woman who must die. She has chained herself to the track. The train cuts her in half like a razor and stops.

Yellowhead is called out to see the body. He sees the face and her tattered dress, her hands flung outward over the third rail, which flickers with blue life under her divided form.

The train pulls into the Bedford Station, and Yellowhead gets off to stand on the platform. The downtown train pulls in and he sees her words written in red across two cars.

I LOVE YOU YELLOWHEAD   MY NAME IS YOY

Then he remembers the time in the train when she had looked up at him, reaching out for his hand as he walked away. He moves to the end of the platform and looks back into the mouth of death, where the blue flashes still light the darkness—on and off, on and off, with the smell of ozone and burnt flesh pushing out at him.

At that moment he leaped down onto the tracks and began walking slowly into the darkness. Those who saw him for the last time remember, finally, only his yellow skull bright in the blackness.

No one ever found a body. No one ever found Yoy. No one knows how he picked her up from the electrified rail without falling down dead beside it. Some say he went down into the maze of tunnels, into the caves beneath the river, to rest with her; and their bones still lie there in dry embrace.

Some say they see Yellowhead grinning at them in the high-speed tunnels of the booster trains. They say his ghost lives in the magnetic field that propels the new trains, that it is summoned away from Yoy's arms when the train passes over their place deep in the undercity.

The songs say that nothing in life moved Yellowhead so much as finding out that she had loved him. Others say that he would not have loved her at all if he had not learned too late that she was lost to him. For him to notice, the missing part of his life had to die.

Now there are trains on the moon, under it and above, boosters and surface monorail. And there is a new song that says that Yellowhead's ghost is in all the metal made on Earth; and wherever trains rush, Yellowhead will slip from Yoy's bony clasp to go and look at them. Recently his giant ghost was seen sitting on the rim of a crater, looking up at the stars, dreaming of tunnels across the heavens. A legend is the loveliest part of the truth.

Other songs say different things.

Introduction

Slow Dancing With Jesus

Gardner Dozois

This story was the result of a social evening when Michael didn't happen to be around, but the dynamics worked out much the same way anyway. Susan and Jack and I had gone out to dinner at Dave Shore's (a family-style Jewish restaurant that I'm still sorry is gone, twenty years after it closed; best roast duck I ever had, and their steak smothered in onions was great too) with our friends Bob Walters and Tess Kissinger, two local artists. During dinner, conversation turned to Tess's weird and wonderful dreams, of which she has a seemingly inexhaustible supply (another favorite of mine is the one where the aliens land and insist that we change the way we've been spelling the word "Mexico"). At my insistence, Tess related my favorite dream of hers, which I'd heard her describe before, about how, when she was an unpopular teenager, she'd dreamed that Jesus had taken her to her high-school prom, and told all the other kids, who'd been scorning her, "She's here with me. And if *I* say she's cool, she's cool."

Jack immediately took fire with this idea, and (after a polite but razor-thin pause to ask a bemused Tess if she minded us stealing her dream) decided that we would write it out as a story that very night. He was already working it out in the cab on the way home. And as soon as he got to our apartment, he rushed to where my battered manual stand-up Remington typewriter sat atop our rickety kitchen table, whipped a piece of paper into it, and began to type furiously.

Another engine that drove these collaborations is that Jack is a fearless writer of great ambition, unafraid of plunging right into any writing project, no matter how daunting and technically difficult it might seem to be at the start, no matter how great the creative challenges to be overcome. Already, in the cab on the way home, I'd been getting cold feet, daunted by the thought of the subtle technical difficulties that would have to be overcome to actually get the story down on paper effectively. If it'd been just me, I'd have thought about it for a day or two, decided it was too difficult, and dropped it. But with Jack pounding away on my typewriter in my living room (which was also the kitchen), this was no longer an option.

Jack wrote furiously for more than an hour, taking the story through the opening scene, up to the point where Jesus and Tess arrive in front of the building where the prom is being held. Then he stood up and made a sweeping gesture toward the typewriter, as if to say, "Your turn."

I did take my turn, and finished the rest of the story, although it took me two days rather than an hour-and-a-half. The biggest technical challenge was to make it something more than just a sacrilegious joke, like a Monty Python routine. I wanted it to be representative of a young girl's longing dreams—that was the quality that had to be brought to the story. It had to be simultaneously sad and funny, bittersweet and strange and driftingly wistful. It was a very difficult mood to create, and I felt throughout that it was so fragile that one false step would shatter it. So I was very careful where I placed my metaphorical feet, avoiding anything that was too facile or too obvious, too ha-ha Monty Pythonish, shaping all the details to maintain the mood, even carefully working out which songs the characters dance to, and the order in which they should be played.

Everybody told us that we didn't have a chance of selling this story. Instead, it sold on the second attempt, to *Penthouse*, to Kathy Green again, who really should be saluted for being willing to take a chance on risky material (later, she took my even riskier solo story "Disciples") during a very conservative and repressive (does this sound familiar?) time in American society. If she didn't buy it, I doubt that anyone else would have.

Jack Dann

Ah, yes, I, too, miss Dave Shore's. Some of the best *Yiddishe* cooking in North America. And I remember Tess discussing her strange, weird, ultraviolet dreams, dreams that were simultaneously effecting, beautiful, and frightening; and, Gardner was spot on—when Tess described her dream about going to the senior prom with Jesus, *this* Jewish boy went wild. I remember the image that flashed in my mind, as strong and distinct and three-dimensional as anything I'd ever experienced. I *saw* Jesus: well-coiffured, shoulder length, chestnut-brown hair parted in the middle. Beard clipped short and neatly trimmed. Face tanned and handsome and sensitive. He wears a one-button white tuxedo jacket, black trousers, and a pale blue cummerbund. He pulls up in front of Tess Kimbrough's house in a vintage, white 1955 Thunderbird convertible. He is movie-star cool; he is James Dean and Marlon Brando and Kirk Douglas and John Fitzgerald Kennedy all rolled into one, and to make it even sweeter, he's the Son of God! And she . . . she is a plain girl with acne, the girl no one wants to be seen with, much less take out on a date. (I should hasten to add that Tess was—and is—the absolute antithesis of a plain Jane. I had, in fact, flashed back to my own adolescence when I had acne so bad that in the summer I wouldn't take off my T-shirts at the beach, lest people see the reefs of ugly acne sores on my back and shoulders.)

God, I had to write that story, transform that numinous, coruscating, three-dimensional image into a painting on the page; and once I recovered myself, once I shook myself out of that fugue state of creative yearning and intention, I did, indeed, see that Tess was looking completely bemused. And Gardner . . . well, Gardner looked rather embarrassed. (However, he often looked like that when we were out in public together.)

But I just couldn't let that story go.

So, generous entrepreneurs that we were, we made a deal with Tess. Let *us* write the story and when (and *if!*) it sells, we'll . . . buy you dinner.

Ah, yes, Jack Dann and Gardner Dozois, the last of the big spenders.

As Gardner recounted, we went home, and I immediately sat down at the typewriter and banged away furiously on Gardner's old Remington typewriter, trying to tease out and trap the ideas and images before they dissipated into the light bulb glow of that soft summer Philadelphia night. At least, I *think* it was summer.

Gardner did write the story through to the end. We passed it back and forth, I think; but Gardner had, indeed, caught the tender poignancy and yearning of adolescence. I remember arguing that the hint of tongue in the last kiss might be construed as too sacrilegious; but after all these years, I think Gardner was right. He maintained exactly the right balance on the tightrope, and the ending —which is Gardner at the top of his form—is a perfect pirouette.

I might mention, though, that there *was* another editor willing to take a chance on one of Gardner's risky stories. It was I, the very one, who commissioned "Disciples" for my Jewish science fiction and fantasy anthology *More Wandering Stars*. Now I mention this only to make a very small point—that Gardner is really the secret master of Jewish guilt, for, you see, when he gave me the finished story he said, "Jack, would you have any objections to using this story as a reprint?"

"A reprint . . . ?" Eyes blinking.

"Yeah. Kathy Green is interested in buying it for *Penthouse*."

"*Penthouse* . . . ?"

"And, frankly, I could really use an extra $2,500.00."

"2,500.00 . . . ?"

So nu? What could I do? Say no . . . ?

But at least *now*, after all these years, the secret is out!

Slow Dancing With Jesus

Gardner Dozois and Jack Dann

J ESUS CHRIST APPEARED AT TESS KIMBROUGH'S DOOR
dressed in a white tuxedo with a blue cummerbund and match-
ing bow tie. His chestnut-brown hair was parted in the middle and
fell down past his shoulders, and his beard and mustache were
close-cropped and neatly combed.

Tess's mother answered the door. "Come right inside. Tess will
be down in a jiffy." She led Jesus into the front room. "Tess," she
called, "your date is here."

Upstairs, Tess checked the bobby pins that held her French
twist together and smoothed imaginary wrinkles out of her dress. It
was the emerald green one, with dyed-green shoes to match, that
her urbane and sophisticated mother had helped her pick out, and
she was somewhat nervous about it. But then, she was so nervous
anyway that her teeth were chattering. She told her image in the
mirror that this was going to be the most perfect night of her life,
but the image in the mirror didn't look convinced. She practiced
breathing evenly for a moment, flaring her nostrils. Then she
walked down the stairs to meet Jesus, remembering not to look
at her feet, and trying to maintain good posture.

Jesus stood up as she entered the room and presented her with a
corsage, a small orchid on a wristlet. She thanked him, kissed her

mother goodbye, promised that she'd be back at a reasonable hour, and then she was sitting beside Jesus in the leatherette seat of his Thunderbird convertible. Jesus refrained from laying rubber in the front of Tess's house, as most kids would have done; instead he shifted smoothly and skillfully through the gears. Tess momentarily forgot about being nervous as the wind rushed by against her face and she thought that she was actually—right now—going to the prom.

"How are you doing?" Jesus asked. "Do you want a cap or something so the wind won't mess your hair?"

"No, thanks," Tess said shyly. She was almost afraid to look at him, and kept stealing sidelong glances at him when she thought his attention was elsewhere.

"You nervous?"

Tess glanced at him again. "You mean, about the prom?"

"Uh-huh," Jesus said, executing a high-speed turn with an easy, expert grace. The buildings were going by very fast now.

"Yeah . . . I guess so."

"Don't be," Jesus said, and winked.

Tess felt herself blushing, but before she could think of something to say, Jesus was bringing the car to a smooth stop in the lower parking lot of the high school. A kid whose Vaseline-smeared hair was combed back into a ducktail opened the door for Tess, and then slid into the driver's seat when Jesus got out. Jesus gave him a five-dollar tip.

"Jeez, thanks," the boy said.

Cinders crunched under their feet as they crossed the parking lot toward the open fire door of the gym, which was now framed by the paper lanterns that glowed in soft pastel colors. Tess walked hesitantly and slowly now that they were really here, already beginning to feel the first sick flutterings of panic. Most of the kids didn't like her—she had long ago been classified as uncool and, worse, a "brain"—and she didn't see any reason why they'd start to like her now. . . .

But then Jesus was surrendering their tickets at the door, and it was too late to flee.

Inside the gym, the bleachers had been pulled back from the dance floor and the basketball nets had been folded up. Paper streamers hung from rafters and water pipes, herds of slowly jostling balloons bumped gently against the ceiling, and crepe-paper roses were everywhere. The band—five sullen, young men in dark-red jackets that had "The Teen-Tones" written on them in sequins—

had set up in the free-throw zone and were aggressively but un-skillfully playing "Yakety Yak." Kids in greasy pompadours, crew cuts, and elephant trunks milled listlessly around the dance floor, looking stiff and uncomfortable in their rented suits. Only a few couples were dancing, and they jerked and twitched in lethargic slow motion, like people slowly drowning on the bottom of the sea.

Most of the girls were still standing by the refreshment tables on the other side of the room, where the punch bowls were, and Tess made her way toward them, feeling her stomach slowly knot with dread. Already she could see some of the kids smirking at her and whispering, and she heard a girl say loudly, "Just look at that *dress!* What a nerd!" One of the class clowns made a yipping, doggy noise as she passed, and someone else broke up into high-pitched, asth-matic laughter. Blindly, she kept walking. As she came up to the group around the punch bowls, her friend Carol gave her an unen-thusiastic smile and said, "Hey, lookin' good," in an insincere voice. Vinnie, Carol's bullet-headed boyfriend, made a snorting sound of derision. "I just don't understand why you have anything to do with that dog," he said to Carol, not even making a pretense of caring whether Tess could hear him or not. Carol looked embar-rassed; she glanced at Tess, smiled weakly, and then looked uneasily away—she genuinely liked Tess, and sometimes hung out with her after school (in the classic teen configuration, encoun-tered everywhere, of one pretty girl and "dog" doing things together), but as a captain of cheerleaders she had her own status to worry about and under the circumstances she'd lose face with the cool kids if she stuck up too vigorously for Tess. "I mean, *look* at her," Vinnie complained, still speaking to Carol as if Tess weren't there. "She's *so* uncool, you know?"

Tess stood frozen, flushing, smiling a frozen smile, feeling her-self go hot and freezing-cold by turns. Should she pretend that she hadn't heard? What else could she do? The clown had drifted over, and was making yipping noises again. . . .

Jesus had been a few steps behind her coming through the crowd, but now he stepped up beside her and took her arm, and all the other kids suddenly fell silent. "Leave her alone," Jesus said. His voice was rich, strong, resonant, and it rang like a mellow, iron bell in the big, empty hall. "She's here with *me*." Vinnie's mouth dropped open, and Carol gasped. All the kids were gaping at them, their faces soft with awe. Tess was intensely aware of Jesus' strong, warm fingers on the bare flesh of her arm. Jesus seemed to have grown larger, to have become huge and puissant, a giant, and his rugged, handsome face had become stern and commanding. He radiated strength and warmth and authority, and an almost tangible light—a clear and terrible light that seemed to reveal every zit and pimple and blackhead in the sallow, shallow faces of her tormentors, each slack mouth and weak chin and watery eye, a light that dwindled them to a petty and insignificant group of grimy children. "She's here with me," Jesus repeated, and then he smiled, suavely, jauntily, almost rakishly, and winked. "And if I say she's cool, believe it, she's cool."

Then, before anyone could speak, Jesus had taken Tess's hand and led her onto the dance floor, and they were dancing, slow dancing, while the band played "A Million to One." She had never been able to dance before, but now she danced with effortless skill, swirling around and around the floor, following Jesus' lead, moving with beauty and flowing, silken grace, shreds of torn paper roses whispering around her feet. One by one the other couples stopped dancing and stood silently to watch them, until they were surrounded by a ring of pale, gaping, awed faces, small as thumbnails and distant as stars, and they drifted and danced within that watching ring as the band played "Good-night, My Love" and "Twilight Time" and "It's All in the Game."

After the dance, Jesus drove her home and kissed her goodnight at her door, gently but with authority, and with just the slightest sweet hint of tongue.

Tess let herself in and went upstairs to her room, moving quietly so that her mother wouldn't realize that she was back. She switched on a soft light and stared at herself in the mirror; her flesh was tingling, and she was sure that she must be glowing in the darkness like freshly hammered steel, but her face looked the same as always, except perhaps for the expression around the eyes. She sat down at her night table and took her diary out from the locked, secret drawer. She sat there silently for a long while, near the open window, feeling the warm, night breeze caress her face and smelling the heavy, sweet perfume of the mimosa trees outside. A dog was barking out there somewhere, far away, at long intervals and cars whined by on the highway, leaving a vibrant silence in their wake. At last she opened her diary, and in a bold neat hand wrote, "*Dear Diary, Tonight I met—Him. . . .*

Introduction

Blues and the Abstract Truth

Barry N. Malzberg

"Blues and the Abstract Truth" did not produce the remarkable amount that *Omni* paid us, only grief in the experience, ease in composition and bemusement in publication . . . here was my life entire (twenty five years spent looking into the cage, twenty-five years looking out) and nothing more to say. It is a collaboration which felt like the single self, one of the definitions of a good collaborative work.

Jack Dann

1987, and author/editor Dennis Etchison asked me for a story for a collection to celebrate the tenth anniversary of the prestigious *Lord John Press*.

I pondered and daydreamed, searching for a story idea; and memories flittered and skittered through my mind, ghostly images on the dark field of the years. I remembered the years of writing novels in a succession of small, home offices; starting businesses or getting jobs to get past the rough patches; and always quitting to write again. And I had the chilling realization that this journey from youth and vigor to middle-aged regret, poignancy, and ennui had taken no time at all. Growing old is essentially and profoundly instantaneous. That age-old idea drenched me like rain, like a sudden, terrifying deluge; and *there* was the story. I could see it flickering frame by frame in my mind's eye: My character: one minute young and vital, the next minute middle-aged and sitting in a cheap, fly-by-night sales pit, options closed, dead-ended. He couldn't get out, couldn't escape through art and artifice.

If memory serves, I wrote the opening in a white heat, then sent it to Barry. This was the metaphor that illuminated so much of the dark terrain we shared. It went a good way toward explaining the way we felt, had felt, and would certainly feel in the future. Barry took the bit, and we passed the story back and forth. I believe I did the final, conforming draft.

Fourteen years after we wrote "Blues and the Abstract Truth," Barry e-mailed me: "BLUES AND THE ABSTRACT TRUTH. Half my life spent staring into the windows wanting to be there, half my life spent in there staring out the window wanting to be free. And never for a moment at peace."

The boiled-down, distilled truth of the story.

Repeated and refracted yet again in Barry's introduction.

Dennis generously gave us permission to publish the story first in the January issue of *The Magazine of Fantasy & Science Fiction*. He then published it in *Lord John 10* and his groundbreaking anthology *Metahorror*.

Blues and the Abstract Truth

Barry N. Malzberg and Jack Dann

THIS ISN'T A SPIRITUAL OR A PRESCRIPTION. IT IS, however, a precise diagnosis.

Bear with me. To explain and explain.

So this is how it happens: It's 1963, and you are with a girl named Mollie. John F. Kennedy was killed three weeks ago on the 22nd (you can look that up), and LBJ is telling us that we will continue . . . continue with what? "Danke Schön" and "Call Me Irresponsible" are playing day and night on the radio, God help us all. You went out to a college bar in Hempstead, Long Island, where they had a guy who played terrific jazz organ, and you picked up this girl who is a freshman at Hofstra and hails from upstate somewhere, maybe Cohoes. She says she was the *only* Jewish girl in her high school, and she makes every other word sound like "aou."

You've brought her back to your rented room on the second floor of Mr. Seitman's rooming house in East Meadow. You thought you'd have to sneak her into the house, but dictatorial, half-blind Mr. Seitman has gone out to play bingo, and now you're safely behind closed doors and impressing the hell out of Mollie with your knowledge of jazz. You're studying music at the same college she's attending (she's a theater major), and you are absolutely certain that one day your name will be listed in *Playboy*'s Annual Jazz Poll. And you're smart because you're studying musicology; worst comes to worst, you can teach during the day and play in the clubs all night. You have a 1-Y draft status because you have a nervous stomach, and right now you're playing the classic recording of Louis Armstrong's "A Monday Date," where he cuts in with a brilliant vocal rendition right after his trumpet solo.

Mollie has been saying something like she's a virgin and that she believes chastity to be the only valid option for a woman in these times, although she's not opposed to oral sex. Not *bitterly* opposed, anyway. In 1963, before and after JFK's extraordinary run of bad luck, it was very chic in college circles to be a virgin, even if you weren't, so this is not surprising or objectionable.

"Sure," you agree, understandingly. "Sure."

She looks like she has nice breasts under her skin-pink mohair sweater, and you are hopeful of seeing them naked soon, but (and this is the kicker) *you* are for sure the virgin in this crowd. You don't know how to tell her this or cover your inexperience.

Luckily, she knows that you want her, and senses your awkwardness, and she takes you off the hook easily by making the first move.

The important thing is, you are going to come.

Coming is definitely not a routine event in your life—with a woman, that is to say. You have been thinking about it all night. Now the black lights are on, and so is the rotating sparkle globe you've installed on the ceiling, and all your posters are glowing like neon: peace signs and astrological signs and all manner of fantastic beasts and Nereids are suddenly brought to radioactive life while the room seems to twirl with every possible color. You and Mollie are smoking some unbelievably good Panama Red, which a buddy from your band has left with you to stash, and Mollie's clothes are off—almost all of them, anyway—and you are so stoned-out now, the two of you, that you are confusing the music with your thoughts, but you're getting it right, sliding your fingers over her goosebumped skin, pushing and grinding against her, tasting her cigarette-soured mouth, thinking musically of this and that and nothing at all and that poor bastard JFK, fucked over now by a Texan, and then you are

Transformed.

You are taken up and out, Stony-o, you are lifted like the bullets lifted JFK in the Continental, you are *yanked*, and then. . . .

You are bearing with me. I am doing what I can to explain. Over and over this goes, but it is vitally important to get it right; there is no understanding without memory, Mollie, and I can still almost feel your arms tight around me, and your tongue, and then

You are somewhere else.

You are *here*.

You are in this *place*.

It's like being six sheets to the wind and falling down the stairs.

It's like being jolted out of a deep sleep.

But here you are, young man, no transition, yank, bang, and you're in a large office separated into cubicles. The pushpin fabric of the five-foot-high cubicle dividers is powder blue, the commercial-grade carpet a dismal brown. The dividers are on your right, and six people are crammed into the cubicles, one to a spot, phoning, until suddenly they all turn to look at you, staring at you, waiting for an explanation. You must have made *some* kind of squawking noise, and who can blame you, what with Mollie's face taking up the field of vision one minute, and now this. . . .

You look at these six people, and what you really want to say is, "What the fuck is going on here?"—but that would expose your position immediately. It's not for nothing that you have a little sixties smarts, a residue of late-fifties cunning. You still have a buzz on from the grass (maybe that pot was *too* good), and you say, keeping your cool, adjusting yourself to the situation, "Back to work, gang. I just got a shock from the computer."

The word just comes to you. *Computer*. In 1963 that was a tech-word like *astronaut* and *New Frontier*, but you somehow had access to it. Be that as it may, you're still new to all this, and as you look at your hands, you can tell you have aged. You are not twenty, that is for sure. (Would that you were!) The hands are solid and bear the heavy imprints of time, and you know, now you know, that if you raise your hand to your face, you will feel texture, wrinkles, a bristly stiff mustache.

Such is the rush of chronology. It is much more than a physical dislocation. Much has shifted.

But under the circumstances, you are amazingly calm.

You have had all of this latter time to think about that, of course; your calm, your amalgamation, your *synchronicity* with the impossible. Because, of course, you are of two parts: there is the strangling, stunned part of you that has come *here*, and there is that distant and cold part with which you have just merged; it is that distant "you" that knows about computers and the precise function of this office, which is to sell the unneeded to the unloved under the guise of love and need.

You're selling entertainment.

This is a cable-television sales pit.

But the young, dislocated part of you asks how the fuck you got *here*, of all places. This is absolutely nowhere. You were supposed to become a goddamn musician. You should be out playing a gig at the Metropole or maybe The Half Note. At the very least, you should be teaching, maybe not at Juilliard, but a decent university wouldn't have been out of the question. You certainly shouldn't be managing six part-time temporaries working on a Friday night. And your distant, older part—the self you are quickly coming to know, the self that has been ground smooth as a stone by forty-two years of experience and frustration—doesn't have a word to say to you.

Because you know, Stony-o. You *know*.

A young woman of about twenty says, "Yeah, I've had that happen to me, too, when I'm putting stuff into the computer. Shocks the hell right out of you, doesn't it?" she says crudely, smiling. She is swarthy and doe-eyed, and it is obvious that her long shock of white-blonde hair is dyed, the ends burned by countless applications of bleach. The part of you with whom you have merged, the worn-out and cynical "you" who knows computers, understands that her name is Franny. She had been here for six months—a long time in the telemarketing game—and not so long ago you asked her to have lunch with you, but she said, "No married men; I've been through that door once, and that was enough." Another humiliation, even though you are the boss, even though you are supposed to be in control.

So now you know of this and other incidents of this man's life. Although everything is new and terrifying, now you *know* that twenty-odd years have passed and that you have merged with an older self, but whether it is really you or a defeated facsimile, you are not yet sure. There is still a tendril of hope in your heart. After all, this couldn't really have happened to *you*. But with dislocation comes instant maturity, and you really do know the truth, just as you know that it would be a kind of death to accept it completely.

Slow and tentative, fast and desperate, you have the answers. And yet you have none.

The buzz from the grass has ebbed—the yanking will do that to you—and you are very cold and very clear on a level of functioning that is so precise that it is the most terrifying thing yet. You are out of control, and yet you are *in* control. JFK, you understand, has been dead for half as long as he was alive, and Phil Specter is gone, gone.

"Come on, now," you say, cheerlessly enough, as you are in a supervisory position, "let's get back to *work*"—just as if you knew what you were doing here, as if you belonged (but you do! you do!)—and you go back to the computer. As one part of you gazed in wonder, the other part is monitoring the telemarketing service reps (you also know they're called TSR's) and at the same time typing names and addresses, answering Y or N to arcane questions coming up on the screen of the monitor, which reminds you of the fluorescent black-light posters in your room in East Meadow, the very same room where, moments before, you were kissing and tasting Mollie's lips, which were sticky and deliciously red from a recent application of strawberry lipstick gloss.

Well, that is how it began. Or how it ended.

Outside looking in . . . inside looking out; my mantra.

One moment I'm twenty and trying to score; the next moment I'm forty-two and supervising cable sales in an upstate district that includes Mollie's hometown of Cohoes. I am married to a woman named Ellen Aimes, my first and only marriage, her second. We have been married for eighteen years and have one daughter, Mollie. (Through the insane coincidence of a malign but stupid fate, Mollie was the name of Ellen's mother.) We have careful sex once a week, always in bed and in a missionary position. Ellen is a mathematics teacher at a junior high school. I make about twenty-five thousand a year; she makes thirty. I drive a 1983 Pontiac Catalina and collect bebop and modern jazz, although I don't play any gigs, nor do we have instruments in the house. I don't need eight hundred pounds of piano to remind me of my failure. In the years since my . . . merging, return, amalgamation, whatever you wish to call it, I have had three adulterous involvements for a total of eight fornications, none of them particularly successful, all of them with younger co-workers. Ellen knows nothing of this, nor does she know that I was recently yanked out of my past and spilled into my future, all middle having been taken away from me.

But I know that if I were to tell this to anyone—anyone at all—I would be in severe trouble. Life would tremble. Life would topple. Life would become dangerous and ill-considered. I cannot manage this. I have bills to pay. I have a life—yes, a life—to lead. Mollie needs a father. She is eleven years old and is beginning to hate me in a healthy, bored sort of way.

How, I ask you, can I tell anyone of this? How, outside of this recollection, can I make my fate, my condition, clear?

Only this: Once I was twenty, and the shot that killed JFK

somehow seemed to have catapulted me into my life; all the years outside looking in, and now I was going to be on the inside myself, and then, and then—

And then another shot, another catapult—and I am forty; married; a father, an unsuccessful adulterer (although perhaps I should count it a success that I haven't been caught); a panting, heavy, sad case of a man on the lip of middle age; and I now *am* on the inside looking out. Evicted and entrapped without a single moment, a single moment in the middle.

But I do have a facility for amalgamation. I could have just as easily lost it in the first moment of middle age, but instead, I interfaced with the future and saved it.

Interfaced. . . .

And I pick up a work order for a sale to a new subscriber in Cohoes (which precipitates all of this, you understand), and I just stare at it and stare at it.

Is that you, Mollie?

Is that you, I see, first name, middle name, new last name? Is that what I have made of you? A name and address on a sales card?

I'll never call you. It would be a disaster.

I will call you. It will be a disaster.

I'll never call you. It would be a disaster.

You think of calling her, don't you, Stony-o?

If you do—oh, you poor bastard—if you do, *will it take you back?*

Will it will it will it?

About the Authors

Jack Dann has written or edited over sixty-five books, including the international bestseller *The Memory Cathedral*, which is published in over ten languages and was #1 on *The Age* Bestseller list. The *San Francisco Chronicle* called it "A grand accomplishment," *Kirkus Reviews* thought it was "An impressive accomplishment," and *True Review* said, "Read this important novel, be challenged by it; you literally haven't seen anything like it." His novel *The Silent* has been compared to Mark Twain's *Huckleberry Finn; Library Journal* chose it as one of their "Hot Picks" and wrote: "This is narrative storytelling at its best—so highly charged emotionally as to constitute a kind of poetry from hell. Most emphatically recommended."

Dann's work has been compared to Jorge Luis Borges, Roald Dahl, Lewis Carroll, Castaneda, J. G. Ballard, Philip K. Dick, and Mark Twain. He is a recipient of the Nebula Award, the World Fantasy Award, the Australian Aurealis Award (twice), the Ditmar Award (three times), the Peter McNamara Achievement Award, and the Premios Gilgames de Narrativa Fantastica award. He has also been honored by the Mark Twain Society (Esteemed Knight). His novel, *Bad Medicine* (retitled *Counting Coup* in the US), has been described by *The Courier Mail* as "perhaps the best road novel since the Easy Rider Days." *Booklist* wrote of Dann's retrospective short story collection *Jubilee:* "This is literary sf of the best sort. Lay in extra copies to accommodate readers taking it slowly and luxuriously."

Dann's latest novel, *The Rebel: an Imagined Life of James Dean* was published by HarperCollins Flamingo in Australia and Morrow in the U.S. (Check out www.ReadTheRebel.com.) *The West Australian* called it "an amazingly evocative and utterly convincing picture of the era, down to details of the smells and sensations—and even more importantly, the way of thinking." *Locus* wrote: "*The Rebel* is a significant and very gripping novel, a welcome addition to Jack Dann's growing oeuvre of speculative historical novels, sustaining further his long-standing contemplation of the modalities of myth and memory. This is alternate history with passion and difference."

Dann is also the co-editor of the groundbreaking anthology of Australian stories, *Dreaming Down-Under*, which won the World Fantasy Award in 1999. He edits the Magic Tales anthology series with Gardner Dozois; and his anthology, *Gathering the Bones*, of which he is a co-editor, was included in *Library Journal*'s Best Genre Fiction of 2003 and was shortlisted for The World Fantasy Award.

Jack Dann lives in Australia on a farm overlooking the sea and "commutes" back and forth to Los Angeles and New York.

☆   ☆   ☆

Susan Casper is a short story author whose works have appeared in such magazines as *Playboy, The Twilight Zone, Amazing, The Year's Best Horror Stories, Series XII, Fears, Whispers, Shadows, In the Fields Of Fire*, and *Journeys To the Twilight Zone*. She is the editor (with Gardner Dozois) of *Ripper!*, an anthology of tales about the infamous Whitechapel murderer. She lives in Philadelphia, Pennsylvania.

☆   ☆   ☆

Gardner Dozois was the editor of *Isaac Asimov's Science Fiction Magazine* for nineteen years (which, under his editorship, has won the *Locus* Award as Best Magazine an unprecedented fifteen years in a row), and also edits the annual anthology series *The Year's Best Science Fiction*, now up to its *Twenty-Second Annual Collection* (and which has won the *Locus* Award for Best Anthology fifteen times, more than any other anthology series in history). He's won the Hugo Award fifteen times as the year's Best Editor, won the *Locus* Award as Best Editor sixteen times in a row, and has won the

Nebula Award twice for his own short fiction. He is the author or editor of more than a hundred books, the most recent of which are *The Best of the Best: Twenty Years of The Year's Best Science Fiction*, a new collection of his own short fiction, *Morning Child and Other Stories*, and a reissue of his novel *Strangers*. He lives in Philadelphia, Pennsylvania.

✻   ✻   ✻

Gregory Frost's latest novel, *Fitcher's Brides* (Tor Books), is a recasting of the fairy tale of Bluebeard as a terrifying story of faith and power in 19th century New York State.

In 2003, between *Fitcher's Brides* and the novelette "Madonna of the Maquiladora," Frost was a finalist for six awards in the fantasy and science fiction fields: Nebula Award, James Tiptree Award, Theodore Sturgeon Memorial Award for Short Fiction, Hugo Award, International Horror Guild Award, and the World Fantasy Award.

His shorter work has appeared in *The Magazine of Fantasy & Science Fiction*, *Isaac Asimov's Science Fiction Magazine*, *Dark Terrors*, *Whispers*, *Realms of Fantasy*, and in anthologies such as Nalo Hopkinson's *Mojo: Conjure Stories*; *Snow White, Blood Red* and *Black Swan, White Raven*, edited by Ellen Datlow and Terri Windling. Some of his work has been included in the *Best New Horror* collections edited by Stephen Jones.

He has twice taught the Clarion Science Fiction & Fantasy Writers Workshop at Michigan State University and acts as one of the Fiction Writing Workshop Directors for Swarthmore College in Swarthmore, PA.

A collection of his shorter work, *Attack of the Jazz Giants and Other Stories*, is also available from Golden Gryphon Press.

✻   ✻   ✻

Jack C. Haldeman II was raised in Alaska. He was a research scientist and worked with artificial intelligence and closed environmental control systems, the latter in connection with NASA's space-station project. A science fiction writer since 1971, he was the author of over a hundred stories and novellas and ten novels, including *Vector Analysis*; *There Is No Darkness* (with his brother Joe Haldeman), *The Fall Of Winter*, and *High Steel* (with Jack Dann). He published articles in scientific journals and poetry in various magazines. Jay, as he was affectionately known to his friends, passed away on January 1st, 2002. He is survived by his brother Joe, daughter Lorena, and his wife, Barbara Delaplace.

✻   ✻   ✻

Barry N. Malzberg is the author of more than ninety books and over three hundred short stories. His novels include *The Falling Astronauts, Beyond Apollo, Underlay, Galaxies, Chorale, The Remaking of Sigmund Freud, Herovit's World, The Men Inside, Guernica Night,* and *The Cross of Fire.* His short story collections include *Final War and Other Fantasies, In the Pocket and Other Science Fiction Stories, Out From Ganymede, The Many Worlds of Barry Malzberg, The Best of Barry N. Malzberg, Down Here In the Dream Quarter, Malzberg At Large,* and *The Man Who Loved the Midnight Lady.* He is the author of the darkly brilliant critique of the genre, *The Engines of the Night.* Barry Malzberg is a former editor of both *Amazing* and *Fantastic,* a multiple Nebula and Hugo nominee, and winner of the very first John W. Campbell Memorial Award for Best Novel.

✳   ✳   ✳

Michael Swanwick is one of the most acclaimed science fiction and fantasy writers of his generation. He has received a Hugo Award for fiction in five out of the last six years—an unprecedented accomplishment!—and he has been honored with the Nebula, Theodore Sturgeon, and World Fantasy Awards as well and receiving nominations for the British Science Fiction Award and the Arthur C. Clarke Award.

His stories have appeared in *Omni, Penthouse, Amazing, Isaac Asimov's Science Fiction Magazine, High Times, New Dimensions, Starlight, Universe, Full Spectrum, Triquarterly,* and elsewhere. Many have been reprinted in Best of the Year anthologies, and translated for Japanese, Croatian, Dutch, Finnish, German, Italian, Portuguese, Russian, Spanish, Swedish, Chinese, and French publications.

His books include *In the Drift,* an Ace Special; *Vacuum Flowers; Griffin's Egg;* the Nebula Award-winning *Stations of the Tide; The Iron Dragon's Daughter,* a New York Times Notable Book, *Jack Faust,* and *Bones Of the Earth;* his short fiction has been collected in *Gravity's Angels, A Geography of Imaginary Lands, Moon Dogs,* and *Tales Of Old Earth.* His flash fiction was collected in *Cigar Box Faust and Other Miniatures.*

He lives in Philadelphia with his wife, Marianne Porter.

✳   ✳   ✳

Janeen Webb has won a World Fantasy Award (for *Dreaming Down-Under*), and the Australian Aurealis and Ditmar awards for her short fiction. Her current work includes a series for young adults, *The Sinbad Chronicles,* which comprises to date: *Sailing to*

Atlantis; The Silken Road to Samarkand, and the forthcoming *Flying to Babylon*. With Andrew Enstice, she has co-authored *Aliens & Savages: Fiction, Politics and Prejudice in Australia*, a controversial book on racism in Australia; *The Yellow Wave*, an annotated critical edition of Kenneth Mackay's important 1895 scientific romance; and *The Fantastic Self*, an edited collection of critical essays on fantasy and science fiction.

Her criticism has appeared in such diverse publications as *Omni, Foundation, The New York Review of Science Fiction, Science-Fiction Studies*, and in standard reference works such as *The Encyclopedia of Science Fiction*, the *St James Guide to Science Fiction Writers*, and *Magill's Guide to Science Fiction & Fantasy Literature*. She was co-editor of *Australian Science Fiction Review: Second Series*, from 1987 to 1991. This bi-monthly journal was the premier science fiction forum in Australia and had a worldwide influence on the genre: it won a Ditmar Award in 1991. She holds a doctorate in literature, and is Reader in Literature at ACU National, Melbourne.

*   *   *

George Zebrowski's nearly forty books include novels, short fiction collections, anthologies, and a book of essays. Science fiction writer Greg Bear calls him "one of those rare speculators who bases his dreams on science as well as inspiration," and the late Terry Carr, one of the most influential science fiction editors of recent years, described him as "an authority in the SF field." Zebrowski has published more than seventy works of short fiction and more than a hundred and forty articles and essays, and has written about science for *Omni*. His short fiction and essays have appeared in *Amazing Stories, The Magazine of Fantasy & Science Fiction, Isaac Asimov's Science Fiction Magazine, Analog, Science Fiction Age, Nature*, the *Bertrand Russell Society News*, and many other publications.

His best-known early novel is *Macrolife*, which Arthur C. Clarke described as "a worthy successor to Olaf Stapledon's *Star Maker*." *Library Journal* chose it as one of the one hundred best science fiction novels, and The Easton Press included it in its "Masterpieces of Science Fiction" series. His other novels include *Stranger Suns*, which was a New York Times Notable Book of the Year; *The Killing Star* with Charles Pellegrino; *Brute Orbits*, an uncompromising novel about the future of the penal system, which was honored with the John W. Campbell Memorial Award for Best Novel of the Year in 1999; and *Cave of Stars*, a novel that is part of his Macrolife mosaic. *Skylife*, an anthology edited by George

Zebrowski with Gregory Benford, was published in 2000. *Swift Thoughts*, a collection of his stories, came out in 2002, and received a starred review in *Publishers Weekly*. A second collection, *In the Distance, and Ahead In Time*, was also published in the same year. The latest volume of his legendary *Synergy* series of original anthologies was published in 2004.

✻   ✻   ✻

Two thousand copies of this book have been printed by the Maple-Vail Book Manufacturing Group, Binghamton, NY, for Golden Gryphon Press, Urbana, IL. The typeset is Electra with Berkeley display, printed on 55# Sebago. Typesetting by The Composing Room, Inc., Kimberly, WI.